THE BIRTH OF IDA

RACHEL GROSVENOR

A Wild Wolf Publication

Published by Wild Wolf Publishing in 2024
Copyright © 2024 Rachel Grosvenor

ISBN: 978-1-907954-89-4
Also available as an E-Book

www.wildwolfpublishing.com

For Sadie Adler

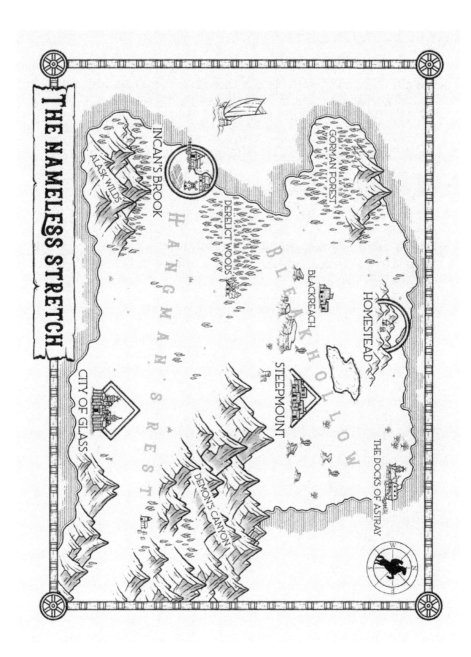

THE NAMELESS STRETCH

ALASK WILDS

INCAN'S BROOK

GORMAN FOREST

DERELICT WOODS

H A N G M A N ' S   R E S T

B L E A K H O L L O W

BLACKREACH

HOMESTEAD

STEEPMOUNT

CITY OF GLASS

DEMON'S CANYON

THE DOCKS OF ASTRAY

1

Prologue

Within The Nameless Stretch there are many tales and years of stories, enough to fill up your bedtimes for eternity. The tale of Ida is the penultimate story of Bleakhollow, a region in the Northwest of the sun-scorched land. Within their dampened walls, the people whisper her story to their children. Be wary of people like Ida, they say, with a knowing glare. Their world is not so different to the one you know, reader, with the skies up top and the ground below, but inside The Nameless Stretch there are things you won't recognise, places, beliefs, and spirits. Not everyone in that land knows the full story of Ida or how she came to be. Reader, there are worse things than being like Ida. This is her origin story.

Chapter 1

Just how asleep was he? He lay beside her, the gentle snore rising and falling with his bony chest. The candlelight flickered, and she watched him, wary. If she were to make a move, would it throw him from his slumber? She shifted, pulling the blanket from her body. It seemed to have no impact on him, so she sniffed hard, pausing again. Nothing.

'Colt,' she whispered, sliding toward the edge of the bed. He snored on. 'Colt, it's Elizabeth here. Colt.' She thought for a moment of what would have awoken any other man. 'You are...about to be robbed.'

Her thin hand flew to her mouth to stop it from bursting open, fearful of his reaction. She had chosen him for this very moment. She knew it as soon as he walked into the bar; his skinny frame and well-worn clothes were exactly what she was looking for. He wasn't much bigger than her, and he was a man who didn't look like he would put up a fight. As soon as he ordered a drink, she sidled up to his sappy body and made her introductions. The other girls were happy to leave her to it; he looked so green. He blinked with those large, fish-like eyes and took a deep sip of his beer. His Adam's apple bobbed comically as he swallowed, and she pulled up a stool.

'You're not from around here, are you, sir?'

Sir. The magic word that the other women had told Ida made all men weak at the knees. He shook his head, taking another sip.

'Well, I hope you won't be scaly to a lady. Would you buy me a drink?'

More blinking. He looked her up and down, trying to take her in without meeting her gaze.

'What'll it be,' he said, more of a statement than a question.

She grinned and nodded at the bartender, mouthing, 'My usual.' All the girls played this trick, the usual being water, disguised as bourbon, in a dark glass.

'So, what's a man like you doing in a dive like this?' she asked, trying again to engage him in some sort of conversation.

'I ain't interested in no entertainment,' he said, giving her a hard stare.

She huffed. 'Well, I don't quite know what to say to that, sir, except that I take offence. I was not trying to 'entertain' you. Simply trying to ascertain what you might be wanting from the kitchen before I knock off for the night.'

His strange, light eyes swivelled across her youthful face. 'You are the cook?'

'I am.'

'Oh...' He removed his hat and placed it on the bar, shrugging. 'I apologise, ma'am. I guess I've had a long sort of journey, and I've been on my own a while. You get sort of funny when you spend too long alone, only the horse and the sky for company. You get a little suspicious of folk.'

She smiled. 'Don't I know it.'

There was a skill to these events, and it was one that Ida had picked up in a matter of months. The flattery was one thing, but a man smarter than a toad could see through that. Any man could be easily flattered by a woman. Some men knew exactly who they were, and Ida saw that they were the toughest ones to crack. They were the men to watch out for – they would use a woman and pay their way to the barman, cutting them out of the picture entirely.

This man, however, was a slightly different breed. He was the type who was nervous, uncertain. He couldn't fathom why a woman might want to be with him, so Ida was careful to give him a reason for the chat. She acted modestly, covering up her chest and ankles, sipping her drink, laughing at his jokes. He was looking for a wife. The other women said that they always were, this kind. A man who already had a wife knew exactly what happened on the other side of that door, and their only concern was their wife not finding out, never mind what type of woman he could find in a bar. But this man was looking for love. So, Ida was careful to show him a little bit. She had done this before and had watched the other women practising the trick of showing a potential client the impression of a good, kind woman. She

4

lowered her age, raised her eyes, and blossomed. She pried a little, asked him what his passions were, matching them with her own. She filled up his glass and delighted in hearing about his horse. A Delath Walker, dark bay. He pointed at him through the grimy window, hitched outside. He was a beaut, all right.

'He is lovely,' Ida gushed, memorising the sight of him.

'Oh, he's just about the best horse I ever had. Raised him from a foal, had him six years. Yep. All's right with the world when it's just Trigger and me.'

'You sure do have some fascinating stories. I could listen to you talk all day long, Colt!'

He grinned in response and drained the last of his sixth beer. She'd counted.

'And Colt,' Ida said, glancing outside. 'It looks like I have spoken to you all day. That sun is dipping in the sky. Where are you staying tonight?'

He nodded, following her gaze and fixing his eyes on the red dusk. 'Thought I'd get myself a room here.'

'Oh sure, that's very wise. We make a breakfast that's worth staying over for!'

The now comfortable Colt grinned and leaned on the bar. 'I'll be heading up then. It's been a long day. Which room will I be staying in?'

'Don't you worry – I'll take you up and show you. We're not the most hospitable bar in town for nothing.'

If there was a pause in his reaction, Ida didn't notice it. He followed her up the stairs, his worn saddlebag swinging over his shoulder, whistling a merry little tune. She showed him into an empty room with all the basics he'd need, observing as he made his way over to the bed. Then, she closed the door behind him and watched him remove his boots, trying not to react to the scent of him in this enclosed space. Filth was a normal part of life, but there was nothing like the smell of a man to turn Ida's stomach.

'You didn't need to show me up, Elizabeth. I could've made my way,' he said, and Ida sighed and merrily waved her hand to show that, really, it was no bother.

'I like to do my bit for guests. Now, what can I do for you to make this your best stay?'

Colt removed his hat and ran his hands through his thinning hair, an awkward laugh playing on his lips. 'I don't have much money, Elizabeth. The pleasure of your company tonight has been enough to keep me satisfied for a good few weeks.'

'Oh hush now, I'm not after your money. Ours is a union born from good communication – a rare thing these days. Am I wrong?'

He blinked as if trying to work out whether or not he heard correctly. There was no word of a lie on her lips, and she really was not after that man's money. She was after something much more valuable.

'Well, I felt it too, Elizabeth, but I can hardly believe my luck…you being such a beautiful woman and an honest one at that.'

'You flatter me.' She smiled, playing her part to the best of her ability. If the last few months had taught her anything at all, it's that she could only survive by playing a part.

There was still no movement from him. Ida smiled in the flickering darkness and reached for his trousers, pulling them on and mouthing a 'thank you' when she discovered that they fitted. She wrapped the bandage she had been hiding for weeks around her breasts, binding them down and tying the material beneath her armpit. Colt's clothing smelled damp and mouldy, as though things were growing inside, but she donned them anyway, doing up the shirt with efficiency.

He was a trusting man. This was proven by the fact that he had placed his holster, guns included, right next to his saddlebag, flung over the end of the bed frame. The only thing he had kept on his person was his hat, Ida noticed, with a grimace. It sat on his stomach, rising and falling with his breath. She wouldn't be able to get out of town without the hat. She needed it to cover up her long mouse-coloured hair, to hide the silhouette of her features, her strong jaw. Ida picked up the holster, did it up around her waist, and then stepped into her boots. She wouldn't take his own – leave the man with something. Besides, they looked too big for her, and there was something about pushing her feet into this man's boots that turned her stomach. A flash appeared in her mind of the night before, his sweating body over hers, and she shook her head, forcing it out of her thoughts. She breathed in, reminding herself to focus.

Ida stepped toward him, pulling out one of the guns and aiming it at Colt's head. He slept untroubled, utterly unaware of the precarious situation he found himself in. With her left hand, she reached for the hat and took a breath. One, two…reach. Her fingers touched the material, and she lifted it gently. It was hers. He didn't wake. She reholstered the gun and piled her hair on her head, securing the worn hat over the top. She was ready. She was going to escape this terrible place. Ida threw the saddlebag onto her shoulder and tipped the hat forward, trying her best to disguise her features. She unlocked the door and stepped out, closing it carefully behind her. The harder it was for Colt to raise the alarm, the better.

Ida started down the hallway and then paused. What was she doing, walking as her usual self? That was a sure-fire way to be caught. No, she had to be Colt. That was the only way to get out of here. She thought of him, but realised that she had no idea how he moved. She had been so concerned with her plan that she had forgotten to pay attention to those finer details. What men did she know? Ida closed her eyes. Her father.

She brought to mind his body, his shape, his voice. With care, she rolled her shoulders forward and took a few practice steps, ambling and dropping her hips with each movement. That was more like it. She dipped her chin and sniffed, doing her best to create a realistic version of the man she remembered. Then, she descended the staircase. With every step, her heartbeat grew louder, threatening to wake the entire saloon. As she reached the bottom few stairs, she looked up. The saloon was basically empty, apart from the few who always sat at the bar, nursing drinks into the early hours. One of them was staring ahead, grumbling to himself. The other was fast asleep, with his head on the wooden table before him. The barman was nowhere to be seen, and Ida was grateful for it. She walked past the grumbling man toward the door, seeing with pure anticipation the Delath Walker still hitched up through the window.

'That your horse?' the grumbling man said, swivelling in his chair.

Ida stopped in her tracks and sniffed. 'Hmmm, mm,' she said softly, holding her breath.

'It's a beaut, all right,' the man spoke again, whistling through his teeth.

'Yup,' Ida said, reaching within herself for the deepest voice she could find, her father's voice. She began to walk forward again, shoulders hunched, head low. The man said no more.

Outside, the sun was just beginning to rise in the sky, and the birds had started their dawn song. The air smelled different to usual, fresh and bright, as though it was aware of the change for Ida personally. The horse was standing with its eyes closed, chomping on his bit. She stepped forward and stroked his muzzle for a second, letting him smell the scent of the clothing, recognise the tones of his master. Of course, Ida knew that Bullet would have known a stranger covered in her scent, but she had to trust that this horse was open to a new owner.

He seemed happy enough, and Ida quickly fastened the saddlebag over his back, pulled the reins from around the hitching rail, and mounted. The trousers were a blessed change from her usual skirts. She turned the horse and nudged him into a steady jog, aware that a stranger galloping out of town at dawn would only attract unwanted attention.

The houses and shops of Steepmount were beginning to wake up, and windows were being pushed open, children running out into the street. To them, Ida looked as she had hoped. Just a stranger heading out of town. Beneath her disguise, she felt different, obvious, as though she were wearing a sandwich board bearing her name, highlighting her shame. She kept her eyes steady. The future beckoned.

Chapter 2

'Bleakhollow is no place for a woman.'

The words of her father rattled in her mind as Ida rode on. The orange sun was now high in the sky, the horse jogging at a steady but slowing gait. Her father was right. She had known it even then when the safety of their homestead seemed to stretch into the distance, the land to be her own one day. Each night, they would sit together on the porch, pipe smoke billowing into the air around them, her father talking of the land, the seasons, and her mother. His stories were always the same, day after day, as though his mind were stuck on an impenetrable loop. Ida listened every now and then. He would talk about how they met, her mother and him. How the stars shone that evening, of the wild way she traded her father's produce. He admired her proud chin, he said, time and again. It was a chin that Ida had inherited. Beneath the scent of smoke and the chilled twilight air lay the promise of a life understood. There were no surprises at the homestead.

After the tale of their meeting, he would move swiftly on, barely a breath taken. Their home, their land. Showing her the bounty, the promise of their future. The blissful eleven months of marriage. So short, he would say, so painfully short. Ida would nod and lean back in her chair, sipping on the strong bourbon that they shared each night. There was nothing that she could say to this. She had tried. She had asked questions, pried into their relationship. She had argued, saying that her chin was nothing like her mother's. It was as though she wasn't there at all, merely a vessel for stories. Then, he would end with her mother's death. Each time, the words were the same. She became pregnant. Then, Ida arrived. A wonderful few months, her father would say, the three of them together. What plans he had for a large family, for more daughters, for sons. And then, one day, she was gone, along with his dreams. There was nothing else to be said.

Sometimes Ida would suggest a change in the routine, that they might ride somewhere together, watch the sun setting from a different location.

'Not tonight, girl.'

She often requested to be shown the land they owned and expressed a hope that she could work in the fields, help her father with the earth, and make them more money.

'A woman's place is in the home.'

Each night, Ida said the same thing before they went to bed.

'Father, tomorrow I shall ride into Blackreach, where I shall trade some of our goods.'

Each night, she was met with a silly grimace from her father and outright refusal.

'You'll be eaten alive, girl. Leave the trading to me. Blackreach is certain death for a young woman. Your mother would turn in her grave at the thought of it.'

But Ida longed for it. She dreamed of the day she would be allowed into the nearest town. She feared and desired it in equal measures, as though it was a paradise created by evil itself. She knew that she was to inherit the land, but how could she make any money if her father wouldn't even teach her how to work it? A week before his death, Ida had grabbed him by the hand and squeezed.

'Father, I am twenty-eight years old. You are ageing. We cannot go on this way for much longer.'

He looked at her then, the dirt of the day's work barely disguising the lines on his face.

'Twenty-eight? You are mistaken, I think.'

Ida blinked in the sunlight and pulled herself back. It was far too easy to drift into her past life. When she allowed her mind to dream, it was as though no time had passed at all, as if she was still sitting in the well-worn groove of her mother's rocking chair. How she had longed for some change, a new way of life. And now, it was here, thrust upon her in one swift movement. Perhaps you couldn't always choose how the change came to you.

The horse had now slowed to a walk, its skin glistening in the sunshine, the bay coat drenched in sweat. Ida glanced at the high sun. When she had escaped Steepmount, she'd had no idea what would exist past the hill, and had chosen a direction indiscriminately – any path but back home. Now, she scrutinised the barren land around her. The dry land stretched for miles, out of which occasionally sprang rocks and shapeless mounds. Ida saw the random bison, an animal that caused her heart to lurch with fear, its shape in the distance hard to recognise as what it was. Twice, she had thought she was coming across a lone rider. That had not yet been the case, though she feared it.

'I should have planned more,' she whispered to the horse. His ears flicked backwards, listening. It was the first thing she had said since they had left. Hours must have passed. Could she have planned more? Mrs Smithe, the madam, was so clever, so tricksy as to get the women in her employ into debt as soon as she possibly could. When Ida had ridden into the town of Steepmount, desperate and afraid, she had been so wonderfully welcomed. Mrs Smithe had fed Ida a decent meal, shown her to a beautiful room, and helped her pick a dress from her late sister's closet, who happened to be the same size as herself. It was later that Ida realised that everything was not as it seemed, when the exact role she was to play was made clear, and her debt was laid out for her to see, her old horse sold off to recoup some of those funds.

'What did your owner call you, boy? I remember him telling me something, but I can't quite bring it to mind.' One ear flicked forward again as though he was bored of listening. What names did she know?

'I'll call you Bullet for now,' she said. The memory of her horse was nothing but that now, a glimmer of history.

She thought of Colt waking up in the empty room, his clothes, guns, saddlebags, nowhere to be found. He would give her the benefit of the doubt at first, choosing to believe that perhaps she had sent his clothing away for cleaning. And what of his hat, that always sat astride him as he slept? He would pull on the door handle a couple of times before his belief of her good intentions turned to confusion, and then rage. His fists would beat against the wood, shaking the frame. The barman would sprint up the stairs and release him, and then shrug. It was nothing to do with him. What woman? Elizabeth? There was no one of that name under this roof. Colt would fly down the stairs in his union suit, swearing as he reached the window. There it was, proof of the crime. His beloved Delath Walker, stolen.

So she was a criminal now, like her brother. The thought of her brother's face made her skin flush and crawl, his image, holding a gun at her father's head. He wasn't meant to die before he retired, wasn't meant to have his secrets come back to kill him. Her brother had arrived at the homestead months ago, while she was darning socks on the porch.

'What business have you here?' she had asked, throwing her sewing onto an abandoned chair.

Her brother shifted in his saddle and stayed astride his horse, and glared at her from beneath his hat. His eyes were as mean as anything she had ever seen, but his age was young, hardly older than herself. 'I don't have any business with you. Where's the man of the…house?' he growled, his stare rolling over the home behind Ida.

'He's working. What business have you here? State the reason for your visit, or I'll get my gun.'

He grinned. 'Last I checked, it wasn't illegal for a man to enter his own land.'

Ida glanced at him. 'What in the Stretch does that mean?'

'What's your name, lady?'

She waited no more and turned, reaching beneath the chair for her Winchester. She always took it everywhere, her father reminding her often that you never knew when you'd run across an intruder or a flighty dinner.

'Wait a minute there, Shooting Shea,' the stranger said as Ida swivelled, holding the barrel to face him.

'You've got ten seconds to tell me why you're here.'

'To see my father,' he said, his smile disappearing. 'And I'm guessing that you're not Shooting Shea. You're Ida.'

She blinked, the gun lowering, and watched as he dismounted in a swift movement, head cocked to one side. 'My father only has one child,' she said, already knowing that this couldn't be true. This man certainly looked like him, with the same deep brow and narrow stare.

'Well, that ain't strictly true. Our father did the dirty on your mother – and he did the expected on mine. Anyway. I don't have much in the way of land, and I am pleasantly surprised to see what I have coming to me.' He nodded, looking around him as though he'd just signed the lease for the house. 'Tell me where he is, Ida. I should like to make myself known.'

'I won't. I don't know if you're telling the truth.'

'Well, how's about this? I'll go find him. You fix us up something nice for dinner.'

With that, he mounted his horse once more and flew away into the surrounding greenery. Ida stood for a moment, dumbfounded, hesitating and fretting. After an unhappy ten minutes, she drew back her shoulders, choosing to leave her gun on the porch. If she approached with kindness, perhaps that would be enough. She stalked to the stable to grab her horse. He was long in the tooth and gentle as a lamb, but he could still move when he needed to. Ida had barely tacked him up once the bit was in his mouth, sensing that there was little time to waste. She pulled her skirts up around her waist and mounted him from a starting block, damning ridiculous decency. Sweet Bullet seemed to understand the urgency, and together, they sprang from the stable and thundered after the wayward brother, a man Ida had never before laid eyes on.

She found him all too quickly. Her father, on his knees, begging for his life, for forgiveness, for his behaviour. Her brother stood over him, pistol aimed at his head. The bang came as she skidded into view and watched her father fall. The brother sensed her presence, and there was nothing that she could do. Ida turned Bullet round and urged him forward, moving through the grass, over the hills, away from her home. She rode until she could ride no more, until the darkness descended and drove them into a dogged trot. Her legs and arms ached, Bullet flagged and dipped. As she was about to relent and fall into the dirt for the night, she saw a glimmer of light on the horizon. This is how she entered the lofty town of Steepmount, high on a hill.

Ida turned around and looked behind her for the hundredth time that hour. They weren't moving quickly enough; she couldn't get the blasted horse to move forward at speed. Riding her old Bullet had always been intuitive, as though he could read her mind, sense her desire for an amble or flight. Ida closed her eyes and whispered.

'Please, Bullet. They'll kill me.'

His gait remained the same. The walk was getting slower, if it were possible. Ida wiped her brow with her sleeve and peered at the damp dirt that stained it. Had she been naïve enough to think that she could escape such a life? Her father was right. A woman in this land would be eaten alive. She felt her eyes sting and a tightness in her chest. What use would crying do? And yet…she was unable to stop. A sob rose, and she leaned forward, burying her face into Bullet's black mane, heated by the intense sunlight. His step suddenly lightened. She lifted her head, frowned, and then sat back in the saddle. He slowed again. She leaned forward once more, pushing herself up and out of the stirrups, kicking him on with her heels. He sprang into life, first breaking into a jog and then a lope.

'Yes, Bullet!' Ida laughed, forgetting her woes momentarily. Clearly, she had trained her own horses differently from Colt. She grinned as the dust and sand beneath Bullet's hooves flew up and hit her in the mouth, grains coating her tongue and teeth. She moved her hands forward on his strong neck, allowing him to stretch and bound across the plain. Finally, they began to get away.

Behind her, a posse was already forming in Steepmount. Colt was now dressed in borrowed clothing, raging about the woman who had robbed him. Mrs Smithe was lamenting that Ida was a poor, sweet thing, and yet significantly in debt. Indeed, it could not have been she who would rob a man in such a way. Those who were at the bar the night before sighed along. It was Ida, all right. There was no doubt.

Chapter 3

As they sprinted away, the land began to transform at speed. Ida was grateful for it, the sun now moving across the sky, chasing them out of the unforgiving desert. She saw that the terrain was changing and leaned back into her seat, slowing Bullet down. They jogged forward, and Ida glanced at the ground beneath them, still dry and dusted but now covered in rocks and jarring holes. She thought of the grassy fields of home, the open stretches of dappled wheat, where she and her old Bullet could ride hard without fear of falling. Here, she would have to take care that Bullet didn't trip or twist an ankle. They slowed a little further, and Ida squinted into the distance. There was a sign up ahead, stuck haphazardly between two large rocks. A sign of life or death?

'Demon's Canyon…' Ida read aloud as they walked toward it. 'Falling probable…falling probable? That's a weird—'

And then the world went black.

Reader, there were many hardships in life on the frontier, or in any frontier, supposing that you don't know which one Ida subscribed to. In this land, The Nameless Stretch (for truthfully, there was no agreement to be had on what it should be called, and every disagreement ended with a gunfight and death), the scenery was so changeable that it could be called one name only.

Beyond Bleakhollow and its many towns and people lay the desert to the south. To the west lay woodland, which is where Ida would have begun had she thought about the map her father had owned. However, all that Ida knew was that she was running away from the north, and at the time, the south seemed the most likely direction. The edge of Bleakhollow ended when the desert met Demon's Canyon, a rocky grave for travellers, escapees, plunderers and fools. Those who entered without knowing where they were going were often surprised by a fall, and even more surprised by death.

Water. Blessed water. A drop hit her lip, and she licked it, frowning. Where was she? Who had found her? Colt?! Ida opened her eyes and took in the image before her. It was Bullet, his head over hers, his muzzle dripping liquid onto her mouth. She groaned and shifted on the hard floor, checking her body mentally for any breakages. It seemed to be okay…she ached, but nothing was screaming out at her, apart from the need for water.

Ida sat up and put her hand to her head, pushing Bullet's muzzle away. There she was, sat in front of the sign. She hadn't moved at all.

'What on earth?' she murmured, staring at the words and then the horse. He was soaking wet, water dripping from his hair and lips. He seemed delighted. Ida got wearily to her feet, looked around her, and then stepped toward the sign again, peering just past it. Behind lay a large canyon, the bottom hidden entirely by distance. Ida gulped and turned to Bullet.

'You knew what lay beyond this sign, didn't you? You've been here before. And clearly, you know where some water is.'

Bullet's ears flicked in the sunshine. Ida reached for the damp saddle, pulling herself up.

'Next time you want to make a stop, take me with you. Don't just throw me off.'

Bullet let out a wet snort.

'Bullet. Go.'

His ears flickered again, and he stomped one hoof as though protesting against his new name. Then, he began to walk slowly, picking his way across the stony ground. He turned to the right of the sign and canyon and moved forward despite a sudden drop ahead. Ida grasped the reins and pulled.

'Bullet – no!'

Bullet shook his head, loosening her grip, and continued. As they reached the edge, Ida saw a small path cut into the side of the canyon wall. It was slim, almost too narrow to fit a horse down, but Bullet seemed not to notice the drop into certain death. Ida shivered, the trembles taking over her body, and she tightened her grip again, reins slipping against her damp hands and weak fingers. She closed her eyes and breathed in through her nose and out through her mouth, a trick her father taught her when she was training a green horse liable to buck.

On they moved, Ida occasionally opening her eyes and squinting through Bullet's ears to see their descent. The shale beneath his hooves caused him to skid now and then, but Ida found that he moved faster when she tensed her body, so she leaned back and did her best to relax. After what seemed like an eternity but was, in fact, just ten minutes, they had arrived. Bullet stopped and snorted, giving Ida a start. She opened her eyes properly. There in front of them stood an archway, just big enough for the two to slip through. Above it was the shape of a teardrop carved into the stone. Ida clicked her tongue, urging Bullet onwards. It was pitch black inside, and the only sound that could be heard was the dripping of water, which was high-pitched and welcome. Ida dismounted and wrinkled her nose, the scent of damp stone new and cold in her nostrils. The dank darkness was a welcome respite from the heavy sun. She stood for a moment and leaned against the horse's wet flank, closing her eyes and holding her feet fast on the ground. The cold air on her skin made her grateful to be alive.

After her heart had slowed a little, and for the first time, Ida reached for and unbuckled one of the saddlebags she had stolen from Colt. What could be in there? She pushed a hand into the worn leather and felt around, grinning with satisfaction after a mere moment. She pulled out a small tin box with rough edges. Exactly what she was looking for – a box of matches. In the darkness, she opened them and lit one, the flame burning bright for a second before settling into the damp conditions. Her immediate surroundings lit up around her, and she moved the light around. It was a compact cave with some definite signs of life. Next to her feet lay a crumpled blanket, a small box, and a handheld lamp.

'Bullet! A lamp!'

Ida got to her knees and turned the dial on the side, holding the flame and whispering pleas beneath her breath. If it had any kerosine left in it, then she would do something spectacular, she whispered, as though the world was listening and watching. The lamp sparked into life, illuminating Ida, Bullet and the cave.

It had definitely been lived in at some point. As Ida moved around the space, she found floor rolls, candles, a small pan, and empty bottles with remnants of whisky. She almost forgot the promise of the water, so fascinated was she by the evidence of other humans. Bullet's behaviour was also interesting. He was completely comfortable there, standing against one wall with his eyes closed and hind leg resting.

'This is where you and Colt lived, isn't it?'

Bullet's eyes remained closed, his nap undisturbed. Ida nodded, answering her own question, the image of her father when he listened to his own stories. She grabbed the lamp and stepped deeper into the cave, moving beyond Colt's discarded items. Beneath her boots, the click of stone changed to the crunch of gravel, and Ida gasped as her eyes settled on the sight before her. It was a lake. She cupped her hand and scooped up a little water, sipping gently. No salt. No wonder Colt had chosen this space to sleep in. Water, shelter from the sun, room for the two of them. Ida placed the lamp down on the gravel and began to undress, removing Colt's stinking clothes from her body. She was still hot, flushed from riding in the burning sun for hours on end, sweating from the ride down the canyon. There was a saying her father had told her; 'The sun will make you drink, but your stink will make you sink.'

Reader, this was the kind of saying that came about when your Uncle Arnold fell asleep in the bathtub at the same time as that friend of a friend's mother took a dip in the local lagoon and didn't come back for supper. Reasons for death in The Nameless Stretch were varied and plentiful, but when the nameless people made up a saying for a situation – you had better pay attention to it. For interest's sake, other expressions included, 'If you pay a peddler before you get your peddle, he'll be peddling your peddle elsewhere and drinking on your dime.' And 'For god's sake, stop shooting strangers just because they look at you funny, or else you'll be forced to marry your cousin before winter is through.' If you're unsure of the meaning of these last two, it's best to plan a visit to The Nameless Stretch to see what's what.

The water was colder than Ida could have dreamed, and though she feared its darkness, the draw of the cool around her was far too strong. She leaned her head back into the lake, feeling the tendrils of cold reach her skull, delving into the pores of her scalp and bringing her back to life. She sat for a moment in the dimming cold and thought of her homestead and her long-lost brother. What would he have done to it by now? She imagined him sitting on the porch, Winchester flung over his arm, waiting for her to come home. Ida cupped her hands together and took a sip of the water, feeling it drip down her front. If he was waiting for her, he could wait forever.

After her swim in the lake, she had gotten ready to leave, gathering the bottles and filling them with water, salvaging what she could from the things that Colt had left behind. There was nothing of interest apart from the bedroll, and she had been disappointed to find that the box contained one lone cigarette. She pocketed it for another time. She had good intentions – they would carry on their journey away from Bleakhollow and keep riding until Demon's Canyon was a memory only. And then, when she stepped out of the cave into the afternoon sun, it was as though the rays were pressing her skin, burning her with its brightness. She stepped back into the darkness, to which her eyes had already become accustomed.

'Just one rest,' she said to Bullet, untacking him with care. 'We'll rest until nightfall and then head back onto the road. They won't expect us to ride at night.'

Bullet peered at her. They could both do with the rest.

Ida shifted her body. The cold was slowly moving from a blessed relief into her bones, causing her to shiver. Her damp hair nestled on her shoulders, and she closed her eyes, choosing to imagine, instead of the heat of the sunshine on her body, the sweat that would pour from both herself and Bullet should they leave now. No, sleep was best for both of them. Later, they would move like shadows in the nighttime, always a step ahead.

Her body began to relax, her mind filling with the nonsensical images of falling asleep. Both Bullets danced in her visions, their bodies moving in time, fluid like water. Like ice-cold water.

Chapter 4

The posse had now split up, looking for clues, teams of three. The Sheriff of Steepmount led two of his men to the border of Bleakhollow, and they stood astride their horses and eyed the beyond.

'If she's unlucky, she'll have come across Demon's Canyon,' said the sheriff, smiling at the thought. Unfortunate deaths were an amusing part of the job for him.

'Yep, yep, yep. That ain't lucky. They don't call it Demon's Canyon for nuthin',' said one of his men, a giddy look of cruel glee stretched across his face. 'Well, is that where we're headed?'

The sheriff sniffed and shrugged. 'I don't know. It's not like that Colt is a member of our town, is it?' he said. 'And yet…she does owe Mrs Smithe a debt of gratitude, never mind of money. And I owe Mrs Smithe a debt of gratitude myself.'

Both of the men began to giggle, and the sheriff rolled his eyes.

One spoke up. 'How far could she have gotten, really? I reckon she'll be back in Steepmount, hiding behind a trough.'

'Anything is possible,' the sheriff murmured. 'But she'd be mighty stupid to stay in town.'

Ida stood, gun to her side, shaking in the midday heat. There he was, riding up toward her, trashing the flowers that had taken years to cultivate. Smashing her efforts for a beautiful existence. She lifted her Winchester, cocked the hammer, and stared down the barrel. The lazy tread of his horse's hooves clicked over her land. She closed her right eye, aimed, and fired. A bullet flew out of the bore, and she saw it swirl through the air in slow motion. It landed within a second, straight into his left arm. His body shifted backwards with the force, his face crumpling in pain. He fell, landing in the dirt with a heavy sigh. Ida nodded and stalked toward him, her rifle still poised.

'You oughta steal somebody else's land, you son of a bitch,' she said, aiming the rifle at his head.

He beheld her and laughed, an easy laugh that was now free of pain. 'And you oughta get going, Ida, they're coming for you. Thief.'

'What?'

'Ida. They're coming for you. Ida. Thief. Ida. They're on their way.'

Ida woke with a start. The darkness welcomed her, enveloping her. She breathed in the dank air and reached for the lantern by her side, hurriedly lighting it with a match. The cave illuminated before her. Bullet was standing close, his eyes watchful.

'Bullet,' she whispered. He didn't move. 'We must get back on the road.'

She got to her feet and dressed, the clothes still attached to the stink of Colt. She had thought about washing them in the water, leaving them out to dry, but was afraid of them being seen by a passer-by. There was nothing like laundry to give away one's location, though the scents of his body bought back some sickening memories of him heaving above her, flushed with hideous effort and carnal pleasure. Ida shuddered and grabbed her hat, and then rolled up the blanket that she had slept on, fastening it to the back of the saddle. She tacked Bullet up, speaking to him in low, gentle whispers the entire time, trying to forge a bond between them. He was easy to tack up, accepting the bit and girth without faces or trouble. Ida was endlessly grateful for it, the warning of her dream lying in her mind.

They left the cave on foot with Ida leading Bullet. The darkness that welcomed them was a different type of darkness to that found within the cave, which closed around you, hiding that which lay before your face. Outside, the air was now cooler, a slight wind whistling through the canyon, dusting the shale beneath their feet. The moon was bright and high in the sky, colouring the land grey and white, its brightness a comfort to Ida. She stepped onto the small ridge and climbed onto Bullet's back, nudging him forward. Even in the night, he took to the thin walkway with a carefree attitude, delivering them back to the relative safety of the ground on the edge of the canyon. She pulled him to a halt next to the sign where they had descended earlier. It felt like a lifetime ago already, when they stood tired and hot, and this world before them looked different. Bathed in moonlight, the harshness of the terrain seemed silky and smooth, like white sand poured over water.

So, which way? Ida knew which way not to go, and that was backwards. There was nothing to be gained from that but hanging. She contemplated the future, the horizon, unsure. They would expect her to move forward, perhaps, toward the towns of Hangman's Rest. If that was the case, she should go west. What lay west anyway? Ida thought of the map that her father used to pore over during trading season and frowned. It was just a map of Bleakhollow. She had memorised it even though she hadn't visited all of it. But the rest of The Nameless Stretch? She knew that Hangman's Rest had towns in it, different lives and people, but she had never dared ask her father if he had ever been. He was always cagey about his past. Ida raised her eyebrows at the thought of this and sighed. He was hesitant with good reason; he knew that beyond the homestead lay a brother for her. Maybe even more siblings sank between the cracks of The Nameless Stretch, just waiting for her to ride past.

Ida gazed at the glistening moon and clicked her tongue, moving Bullet forward into a light jog. Beneath the celestial glow, she felt safer. Perhaps they should become nocturnal? She leaned forward in her seat and allowed Bullet to lope onwards, speeding up with each beat of his hooves. The air whipped about Ida's face, and she kept her eyes focused on the steady horizon, the ever-constant area of hope: away from everywhere.

The landscape of Ida's home had always been a familiar sight. In summer, the green of the hills grew strong, and the house and porch bathed in a strange yellow light as though the home were a piece of glass reflecting the sun. The days were long, her father working in the fields, harvesting, struggling alone. Ida would prepare lunch each day and ride to meet him, where they would sit beneath an old oak tree and enjoy cider, bread and dried fruit in veritable silence, after her father's daily quip; 'It's okay to eat with your fingers, the food is clean.'

At home, Ida would dry flowers, clean clothes, and generally busy herself with the never-ending supply of work that came from running a household. Sometimes, in the summer, she made tasks last longer than they had to, working the clothes through the lake for hours at a time, the water up to her waist cooling her burning skin.

There was no season like the summer for staring at the horizon, and Ida had come to recognise each bump and dip and familiar tree that lay in the distance. Now, she stared at the hard grey line with an anxious heart. Her father's words were heavy in her mind. The majority of all the words she had ever heard had come from his lips. And so far, hadn't they proven to be true? When he told of the myriad of ways she might come to harm if she left the farm – and there had been plenty – they included some of the horrors that she had already experienced. Men who didn't care if you weren't married didn't see a human being as anything but a vessel. People who weren't who they said they were. And yet, nothing he said had truly prepared her for the real world. Ida felt a shudder crawl up her spine as she thought of her naivety when she first rode into Steepmount. She pulled the air through her nostrils, enjoying the dusted, cold air of freedom. Sometimes, she felt as though she collected scents. The lavender scents of her first room at Mrs Smithes', the luxurious perfume and clothing. The saloon, a steady mix of beans and pork drifting up from the kitchen, seeping through the floorboards beneath the beds where men who hadn't washed in days sweat over her. And home, the farm, the scent of everything she knew, tough to put a name to. Dirt, sugar, hard work. The sweetness of the roses and the homemade petal perfume that she created when they were dying. This journey, she thought, would always be synonymous with the scent of Colt. Until she could wash the clothes, at least.

They continued forward, Bullet now in a rhythm and moving soundly, and Ida beginning to relax in the moonlight. The landscape started to shift, the ground still dry stone, sand and shale, but the surrounding bareness added the occasional dying tree, roots shovelling through the earth. Ida watched the trees grow thicker, more and more clinging together, going from brown to a strange and pale swamp-like green. It was turning into a sort of woods, the horizon becoming harder and harder to see before them. As Ida shifted her body back in the saddle, Bullet tensed, his ears flattening back on his head, the whites of his eyes becoming visible. Ida's grip tightened in response, and she grasped hold of his mane for support, clinging on as he lurched sideways.

'Whoa, whoa, Bullet,' Ida hissed, trying to keep calm as he danced across the earth. She glanced around them, staring at the trees, the moonlight shining a spotlight. After a moment, Bullet calmed and stopped still, ears still flickering, listening. Ida held her breath and did the same. She saw nothing in the moonlight, even in the shadows that played across the branches of the trees, but she heard exactly what she feared. The cock of a hammer, a footstep on a leaf. Ida held her hands in the air, a trick she had learned from her father's stories.

'You give up so easy?' a deep voice said, barrelling through the air behind her, and Ida swivelled in her saddle to see the speaker, causing Bullet to turn to face him. It was an old man leaning against a tree bathed in shadow, a phantasm in the milky darkness. His gun was pointed at them, though lazily, his wrist bent to the side as if it were too much of an ask to point it. Behind him, Ida could see the flickers of fire.

'I am just passing through,' she said, forgetting momentarily that she was supposed to be someone else, her voice coming out as her own. She cleared her throat dramatically, deepening the cough. The man frowned.

'Passing through to where?' he said, stepping out into the moonlight.

Ida looked at his long, unkempt beard, his ageing skin, and worn clothes. She shrugged.

The man shook his head. 'You don't know? If you don't know, I'm going to take that as a threat.' The gun waved in his hand.

'I'm just riding through here, sir,' she said, keeping her voice low and gruff. 'I don't mean to cause you any offence.'

The man laughed, a single, barking noise that made Ida jump. 'Oh, put your hands down, fool; I'm just giving you a taste of these parts,' he said, lowering his gun.

Ida dropped her hands, regathering her reins. She nodded at him curtly.

'I know the reasons why a man such as yourself might be riding through these woods at night. She hides a lot, don't she?'

Ida frowned and placed her right hand on the handle of the gun in her holster. 'Who?' she asked.

'The darkness. She hides a lot of sins. A lot of your type, skulking through the night, running from something or another.'

Ida shook her head. 'I'm not running. I'm just passing through,' she lied, keeping her gaze hard and steady.

'Just passing through,' the man repeated, glancing up at the moon.

'Yep.'

'Well, in that case, you'll join me for supper. I've got 'Son of a Gun stew' on the fire over there and not a lot of company.'

Ida winced, torn. Her stomach had been rumbling since the meagre meal of crackers she had shared with Bullet earlier that evening, and yet this was a risk. A feed with a strange man? What if it was some sort of trap? She said nothing. He stepped forward.

'What's your name? I'm Brigg.'

'I'm C-Colton,' Ida said, growing used to the deepening cadence she had adopted, her father's voice that she was doing her best to mimic. 'And Brigg, I'm going to remain armed throughout our meal.'

Brigg laughed that single bark once more. 'Listen – you're a stranger, I'm armed to my teeth just lookin' at ya.'

Ida smiled. He was right. Brigg was a strange man, and so was she. This was a different world to the one she existed in as Ida. This was a man's world. She dismounted in a single, swift movement and led Bullet toward the fire, flanked by Brigg.

'That's a beautiful horse,' he said.

'Yup. Raised him from a foal. Delath Walker,' Ida responded, doing her best impression of Colt, mimicking his words. They reached the fire, and Ida hitched Bullet to a tree, patting him on the shoulder.

'You a bourbon drinker, Colton?' Brigg asked, passing over a tin cup.

Ida nodded and took it, bringing it to her lips for a long sip. It was her first real taste of bourbon since she'd drunk it beside her father, if you didn't count the second-hand bourbon fumes that filled her senses when she was roughly kissed by one of Mrs Smithes' clients.

She sat beside the fire for a moment, a semblance of calm taking over her. She didn't know the man sitting opposite her, but it was a relief just to have someone else there before her, not to be on the move. The flames licked and stretched to the sky. Was it possible that it had only been twenty-four hours? Surely not. Time was beginning to extend into the unknown, bending and moving as she had never known it before.

Brigg ladled out the stew into a misshapen wooden bowl and handed it to her. She brought it to her lips and took a sip, eyes on the man in front of her. He produced a spoon from his pocket and then began to take a huge spoonful of the stew, oily splashes dripping down his chin and beard. Ida's first response was one of disgust, but then she paused. For the first time in her life, there was no standing on ceremony, no father to warn her of her manners, no madam to ask her to improve her attentions. The life of a man truly was better. Ida leaned forward and ate hungrily, picking the bits of tripe out and shovelling them into her mouth. Brigg watched her with an expression of satisfaction.

'You see, I knew it when I saw you. That, I said to myself, is a hungry man.'

She nodded, shrugging, continuing to eat.

'Yup, I don't mind sharing what little I have. I lack a bit of company, you see. The life of a prospector ain't all it's cracked up to be.'

Ida wiped her mouth. 'You're a prospector?' she said with interest, her deep voice wavering. 'I've never met one before. My father used to tell me stories, though.'

'Of the prospecting life? All gold and adventure, I'll wager,' Brigg said, rolling his eyes.

Ida laughed, reminding herself to deepen it at the last minute. 'Quite the opposite. He said he'd only ever met prospectors who were tough and…well, a bit…'

Brigg grinned. 'Yeah. If you don't like the mining camps – which lad, no one does – you end up 'a bit'. It's all that time spent alone, thinking of the gold. Well, alone. Not alone. I've got Stinky Hoss for company.' Brigg motioned to the left of him, and Ida noticed a donkey hitched to a tree for the first time. She tipped her hat to him with one hand and then helped herself to another ladle of stew without asking. She was beginning to get used to the life of a man, taking what she liked.

'So, Brigg. Where you headed?'

He put his bowl down on the floor beside him and scratched his beard. 'I'm headed to Bleakhollow.'

Ida's heart clenched. She did her best to look normal, relaxed. 'Is that right?'

'Yep. Not too far out now. I should say it's a couple of days of easy riding. Is that where you've come from?'

Ida shook her head. 'No. What business do you have in Bleakhollow?'

Brigg laughed a deep booming laugh, longer than his previous efforts. 'Trade, of course. What use is gold if you can't sell it? It ain't edible, you know.'

'No…no, I know that.'

'So what's your business? Riding around in the nighttime ain't much of a business. You gotta be headed somewhere.'

'I'm a…I'm…' Ida stuttered, struggling to think. A farmer? No, why would she have left the farm?

'You a bounty hunter?' Brigg asked, his face serious.

Ida nodded, hesitating.

'Tough job. Tougher job than mine. Choosing to mix with criminals?'

'I don't mix with them,' she responded quietly. She took a sip of the cooling stew and picked out a piece of liver, placing it into her mouth. The fire crackled in the silence.

Brigg leaned forward, scooped more stew into his bowl, and put it down next to the fire. 'For the tommyknockers,' he said with a knowing smile.

Ida nodded. She had never heard of such superstitions before working in the saloon when she received the occasional, and it was rare, prospector. They were superstitious, the lot of them, and Ida had scoffed inwardly at the tales of the tiny men that caused trouble in their lives, swapping their gold with pyrite, directing their dowsing rods to stone. She said nothing about it, finishing her stew and placing the bowl down beside her.

'Thank you for the meal.'

'You got it,' Brigg replied. 'I ain't chatted to anyone in days, apart from Stinky Hoss. Listen, you wanna be careful riding about in the nighttime. I gotta feeling you're a tenderfoot.'

'I've got guns. I've got a horse. I'll be fine,' Ida said, sniffing hard.

'No offence meant there. There are always more eyes watching you than you think.'

Ida scratched her chin in irritation. She could travel the land over and still get told what to do by complete strangers. 'And what about you? Aren't you a sitting duck, out here on your own, gold on your person, a donkey as an escape aid?' she snapped.

Brigg raised his hands and laughed, his eyes remaining unsmiling. 'An old man making his way to Bleakhollow? I ain't got nothing worth taking, trust me. But you...you got something worth taking.'

The fire was dying between them. Did he know? Was he referring to her womanhood? They looked at each other, and Ida shook her head. He did. He knew. He knew who she was. She blinked purposefully, her right hand moving to her side. Ida rested her fingers on top of her gun and raised her eyebrows. Brigg frowned.

'What have I got that's worth taking?' she asked, keeping her voice low and strong.

Brigg shrugged, his right eye twitching. 'Your nice horse, for a start. I'm just saying. There something off about you, Colton – I ain't figured it out yet.'

'It ain't yours to figure.' Ida stood up and dusted the dirt off her trousers with her left hand, a casual move that was meant to distract from the still-hovering right hand that paused on the handle of her gun. 'I'll be off now.'

'As you please. I didn't mean you no offence, but I gotta say, the mood has soured a bit.' Brigg scratched his beard and shrugged. 'Listen, there's a little town on a hill in Bleakhollow, name of Steepmount. If they ain't got the prettiest whores!'

Ida didn't hesitate. This was confirmation. She pulled her gun in one swift movement and cocked the hammer, aiming it at Brigg. He stared at her, mouth open, hands flying to the air.

'What about them?' she growled.

Brigg regarded the gun in surprise and swallowed. 'I was just saying – next time you're in town, ask for Mrs Smithe and mention my name – she'll get you a discount!'

Ida nodded and then reholstered the gun as quickly as she had pulled it. 'All right.' She touched her hat with the tip of her finger. 'Thanks for the stew.'

Brigg responded with the same action and watched as Ida mounted.

'Colton, if you're headed in the way you were going originally – a word of warning. You want to get yourself some long boots. Hangman's Rest is lousy with snakes.'

'Yessir. Anything else?' Ida bit her tongue. She wanted to tell him that she didn't need any more advice, that her whole life was made up of unwanted and unfrequented titbits that she could do without.

'Anything else?' Brigg said, thinking for a moment, his wits not registering the sarcasm in her voice. 'Well, if you come along a trading post…oh, around three hours from here, there's usually a bit of gold to be won in a card game. And once you reach it, head south. Don't keep going west. There are more rumours about what happens that way than I'd care to relate.'

Bullet shifted beneath Ida in the darkness, and she placed a calming hand on his shoulder. 'Rumours of what?' she asked.

Brigg leaned forward toward the fire, the crevices in his face lighting up. 'Of witchcraft. It's the Derelict Woods – they're full of it.'

Ida thought of her father, a man for whom witchcraft and spiritualism were nonsense. She thought of the time that she had found pennies beneath the floorboards of the farmhouse and asked her father what they were for. He had cursed, calling her mother a superstitious woman, and rubbed his head at the notion of what secrets the house might be holding. And then there were the women in the saloon, who had told her witchcraft was a thing of the past, some of them disappointed to mention it.

'There's no such thing,' Ida said, gathering her reins.

'Ah, what would you know?' Brigg said, more to himself than to Ida. She frowned at him and tipped her head again, the silent goodbye.

Bullet and Ida moved through the sparse woods at a more gentle speed than before, nervously at first, with Ida checking behind them at every opportunity. But no, Brigg was not following them, whether or not he had suspected her truth.

Chapter 5

Colt held his head in his hands as he sat in front of the sheriff. The sheriff had his feet resting on his desk before him, central in the small jailhouse of Steepmount. Around him were two cells holding beds and buckets, only one of them with somebody inside. The sheriff took his hat off and inspected the seams with faux interest, a yawn threatening to rise in his mouth. It was late, or early, depending on how you looked at it. He looked at it as late and thought about the bed frame waiting for him in the room next door. Damn it, he'd even lock himself into one of the cells for the night to get some kip; not even that straw mattress would stop him. Colt raised his head.

'So you didn't ride past the Bleakhollow threshold?'

The sheriff stared at Colt. He was a man who understood the meaning of power and prestige. He hadn't killed the former sheriff for nothing. He'd earned this position, and here was this little snivelling dweeb with the audacity to talk to him as though he hadn't.

'Listen, mister, none of my men found anything. No traces. Hoof marks, there are plenty. If she went the direction we did, and that's a strong if, she would have headed straight into Demon's Canyon. Few realise the drop that awaits them.'

Colt looked to the ceiling as though he were talking to the sky and shook his head. 'You're wrong. My horse knew Demon's Canyon, knew it well.'

The sheriff snorted a small laugh and put his hat back on his balding head. 'Horses, you know, ain't really that bright.'

'That's it then. I get robbed in your town, and the only thing that you have to say about it is, 'Horses ain't that bright?' You do know that she stole the clothes off my back? The woman stole my hat! She left me with nothing.'

'And yet, no one saw her leave. There were people in the bar. Now I find that sort of interesting,' the sheriff said, nodding.

'I find that of interest too,' said another voice. Colt and the sheriff turned to the direction from which it came and glanced at the gruff man behind bars. He grinned.

'You find that interesting?' spat Colt.

'Surely do. She robbed you, took everything you got, ain't no one saw her leave? Well, why on earth is that? Where did she go? That's the question.'

The sheriff laughed, a real chuckle, as though he were a child sitting in the schoolyard with his friends.

Colt stood, pushing the chair back and knocking it over. 'What you in for, sir?' he asked the prisoner.

'Conspir…sheriff?'

'Yeah, you got it, a conspiracy, wasn't it? Planning on murdering that neighbour of yours.'

'Yeah, that's it,' agreed the prisoner, shaking his head. 'That no-good sonofabitch.'

Colt grinned at the sheriff and then back at the prisoner. 'If I pay your bail, would you track down this woman for me?'

The prisoner glanced nervously between the two men and thought for a moment. 'Well, you might not think that I got much going on here, boy, the fact of the matter is, I got a bed, I got meals, and I got some fair company in the sheriff here.'

'Well, that's mighty kind of you to say.' The sheriff tipped his hat in recognition.

'So, what are you asking for?' said Colt, his temper fraying.

'I'm just saying, you pay the bail, that's one thing. Then you gotta give me the money for my troubles. I'm talking…for the journey. Food. Hay. Provi…tio…'

'Provisions,' the sheriff finished for him, nodding. 'That's right. It's a poor deal just to pay the man's bail. Why, I might decide to let him out in a couple of days or so. He didn't actually do any murdering.'

'I did not,' the prisoner agreed.

'You did not,' echoed the sheriff.

Colt gaped at the prisoner and then at the sheriff in disbelief. 'Are you joking?'

'Of course he's not joking. Steepmount Jailhouse is not a bad place to be. And anyway, what money do you have? I thought she took you for all you're worth?'

'I always keep something in my union,' Colt said. Reader, between us, Colt didn't have much money to begin with, and Ida had taken nothing but pennies from him.

The prisoner murmured a noise of agreement. 'Wise.'

'Anyway, son, if you're so bothered about catching the woman, why don't you go do it? You don't own any land in Steepmount. You're not from here.'

Colt dragged the chair back up behind him and sat down in silence, his eyes averted from the other man's gaze. There was tension in the room, and the sheriff pulled a bored face at the prisoner, who shrugged. After a moment, the prisoner spoke first.

'You scared, boy?'

Colt's head snapped up, and he glowered at the man behind bars. 'I'm just looking for a gun for hire.'

'Well, Jonesy here might not be your man for that. Eh, Jonesy?' the sheriff said, a kind smile alighting his face.

'I'm a sheep farmer by trade. That murder business wasn't really my regular job. That was because my sonofabitch neighbour was bothering my herd. And my daughter. But I reckon, if your price is sweet enough, that I could do the job for you. I've tracked a few rogue sheep in my time.'

Colt widened his eyes sarcastically. 'Oh yeah? Any of those sheep carry guns?'

The sheriff sniggered. 'Listen, boy, there's no need to get yourself in a stress here. There's guns for hire in this town, but here's a word of advice…there's not many men that'll go far wrong just forgetting about a robbery and getting on with their lives. We all know she ain't going to be back in Steepmount – she owes Mrs Smithe more in debt than she owes you. Heck, I'd doubt if she was even back in Bleakhollow. Her brother ran her out of that farmland her daddy had – she's too old to be a wife. She ain't got nothing round these parts but trouble and danger. Hangman's Rest is where she's headed, if she's even alive still.

And there ain't nothing out there for you but expense and trouble, without any guaranteed results.'

The prisoner whistled low and long and nodded his head. 'Yup, yup, yup.'

Colt licked his lips and scratched his chin. 'That's that then. That's your motto, is it? 'Leave it alone', 'oh well?' What kind of a sheriff don't fight to hang those who have done wrong?'

The sheriff raised his eyebrows, his eyes hardening. 'I hung a man only last week for stealing lemonade from the saloon. Born and bred here he was, but stealing ain't right. What I don't have time for is tracking thieves across lands that I ain't a sheriff in. You better believe that the whole of The Nameless Stretch is lousy with criminals. If this is your first time as a victim, well, you are a lucky bastard. Count yourself as lucky and get yourself a new horse.'

Colt shook his head and stood up, stepping behind his chair and pushing it in dramatically. 'Well, both of you, sirs, have been absolutely no help at all. I'm going to get posters made – Wanted posters. I'm going to send them from door to door, town to town. The Nameless Stretch is about to shrink, and that bitch ain't going to get out alive.' He turned on his heel and marched out of the jailhouse, the large wooden door slamming behind him.

'He's got more money than sense,' the prisoner said.

'I don't think he's even got much money.' The sheriff stood up and sniffed, chuckling to himself. 'Well, Jonesy, I'm going to head off to bed, and I suggest you do the same. I'll get that coffee brewing first thing.'

'Yessir,' said the prisoner, giving a small thumbs-up and turning toward his bed.

'Yup. You want I should turn this light out or leave it on?'

'Oh, leave it on, sir, if you could. It's them rats that I don't like hearing in the darkness. I've a feeling they know to stay away when the lamp is lit.'

'I don't doubt it,' the sheriff replied, smiling to himself. Yes, Steepmount was a good sort of place to be a prisoner, he thought. Shame that young lady didn't seem to know it…although doubtlessly, it'd be a hanging for her.

The sun was beginning to rise, causing the sparse trees to shift from grey to orange in slow motion. Bullet was tired, as was Ida. The tiredness was making Ida jumpy, which in turn was provoking Bullet to dance a little beneath the saddle, sensing her nerves through the air. She rubbed her neck and shook herself.

'We should stop for coffee,' she said aloud, as though Bullet could respond and agree. He said nothing, of course. Ida yawned and blinked at the distance. The trees were becoming thinner, their green leaves wilting and darkening as though they had been burned in a fire. It was a strange sight. Then, between them, Ida saw a building. Was this the trading post? She nudged Bullet forward, and he ignored her, his pace barely increasing.

They got closer, the building looming large on their horizon. Ida could see a light shining through the window, and her heart clenched at it. It was almost a reminder of a home, though she tried to think of a time that she had returned home to her father. That was never the case. It was always the other way around. He would return home to her, and she would light the lamps and candles to guide him. To see the sight from the other side was warming, as though there were treats within. As they arrived, Ida pulled Bullet to a walk and then a halt, dismounting and securing him to the hitching post beside two other horses. She looked at the small hut, the sunlight beginning to shine on the wooden slats that came together to be its walls. The door flew open and smashed against the wooden wall, causing Ida to flinch.

'And if you think I'm just gonna sit here and be robbed – well, you got another think coming!' A man dressed in a long brown fur coat and ludicrously wide-brimmed hat appeared in the doorway and spat on the ground, stomping down the steps. With each movement, his boots rang through the air, the large spurs behind him like wind chimes. Ida had never seen a man dressed like him. He looked as though he was dripping in wealth and wanted the world to know it. 'Who're you?' he said, his voice a shiver of anger.

'I- I'm Colton,' she said, almost forgetting to change her name.

'Colton who? From where?' he asked, hands hovering over his hips. The day was already beginning to warm, and the sun was barely up. How did he survive in such a coat?

Ida hesitated. 'Colton John,' she said, thinking of her father's name. It was not believable. She thought of her father's map of Bleakhollow. 'From the Docks of Astray.'

The man burped as though that were a normal response. Ida wrinkled her nose.

'Well, Colton John, with your backward name. It's early in the season for me, so I don't have much to show, but what I do have is on my horse. What was it you were looking for?'

Ida shook her head, baffled. The man tapped his foot and sighed.

'A coat, is it? You'll need one if you're heading south.'

'I've just come to visit the trading post, sir,' she responded.

'Most folks who come through here do so intending to buy from a trapper. This here is where I do most of my trade. You heading to Hangman's Rest?'

Ida nodded.

'So you'll need a coat. Or you'll die. Trust me, Docks of Astray, you're used to warmer climes than we are.' He stepped past her and walked to his horse, who stood beneath a tree away from the hitching post. The horse was a large bay cob, laden with materials and furs but seemingly unbothered, as though he didn't see the other horses standing beneath anything but a saddle. The man pulled a fur off the back of his steed and shook it out before him, revealing it to be a long coat. Ida watched in genuine admiration. She had never bought herself an item of clothing, not once. She was dressed in the clothes that were left in her mother's wardrobe right up until her brother arrived, and then she was dressed by Mrs Smithe and her cronies. This was a spectacular coat, thick and dark.

'This is a grizzly bear – perfect condition. You'll not find a hole in it.'

Ida stepped forward and reached her hand out, touching the soft fur. It felt so luscious and smooth beneath her fingers that she audibly gasped a little. The trapper grinned.

'Yup. It's a beauty. Worth every dime. Every dime.'

Ida paused. She had no money, apart from the few cents she'd found in the bottom of the saddlebags. There was a heavy silence between the two of them as the trapper waited for her offer.

'I'm… I don't have much,' she said.

'No? Okay. Well, I have a flawless buckskin coat, not nearly as warm, but it'll do the trick.' The trapper leaned a hand on another skin that was thrown over the saddle of his horse.

Ida stared at the beautiful skins and sighed. The trapper appeared to know precisely what this meant. 'All right. I got a poor bull-skin duster – it's got a grand total of five bullet holes in it. Don't ask why.' He folded the bearskin coat back up and secured it to his horse, and then removed the duster with a flourish. Around the bullet holes were traces of blood. The trapper followed her gaze and laughed. 'Oh, that'll clean right off.'

Ida shook her head. 'No, that's not for me.'

'All right. How about this…you seem like an honest lad. That postal worker in there is tryna' take me for a fool. We been playin' cards, and he's been cheatin'. But what I care about ain't the cards as much as what's behind those bars in there.' The trapper leaned forward and lowered his voice conspiratorially. 'I know for a fact that the man in there siphons off a little cream from each envelope that comes through here. I'm talking a little a time – from this town to the next, from one aunt to a niece, he takes what he likes but not enough to cause suspicion. And that's on top of his wages. He's been playing this game for years, boy, while folks like you and me struggle to earn an honest living.' The trapper paused for effect and watched Ida for her reaction.

'Oh, dear,' she said, shaking her head, unsure as to what her reaction should be.

'Exactly. Now here's my thinking – you ain't going come by here again, I shouldn't think. You're headed to Hangman's

Rest, where the bountiful land lies – oh, rarely do traders go back to Bleakhollow.'

Ida sighed, sensing the question that was looming above her. 'And you want me to...'

'That's right. You're a small lad. If you can get in there, get the envelope while he's distracted, and come back out here – that buckskin coat is yours.'

Ida nodded. She thought for a moment, thought of Colt, of the cave that she had spent the night in, of her swift pistol aiming at Brigg's head. She was pretending to be a man. She would do what men did.

'I want a bear,' she said, staring at his pockmarked face with determination. He scoffed.

'That ain't no deal,' he responded.

'All right then, I'll just do what I was intending, head in there for a cup of coffee and a break from my ride.'

'It ain't a canteen.'

'All the same.' Ida touched the tip of her hat with a finger and nodded, turning toward the trading post.

The trapper rolled his eyes. 'All right, boy. You do it, and I won't give you the bear...but you can have this...'

Ida turned as the trapper began to undo something on his saddle. He twisted around and shook it out before her. The grey fur rippled in the air, flowing and moving before her. 'This here is made up of wolf pelts. It ain't perfect, the bastards attacked me on my last trip, and I made this coat here to spite 'em as much as anything. But, bullet holes aside, it's warmer than the buckskin and smarter than the duster.' He held it out to her, and Ida stepped back toward him and felt its weight beneath her fingers. It was soft and warm, heavy to the touch. She glanced at the trapper.

'It snows in Hangman's Rest?'

The trapper laughed. 'Are you joking? Yes. You'll not need that coat here, but when you cross that threshold down south, the air becomes thick with ice. And thank god, otherwise, I wouldn't have myself much of a profession.'

Ida nodded. She was already a criminal, she thought. And was this even her? This was Colton John, a new man, a new person. Separate. 'All right. I'll do it.'

'Shake my hand, son. You got a deal. Listen, I'll distract him. You gotta get in there, get the key off the side, and find the envelope. It's got marks all over it, numbers crossed out. It's thick. It'll be behind them bars somewhere.'

Ida paused, afraid. The trapper narrowed his eyes and lowered his voice again.

'As far as men go, he ain't much of one. He's got the bark of a mean dog, but I'd be surprised if he had teeth to match. He's a lazy bastard, truth be told. And he won't suspect—'

A noise clattered behind them, the sound of footsteps treading down wooden steps. The trapper glanced up past Ida's head and nodded.

'All right, Smidge? Just explainin' to this 'ere lad about mindin' Demon's Canyon on the way to Bleakhollow,' he said with a tight smile.

Ida turned and nodded at the man that had exited the trading post. He was a short, ruddy skinned, middle-aged man, shaped like a barrel. He was dressed as though he worked for a bank, a waistcoat stretching across his round stomach, a golden pocket watch chain attached to one of the shiny buttons. He tipped his crisp-edged hat towards Ida.

'You heading to Bleakhollow, are you?'

Ida nodded. 'Yup.'

'That could actually work out quite nicely for me. I got some post to be delivered to Steepmount. Postal service ain't supposed to be coming for a week. You fancy earning a buck and taking it for me?'

Ida shrugged. 'Can do,' she said. The trapper raised his eyebrows at her.

'Smidge, you're best to leave it for the postal service – you can't go trusting important letters to a stranger,' he said, tutting. Ida was surprised. His morals were baffling.

'I earn an extra dime if they're delivered early,' Smidge responded, pulling down his waistcoat as though that might impact its fitting around his ample stomach.

The trapper shook his head. 'Your funeral. I'm going to get myself a coffee from indoors. That sun is starting to rise, and I don't like the look of it.'

Both Ida and Smidge turned to look at the burgeoning sun climbing in the sky.

'You a coffee drinker, lad?' Smidge asked Ida, pulling at his waistcoat again.

She nodded.

Once coffee had been drunk, the three sat in silence around the card table. Ida had never been inside a trading post before, and it was much as she had imagined. At the far end was a desk, pigeonholes covering the wall behind it, bars at the front, like a bank. The door behind the desk was an outdoor one, so you had to go outside and come back in that way if you wanted to access it. Apart from that, the room was fairly bare, apart from an iron bed frame holding a thin mattress and blankets, a small cooker, and a card table. On the floor beside the table were more blankets and fur. Ida imagined that this was where the trapper slept on occasion.

'So you don't play cards?' he asked Ida, a sigh escaping his lips. Ida shook her head. Truthfully, she knew no games. She had watched the men at the saloon in Steepmount many times but had not been able to gather the whys and wherefores of their actions. The trapper shrugged, his coffee cup long empty. 'You should head off then, lad, hit Demon's Canyon while it's still light. Only a fool would go in the dark.'

Ida nodded and stood. She was happy to get out of there. The conversation between Smidge and the trapper was stilted and awkward, their previous argument over cards and money still not settled. 'I'm grateful for the coffee.'

Smidge yawned. 'Yup.'

'You still want that pelt?' the trapper asked suddenly. Ida glanced at him, noticing the coldness in his eyes. She nodded. 'Good. I'll get it for you now. You can secure it to your horse.'

They went outside together, leaving Smidge sitting at the table, shuffling his cards.

'You're out-staying your welcome, lad,' the trapper said as soon as they were out of earshot. 'We need to get that job done and fast before anyone else rides by.' He pulled the wolf pelt coat from his horse and strode over to Bullet, securing it over his smooth rump. Bullet shuffled at the sensation of sudden warmth against his skin. The trapper turned back to Ida. 'I'll go back in there now and cause a distrac—'

'Oi, lad! Here are those letters I told you 'bout.' Ida saw the trapper mouth a swear word and turned to see Smidge drop down the steps with a grin, a bag over his shoulder. He walked over and pushed it into her arms. 'There's a sweetener in there for you.'

The trapper rolled his eyes. 'Ain't we playing cards, fat boy?'

'What is your problem today – you lose one game, and it's the end of the world,' Smidge growled in response.

Ida watched the two men head back into the trading post and turned to Bullet, securing the bag onto his saddle. They would have to make a quick getaway at any moment.

Within seconds, there was a large crash from inside the trading post. Ida flinched. That must be the distraction she was waiting for. Yells began to fly between the cracks in the walls, the trapper's voice ringing out above all. She thought she could make out the words 'cheater' and 'scoundrel.' Rather him than herself, Ida mused, crouching and stepping toward the secondary door on the side of the building. There was only one large step up toward it, and Ida took it with a sharp breath, holding it as she grasped the handle. She prayed that it was locked, and then she could just go about her business. Ah, but the wolf pelt would no longer be hers. She pulled and turned it, and to her dismay and excitement, a curious mix of emotions, the door opened.

The volume of the men's argument was instantly turned up, and Ida breathed out as though she were breaking in a colt. She stepped in, still doubled over. She allowed the angry words behind the bars to cascade over her, and not recognising or engaging with their meaning or volume, just let them be. It was a trick she had learned when she began to bore of her father's endless stories, the same every evening. To her right were the pigeonholes, some empty, some stuffed with papers. To her left was the desk, a stool pushed in beneath it. There was nothing but single documents on top, so she moved to the two large drawers on either side. First, the left, closest to the door. Ida pulled it open, grateful that it didn't squeak and stared at the insides. It was a mass of envelopes. This man was not an organised postal worker. Bullet could have done a better job.

Ida began rifling through the envelopes, looking for one with numbers scrawled over it, thick with cash. The ones that slipped through her fingers were simply addressed envelopes, nothing out of the ordinary. Ida shook her head, her heart beating hard. The shouting was ongoing, the anger throbbing through the room. She moved to the next drawer and pulled it open. Inside were only a few papers, a rotting apple and a knife placed precariously on top. Ida bit her lip and then grabbed the knife. She shifted to her hands and knees and thought for a moment. Where did her father keep the money? Beneath his mattress, that was no help. Then, as though the sky was on her side, a bright beam of light shone through a far window, reflecting off the knife and shining a spot onto the floor. It was a floorboard, of course, but one with a difference. This one was short, as though it had been sawn to two bits, with a small hole in the corner. Jackpot. She pushed the knife into her pocket and stuffed a finger inside the hole, pulling on the board. It came loose.

Beneath it was the envelope, scrawled with figures and sums, fat with cash, as the trapper had said. Ida grasped it and then pushed it into her pocket just as a sound that terrified her reached her ears. A gunshot rang through the trading post, piercing the argument. Silence descended. Ida took a breath in, the scent of gunpowder filling her nostrils. Should she look? Her hands began to tremble. She pulled her gun out of her holster, took a breath, and then peeked over the desk. There was Smidge, standing over the great trapper, his face concealed by his hat. That was all Ida needed to know. She reholstered her gun and crawled toward the door, which was mercifully still a little ajar. With one hand, she pushed it further open and then crawled out of the building, praying that the door wouldn't attract Smidge's attention. With a deep breath, she stood in the morning air and jumped down the large step.

Bullet was waiting for her at the hitching post. Ida ran toward him, untying his reins and mounting swiftly. She turned him, and then her eyes fell onto the trapper's horse. The cob stood, unaware of the death of his master. Over his saddle lay the bear coat that Ida had coveted earlier. Exactly how much of a criminal was she now? How much of a thief was Colton John? A noise came from within the trading post, and Ida snapped her head toward the main door, fearful of the postal worker. It was still closed. He must be fretting within. She nudged Bullet toward the large cob and took her left foot out of her stirrup, hooking her leg behind her onto Bullet's rump, still covered in the wolf and post. With her balance secured, she leaned over and grasped the soft bear pelt and pulled it. The door squeaked open behind her.

'What the hell?' Smidge's voice rang through the air, and Ida took no time to look. Before she could even unhook her leg, she growled at Bullet to fly, grasping a fistful of mane in her hand. He did just that, compensating for her unbalance in the saddle.

Reader, had Ida waited, she would have heard the warning of the postal worker, and this might be a very different story. Smidge watched them depart at speed and shook his head, gun still in hand. 'He's heading toward the Derelict Woods, the idiot.' He thought for a moment. 'With my bloody post.'

Chapter 6

'Describe her then,' the sketch artist said, his eyes bored and dull.

'I told you, she's dressed as me,' Colt said, already fed up with dealing with the people of Steepmount.

'Yeah, but what does that mean? You want me to draw you?'

'I want you to draw a woman's face underneath my hat. She had…big eyes.'

'Big eyes. Frogs have big eyes. You want me to draw a frog in a hat, or you got some more pointers?' The sketch artist raised his eyebrows. 'Anyone got a photo of this woman?'

'If they had a photo, don't you think I'd be using that?!' Colt barked, rolling his eyes.

'Who knows? All right, big eyes. Nose? Mouth? Chin? Age?'

Colt scratched his head. 'She must have been nearing thirty, although she didn't look like it. I had a few drinks if I could be um…frank.' He glared into the distance, downcast. 'Straight, small nose, I think. I remember it being slightly upturned. The silhouette of her face was so…ideal. I remember thinking…that face. I'd be satisfied with that face for the rest of my days.'

'Oh boy,' said the sketch artist beneath his breath. It wasn't often he drew a picture for someone who wanted the perpetrator to be both hanged and made his wife.

There was a reason that not many wandered into the Derelict Woods. The rumours about the place were as thick as the trees, their canopies creating a dark and dismal swamp-like floor that inspired poetry across the divide between Bleakhollow and Hangman's Rest. Having only seen a map of the north of The Nameless Stretch, Ida had never heard these words. Some wrote them down, most famously in the poetry chapbook *The Killing Trees*, written by M. Forrester. This had been shared and reproduced for almost a hundred years. Had Ida browsed the bookcase in her original room at Mrs Smithes', she would have found a well-worn copy nestled between tales of triumph and courage. Had she read the following poem, she may not have chosen to ride through the dim and damp woods alone.

The sound you hear from over there
Is trying in its knowing.
They're watching you; you should take care,
Your blood will soon be flowing.

It is the night, even in day,
They'll trip you, trap you, pluck.
She's waiting in the poisoned grey,
You've plum run out of luck.

This was one of the most popular poems in the chapbook, for its simplicity and rhyming scheme was easy to remember. It was especially popular with children of learning ages, who found that the last word of the last line could easily be swapped for something ruder and more amusing. Nobody knew if the writer, M. Forrester, had indeed visited the Derelict Woods – but that didn't matter. Everyone knew that the stories were better than the truth, and that was just fine by them.

Ida had noticed a change in atmosphere as she rode from the trading post and crossed the threshold into the Derelict Woods. Her escape had been quick, the earth beneath Bullet's feet firm and dusty, allowing them to leave the dead trapper and the guilty Smidge behind them. The sun was rising fast in the sky, causing Bullet to slow a little, and then…it was as though the lights had been blown out. They entered the woods with such speed that it took both of them by surprise. Bullet slowed as though he were galloping into a brick wall, and Ida grabbed onto his mane to stop herself from flying over his head. Their eyes adjusted quickly to the light.

'It's just the trees, Bullet,' Ida said in a soothing voice. 'Trees are nothing to be afraid of.' Though she heard the words, she couldn't even convince herself. The branches moving in the dimness seemed to hide people, and Ida feared them making themselves known. Was it Colt who hit away in the trees, watching her? Ida urged Bullet back into a walk, the boggy ground pulling at his hooves and fetlocks. 'Have courage,' she murmured, more to herself than her horse.

The air was damp and freezing cold, a stink of sulphur lingering as though the sun had never touched this part of the world before. Ida wrapped the bear pelt coat around her, gratefully feeling its warmth. They continued, observing their surroundings. Ida felt turned around. Was this west? She had left the trading post in such a hurry that it was hard to say which way was which. The branches of the trees stretched out and brushed them like strange spindly claws, reaching out to grasp their skin. How long had it been since she had slept? Her eyelids were beginning to droop.

'Bullet, hold,' she said, bringing him to a halt among the dark trees. She dismounted, her boots sinking in mud, and stared at the ground. How could she set up to sleep in this? It would be impossible. Bullet blinked at her inquisitively.

'I don't know, boy. How can we get some rest here? Perhaps I could…' Ida looked upwards at the trees, wondering for a moment about sleeping in their branches, away from the ground. It was surely a ridiculous idea. Bullet snorted, and the trees whispered and gathered around them, their leaves ruffling in the wind. The noise was hypnotic, almost beautiful, like a sing-song voice folding through the branches, fluid and motionless at the same time. Ida touched Bullet on his soft neck as the words formed in her ears.

Looking for a place to rest?

She turned her head. There was nobody around. Who had spoken?

Need to rest your weary bones? I have space for both of you.

Ida swallowed hard and remounted Bullet, her muddy boots shoved into the stirrups. The air seemed to change around them, the scent of sulphur floating away. Rose petals stretched before her nostrils. The looming trees shook themselves like a line of dogs after a bath, and Ida watched open-mouthed as their branches swept aside, creating a path between them.

Do not be afraid; I mean you no harm.

Ida felt Bullet tense beneath her. The voice may not mean them harm, but she was afraid. But what choice did she have? With the swamp-like floor and closed canopy roof, she could barely track her way out in a hurry. And, so far, she had put faith in a few strangers, and it had been worthwhile. Her tiredness was beginning to take over her entire body, her stomach rumbling and arguing beneath her. The risk of continuing was worth the potential of food and rest, worth the opportunity to hide from Colt and whoever he may have collected to find her.

The sketch artist held up the picture, and Colt snatched it from his hands. It wasn't half bad, actually, despite the fact that the bastard was ripping him off. That much for a doodle? He'd even had Mrs Smithe come in and describe some of Ida's features. Now, he stared into the face of the woman who had robbed him. She looked so innocent. Had the artist done that on purpose? It was as though she was the woman he had initially thought she was, Elizabeth. She even lied about her name. Colt grimaced at the picture and then spat on the floor, filled with rage.

'Oh, take it outside, boy,' said the artist, a sigh escaping his lungs.

'Where's the nearest printing press?' Colt asked, unable to take his eyes off the picture.

'There's one between here and Blackreach. Services both towns.'

Colt said nothing in response, a courteous thank you unable to leave his lips. He stormed back into the midday sun and glared up the street. There, at the end, stood the stagecoach sign. He marched toward it with purpose, his borrowed trousers too long and gathering dust beneath his boots. The only thing the woman had left him, his boots. Not even his hat! How had it come to this, him out of pocket and paying to catch a thief? When this was over, they'd all hang. Ida, the sheriff, the lot of them.

The stagecoach sign was hand-painted, clearly fancy in its day, but now worn and faded. There was no one behind it at all.

'What, you wanting the stagecoach?' a voice called to the side of Colt. He turned to the speaker, an old man who was sitting in a rocking chair on his porch, chewing on a piece of hay.

'Yup,' said Colt.

'Yup,' repeated the old man, nodding. 'He's took a traveller to the Docks of Astray, should be back soon.'

'Right. How long?'

'Oh, soon, I should say.' The old man nodded again, agreeing with his own words.

'Today?' Colt asked, cursing the town of Steepmount silently.

'If that's what soon means to you, I dare say that's correct.'

Colt shifted toward him and turned, sitting on the step up to the porch. The old man chuckled.

'She your girlfriend?'

'What?' Colt snapped, his head swivelling on his weedy neck.

'The picture. That your girlfriend? She looks beautiful, like a rose or—'

'She ain't my girlfriend. She's a thief.'

'Yup,' the old man chuckled again, oblivious to Colt's tone. 'They steal your heart, and they get away with it. They're all like that. But where would we be without 'em?'

Colt said nothing and just listened to the incessant creaking of the rocking chair, back and forth, back and forth, clogging up the anger in his mind. I'll add him to the list, Colt thought, staring at the old man. He can be hanged with the rest of 'em.

The path stretched in the distance, and though they kept following, there seemed to be no end in sight. Ida's body was weary and worn, the warmth of the bear pelt like a blanket around her, the gait of Bullet rocking her gently. Sleep was coming. It began in her mind, her eyes still open, watching, and fearful.

Not far to go, the voice said. Ida had noticed that each time it appeared in her mind, Bullet's ears flattened against his head.

He could hear it too, speaking to them. Ida closed her eyes for a moment, her brain beginning to lull her to sleep. It filled with nonsensical thoughts, dragging memories and lies into dreams. Her father, dancing in the saloon before her, his hat thrown up in the air and never coming back down. Mrs Smithe comforting Bullet, stroking his long, dark mane with care. Her brother, strange and faceless, soothing her woes. Darkness.

The next time Ida opened her eyes, she felt only comfort. She blinked in the dim light, staring at the ceiling above her. To her surprise, the ceiling was patterned, complicated wallpaper that she had never seen before, swirled shapes mixing in gold and brown above her head. She felt the weight of blankets on her body and rolled over. A dying candle was lit beside her on a wooden table, flickering in the air. Where was she? In some ways, it didn't matter. The bed was soft and warm, and though her stomach rumbled, she felt safe. Ida yawned and rolled over, drifting back to sleep with ease.

Hoof on dirt, weight-bearing down onto petals. Ida felt the heft of her Winchester in her hands. His smug smile and hard eyes were unwavering beneath the brim of his hat. The horse pounded at the ground, pulling up her work, her years of growth, of effort. The man was speaking, but his voice was distorted in the wind, echoing strangely in her ears. What were the words he was saying?

Betrayal.

Ida lifted her Winchester and stared down the barrel, cocking the hammer. She breathed in and fired. The bullet landed straight through the centre of his hat. He laughed as if in slow motion and pulled his hat off, holding it aloft. His head was smoking, a strange fog emitting from his temples. He was laughing, laughing, laughing.

Betrayal.

Clink. Clink.

The noise dragged Ida out of her sleep. The room was brighter, a fresh breeze drifting in. She pulled herself up. There was an elderly woman at the end of the bed, busying herself with a pot and a cup. She was dressed in flowing black clothes, of an unusual style that Ida had never before seen.

'Hello?' said Ida warily. She held the blanket up against herself, some strange protection from the stranger. Then, she noticed with a shock that she was not wearing her hat. Her long, brindled hair fell about her shoulders. Ida's breath caught in her throat.

'Hello,' the woman said, turning to face her. Her skin was creased and old, but that was not what shocked Ida. She was covered in tattoos, every corner of her visible skin inked and marked. Ida had never seen a tattoo, not really. The woman's eyes were bright and clear, and she smiled, causing the ink on her cheeks to ripple and dimple like water, fluid.

'Where am I?' Ida whispered, her authentic voice coming out for the first time in days. She took a deep breath, trying to find a braveness within.

'You're at my home. You arrived yesterday with your horse, barely conscious. He's outside, enjoying some oats. You both need to eat more,' she said, her voice crisp and well-spoken. She stepped toward Ida with a cup of coffee and nodded. 'Drink.'

Ida took it and sipped, watching the woman sit on the end of the bed with her own cup. She nodded to thin air, her face expressive.

'What's your name?' asked Ida, taking another sip. The coffee was strong and hot, with a hint of almond. It was everything she could have wanted at that moment.

'Oh, I have many names. You may call me Fae.' The woman took a gulp of her drink and nodded at Ida. 'And you also go by many names, do you not?'

'My name is Col—'

'Ah, Colton. Yes, that is one of them,' Fae interrupted, a strange smile on her lips. The tattoos rippled again as though a wind were blowing them across her face. Ida watched and said nothing. She did not know what to say. This woman had a strange presence about her, as though she already knew everything there was to know about Ida.

'Ida,' Fae said. 'Ida Vale. That is your name.' She glanced to the left of Ida as though staring at the wall and nodded primly as if she had been asked a question.

'How do you know…?'

Fae smiled. 'Because I know. Your mother told me.'

Instantly, Ida threw back the covers, emerging from within their soft protective barrier. Some of the coffee in her cup spilt over the edge and landed on the wooden floorboards beside her. Fae watched in mild amusement.

'You knew my mother?' Ida asked, amazed. She had never met anyone who knew her mother but her father.

Fae patted her hand and took another hearty mouthful of her drink. 'Yes, in a sense. Come, join me in the kitchen for breakfast. You are hungry.'

Ida had almost entirely forgotten about food, but now that it was brought up, she became ravenous in an instant. She climbed out of bed, still wearing Colt's clothes, and watched as Fae stood. The old woman appraised her for a moment.

'These clothes are rotten,' she said. 'You must buy new clothing at the next town you reach – these will never do.' With this, she turned and left the room, Ida following sheepishly behind, feeling as though she were carrying a stench along with her.

The rumbling wheels of the stagecoach slowed before Colt. He had been waiting all day and long into the night. He'd even given up and gotten some rest at one point, and then come back to be told by the old man that the stagecoach had actually reappeared, changed drivers, and trundled off again. And now, the sun was rising through the sky, and it was finally here.

'Where the bloody hell have you been?' Colt yelled to the driver, who turned around and looked behind him, unsure if he was being spoken to.

'Eh?'

'You!' Colt marched over and shook his head. 'Where the hell have you been?'

The driver caught eyes with the old man, repositioned in his chair, and gave him a look that clearly meant, 'Who the hell is this guy?' The old man shrugged and scratched his head. 'I've been up at Blackreach, delivering a chap. What's your problem?'

'I've been waiting for a day,' Colt responded, throwing his hands up in the air. Reader, he could have walked it in less time.

'Well, with all due respect, sir, you should have just ridden. Now, I can take you, but you can keep that attitude right here.'

'I would have ridden if my bloody horse wasn't stolen. Nobody in this godforsaken town will help me, and it is really getting old.'

A look of recognition began to shine across the driver's face, and he grinned. 'Oh yeah, you're the one that got robbed by the whore, ain't ya? Get in, son. I'll take you to where you need to go. No need to get so upset.'

'I want to go to the printing press between here and Blackreach,' Colt responded through clenched teeth, his eyes boring into the man sitting above him.

'Ah, yeah. Run by an old farmer and his son, ain't it? Salt of the—'

'JUST TAKE ME,' Colt yelled, causing the stagecoach horses to flatten their ears and dance before the coach. The driver watched him in silence, shaking his head. Colt pulled the door and stepped inside, banging on the ceiling before he'd even sat down. The coach began moving with such a start that he was flung back against the seats, his thigh bruising on impact. He swore beneath his breath. Up above, the driver grinned and flicked his reins again, urging the horses onwards.

Ida sat at the large kitchen table and watched Fae prepare the meal. She did so in a strange sort of silence, occasionally narrating her actions as though for an audience.

'She'll have two eggs if she hasn't eaten in a while,' she said to the pan, 'but I'll only have one. The chickens won't be able to keep up.'

At first, Ida had attempted to answer the comments, feeling as though she was being rude by saying nothing, but quickly found that she was ignored. She sipped at her coffee and waited, desperate to talk about her mother, to eat some food, to find out where she was. The thought had also passed her mind that the woman might be in cahoots with Colt, that some plan was afoot, but she pushed it out. She would take what she could get, to survive.

The kitchen was large and strange, as though Fae's goal was to squeeze an item into every available space. It resulted in an odd sort of atmosphere, both cramped and spacious at the same time. On the walls were old portraits of all kinds of people, some painted, some black and white photographs. They stared out from dusty frames, watching the entire room.

Eventually, Fae turned, placing a plate before Ida. Eggs, bread, cheese, meat. It was perfect. She began to eat, shovelling the food into her mouth with abandon, not even waiting for Fae to sit down. Opposite her, Fae did sit, watching her guest with a smile. She picked at her own plate, chewing thoughtfully. After around five minutes, with the food starting to settle in Ida's stomach, she sat up straight and rejoined the room. Fae's eyes sparkled.

'Thank you. Apologies, I was starving. I haven't eaten since a miner shared his stew with me, and that was some time ago,' Ida said.

Fae nodded. 'You've been travelling without rest and food, and that's a recipe for danger. They're further away than you think.'

Ida paused. 'Who?' she asked.

'Come, Ida. You know who, let us not waste time. You are safe here for the moment. Not many people travel through these woods since M. Forrester wrote his chapbook, and even fewer make it to my door.'

Ida swallowed. This woman certainly seemed to know a lot. She watched as Fae reached toward her cup, her clothing shifting over her skin and revealing more tattoos. Fae caught her eye, and Ida smiled sheepishly.

'I have never seen anyone with tattoos.'

'Ah, that is not true. Plenty of people have them and cover them. You've seen them, though you might not be aware of it.'

'Yours seem to…they're not…' Ida began, worried that it was her mind playing tricks on her.

'They are fluid. These tattoos were not earned in ink but in a different way. They are not the same as those that you buy.'

'How were they earned?' Ida asked, watching them shift again.

'They were given to me by friends. Do you see these portraits? These are my friends. Not all of them are with me now, but they visit from time to time. It is rare, Ida, that I meet someone who has the same types of friends that I have. But you do.' Fae widened her eyes as though Ida might know what she was referring to.

'I don't have any friends. I don't have any friends at all,' Ida responded. It was true. Not even the women in the saloon counted her among their friends. She was the outsider, always.

'You have one person with you at all times. But I think that you're not aware of it.' Fae glanced to the right of Ida as though someone was standing there. It caused Ida's skin to tingle and chill, and she flicked her head to the side to see what she was looking at. There was nothing there. A curtain at the open window flickered in the breeze, and Ida watched it move and then turned back to Fae, frowning.

'How did you know my mother?' she asked.

'Your mother brought you to me, Ida. She is with you now. She brought you here because she wanted me to tell you this,' Fae said matter-of-factly. She took a bite out of a piece of bread and chewed as though they were talking about the weather, mundane and ordinary.

'Fae. I don't know what you're talking about,' Ida said, summoning back some of the courage that she felt as Colton.

'That's because you're not concentrating. You've never been told what to concentrate on, perhaps. Not many people know, but then, not many have the gift. Let's see what we can do here. Close your eyes.'

Ida did as she was told and closed her eyes. She listened to Fae's voice, recognising the smell of roses.

'Think of your mother. Her name was Anne, wasn't it? Think of that photograph your father had of her, sitting on his bedside table. Her head cocked to one side, her straight-faced stare. Think of her scent. The scent of your mother. Oh…hang on. My apologies. You never met her. Well, perhaps that's best.'

Ida opened her eyes. 'What? I did meet her. She died when I was a few months old.'

'Oh…' Fae said, her eyes darting to the side again. 'Oh, dear. That's not the impression your mother is giving me. She is beside you, you know. Look again.'

Ida's eyes began to sting, filling with tears. She turned and looked to the left of her again, where Fae's eyes kept resting. This time, there was something. She blinked, causing a tear to launch from the edge of her eye and fall onto the skin below. It wasn't quite her mother…but it was a shape – the shape of a human.

'Focus. Your mother is beside you. She is wearing a white shirt, high collar. A black skirt, thick belt. Your mother is beside you, Ida. Look at her,' Fae continued.

Ida focused as hard as she could, imagining her mother's face in the photograph, trying to hold her image clear in her mind. She wanted nothing more than to see her again, than to bring her back, to hold her. The shape began to indent slightly, as though the air was sketching with smoke and dust, imprinting on the space before her.

'Your mother is beside you, Ida,' Fae said again, 'think of how knowing her would enrich your life. She wants to see you.'

The air shuddered and shook before her, and slowly, as if she would disappear in the blink of an eye, Ida saw her. It was the image of her mother, smiling and standing, moving and watching. She was faint, as though she had been copied many times over by a printing press, a memory of a photograph. Ida spoke.

'I see her.'

Before her, her mother began to laugh, gleeful and bright. Ida could hear nothing; there was no noise at all.

'Why can't I hear her?' she asked, not taking her eyes off the image. Her mother stopped laughing and smiled sadly, nodding her head.

'Ah, it is early days, Ida. It takes time to build a strong connection. I can hear her faintly, though I have spent years forging a relationship with the spirits, and in all fairness, she and I do not know each other at all.'

Ida stared at the strange image of her mother. She couldn't look away. 'How long has she been here?'

'With you? She's been with you since she died, Ida,' Fae said.

Ida watched as her mother spoke silent words and dared to look away from her image to see Fae leaning in, holding a golden ear-horn to her right ear and nodding.

'What does she say?' Ida asked, nervous, afraid to hear words from her mother's mouth.

'She says that she is sorry, sorry that she left, sorry that your father was not more capable of moving on. She thinks that you have been held far too long at the farmhouse. She thinks that your brother's arrival, though not ideal, was perhaps a blessing in disguise.'

Ida examined Fae for a second and frowned. 'Though not ideal?'

'Oh…I'm paraphrasing, Ida. She thinks that, and I would agree with this…revenge is not a good plan.'

Ida glanced at the shadow of her mother, who was nodding slowly with serious eyes. She looked so strange to Ida, familiar and yet distant. Ida thought of the photograph that she used to pore over, of the times she would carefully clean its frame while her father was out in the field. She looked like her but sadder, if such a thing was possible. The photograph was not of a smiling woman, but of a serious, thoughtful one.

'I hadn't thought of revenge,' Ida said, looking back to Fae.

Fae smiled and raised her eyebrows. 'I have many gifts, Ida. You dreamt of your brother last night, of shooting him. I could see that dream. I can see it now, written across your face.'

'That was not so much a dream as a memory,' Ida replied, watching the shapes on Fae's hands dance across her skin.

'No, it was not a memory. Leave your brother to the land. He will get his comeuppance.'

Ida chewed the inside of her cheek and sighed. She hadn't actually thought of revenge, not against anybody. Fae was watching her, eyes sparkling. Was this some strange sort of trick?

'Ida. Can I give you some advice?' Fae said suddenly.

'Yes.'

'When you arrived here, it was clear to me that you were trying to pass yourself off as someone else. Your hat was hiding your hair. As I helped you to bed and removed that bear pelt from your shoulders, an envelope fell out of the pocket.'

Ida became aware of her heartbeat, loud in her ears. Some of the money she had stolen. The trading post almost seemed like a lifetime ago.

'Yes, I can see from your expression that you know what I am talking about. You have had some semblance of adventure since you left home, though not all good. Perhaps the best bits are down to who you are pretending to be. It isn't easy to be a woman in this world. Your mother tells me that your father was not the greatest supporter of women leaving the house. He was this way with her, too. My advice is two-fold. Be whoever you need to be to get living. If you find strength in being someone else – do it. I don't doubt that one day, you will realise that your strength was within you all along. You can ride, you can shoot, and what do you have that a man doesn't?' Fae narrowed her eyes and leaned in slightly. 'You have the gift of a woman's perspective. You'll be just fine.'

Ida nodded. 'And the second piece of advice?'

'Get yourself to a town. You're in the west of The Nameless Stretch, head south to Hangman's Rest. Use some of that money to get kitted up – long boots, a wax coat, things that will keep you warm. You should burn the clothes you're wearing now – it's not just the scent.'

'Okay.' She glanced at her mother again, who was still sitting and smiling placidly at her. Ida smiled back. 'I don't know how to say this, but…'

Fae shook her head. 'You know what you're looking for now, Ida. There will be times when you are focusing on something else, and your concentration will lapse. Not to mention, the spirit power in this house is very strong. But if you really want to know, you're never alone. They are there, always. This whole room is filled with more spirits than your mother, let me tell you. Haven't you ever had the feeling that someone is watching you? Standing over you?'

Ida nodded. She had, it was true. Reader, perhaps you have, too.

'That's because they were. Or rather, she was. You'll not find anybody else with my connections, of course. They come to me when they can find no satisfaction with their killer. Sometimes I can help.'

'What?' Ida said, wide-eyed. 'With their killer?'

Fae shook her head and laughed, her entire expression lightening. 'Oh, don't worry yourself with the fine print of spirits. Your case is quite different, I assure you. The spirits make their own rules, I am convinced of it. Or perhaps that was just your mother's determination. Come, if you have had enough breakfast, I must give you something for your journey.' She stood and gestured to Ida with both hands and then swept away, her black clothes billowing behind her.

Ida took one last look at her smiling mother and stood, following Fae out of the room. She checked behind her to see her mother still at the table, watching her. Just how long had she been watching her every move? She thought of herself in the saloon, the men who lay on top of her and winced. Surely, each humiliating moment that had burned into her memory was not also her mother's. The thought was too much to bear. 'Oh,' she said aloud, holding her stomach as it shrank and dipped. Fae was just ahead of her, leading her down a dark wood-panelled hallway. She turned.

'The spirits see only what they wish to see. Your mother would not have seen you at your darkest moments. Not always,' Fae said.

Ida stared at her. 'You can read my mind.'

'No.' She shook her head once. 'I can sense an atmosphere, and I am older than you think. What I guess is usually correct – when I have the opportunity to meet people. Come.'

Fae continued to a small almond-shaped door and pushed it open gently. She stepped inside and held the door open, waiting for Ida to do the same. Ida followed. It was a library, shelves covering not only the walls but the close ceiling too. The scent was strong: parchment, dust…and still the faintest smell of roses. Ida looked upwards at the suspended books held in by bars and read some of the titles. *Runes for the Modern Witch. A Spell a Day for Life. Inspirational Women and their Familiars. Telling the Spirit to Hush Up. Building a House of Spells.*

'I wrote all of those on the ceiling, I'm pleased to say. Not that I sell many, obviously. These…' Fae ran a hand along the spines of books to her right, 'are not written by me. But they are quite useful.'

'You're a witch,' Ida said, staring at the woman. Fae laughed brightly, the tattoos on her skin scattering and then coming back like sand on a bedspread.

'Yes, Ida. Come now, you heard me invite you to my home when you were riding through the woods. What did you think was happening?' she asked, curious mirth playing across her face.

'I don't know. I thought that…perhaps I was dreaming it.'

'Dreams. Yes. You, by the way, have some powers of your own – as you have already seen. Your mother, too. She passed them on to you, as all good witches do. Your father would have none of it, believing that witches were a thing of the past. Had your mother still been alive, you would have had a very different upbringing. Now listen, sit.' Fae pointed at an oversized leather chair that sat behind a desk by the window. Ida nodded hastily and sat down, all too aware that she was now sitting in a witch's house and fearful for it.

'You are…a good witch?' she asked.

Fae frowned. 'I am a witch. There is no good or bad. There is no good or bad in The Nameless Stretch; there are just people trying to get by and spirits seeking revenge. Have I done bad things? Of course, I don't want just anybody turning up at my house, and stupid people have a habit of wandering where they're not meant to. Right! Pay attention. Runes. Pull open the top left drawer of that desk there.'

Ida did as she was told and revealed three stones resting on a cotton sheet. Each stone had a carving on it, edged in white, and the breath in Ida's throat caught as she looked at one in particular. She knew that sign. She knew it very well. It was the same as the one carved beneath the kitchen table at her homestead. She had seen it for the first time when she was around ten years old, cleaning the dust and dirt. There, in the wood, was a strange group of uneven triangles. She had spent time staring at it, wondering about it, and had then made the mistake of asking her father. He had told her instantly not to fill her head with nonsense, but later on that evening, she had passed by the kitchen window to see him beneath the table on his hands and knees. The next time she looked, the markings were fainter, sanded down, though not gone completely. His efforts to remove them had seemed odd, but eventually, Ida had forgotten about it, leaving it to the mystery and memory of her father and his strange, grief-stricken ways.

She picked up the stone that she recognised and held it in her palm. Fae moved closer toward her.

'That is a protection rune. Why did you select that?'

'My mother carved it beneath the table in our kitchen.'

Fae nodded. 'Trying to protect the house. Sensible woman.'

Ida felt the weight of the stone in her palm and then looked to the other two. One had a deep cross carved into the centre, with engraved flecks surrounding it, as though it was in the centre of a fire. The other had three stripes of the same size, the centre deepest than the others.

'You can make your own runes, but those from a practised witch, as I am, are more powerful. This is the one that I have selected to give to you, Ida.' Fae leaned forward, picked up the rune with a cross in the centre, and looked at Ida very seriously.

'This holds a great deal of power. It is not for the faint-hearted. I give it to you, knowing that you may use it to protect yourself, but you should know that you will not always be able to control the outcome. If it is used in rage, death may follow.'

Ida hastily put the other rune she was holding back in the drawer. 'My death?'

Fae shook her head. 'Hard to predict. Think of it as a loaded gun, albeit one that won't land you in the hangman's noose. Here, take it.'

Ida took the rune, uncomfortable. It felt heavier than the other. 'Where do I put it?'

'Against your flesh, if possible. Hide it away. You must be going soon. Ida, I say again, and I cannot impress upon you the importance of this. You must visit a town and get new clothing. Ready yourself for the storm, for it is coming.' Fae turned to walk out of the room, pausing at the door. 'Come, you must leave now. I've work to do.'

Ida stood and reached inside her shirt, pushing the rune beneath the bandages against her skin. It tingled as though it was hot, the beginning of a burn. She followed Fae back down the dark corridor and into the kitchen, staring at where her mother was previously.

'She's gone,' Ida said, the empty space widening before her.

Fae glanced at the space and shook her head. 'She's still there, but you have lost your concentration. It'll come back. Your bear pelt is on your horse already. He waits for you outside. Go, get yourself to the next town along. Head south, out of the woods, along the coast. There's a small town called Incan's Brook. They'll have everything that you need there.'

Ida nodded, the burn of the rune subsiding.

Chapter 7

The printer eyed the image of Ida and smiled.

'Do you know, I swear I recognise this lass. Works at the saloon over in Steepmount, doesn't she?'

'She did. Ida Vale, they tell me her name is. She told me it was Elizabeth,' Colt said quietly. His rage was beginning to subside, turning into tiredness, sadness, weariness. He'd always been an affable fellow, he thought. He'd worked for his whole life before taking this trip. He should never have left his town. All he wanted was a taste of adventure, just a taste. A moment of freedom, to explore the land he called home. He'd trained Trigger for this very experience, worked with him night after night, perfecting his lope, his speed, his jog. And for what? To be robbed within a couple of months. And he was wary, that was the worst of it.

He didn't trust anybody. He saw everyone as a threat, and he knew that was how you stayed safe in a land full of criminals – quick to draw, stay alive, that was what his father had told him. But his father had also had his mother, the serious creature who cared for him, talked to him, blessed him with her presence. And he had nothing. No one. That was another reason, a deeper reason, for this journey. He thought he might meet a woman like his mother…although kinder, if possible. Someone he could take home to the farm, show the sights, let loose in the kitchen. And how had this whore, Ida Vale, tricked him into falling so quickly? She was a devil, with her simpering and giggling, sipping whisky through her whore mouth. She had looked at him like she truly loved him. And that was that. He thought it was all worthwhile. The journey was complete. He would ask Elizabeth to marry him the next day, pack up her belongings, buy her an old nag and head back home. But the rage that had taken over him since he had woken up that day was something new. He had never felt anything like it – as though hatred was pumping through his veins, his heartbeat fuelled by the desire for revenge. He had no idea that he could be this man.

'So what's this a poster for, son? What do you want written?' The printer snapped Colt out of his thoughts.

'Wanted for robbery. Dead or alive. Reward offered,' Colt responded.

'What's the reward?'

'Why, you heading out there yourself?'

'Nope, but you'll get more interest if you name the price.'

Colt sighed and thought for a moment. 'Oh, just put reward offered…five hundred dollars – the sheriff is dragging his heels.'

'All right. But listen…just a word of warning. You get some bad folks responding to these here posters. If you don't have that reward ready when they deliver, they'll be trying to find your body, and no one will give a hoot about Ida Vale.'

Colt removed his hat and wiped his sweating brow. 'Just make the poster, will you? I didn't come here for advice.'

The printer shook his head at Colt as though he were looking into the future. 'Fine. How many copies you after?'

'How many do you usually make? I want them to reach across all of the towns.'

The printer paused. 'Listen, usually, it's the sheriff of whatever town you're coming from that pays for this stuff…and the Sheriff of Steepmount has never told me to flyer the whole of The Nameless Stretch. That's an expensive job. Do you have his go-ahead on this?'

'You'll get paid.'

'How? How will I get paid?'

'The sheriff gave his go-ahead, okay? He'll be round here with the money once you've sent out the flyers.'

The two men stared at each other for a moment, and the printer shook his head. 'Son, I don't trust a word that comes out of your mouth. How much you got on you now?'

Colt swallowed and thought of the money he had secreted in his undergarments. 'How much is each copy?'

'We're talking printing, postal. Even postage to The City of Glass – that'll cost you. Those roads sure are slippy. What you got, son?'

'I can give you forty.'

The printer stopped for a moment and grinned, a gentle laugh coming from his lips. Then, he straightened up. 'You know what? Fine. You'll get a copy sent to each town, and here's hoping that someone sees it. But I want that money up front, right now, and you better pray that you get some reward money from the sheriff – otherwise, you're going to have a tough year.'

It took them all day to get to the threshold of the Derelict Woods. The trees were still behaving, moving aside for each step, and Bullet moved carefully, as though fearful of sinking into the already fetlock-deep sludge. Ida could feel the rune against her skin and the unmistakable feeling of being watched. Was it her mother only, or had some of the spirits from the house followed her? She shook her head. She wasn't sure she wanted the ability to see her mother, not really. Though the thought of it was nice, the reality of being surrounded by spirits chilled her. She shuddered and considered the idea of her mother walking beside her. Or did she float? She checked around her in the dim light but could see nothing.

'Mother, I know that you're there. It's something that I'm trying to get used to. I'm not trying to ignore you.'

There was no response apart from the flicker of Bullet's ears at the noise. Ida pulled the bearskin closer to her. She was pretending to be Colton now. She tried to push away the hidden daughter, the whore, the naïve woman she was. She was Colton, the brave bounty hunter without a home. She would ride into Incan's Brook as Colton, who in her mind was still very similar to her father, and she would take no prisoners, even if Colt did track her down. And one day, she would revisit her homestead, and introduce her brother to the barrel of her gun. Yes, perhaps revenge was a good idea, whatever her mother and Fae thought about it. Ida grinned and rounded her shoulders. She would fake it until Ida had embodied the strength of Colton, swapping her old memories for new ones.

The roots of the trees in the Derelict Woods spoke to each other constantly. Their tendrils hooked and looped beneath the damp soil, holding each other, whispering plans and plots and news. They had watched Ida leave the forest, had felt her tiredness, and watched her progress. Now, they were silent, waiting, observing. Who was next?

The printing press was fired up as soon as money exchanged hands. The posters were sent on their way. Colt organised for a receipt to be sent to the Sheriff of Steepmount, the amount owed underlined twice. In the stagecoach on the way home, he smiled through the window. Ida was about to be outed to the entire land.

The town of Incan's Brook was small but mighty. It was one of the oldest towns in The Nameless Stretch, a fact that was advertised by a large wooden sign as soon as you neared. They were self-important folks, tracing their ancestry back to the roots of The Nameless Stretch, proudly pointing to history books and famous Brookonians.

The actual town was made up of about five streets, a saloon (as every town in The Nameless Stretch could claim), tailors, a pawn shop, a bank, a grocery market and stables. The Brookonians protected their land with vigour. You weren't allowed to build a dwelling there until you could prove that your ancestry was in some way worthy. What this actually meant was that you had to write a letter to the mayor, who decided what he thought based on several factors, e.g. were you rich, what could you offer him in return for his agreement, and did you have a nice looking daughter because his son was in the market for a wife? In actual fact, the Brookonians were far prouder than they should have been, and nobody was knocking on the mayor's door to move there.

Adjacent to the sea, the town had a history of being flooded, the buildings battered and whitewashed. There was also the fish market that had sprung up in recent years, which festered in the hot sunshine, causing a rather unpleasant scent to descend on the town. However, its people remained proud and assured. There was nothing like a good day in Incan's Brook, they said, and indeed, also wrote. They plastered posters up on buildings and houses that named it the 'Prettiest Town in The Nameless Stretch', although no one was sure when an official poll had actually been taken. The mayor took to wearing an overly large hat edged in gold, embroidered with the words 'Mayor of the great Incan's Brook'. He had cheap knock-offs made and sold at the market for tourists and took great pleasure in telling visitors that a safe town like this one did not need a sheriff. A mayor was the thing.

Ida entered the town at a steady jog, now without the bear pelt covering her shoulders. Bullet's skin glistened in the strange heat of the early evening, and they slowed as they reached the first building of the town. The sea was still, barely a breeze running through the now closed market, and Ida wrinkled her nose at the strong scent of fish. A saloon sign stuck out of a building up ahead, and she purposefully aimed Bullet at it. Her stomach was emptying again now, and she had a strong desire for a neat bourbon. Outside the saloon, men and women sat on wooden benches, smoking pipes and drinking deeply from their cups. They watched Ida ride up to the hitching post in silence, a few of the men nodding at her from beneath their hats. A woman waved her fingers and giggled. Ida nodded back and dismounted lazily, showing that she was in no hurry, that she didn't mind that they watched her arrival. She wound Bullet's reins around the hitching post and stepped up to the doors of the saloon.

'Evenin',' said a man closest to the door. 'First time in town, is it?'

Ida paused to look at him. He was young, perhaps younger than her, with a long, healed scar winding its way across his eye. 'Yup,' she replied, using Colton's voice again, the deepness coming more naturally to her now. 'They serve food here?'

The man looked her up and down and nodded. 'Finest food you'll get in The Nameless Stretch,' he said, and the others on the porch hummed in agreement, throwing in the occasional 'yep.'

Ida smiled at the response. 'Is that right?'

'Yup. You got your fresh fish. That's what I'd recommend,' the man said, staring out at the sea.

'All right. Whatever goes with bourbon.'

The murmurs died down, and Ida realised that all of the faces on the porch were now staring at her. 'No, sir,' said an older woman, pipe in mouth. 'We're a dry town. You'll find no bourbon here.'

More murmurs of agreement.

'That's right,' said the man with the scar, 'and we don't welcome none either. So if that's what you're after, you'll have to keep on riding.'

Ida frowned and held up her hands. 'I can live without the stuff.'

'Well, I would hope so!' The older woman spoke up again, shaking her head as though Ida had personally insulted her. 'Our ancestors would not have been able to found this great land without the power of clear thought!'

'I meant no offence, ma'am. I'll be just as happy with a fish supper.' Ida dipped her hat forward and smiled in a placating manner, pushing open the doors.

'And just you leave those guns at the front of the shop, we ain't got no time for a shoot-out!' the old woman shouted after her. Ida rolled her eyes and came face to face with a wall of guns. A small old man with white hair and a tight, wrinkled face stood before them, a desk in front of him. To his right was a closed purple velvet curtain, with piano music drifting between the material.

'All right, heading to the saloon, are you? We ask that all guns are left at the door. You'll see the sign here.' He pointed at a large hand-painted sign that read: *We ask that all guns are left at the door.* 'Keeps us safe, keeps you safe. Means you can have your dinner in peace, not having to watch your back.'

Ida pulled her guns from her holster and laid them on the desk in front of her. 'Don't you go losing them,' she said, the spirit of Colton maintaining her confidence.

The old man grinned. 'I ain't never lost, misplaced, or confused a pair yet. I use the cubby system. You'll be number six. Just remember that, and all will be well.'

Ida nodded. 'Number six,' she repeated and then stepped toward the curtain and pushed it aside. The scent of a kitchen hit her immediately, something burning somewhere in the background. The scene before her was fairly typical for a saloon, with the piano player sorting a nifty tune and women watching from the balcony above. The room was extraordinary in its opulence, though. There was a quality to the wood of the bar, a luminous, buffed glow. The wallpaper was embossed, the pattern complicated and yet delicate. Clientele sat on cushions, leaning on tables that were clean and in good condition. The barman was wearing a shirt. Ida suddenly felt out of place, her dirty clothes giving the impression that she was a scoundrel, a thief. Which she was, she thought. She walked toward the barman and tipped her hat forward. He gave her a tight smile and glanced at her clothes.

'Sir. What will you be having today?'

'I'm after supper, a bath and a room.'

The barman nodded curtly. 'Absolutely. I can have one of the ladies sort you a bath. Would you be acquiring assistance for fifty cents more?'

Ida paused for a moment, unsure as to what he meant. 'I um…no thank you.'

'As you wish. Today, we have a choice of fish or pork.'

'Fish.'

'As you wish. Take a seat, and we'll get that cooked up for you. Your room will be upstairs on the left. 3A.'

Ida scratched her cheek and then leaned forward in a conspiratorial way. 'I hear this is a dry town. If an exception could be made…' She pulled a note from her pocket, one of the many that the envelope had contained, and slid it across the counter.

The barman collected it with a single wipe of the wood before saying loudly, 'This here is a dry town, sir. You'll have to wait until you leave.' There was a twinkle in his eye that let Ida know, however, that she should expect a tipple with her dinner.

She turned and scrutinised the room, the round tables mostly taken up. Card games, loose women, clearly – despite the fact that firearms and alcohol were banned – there was no shortage of vice here. She spied a spare seat on the right side of the room, with its back to the wall. There was only one middle-aged man sitting at the table, eating his supper in silence, a book laid out before him. Ida walked over, pulled out the chair and sat down with a sigh. The man glanced up, nodded, and then went back to his book. The barman came over with a tin cup and placed it down next to her.

'Your milk, sir,' he said before walking away.

Ida picked the cup up and then took a swig. Bourbon. Perfect. The fiery liquid slipped down her throat and soothed her aches. She thought for a moment of her mother, standing beside her. She must have been right there, among all the other spirits that stood within the room and could not be seen. The rune had stopped burning against her skin, and Ida had all but forgotten its existence.

'Read much?' the man before her said suddenly, glancing up.

Ida shook her head. 'Nope.'

'But you can read,' the man responded, his words drawling and long. It wasn't a question, so Ida said nothing. 'This book here, this will change your life.' He grinned, giving a brief indication to the cover. His hair was ragged, as though not cut in six months. However, his skin was freshly shaven, as though he only had the money for one bit of personal grooming.

Ida stared at the book but, unable to see the spine, just nodded. 'All right.'

There was silence for a moment, and the man frowned, leaning forward. 'Don't you want to know how this book can change your life?'

Ida shook her head. 'Not as much as you want to tell me, I'm sure. What is it, religion? Money? Politics? What are you peddling?'

He laughed without humour and shook his head. 'I ain't peddling nothing.'

'Well, all right then. Here's my supper,' Ida said as the barman came over with her fish and a couple of potatoes. She nodded at the man before she started to eat, closing their conversation down. The man watched her for a second.

'Ain't it rude to eat with your hat on? I'm pretty sure it ain't polite that. You'll notice that no one else in this room is eating with their hat on.'

Ida paused mid-chew and looked around the room. The man was quite right. She swallowed quickly and smiled. 'The truth of it is, I haven't been to the barbers in some time. I'd rather keep it on if it's all the same to you.'

'I don't believe it's polite myself. And here you don't wanna talk about my life-changing book. You won't remove your hat. Where you from anyway? You ain't from Hangman's Rest, I'll wager. We raise our kids up right on the south side of The Nameless Stretch.'

Ida picked up a napkin and wiped her mouth. 'Sir, I am not from around here, no. Does it offend you that much, or would you allow me to get on with my supper?'

The man pulled a disgruntled face and sniffed. 'It offends me, it offends me. I am greatly offended by those with a lack of etiquette.'

'I'll bet you wouldn't be so offended if I hadn't had to give my guns at the door,' Ida hissed, cutting her fish with menace.

'And what does that mean?' the man responded.

'It means that a land without firearms is a world where men can be offended by the slightest things and not get shot for it.' Ida listened to the words as they appeared in front of her, fully formed. She had never said such a thing in her entire life. Her skin pricked in shock, and she silently acknowledged the change Colton was having on her.

'You are rude, sir, and I don't mind saying it.'

'Exactly,' Ida retorted, 'and you should mind saying it.'

There was silence for a moment, and Ida noticed that a few people from the other tables were looking over at them. She rolled her eyes and sighed, then beckoned to the barman. He gave her the look of a man who was not used to being beckoned and certainly did not approve of it just because he was in the service industry. He finished wiping the glass he had in his hands in a leisurely manner before sauntering over. He pursed his lips in an expectant way.

'Do you happen to have a pair of scissors that I might borrow, sir?' Ida asked, being careful to be courteous.

He went back behind the bar and then came over with them. Ida took them with thanks and downed the contents of the tin cup on her table.

'I am coming back for this food, so don't clean it away,' she said, looking at the man with daggers in her eyes. Ida stood, pushed her chair back, and then marched through the back door, following the handwritten 'Toilet' sign. The outhouse was beside a tree behind the building, and Ida walked crossly over, irritated that her supper had been interrupted. The sun was beginning to set in the sky, throwing an orange glaze across the world.

Ida stepped behind the outhouse, away from prying eyes, and removed her hat, placing it on the dirt floor beside her. Her father was the only one who had ever cut her hair, and he had done so with precision, careful not to cut off an inch more than was needed. Now, she was going to do something she had never done before. She stared at the scissors and then caught her breath. A shadow had appeared next to her. Ida tried to focus and watched the shape of a person become sketched through the air, just like in Fae's kitchen. It was her mother. It was fainter than before, like smoke. Ida smiled at her, grasped a piece of hair, and cut near the root. She repeated the action, hacking at some bits with the blunt scissors until it was short all over. Her long dark hair lay in a pile by her feet, and Ida nudged it with her boot.

'So long.' She ran a hand over her shorn scalp. It felt uneven, but she marvelled at the feeling of pure freedom that followed. Her head was noticeably lighter. She moved her neck from side to side to feel the lack of hair hitting her skin and laughed. The air swam about her scalp, and it felt glorious. Ida put on her hat. It was looser now. As she turned to go back, she looked for the shadow of her mother but saw only trees. What had made her appear so suddenly and then disappear again? Was it the memory of her father cutting her hair?

'Hi, Mother,' she said, aiming the words into the empty air.

Ida strode back to the saloon with purpose, marching through the back door and depositing the scissors onto the bar with a flourish, before retaking her seat. The middle-aged man was back reading his book, holding it in his hands, and he frowned at her over the top of it as she sat down. Ida removed her hat with a crazed grin on her face and placed it down beside her purposefully.

'That's…well, that's a look,' the man said, blinking at the spectacle.

'That's right,' Ida responded, cutting a potato.

'There's a barber over the other side of this street, you know, he'll be working tomorrow.'

'Well, perhaps I'll pay him a visit,' Ida said. She noticed that she could now see the book's spine in the man's hand and squinted to read it. She nodded. 'It's a religion then. That's what you're peddling.'

The man shook his head. 'I don't peddle the words of the gods – they do that themselves. I'm just a humble vessel waiting to be filled with their love.'

Ida took a bite of food and chewed thoughtfully. 'That's a strange way to put it, sir. I think that you are a strange person.'

The man burst out laughing and lifted his own tin cup toward her, offering a cheer. 'So says the stranger who practically scalped himself for a fish supper. If I'm strange, I ain't the only one at this table.'

Ida smiled a genuine smile and raised her cup, clinking it against the man's. Something told her that he wasn't drinking milk either.

The sheriff glared at the wanted poster plastered to the wall and spat on the ground, kicking dust up with his boot in irritation.

'That goddamn—'

'You want me to find him for you, sir?' his colleague said, shaking his head in anger.

'That goddamn son of a bitch. He ain't got no reward to give, and I know it. And what's more, we're going to get bounty hunters here asking for a payout. You know as well as I do that I didn't approve this – I ain't got the spare dollar to pay for some whore. She could be as far away as the goddamn City of Glass.

She could be buried in their graveyard for all I care.' The sheriff took his hat off and wiped his brow before replacing it.

'Sheriff?' a voice said, causing him to turn. It was Mrs Smithe, wrapped in a shawl and shivering in the hot night air.

'Mrs Smithe, hello,' he said.

'I just wanted to thank you, Sheriff. I can't tell you what it means to me that you care about my debt this way.' Mrs Smithe smiled warmly and reached out, taking the sheriff by the hand. He swallowed and nodded.

'Yes, ma'am, well. You have served our community here for quite some time. We'll do what we can.'

'And don't I know it. I feel safe here in Steepmount, sir, and I must say that you do a good job. A good, honest job. You're much better than that old officer. And I would like to extend to you the offer of a night at the saloon on the house, if you catch my drift.' She smiled a wide, gap-toothed smile and patted his hand.

'I appreciate that, Mrs Smithe, but that is what they call a "conflict of interests", so I will decline at this time,' he said, his mind filling with images of her naked. His colleague cleared his throat purposefully and smiled. The sheriff rolled his eyes.

'Oh, sir,' Mrs Smithe said, turning her attentions to the man beside the sheriff, 'you know that I cannot you offer a free evening with the ladies. I can offer you a fair discount, though, for one night only.'

'I'll take it,' the colleague responded quickly, a large, stupid smile settling on his face.

The room that Ida had been given had certainly seen better days. She pushed the door closed behind her, smelling the bourbon on her breath. She had stayed in the bar area for a few more drinks with the religious gentleman, listening to his tales of glory from up above and accepting his offer of a drink. Life as a man was better in this world. The working women had observed them, cooing and laughing at jokes, pressing against Ida as they walked past with knowing eyes. At first, she had worried that it was because they recognised another of their kind, but she quickly found that this wasn't the case. Ida set her jaw firm whenever they glanced over, rolling her shoulders back and sniffing hard. She tried to embody her image of Colton. It appeared to work.

Ida stepped forward and sat down on the bed, surprised by its softness. The room was decorated as the bar was downstairs, but it was as though it had been made fancy and then left alone for years. The wallpaper was coming off the walls, a nice layer of dust sat on the lamps. It would do for a night. Ida scanned the room for any signs of her mother but could see none.

There was a knock at the door. 'Sir, will you be ready to take your bath now?' a voice said, drifting through the cracks.

Ida started, having forgotten. She stood and walked toward the door, dragging it open. A woman stood on the other side, with large, soft eyes, smiling.

'Your bath is ready, just down the hall here.'

'Thank you,' Ida said, her voice catching. The woman was undeniably beautiful, with soft golden curls framing her face and rosy cheeks flushing before her.

'You're welcome. Come, let me show you.' She took Ida's hand and turned, leading the way down the corridor. Ida let herself be taken. At the door, the woman led her to a room with a large tin bath, steaming. Ida gazed at it, almost giddy with excitement. She hadn't washed properly since the cave, and even then, it was without soap. The woman handed her a towel, her face bright and open.

'Will you be wanting assistance with your bath? It's only fifty cents extra.'

Ida shook her head, saying nothing. She didn't want to breathe her bourbon breath on the woman, and she was slightly afraid. For the first time, she felt something more than repulse at the thought of another person touching her. What was this strange feeling? It was as though butterflies were settling in her chest, her hands clammy and face hot. She did want assistance from this woman, but honestly, she would never ask for it. She had learned the hard way that there was nothing worse than offering yourself to a stranger, especially one who hadn't washed in days, who wore visibly dirty clothes. Ida wasn't stupid. She couldn't trick herself into believing that this woman felt more for her than duty and fear. She smiled, set her jaw, and shook her head again. The woman nodded.

'All right, should you change your mind, I'll be just outside. All you have to do is holler.'

The woman stepped out, closing the door behind her with a click. Ida stepped forward and turned the key, locking it. She removed her clothes, excited to be rid of them. Tomorrow she would buy new ones and burn those that had carried Colt's scent from Steepmount to here. Once down to her skin, Ida began to unwrap the bandages that kept her breasts flat against her body. She did so quickly, in anticipation of feeling the warm water on her skin. A clatter stopped her in her tracks. Ida looked down to see the rune by her feet, its colour dull and lifeless. She reached to pick it up, feeling its weight. It no longer burned her skin, no longer pulled on her. She placed it next to her clothes and stepped into the bath, the warm water engulfing her.

It felt like years since she had last settled into a bath. She closed her eyes and rested for a moment, listening to the far-off noises in the bar, the men chatting, the women laughing. A dry town, she thought to herself. That was a joke in itself. There was no way that this was a dry town. The barman had found that bourbon far too easily. She wouldn't doubt that nearly every man in that bar was drinking liquor, not to mention carrying a concealed weapon.

Ida held her breath without opening her eyes and let herself sink under the water. The warmth spread onto her scalp, soothing the skin. She pushed her face back out into the air and took a deep, long breath, then reached for the soap. The suds bubbled from her skin and hair to the surface, the water turning a murky grey within moments. Ida thought of the soft bed that awaited her, the warm calm of being somebody else. For a couple of minutes, she felt completely free.

Chapter 8

The posters were sent out to all the corners of The Nameless Stretch, from the Docks of Astray to The City of Glass. They were plastered up in various places, onto saloon walls, in post offices, on fences, as soon as they arrived. Some were copied and handed out, murmurs over the reward and what that might entail ensued. Colt sat with a whisky at the bar of the saloon in Steepmount; eyes focused on nothing but the wood in front of him.

'You doin' all right there, sir?' One of the working women sat beside him with a smile, placing a hand on his shoulder. He flinched as though he had been burned and shook her hand off.

'I don't want nothing to do with your sort.'

'Oh goodness, Colt, you can't let one woman ruin your relationship with all of them. There's plenty of people in this world, and not all of them are good 'uns, but that don't mean that we oughta live a life of solitude,' the woman said, motioning to the barman.

'I fell for that once before, and I won't fall for it again,' Colt said, eyes still staring ahead.

'It's a lesson all men must go through, don't fall in love too easy. You could ask any man in this room, and they would all have a tale to tell like yours,' she said, smiling at the barman as he placed a drink down in front of her.

'She's quite right,' the barman said, topping up Colt's glass. 'It's a rarity that it happens quite like your story, but everyone has a tale like it. That's life for you.'

'That's love for you,' the woman said, raising her cup.

Colt glared at the two. 'You're just trying to get me to spend money.'

The barman rolled his eyes and walked away, his attention shifting to somebody else.

'That ain't incorrect, Colt, but the fact is that we've all watched you night after night, sitting at this bar, complaining and drinking. Now, what is the point of that? It don't sound like a happy life to me. Life is there for the living, and you're living it like a dead man.' The woman sighed and took a sip of her drink. Colt watched her.

'I ain't treating life like a dead man. I got a focus, that's all. When you got a focus, you don't worry about anyone else. You just focus on what you got to do, and you get it done.'

'Your focus is finding a woman in The Nameless Stretch. She'll be long gone by now. She could have gone to the docks and got a boat out of here, although that would have been a big decision. Or she could be living it up in The City of Glass, where they say it's so cold that everyone covers their face for most of the hours of the day. No one would know.'

'They've caught people before,' Colt said, 'and the offer of a five hundred dollar reward is too much to ignore for most bounty hunters.'

The woman pulled a face and shook her head. 'Maybe you're right. It ain't for me to say.'

'That's right,' Colt said, emptying his glass. The whisky stung his throat, and he coughed, his skin going red.

'Listen, Colt, if you're gonna be around the saloon night after night like this, what's the harm in treating yourself? We none of us are gonna rob you. Heck, I've worked here for long enough – you can ask my clients.'

Colt turned his head and looked at the woman. She was okay to look at in a plain sort of way. Pretty but plain. Her hair was a muddy brown, and when she opened her mouth, you could just about see that her teeth were missing at the back. He sighed. 'I don't know.'

'Well, my name is Helen. You can call on me anytime. Just don't leave it too long.' She smiled and stood up, pushing the stool beneath the bar. 'My mama always used to say to me, if you let bad thoughts take over your mind, you're asking to turn into a bad person. And bad people don't have any luck when they die. They die horrid and painful deaths, filled with the hatred of others. It's just something to think about. If you wanna live a beautiful life, you gotta think beautiful thoughts, Colt.' She raised her eyebrows suggestively and went to sit by another man at a table behind them, introducing herself with a flourish.

Colt glanced at her. Was she right? No. She was just trying to trick him, another woman trying to cheat her way to his bedroom, steal what little he had left, his borrowed clothes, his dwindling supply of money. Maybe it was time he took matters into his own hands. Perhaps it was time he did some tracking himself.

Ida woke with a start, sitting up in the soft bed. The noises of the bar downstairs had quietened down, and the street outside made no sound. And yet, her heart pounded beneath her skin. She stared at the room, the moonlight creating shadows. Ida looked at the carriage clock on the bedside table. It was three in the morning. Her mother. Was she in the room? Had she woken her? Ida focused, bringing back the moment that she had sat in the witch's kitchen. She took a deep breath and scrutinised the space at the end of her bed. There, certainly magic, the air began to sketch in the soft glow of light, the image of her mother being drawn before her. Ida smiled. Her heart felt as though it was a bucket filling with water. Her mother's face became clearer still, more defined than ever before. The woman stood at the end of the bed, her hands over her heart. She nodded and said the word 'Ida', the noise barely audible.

'Mother,' Ida said. She watched as she moved around the side of the bed and sat down, the sheets not even creasing beneath them. Ida had always dreamed of her mother in the nighttime, of cool hands soothing the skin on her face, stroking back the hair on her forehead. For the first time, it occurred to her that perhaps these were not dreams after all, but a type of reality.

'Ida,' her mother said again, and this time it was a little louder, and Ida strained less to hear it.

'I wish I could take your hand,' Ida said sadly.

Her mother nodded. 'I have had that wish since I entered this realm.' The words floated on the air.

'I am so sad that I never got to know you, that you left so early.'

'We cannot all be long for this earth. I was but your age when I left,' her mother responded, her words clearer and more transparent.

'Is father with you now?' Ida asked, frowning, looking about the room for any clues of his existence.

Her mother shook her head. 'No. He will be with your brother, of course.'

Ida leaned forward, confused. 'With my brother? Why?'

'Ah. You have not worked it out. Not all dead turn into beings such as myself; those who die by accident are destined for greater things. However, those who die at the hands of another are tied to that living being until their death. Many wait for that time so that they can exact revenge in the afterlife. Fae has the only inner strength that I know of, which removes a spirit from their living killer. This is why she has such a full house – they have decided to leave revenge alone.'

Ida shook her head, frowning. 'Fae helped you…but that means…father? He murdered you?'

Her mother shook her head, her spirit appearing to breathe in deeply.

'No?' Ida said, confused. 'But you died when I was a few months old. Who did this to you?'

'Ida, I did not die when you were a few months old. Your father told you that in a misguided attempt at protecting you. I died when you were born. I did not ask Fae to separate me from my living being.'

Ida put her hand over her mouth, a sob rising in her throat. Tears pushed themselves from the threshold of her tear ducts, diving onto the skin below.

'Me? It was…me?' she stuttered, the words wobbling in the air.

Her mother smiled kindly, the air around her image making her clearer and more precise. 'I believe that the system was shaken by the love I felt for you. Birth and death are closely aligned. I became bound to you, perhaps because I could not bear to let go of you.'

Ida continued crying, pulling the bedsheets up to her face. 'So you are bound to me for life?'

Her mother nodded.

'If you wish to leave, we can revisit Fae. I don't care if they catch me retracing my steps. It's the least I could do.'

Her mother shook her head. 'I would still be a spirit until your death. However, I would be living at Fae's, and that's not how I would spend my time. At least this way, I have been able to watch you grow. Your father didn't give you enough information about me. The same stories, night after night. They weren't helpful. I was a homestead witch, and I knew all about your brother and the other woman he kept at Blackreach. I worked hard to keep his other family at bay. You found only a few ways that I protected the land. The day before your brother came, your father dug up some land at the front of the driveway. You were busy indoors. I watched him from the porch, and I knew when I saw him pause what he had found. My runes. Protection runes. He dug them up and threw them in the river. I knew instantly that the spell was broken and that you would no longer be safe. I knew that man would come, I could only hope that you would be able to get away with your life. Your father was not so lucky, but then, he was never a lucky man.'

Ida stared at her mother. 'How would my brother have known that the runes were gone?'

'I do not know. I knew that there was another woman, but I didn't know who she was. It is possible that she was a greater witch than I. And the many years had passed. I don't doubt that the protection weakened.'

Ida noticed that her mother's voice was becoming louder, and she was almost able to not strain to hear her. 'So Father is bound to that man for life.'

Her mother nodded.

'And in the afterlife, he will be able to exact revenge.'

'So they say.'

'What if I kill my brother, and he is then bound to me? What of my father's spirit?'

'Your father's spirit life would end. Revenge would be exacted should the man be killed. What greater revenge is there for those killed than to see the killer meet the same end?'

Ida nodded, staring at the image of her mother. She looked so young still, almost like her sister. 'I understand.'

The moonlight was brightening, clouds parting before it. Ida heard a far-off whinny, a lone horse perhaps, waiting in a stable below. 'The more I think on it, the more I think I should revisit that brother of mine.'

Ida's mother shook her head. 'I should fear for your life.'

'For what life?' Ida said, the words coming out harsher than she had intended. 'What life did I have there, at home, hidden away from the world and existing only to look after my father?'

Her mother smiled. 'But look at you now.'

'Yes, look at me now.' She reached up to her and grasped the sprouts of hair.

Her mother reached her hand forward as if she wished to touch her. Of course, she could not. 'There is more to this world than the homestead and revenge. And now, at least, you are aware of your powers.'

Ida sighed. 'All right.'

They watched each other, the moonlight streaming through the shape of her mother and bouncing off Ida's skin.

The morning arrived with fanfare, bright and beautiful sunshine flooding Ida's worn-down room. She awoke, blinking wearily at the window. She could no longer see her mother. Had she even seen her mother last night, or had that whole thing been a strange dream? Her head ached a little from the evening's bourbon. She wouldn't be surprised if it turned out that it was, in fact, an illusion. Alcohol had done worse. She couldn't even remember falling asleep.

Ida got out of bed and dressed hurriedly in her worn-out clothes, excited at the prospect of throwing them out. She stared into the tarnished mirror hanging from a rusted chain on the wall. In the bright morning daylight, this room looked even worse than it had before, and her hair was a horror show. First, she'd head to the barber, see if he could give her some kind of short crop and get rid of the mop on top of her head. Then, the tailors. By the end of the day, she'd be more Colton than Ida, more Colton than Colt. The stinking clothes she'd worn on her back for too long would be burned.

She left the room open, dropping her feet down the wooden steps of the saloon with a stilted heaviness, the noise of her boots causing people to swivel and stare as she entered the bar. The same barman from the night before stood behind the polished wood, yawning against his hand. Ida nodded at a few of the patrons as she made her way toward him.

'Hello,' he said sleepily.

'Morning. You got coffee?' Ida replied, leaning on the bar.

'Yup. We got coffee.'

'Great, then pour me a cup,' Ida said. 'I might stay another night – but we'll straighten up my bill at the end.'

The barman shrugged, truly looking as though he couldn't care less about anything in the world, and poured a cup of coffee from a tall silver pot waiting on the bar. Ida took the cup from him.

'You don't own this place, do you?' she asked, taking a sip of the bitter and lukewarm drink.

The barman filled a cup for himself. 'Why on earth would I want to?' he said beneath his breath, downing the coffee. Ida took another sip, frowned at his manners, and then downed her cup, too, giving him a wry smile.

'Anything else? The cook can get some meat on the grill,' the barman asked, barely looking at her.

'Nope. I got errands to run.'

'Suit yourself.'

Ida nodded and turned, walking out through the heavy purple curtains. The old man was there, reading the newspaper in front of his cubbies.

'Number six,' Ida said.

'Morning there. Number six, is it? Ah yes, I remember you.' He turned and pulled her guns from one of the cubbies and slid them over the counter. Ida took them and reholstered her weapons, feeling more confident immediately.

'Told you I'd get the right ones, didn't I?' The old man grinned a wrinkled smile.

'You did.'

'Leaving town now, are you?'

'Not directly,' Ida responded, 'I got some business to take care of first. Might stay another night, depends.'

'Cooooeee, you got the bug already! I knew it. It happens so often with these visitors.' The old man clapped his hands and hopped momentarily from foot to foot. Ida watched him with a scowl.

'What do you mean?' she said.

'You got the Incan's Brook bug! It happens to the best of us. Why, I was from the Glass City myself, though you would never know it now. Once you see the sights of this place, why would you want to go anywhere else?'

'Well, sir, I've only seen the saloon so far, so I'm not going to move in lock, stock and barrel yet.'

'You'll get there, trust me. What's your name?'

'My name is Colton.'

'Colton, what?'

'Colton is all you need right now,' Ida said, touching her hat and turning her back on the gunkeeper.

Colt pushed the door of the sheriff's office open with a firm hand and stepped inside. The sheriff was leaning against the jail cell bars, chatting to a prisoner about what sounded like cattle and the best way to breed a good cow. Colt cleared his throat, and the sheriff turned, his face dropping as he saw who the visitor was.

'What do you want, Colt?' he said gruffly, rolling his eyes.

'I want to know if there's any news,' Colt said, standing with hands on his hips, a firm look of determination set on his weaselly face.

'News? Sure is. Farmer Grough is pretty sure that someone has been stealing his cattle – not all at once now, because that would be a certain misdemeanour – but subtle like. One at a time. Have you ever heard of anything like it?'

Colt scratched his chin in annoyance. 'Why the hell would I be here to discuss some farmer's cattle?' he screeched.

The sheriff flinched at the noise. 'Well, the way you've been hanging around here, I thought you might have had the presence of mind to be a little bit helpful to folk. We don't accept just anyone, you know.'

'Now that ain't true, is it? You do accept just anyone here – take a look at the whores who frequent your saloon.'

'Sir,' the sheriff dug his thumbs into his belt and stepped toward Colt, squarely standing in front of him. 'I think it's about time you left this town. You're no longer welcome. The problem is that you seem to have an opinion about everything, even when nobody asked. We're just about sick of your attitude.'

'I was robbed!' growled Colt, incandescent with rage.

'And so what? You never been robbed before? I can barely believe that – it's such luck. Look at Jonesy here – behind those bars. Jonesy is in here for at least another month, and he ain't complaining.'

Both men turned to look at the prisoner, who grinned and nodded. 'That's right. And I been robbed before too. No point in whining about it, is there? That's just the way of the world.'

'That's just the way of the world…' Colt said, 'is a phrase that only losers use.'

The sheriff blew out a long whistle, irritated. 'Sir, you have outstayed your welcome indeed.'

'Have you heard anything from the posters?' Colt responded, ignoring the sheriff's words entirely.

'We do not fund those posters, and so I would not have heard anything regarding that matter. And what's more, if I had heard, I don't think I would have told you anyway. Ida might be a thief, but she's a damn sight more agreeable than you are.'

Colt hocked some phlegm in the back of his throat and spat on the wooden floor of the small jailhouse. The sheriff shook his head and pulled his gun in one swift and frightful movement.

'Colt, I will shoot you where you stand, you goddamn sonofabitch. I will shoot the hell out of you, and as the sheriff, I won't have nobody to answer to. You want a second chance? There's an old nag for sale up the way – she ain't much, but she's good for a few miles. Go buy her. Old farmer Huss won't ask for much in the way of reparation. Once you've got her, clear yourself outta here.'

Colt shook his head. 'How about this…you don't shoot, but you put me in one of these cells. I won't cause any more trouble in there, will I?' His face twisted from the strange anger to a pleasant smile. The sheriff frowned, lowering the aim of his gun.

'What are you talking about?' he said, surprised at this sudden change of events. The prisoner in the cell behind him echoed this thought, his words lost to the confusion.

'If I'm breaking the law enough for you to shoot me, I'm breaking it enough for you to lock me up. Ain't that so?' Colt said.

The sheriff scratched his head with one hand, lowering the gun even more. 'What do you want, you devil? Hey, Jonesy, you following this?' he said, throwing the question behind him to the prisoner.

'He is a devil,' Jonesy said. 'He's planning something, and I don't mind saying it. He's planning something wicked, I'll wager. What do you want to be locked up for, boy?'

Colt shrugged. 'I believe that Ida Vale will be coming back to this town – whether by design or through force. I would like to be here when she arrives. That is all there is to it. I am not trying to be disagreeable.'

'Even if she does come back, what makes you think that you'll still be around to see her?' the sheriff responded, a smile creeping onto his face.

'Where am I going? I haven't broken the law.'

'Well, that's to be seen.' The sheriff grinned, his teeth showing. 'Hop on into that cell there and keep it quiet. We like the quiet round here.' He aimed his gun once more and directed Colt into the prison cell, who went without fuss. Once inside, the sheriff closed the heavy iron door and locked it with glee. 'You know, Colt, I like this idea. This is a good idea. You ain't had many good ideas since you got here. But this, this is all right. Don't you think, Jonesy?'

The other prisoner came to life at the sound of his name and hooted a great laugh, as though a joke had been told and he had truly appreciated it. 'I'll tell you what I like, Sheriff, if I may.'

'Go right ahead.'

'I like the sweet drop of judgement for any ne'er-do-well,' Jonesy said. He and the sheriff fell silent and turned their full attention back to Colt, who sat on the straw bed in his cell with a blank look on his face. The sheriff nodded and reholstered his gun.

'Well, that is my favourite thing in the entire land. Nothing like it.'

Ida sat in the barber's chair and raised her eyebrows.

'Just shave it clean off, boy. Give me a blank slate to be working with,' she said, her voice gruff and deep almost naturally now, the second thought of being Colton barely registering as she spoke.

'You want it to be a close shave?' the barber asked, his hands shaking slightly. He was an old man, well beyond what Ida would have imagined being his best barbering years.

'That's what I said, right?'

'All right, sir. You don't want a face shaving today, though?' He frowned at her in the tarnished mirror.

'I don't look like I need one, do I?'

'Well, if you don't mind my saying, you got the skin of a prepubescent boy. Or a woman. I don't see a single—'

'Would you mind your business? I asked you to shave my head, and here we are talking about it like it's the statement of the century. You are a barber, are you not?' Ida snapped. It was true, and it had occurred to her since changing her clothing that there were parts of her that were not believable as Colton. But as it was, confidence seemed to make up for that fact. It almost didn't seem to occur to people that a woman would be so brazen as to disguise herself. There was just no considering it.

The barber shrugged and got to work, first evening up the ragged cut that Ida had already performed and then beginning to shave the head with a cut-throat razor. He mumbled to himself the entire time, though Ida could not make out a single word, just a low hum of nonsense and silliness. She watched him in the mirror, almost forgetting to watch herself transform. When he had finished, she laid eyes on the person in front of her and jumped slightly. It was a shock. There, before her, sat the image of her father. She gasped and leaned forward, taking in the strange portrait. It moved as she did, not another spirit like her mother. The barber frowned.

'That's what you asked for. There's no refunds here.'

'No, no – it's fine. It's just a bit of a...shock,' Ida responded.

'Well, it isn't the style, if I could be honest. We don't sell many of these. You'll have to make sure you wear your hat. That sun can be mighty cruel.'

'Hmmm,' Ida said, running her hand along the strange smoothness, marvelling at its bareness.

'You hear me? You'll have to be careful with that s—'

'Yes, sir, I can hear you. I'm aware of the sun,' Ida said.

'Even in The City of Glass, I would be careful. I mean, it's cold there, but it's got a bright—'

'How much do I owe you?' Ida interrupted, not wanting to carry on the fruitless conversation. The power of interrupting a man still gave her a buzz, something that she would have never done before.

'Oh, it's fifty cents,' the barber said, his expression turning into one of mild hurt.

Ida reached inside her pocket, pulled out a coin, and placed it into his hand.

'Them clothes have seen better days,' the barber said, not unkindly.

Ida rolled her eyes and placed her hat back on her newly skinned head. It felt strange, as though it was suctioned onto her scalp. She nodded at the barber and stepped out into the midday sun. It was bright in the sky and shone down on the market stalls that were being set up before her. The scent of fish was ever-present. Ida's nose wrinkled, and she peered up the street, eyes resting on the swinging wooden signs that betrayed the insides of each shop. There, at the end, she saw one with a hand-painted needle and thread on it. She felt the weight of Colt's old clothes on her back and began to walk toward the sign, excited to brand herself anew.

Chapter 9

Colt sat behind bars in silence, watching the other prisoner go about his business. Jonesy seemed to know everything about the place. He knew what time to expect a coffee, the daily occurrence of particular locals complaining about the noise, but most importantly – he knew the sheriff very well. The sheriff had just left, pushing his hat on his head with the whistle of a tune, telling the men that he'd be back after he'd had a bite to eat. Colt heard his stomach rumble and wondered for a moment whether his grand plans were not so great after all. Perhaps he'd made an error here. He stared at Jonesy as the criminal organised a small stack of paperbacks beside his bed. He was irritatingly cheerful, Colt thought. Annoyingly buoyant.

'Where did you get the books?' he asked. Jonesy started as though he had forgotten that he was there at all.

'Eh? Oh. The sheriff gave these to me. Helps pass the time. Got some real good 'uns, Tales of the Stretch, that sort of thing. Can you read?'

Colt scoffed. 'Of course, I can read. What am I, a moron?'

'No shame in not being able to read. There's plenty more lessons in life than what you can find in books. I didn't know how to read proper until I came in here. The sheriff helped me a little, and they got old Mrs Reeble from the local school. She comes by every few weeks to give a lesson.' Jonesy grinned.

'That's a waste of time, educating men who are being sent to the gallows,' Colt responded, inspecting his nails.

'That ain't so. I ain't going to the gallows, first of all, and second of all, you're less likely to try and escape if you got other worlds you can visit.' Jonesy picked up a thin book from the pile and held it up. It was greying and dog-eared, the cover a little torn. He scratched his beard and sniffed. 'This one is my favourite. It's all about this girl – she's young, but she's tough as old boots. She knows how to ride and shoot, takes off across the Stretch…well, I won't ruin it for you.'

Colt shrugged. 'I won't read it.'

'So what will you do? I don't know why you even asked to be put in here. I think it's awful strange of you.'

'I ain't in the habit of explaining myself to criminals,' Colt hissed.

Jonesy grinned at this and chuckled. Then, he lay back on his bed, opening the dog-eared book in the middle. Colt continued to watch him.

The tailor's shop was larger than Ida had expected. She stood in a changing room off to one side, listening to the seamstress hum and move hangers around. The air smelled strongly of cologne, an almost gagging scent that seemed to be attached to all of the fabric in the shop. Ida contemplated the outfit that she had just put on. She had been careful to keep the rune against her skin, still inside the bandage that hid her female secret. It was perhaps the first brand-new outfit that she had ever worn. Her father had given her hand-me-downs of her mother's clothing from when she was small, and she had always learned to make do. Even the clothes that she had gotten herself so in debt for with Mrs Smithe held the scent of another couple of women. The image in the mirror looked back at her. Colton was a strange-looking sort of chap, Ida decided. His face held the same weary look of her father. She could see almost none of her mother in there. The outfit consisted of too-large maroon canvas trousers, a soft off-white shirt, a maroon waistcoat and a matching duster jacket. Ida kept the old hat on, liking its looser fit. There was something untrustworthy, she thought, about a man dressed entirely in new clothes. The worn hat loaned a more natural element to the outfit. Her boots remained, too. It seemed like a tremendous waste of money to buy new boots when the old ones fit well and were free of holes.

'How are you getting on in there?' The seamstress's voice drifted over the top of the door.

Ida shrugged despite not being able to be seen. 'Yeah, okay. I'll take this one. Maybe fold up another of these shirts if there is one. They're always the first to go.'

'Yes, sir. We've got a beautiful selection of silk bandanas that might interest a discerning gentleman like yourself?'

'Silk? What need have I for silk? I need something that'll take the sweat off my brow, not something that'll look fancy,' Ida responded, shifting the waistband of her trousers.

'We've got cotton too, sir, if that takes your interest.'

'Oh, add one as you please. I care not for pattern, as long as it isn't floral. For that, I cannot abide.' Ida waved her hand as though the woman were in front of her. 'I tell you, that tailor of yours wears a strong cologne. It sticks in your throat,' she said with a slight cough.

'I don't know nothing about that,' the answer came. The humming of the seamstress began again, this time of a slightly more jaunty tune, no doubt related to the sale that she had just made. Ida collected the old clothes from the floor of the changing room, the scent of Colt no longer spiking her nose, as if it would have had a chance among the smell of the tailor's cologne. She pushed open the door and nodded at the seamstress, a plump middle-aged woman who was fussing about the clothes like a fly around honey.

'Will you dispose of these for me, ma'am?' Ida asked, indicating the pile in her arms.

'Oh, I certainly will. They have had their day. It was a good decision to visit us, sir. You look much better than when you arrived!' The woman took Colt's clothes with a flourish and grinned, taking them out the back. Ida stood alone for a moment in the shop, waiting for the woman to return and charge for her items. The air, still thick with that pungent scent, changed slightly, and Ida felt the presence of another person. She glanced around her. There was no one to be seen. She strained her eyes, trying to focus them on the image of her mother. There was no shape in the air before her, and this feeling was different to her mother's; it was stilted, angry. Ida felt the air hasten past her ear, a breeze indoors. She turned and caught the sight of someone at the side of the room, a man. His image disappeared almost as soon as she saw it. Ida's heart began to thump in her ears.

'Are you being dealt with?' a deep voice said. Ida jumped and turned to see a spindly middle-aged man behind the tailor's desk, the undeniable culprit of the scent. It grew more potent by the second. The man gaped at her expectantly, small circular glasses perched on the end of his nose. Beneath that, a long moustache twitched.

'Yes…your assistant.'

'Mrs Perth.'

'Mrs Perth, yes.'

'You have paid?' the tailor asked, moustache still moving.

'Not yet,' Ida responded.

'The outfit is a little big on you. I can take it in.'

Ida considered this for a moment and then shook her head. 'It'll do fine.' Out of the corner of her eye, she saw the shape again, the man, moving past her. She flicked her head and stared upon nothing once more, as though it was never there.

'It's a shame not to have it taken in to fit you,' the tailor said.

Ida stepped forward and frowned, looking into his eyes. They were bloodshot and worn, bags beneath them.

'What are you staring at?' the tailor asked, his voice irritated and clipped.

'I get a funny feeling about this place, this shop. Has it always belonged to you?' Ida asked, her head cocked to one side.

Mrs Perth came bustling back into the room at that very moment and clapped her hands together as she looked upon the image of Colton, grinning. 'That outfit becomes you very well, sir, very well.'

Ida nodded in her direction, still keeping her eyes on the tailor. 'Has this shop always belonged to you?' she asked him again, refusing to be distracted by the seamstress.

'It has been in my possession for long enough,' the tailor said carefully, his eyes narrowing. 'You owe us twenty for the clothing.'

'A bargain,' Mrs Perth sang, 'a bargain indeed!'

'And you, Mrs Perth, how long have you worked here?' Ida asked, glancing at the jolly woman.

'Me? Oh, I've been here a good few years now, worked for the old gent before his—'

'Do you have the twenty, sir?' the tailor interrupted. Ida grinned. It was as she thought. She leaned down and pulled the notes from her right boot, counting out the correct amount and placing it on the desk.

'Do go on, Mrs Perth, you worked for the old gent before his…?'

'Oh, sir, you didn't hear?' Mrs Perth widened her eyes and moved forward conspiratorially. 'Mr Wisscom, he disappeared a few years ago. I worked for him sin—'

'Twenty. All is correct. Mrs Perth, go out back and check on the girl, will you? Some of those chores are taking longer than usual.'

The tailor and Ida looked at each other in silence as Mrs Perth made her way back out of the room. As soon as the door closed behind her, the tailor leaned forward over the desk, the measuring tape around his shoulders click-clacking into the wood. 'Who sent you?' he hissed.

Ida laughed without joy, the deep laugh of Colton that was now becoming her own. 'Who sent me? Nobody. I've just got this feeling…' She paused, feeling the rune beneath her clothing grow hot against her skin. The air behind the tailor shifted, the ghostly image of the man once more coming and going. Ida frowned. What strangeness was this that she could no longer see her mother but was seeing other spirits? Had the powers of the rune's creator begun to become her own? She wished it was not so; the thought of seeing others' criminal responsibilities was a hideous one.

'You've got a feeling that what…?' the tailor asked, bloodshot eyes hesitant behind his glasses.

'You're being haunted, sir. Perhaps it is the previous owner of this place – I do not know myself, but I've a feeling that you're quite aware of it.'

The tailor scratched his head. 'Oh…oh, you're…what are you a…spirit guide or something like that?'

Ida shook her head. 'Nothing like that. I just got a feeling for these matters.'

'Okay…okay.' The tailor shifted around as though he was trying to work something out, and then grabbed the money he had just counted and slammed it back down in front of Ida. She frowned at it and then back at him. 'You can have the outfit for free if you get rid of him for me,' the tailor whispered, checking behind him, the empty air swivelling.

Ida laughed. 'Get rid of him? How in the hell would I do that? You got yourself in this mess.' The rune was getting hotter by the second, and she sucked air in through her mouth sharply, trying to control it.

'What do you mean I got myself in this mess? He's been haunting me. I took over the business, and he's been haunting me, but nobody believes me. He's been doing stuff at night – knocking over the furniture, changing things up. I can't abide by it – I can barely sleep!' His eyes widened, his voice strangled and strange.

The air was growing so thick with the scent of cologne that Ida could feel it choking her, lingering in her throat. The rune throbbed over her skin, and she took a step back from the tailor, rubbing her hand over her forehead and readjusting the hat that sat on top of her freshly shaved scalp. 'You need to put less of that scent on you, sir; I can barely think straight.'

The tailor paused, eyes wider still. It was like looking at the face of a dead owl, Ida thought. 'You can smell that?' he asked, leaning over the desk with abandon.

'Of course I can.'

'You're the first person to smell it since I took over. It's been choking me for years. It's him…did you see him?' The tailor glanced around again, searching the air.

'I saw him…at least, I think I did. Sir, I'm gonna ask you this only once, and then I'm gonna head out because this situation is not my ideal. Did you kill the man?'

The tailor shook his head instantaneously, a practised movement to the question that Ida guessed he had been asked many times before.

'Sir,' Ida said plainly, 'I am not going to tell. I must say – the only reason that you would be experiencing a haunting of this kind is if you killed the man. Now, you don't need to tell me a thing because, in many ways, I already know the answer, but if what I say is so – then this is you for life.'

The tailor shook his head and came around the side of the desk, grasping Ida's jacket with his hands. Ida rested her right hand on her gun, ready to pull, cock and shoot.

'There's nothing I can do?' asked the tailor, his skin pale and yellowing in the light.

'You can die – that is all you can do.' She took a step back and pulled her gun, raising her eyebrows at the wild man. He seemed to realise that he was holding onto her lapels and let go hesitantly, stepping backwards. The ghostly image of the victim hovered in the air behind him again, for a second longer this time. Ida glanced at him, surprised that his depiction was not sketched through the air as her mother often was. He was clearer, somehow, more solid.

'Sir, there is nothing you can do. He has decided that you have not repented. He will, therefore, not relent in his haunting of you,' she said, reholstering her pistol. 'I do not want to harm you – I myself cannot see my way to a lifetime of being followed by a stranger.'

The door dinged at that very moment, the bell above it ringing out and causing the tailor to jump. His eyes didn't shift from Ida. She grinned and took a fleeting glance away.

'"Tis the postman, sir, that's all,' Ida said softly. Her hand reached up, and she touched the tip of her hat. She picked her twenty dollar bill up from the desk beside them and pocketed it with a wink, turning toward the door. She stalked out, shoulders rounded back, chin high.

Reader, she left just when she should have. The tailor shivered as the door slammed closed and looked at the postman, who stood quite still as if in shock.

'What's with you?' the tailor asked grimly. 'You look like you've seen a ghost.'

'I don't think she was a ghost...' the postman said, shaking his head. He reached inside his pocket and pulled out a sheet of paper.

'What?' the tailor inquired, stepping toward the man to see what kept him so captivated.

'That woman who just left,' the postman responded.

'Oh...'

'You tell me that it ain't her…' The postman stared at the image in front of him, a well-to-do sort of woman with a strong jawline. 'She's changed her appearance somewhat – but it says right here that that's what we should be looking out for. Lookit!'

The tailor scratched his head and regarded the wanted poster. 'It sure does say that. And I see what you're saying, but I'm not certain.'

Mrs Perth came bustling into the room, clucking to herself about the girl out back. The tailor glanced up and beckoned her over.

'Mrs Perth, that person that we just fitted…well, come and have a look at this.'

She came over with great purpose, the movement of a woman utterly sure of herself. The postman handed the wanted poster to her, and she squinted at it.

'Well, well…I couldn't say for certain, but she certainly bears a likeness. Perhaps related. Brother, was it?'

'What?' the postman asked, shaking his head. 'That was the woman who just left here. You two couldn't see that?'

'Well, it ain't up to me, Mr Defold, and it ain't up to the tailor here.' Mrs Perth shrugged and handed the poster back.

'I am telling you that this is her. Look here – there's a reward. What do you say?' The postman's eyes lit up, and he licked his lips greedily.

'I want nothing to do with that person. They know…too much,' the tailor said, shivering again at the memory of Ida's words.

'I know who won't be so precious,' the postman said under his breath, pocketing the poster.

'Now, just you listen here, Larry – we've had this issue with you before. Those posters are supposed to go right to the mayor – you shouldn't be getting any special compensation for your knowledge of it.' Mrs Perth put her hands on her hips, a step away from waggling her finger at the man.

'Oh, take a day off, Mrs Perth, you take this town too seriously.' The postman pulled some letters from his bag and shoved them into the tailor's hands before turning and stepping out the door with a flourish.

'That man is trouble. He does not represent Incan's Brook,' Mrs Perth said bluntly. The tailor said nothing but stared into space beside her. 'Don't you think, sir?' she said, snapping him out of his daze.

'Hmmm? Yes, something like that,' he replied, his eyes darting around the room.

Chapter 10

Jonesy took a sip of his coffee and grinned, nodding at Colt. Colt sighed into his cup. It was intense, much stronger than he was used to. It was not his thing. His mother used to make it in a way that he loved, thin and gentle, the water having a slight hue of dirt to it. It was more of a suggestion of coffee, a mere mention. This stuff looked like it could be used to grout tiles. He took a sip and winced. It was disconcerting to have a coffee so thick and dark…what if the sheriff was trying to poison him or something? He'd never know with this stuff.

He placed the enamel cup down on the small table in his cell and sat heavily on the bed. Jonesy was humming again. He was always bloody humming, as though being in jail was the sweetest thing ever to happen to the man. What an idiot, thought Colt. What a situation to find oneself in.

He lay back on the bed. Spiders danced above him. There was an influx of them above his cell, the webs intricate and far-reaching. Sometimes, the spiders swung on their threads through the highest point of the bars, freeing themselves from within. It pleased Colt to see this, their freedom, a beautiful and inspiring sight, as though he hadn't chosen to be locked up himself. Which he had, he reminded himself with a grimace. So what was his plan? Jonesy slurped and made a self-satisfied, 'hmm' noise that irritated Colt to his core.

The wanted posters would be arriving right about now if they hadn't already. They were travelling to each town and city in The Nameless Stretch, sharing her face far and wide. Soon there would be an influx of bounty hunters scouring the land, doing the hard work for him. Then, they would arrive, Ida Vale in tow. Dead or alive, Colt thought. He wouldn't care either way. The money, though, could be an issue. It was the money they would want, and it was the money he didn't have. But would it matter? The sheriff would have to deal with it, not him. He could just slip out the back, having seen justice done. And hopefully, beautiful Trigger would be right there waiting. He scratched his hip, the skin tickling beneath the borrowed cotton trousers he wore.

'Where you from?' Jonesy said, his coffee now finished. Colt sighed and let his head fall to the left, staring at the prisoner from his horizontal position on the bed.

'A small farm in the south,' he responded.

'I'm from here. Both my 'rents were from here too. And their 'rents before them.'

'Is that so?'

'It is. Your mama still alive?' Jonesy asked, standing up and resting an arm on the bars of the cell.

'I'm feeling tired,' Colt said, turning his back on the man. He stared at the wall before him and tucked his feet up, foetus-like. He heard Jonesy grumble, saying something about company and politeness, and then listened to the heavy drop of his body onto his bed.

Colt thought of his mother. She was still alive. She was back at the farm, alone without adult company. His father had died a year back, leaving the two of them with the burden of the land. His brother was younger, smaller, stupider. The three of them sat around the table the evening after their patriarch's death and discussed the future with slow deliberation, no tears, no tantrums. His mother was a cold woman, experienced in frugal living. There was no garment that could not be restitched, not a leftover that could not be saved. She gazed at Colt behind glassy blue eyes, tired from the day before, and sighed.

'You must take over the farm as the new man of the house.'

Colt glared back at her. She knew, without doubt, that this was not his design. He was a man of action, or at least, he aimed to be. That was where his future lay, undoubtedly. He had read the stories for as long as he remembered, soaking in the adventure and travel, dreaming of the vast open plains and the lack of responsibility. This is what he had been working toward for years, training up Trigger and occasionally sleeping outside to toughen himself up.

'My plans remain the same, Mother,' Colt said in response, his eyebrows furrowing.

She sniffed, a grim smile playing on her lips. 'The hell they do. You are the eldest. When your father was alive, we were happy to play along with your little games, but if you think for a single minute that you're abandoning me, your brother, and this farm, then you have another think coming, boy.'

Colt glanced from her to his brother, who sat awkwardly between them. He was sixteen, but he looked about fourteen, as though his body hadn't realised his age yet. 'Don't you think you can take over the farm?' he asked him. His brother's eyes darted from Colt's to his mother's, and he opened his mouth to speak but was silenced by her raised hand.

'Don't you go asking him for his opinion. I am telling you what needs to be done, and you will obey me. This farm has been in our family for generations, and it's because our ancestors stepped up and took control whether they liked it or not,' she said. His mother always spoke like this when angry. There was a calm, cold edge to her voice that shivered through the recipient of her speech. Rarely did people disobey her for fear of what lay on the other side of her strange stone-like demeanour.

'Mother,' Colt began, licking his lips as he considered his words, 'I am not asking you for permission. I am a grown man. I will stick around for a month or so to help the boy understand what needs to be done, but you will have to hire someone to do the brute work. I am not willing to do it.'

His mother's foreboding smile did not falter but remained on her face. Her dark eyes were sharp and unblinking. 'Son,' she glanced at Colt's brother, 'go and make a fire in the drawing room. We shall be through presently.' A look of relief swam across his features, and he stood quickly and exited the room.

The mother and son stared at each other in silence for a moment. Colt raised his chin and gave a dismissive dip of the head. 'I don't have anything more to say on the matter,' he said.

'You will stop at nothing until your brother and I starve, is that it?'

'What? Mother, you are quite capable of controlling the books as you always have. You just want free labour – and the boy is old enough to learn. I was in the fields at a far younger age.'

She splayed her hands before her as if in worship. 'Why have I been cursed with a dead husband and an ungrateful son?'

'Who knows?' Colt replied, standing. The legs of the wooden chair screeched across the worn floor. He stepped toward the kitchen door and placed a hand on the handle, about to push, when something stopped him. It was a crackle in the air, a strange sort of tension.

'Colt,' his mother said in a low voice, 'if you step out of the door, you will be disowned.'

He turned and ran a hand through his thinning hair, shaking his head in exasperation. 'I cannot throw my life away here, on this farm. I'll never do any of the things I'm supposed to, can't you see that? I won't find a wife, won't ride through the open plains, won't make a name of any type for myself. I'll just be nothing.'

His mother snorted derisively. She picked up a mug that was on the table before her and held it high above her head, then let it fall. It smashed violently onto the wooden floorboards, shattering into countless pieces.

Colt jolted awake and sat up in bed, eyes wide. Jonesy was messing around with his pile of books and had knocked his enamel plate and mug to the floor. He grinned at Colt and shrugged, no apology forthcoming. Colt swung his legs over the side of the bed and placed his feet on the cold floor, his heart still hammering.

Being a postal worker in Incan's Brook was not the position Larry Defold had imagined it to be. As a child, he had watched the local postman riding to and fro, packages delivered with a wide smile. He was on a first-name basis with his neighbours and often stopped to regale Larry with tales of his travels – the far-flung corners of The Nameless Stretch that he had delivered mail to, his brave and bolt-proof horse that carried him to adventure. Larry was bewitched. His father was a fisherman, but Larry knew from childhood what his profession was to be – and if it wasn't a mailman, he didn't want anything to do with it. So, on his eighteenth birthday, he applied. The post office was quick to accept. They didn't usually have an application sent to them that was so…well, detailed. Larry had even written up his own postal guidelines to keep him honest, complete with a rhyming oath. This was unusual, to say the least. Indeed, for the first ten years of the job, Larry was the most loyal, hard-working, and downright proudest mailman Incan's Brook had ever seen. He collected mail and dropped off parcels from all over, caring not for distance nor weather. As the years went by, more post offices began to spring up, causing Larry's journeys to shorten significantly. Eventually, he was hardly ever called upon to go outside of Incan's Brook, and he lamented that the adventure he had signed up for was no longer not just available to him – it didn't even exist. His manager watched him go from a chirpy, encouraging sort of fellow to a miserable man who no longer bothered to learn the names of his townspeople.

'Larry, what can I do for you to make this job a happier one?' he asked him one day while sorting the local influx of wanted posters for the mayor.

'You can give me a pay rise,' Larry said. He leaned forward and wrote an amount on a piece of paper and slid it across the desk to the postmaster, who read it in silence.

'That's more than I earn,' he said mildly, surprised at the amount.

Larry quickly learned that there was no pay rise. What's more, there was not any position of authority that he could move into. He felt as though his life of adventure had been stripped away from him, and he had not a jot to show for it except an ageing horse. It was then that Larry began to consider ways to earn a little money on the side. He started off fairly gently, picking up bits of groceries and items for those who could not travel, marking up the cost at the door. This was well and good, but it wasn't going to put much money in his pocket.

Then, one day, he began to pay attention to the figures on the bounty posters that were heading to the mayor's office. The usual way of it was that the posters would be pinned onto the notice board just outside the office, so that any bounty hunters could visit and take down the details of those that they were interested in hunting. Larry knew that it was frowned upon to take down the posters or to show favouritism in any way by delivering them solely to individuals. But frowned upon wasn't strictly illegal, was it? That day, Larry began a little racket. The word quickly spread among the bounty hunters that in Incan's Brook, one could be guaranteed sole knowledge of a bounty, a head start that delivered an excellent cut of profit for Larry. Since then, the mailman largely ignored his original oath and guidelines, leaning instead on the much more generous motto: if it makes money, do it.

This time, he thought, holding Ida's wanted poster in his hand, was a little different. Larry couldn't just guarantee sole knowledge of the bounty; he could show the hunters the location of the criminal, too. Now, that was worth something. He was not a man to attempt to capture wayward bounty himself, his powers being of the mind rather than the strength of arm. Larry whistled a merry little tune as he walked down a dirt side alley just off the road from the main street. In a small, dark and drab old barn, there was a bar that everyone well-to-do pretended didn't exist. It was frequented by bounty hunters, criminals, and those who weren't brave enough to tip the bartender in the saloon for a tipple. Larry knew exactly who to find there.

The bar was fairly empty, and they all turned to stare at Larry when he walked in. He tipped his hat to the general room, nobody in particular and everybody at once. The scent differed significantly from the saloon. It was one of hot air, body odour, yeasty drinks and fish. Larry's nostrils flinched. There was one man in particular that Larry was hoping to talk to. He glanced around the room fervently, eyes eager and beady. The barman nodded over.

'What'll it be?'

'Beer. You seen Phoney about?' Larry replied, scratching his head.

'He was in earlier,' the barman said, pulling a pint into a beer glass that looked as if it had already had multiple drinks poured in it that day.

'Oh. Any of his—?'

'Over by the window.' The barman placed the full glass down on the table and nodded. Larry placed down a single, grubby coin and took the beer, turning to face the only window in the room. In front of the streaked glass, a woman was sitting, a whisky before her. Larry walked over.

'Ma'am?'

'Hmmm?' she said, not looking up. Larry glanced at the messy blonde bun scraped up on top of her head, the worn dress that fell about her, held in place with a holster, two guns shining inside.

'Ma'am, you are part of Ph— um, Billy's gang, is it so?' he tried again.

The woman glanced upward and met his eyes. Hers were dark and glassy, the sign of one too many. 'He ain't here.'

'No, well, I can see that. I've got something I'd like to discuss with him. Where can I find him?'

The woman looked Larry up and down in a slow, lazy way that made him question her motives. She seemed as though she might draw a gun on him at any moment, the tension surrounding her was electric. He frowned.

'Who's asking?' she said.

'Well – I'm the local—'

'Postman,' she said, finishing the sentence with an air of derision.

'That's right…listen, I got a bounty, and I know where the Phoney – I mean, Billy – can find the mark.'

The woman took a sip of her whisky. 'Is that so? How about you give that information to me, and I can pass it on.'

Larry hesitated and smiled. 'Listen, lady, just tell me where he is, all right? There are plenty of other people I could pass this information to.'

The woman tutted. 'Ain't that so. Well, postie, you better follow me then. Billy would hate to be left out.' She stood up with a strange snarl and led Larry to the only other door in the place, the back door. It creaked open. Larry had never ventured this far through before and was surprised when he felt the sunshine beat down on his skin again. There, in a small courtyard, stood three men, one of them Larry recognised as Billy.

'Mr Defold,' said Billy, tipping his hat. He was the shortest of all there but carried himself in such a way that you would never think to mention it.

'Yessir,' Larry said, mirroring his movement. Those of The Nameless Stretch had long given up handshakes ever since a bandit nicknamed Handy Rose had ridden the lands many years ago. Rumours abounded that the woman collected the hands of men she found attractive, distinguishing them by a handshake. The practice was swiftly dropped as a foolish endeavour between any sex.

'He's got a bounty for you – knows where the mark is,' the woman said by way of introduction, rolling her eyes over to Larry.

Billy simply nodded. It was an indication that Larry should remove the bounty poster immediately, and he did so with a smile. He held it up to show the group the image.

'Five hundred dollars,' he said.

'I can read,' Billy responded.

'Of course.' Larry hesitated, swallowing. Even after all this time, he still feared the leaders of these gangs. They were somehow above the law entirely, bounty hunters, as though anyone they killed were legal tender – viewing humans as dollar signs only. 'I saw this woman in the tailors about an hour ago. She's right here in Incan's Brook.'

'Is that so?' Billy said, reaching for the poster. Larry pulled it back, smiling in a faux apologetic way.

'It's the fee I'll need before I hand it over. I've got some good information. I think I know where she's staying. I'm asking for $100.'

The men beside Billy smirked in unison. Billy blinked exaggeratedly, meaning to show amusement. 'That's a big cut. Let's see…she's staying at the saloon, am I right?'

Larry fumbled with the poster, and Billy nodded in response as though that was all the information he required. 'Excellent. Here's your cut.' He pulled a thirty dollar note out of his pocket and pushed it into Larry's coat, a tight smile on his lips. One of the men stepped forward and held out his hand.

Larry sighed. He knew his jig was up immediately. It was barely more than he usually got.

'Okay,' he said, handing over the piece of paper with a grimace.

Chapter 11

Ida stood before the tarnished mirror in her room, her hat and boots abandoned behind her, the new clothes soft against her skin. She pulled at them a little, trying to rough them up. She didn't want to look so wholly brand new. It was illuminating somehow, as though she were holding a torch above her head, asking for the world to see her.

The sun was dropping in the sky outside, filling the space with dusk. Ida looked at the room behind her in the mirror, the strange otherworldliness of the sight. It was empty, or so it seemed. Her mother must be there, she thought, and shuddered slightly at the memory of the tailors. It was strange how she had seen the man behind him, how the air had moved in a different, more violent way. Perhaps, she mused, it was indicative of how one died. Perhaps the hauntings could be gentle or fierce. And yet, why was she now seeing the image of others' hauntings, especially if the tailor was not? Why had she developed this sixth sense? The rune burned suddenly against her skin, as though it were tapping her on the shoulder, a reminder of its existence. Ida did not want the powers of the old witch. She didn't want to live a life haunted by strangers and the murdered. She didn't even want, she thought sadly, to be haunted by her mother. An everyday life, the life of a free woman, was the goal.

The noise of a piano began to drift up to her room, tinkling in the dimming light. The saloon was readying itself for another evening of pleasure, of food, of light. What was the life of a free woman anyway? she wondered. Hadn't she lived that life and found it full of pain and misery, of others destroying the fabric of her existence? No, life as a free woman was not what she desired. Life as a free man, now there was the ideal.

So, what was her plan? Ida thought of Incan's Brook, the false cheer of it all. A dry town that served alcohol, what hypocrites. If Colt were not searching for her, perhaps she could settle somewhere. And yet, if he were searching for her, and she imagined this scenario was more realistic, where could she go? Perhaps to The City of Glass, the furthest place on the map. She had heard the tales of the city, how the cold forced people indoors, how they covered their faces up to protect from frostbite, their features invisible to those around them.

But then, there was always revenge – an intriguing thought. The entire town of Steepmount was guilty, in her opinion. From those who took advantage of her to those who turned their faces, they were criminals all right, and they should pay. A shout from outside caught her attention, and she swivelled toward the window. There, she saw the image of her mother, staring out from the second-story room into the street. Ida let out a breath of surprise, still not used to seeing her likeness before her. Her mother turned and then gestured beyond. Ida stepped toward the window and peered out.

Below, in the street outside the saloon, stood three men arguing with the small gunkeeper from the entrance. The shortest of the three men was waving a piece of paper around wildly, gesturing at the saloon in general. The gunkeeper kept raising his hands, pointing to their weapons, and shaking his head. Ida unclipped the latch on the window and pushed it outwards, just a fraction, to turn up the dialogue.

'You are harbouring a fugitive in this establishment!' the short man yelled, 'and I am a man of the law. You will allow me to come in and collect my bounty immediately, sir!'

'I ain't letting you in with those weapons – you could shoot someone's eye out. If you are truly a man of the law, you can fetch the mayor to override my decision. That is all.' The gunkeeper went to turn away but paused as the short man's right hand hovered over the handle of his gun.

'Listen to me,' he said bluntly. 'I cannot waste time fetching the mayor when there is a wanted fugitive in there. I cannot collect a bounty without weapons – of course. I cannot. How would such a thing work?'

'You could use your sweet words,' the gunkeeper said to the irate man, a cluck of sarcasm in his voice. 'And anyway – let me have a look at that picture. I know each and every person who has gone inside that saloon today – I have a memory that is stronger than a bullet.' He snatched the poster out of the short man's hands, and to Ida's surprise, the man let him. 'Ida Vale,' he read.

Ida flinched. Surely not?

'Let's see here…' the gunkeeper continued. 'It's mostly men in there. I ain't seen a well-to-do lady in there all day, apart from the employed, of course. You know that a lady of this description would usually stay at Mrs Fudd's B&B, don't you? They don't often come and stay in a saloon – a dangerous place for a lady.'

'She looks like a common whore to me,' said the short man, spitting into the dirt.

Ida shifted out the way of the window, her back to the wall. The image of her mother was gone again, and she sniffed hard, staring at the room. She had to get out of there. How long could that gunkeeper hold those men away?

'Five hundred dollars, is it? That's a pretty penny, although Bleakhollow is far enough away and—'

And her guns. Ida thought of her weapons, sitting in their own private cubby right behind the gunkeeper. How would she get those back without being caught?

'The postman said that this is where she was staying.' The short man's voice floated up to the window.

'Larry? I don't see why he should know better than I do.'

Ida took a deep breath and stepped back into the room. It was time for action. She grabbed her hat and quickly put on her boots, lacing them up with abandon. The voices continued outside, the sun setting and plunging their scene into darkness, lit only by kerosene. Ida began throwing her small items into her saddlebag, glancing longingly at the bed. She had hoped to spend another night in this semi-luxury, not a night on the road. She threw the double-ended satchels over her shoulder and stepped toward the door, pulling it open. In the hallway stood a saloon girl, grinning at her as though she knew that the door was about to be opened.

'Looking for company?' she said softly.

Ida stepped forward and glanced around her. 'I would like your assistance, ma'am,' she said to her.

'It is not a problem. How much you got?' The woman began to step toward the bedroom, and Ida lay a hand on her arm, halting her.

'No, I will pay you, but what I require is a little different. There are some men outside, shouting. I would like you to go out there and distract them.'

The woman frowned and curled her top lip, her eyes narrowing. 'You a criminal?'

Ida laughed without humour and shook her head. 'No! I had a falling out with the gentlemen outside, that's all. I should like to leave without their accosting me.'

The saloon girl widened her eyes in a disbelieving way. 'That sounds suspicious to me. It'll cost you.'

'That's fine. I'll pay.'

'All right,' the girl said, raising her chin in defiance. 'It'll be fifty dollars.'

Ida nodded and reached into her shirt, pulling out a wad of cash. She counted fifty out in front of the shocked eyes of the girl and handed it over.

'I meant sixty,' she said, taking the money and pocketing it.

Ida raised her eyebrow. 'You have what you asked for. I am not asking you to do something that I could not ask any one of the women here to do.'

The girl grunted, 'Fine. I shall head out now.'

'Get them away from the door if you can. My horse is in the stable next door. I'll need to get past without them seeing and collect my guns on the way.'

'As you wish.'

Ida watched her stroll down the hallway as though she were in no great hurry and followed behind at a distance. The woman made her way down the stairs, occasionally stopping to chat idly to a friend or client, and Ida hung back, paying particularly close attention to the threads on her sleeve or the woodwork on the banister when paused – as though she were fascinated by these mundane details. Eventually, they reached the saloon, and the woman sauntered across the floor, waving to a gentleman every now and then, grinning at the barman. Ida kept her hat dipped low over her face and tried to walk at an average pace behind her. As they reached the velvet curtain, she watched the woman roll her shoulders back and breathe in deeply. Then, she pushed the curtains aside with a flick of her wrist and ran full pelt through them. Ida heard a scream and a shout, the words, 'he's getting away!' drifting through into the saloon and making some of the clientele look up from their drinks with mild interest.

Ida took a breath. The words, 'Have faith, child', suddenly appeared in her mind as though they had been whispered to her. She pushed aside the curtains. The gun cubby and desk were left unattended, as she had hoped, and she slid behind the wooden divide and hastily located her weapons, holstering one and, much to her dismay, dropping the other. It made a great clatter but, and she was grateful for it, didn't go off. She bent down to retrieve it and paused, taking a moment to steady her breathing and calm herself. She could hear the saloon girl outside, random sentences floating through the air.

'He ran right past you – didn't you see him? Aren't you supposed to be the law?!'

The deeper, duller tone of the short man was harder to hear, his responses lost to grunts and murmurs in the air. Ida stood and holstered the fallen gun and then moved toward the door. Keeping her back to the wall so that they could not see her from outside, she took a breath and checked the situation. The saloon girl was talking wildly, throwing her hands up and shaking her head, pointing in the opposite direction. The gunkeeper was scratching his head, the picture of confusion, as though he knew that the saloon girl was putting on a show but couldn't work out why. The short man was holding the poster of Ida in his hand, but was now paying little attention to it.

'Oh, for goodness sake – why aren't you chasing him?' the girl shouted.

The short man shook his head and put his hand to his hat, 'I don't know what you're talking about, woman! I ain't seen anyone come out of that saloon!'

'Well, then, you must be daft. I mean it. No wonder the criminals are running riot in this town.' She glanced at the paper the man held and tutted. 'There'll be a bounty on his head by the end of the day, and you will have given it away.'

'Lady, I've got a bounty waiting for me right in there.'

'I don't think that Mr Grebus here will mind stopping anyone from coming out, if you would do me this kindness, sir. He took my gold necklace. It was my mother's. Can you imagine how I would feel should I lose it?'

'Oh fuck it,' the short man said, handing the bounty poster roughly to the gunkeeper. 'Mr Grebus, if I come back here and you have let anybody – whether it's this woman or not – out of this saloon, then you will be praying for mercy. Do you understand?'

The gunkeeper nodded. Ida took a breath and watched as the short man swore again. He ran off in the direction of the saloon girl's pointed finger, followed closely by his two men. The gunkeeper turned to come back inside, and Ida stopped.

'Oh, Mr Grebus!' cried the saloon girl suddenly, 'I was frightened for my life!' she wailed, and grabbed the man by the arms, pulling him away from the direction of the door. She began to sob loudly and theatrically, as though she were taking great pleasure in the new role life had thrown her way, and hiccupped a loud cry before burying her face into his shirt.

'Oh dear, dear,' the gunkeeper said, uncomfortable. Ida took her chance, slipping past the two, out into the air. She stepped, walking but not running, to the stable and ducked inside. There was Bullet, chewing hay in the dimming warmth. Ida grabbed his tack and put it on him, leading him out to the open air. She mounted, pushing him into a jog from a standstill, following the path out of the town. Behind her, life carried on as usual in Incan's Brook, the saloon heaving with hypocrites, all wishing each other a sober evening while disguising the drink in their cups.

Chapter 12

Colt watched the sheriff from his bed, who was going through his post with a noisy concentration, humming as he skimmed letter after letter. The morning coffee had been poured already, and it waited by the bars of the cells in the badly washed enamel cups, the thick gravy-like liquid cooling. Jonesy slept. The sun was still low in the sky, the room barely lit by its orange glow. The sheriff was sitting with his feet up on his desk, a lazy yet powerful position that Colt both admired and viewed derisively. He sat up on his bed, about to collect his coffee (to which he was now becoming habituated), as the sheriff suddenly went silent. His feet dropped from the desk as he read, and then he glanced over the top of the paper, staring at Colt. He stood, moving his feet across the tiles with the languid step of a man enjoying the threat of his presence. Colt was not as threatened as the sheriff liked to believe, of course.

'Do you know what this says, boy?' The sheriff squared up to the cell bars and raised his eyebrows expectantly.

'Of course not,' Colt responded, standing.

'It says that there are bounty hunters on their way here, with Ida Vale. They are writing to us so that we might make space in the cells, get the reward money ready, etcetera, etcetera.'

Colt grinned and stepped forward, just as the sheriff lifted one boot and kicked the coffee cup straight into the cell, causing the enamel cup to clatter onto the tiles, and the dark liquid to cast itself across the floor and bed, and a little on Colt. He said nothing and paused. Jonesy was shocked awake and sat up with a small cry, his hands held before him as though he were dreaming that he was in a fight and he was the victim.

'Do you have five hundred dollars, boy?' the sheriff asked, his stare brutal and unflinching.

'I do not,' said Colt, concern creeping onto his face. 'But it is right that she should be caught and brought here. She is a criminal, Sheriff, and I have done the right thing.'

'You know,' the sheriff continued, as though no words had been spoken at all by the prisoner. 'If you had not handed yourself in for whatever plan you think you're going to accomplish, I would be tracking you at this very moment. So either way, you can be satisfied that you are in the right place.'

Colt swallowed. 'She is a crim—'

'You are a criminal,' the sheriff said firmly, cutting him off. 'I do not care what happens to Ida Vale. I care what happens to you. So these bounty hunters, they tell me that they're riding from the Docks of Astray. Do you know how far away that is, boy?' He held up the letter as though that might give some indication, although Colt could not see what was written on it.

'That's northeast,' he replied, rounding his shoulders. He was beginning to feel nervous and tried to imagine his mother's face in place of the sheriff's, a person he would never allow to disregard and speak to him in such a way.

'It is northeast. So it won't take long, will it? Maybe…two days if they stop for rest and food. But why would they stop to rest when they could be living the life here? When they could be eating at the saloon, seeing our famous women, enjoying all the hospitality that five hundred dollars can afford a man. Why would they sleep on the dirt ground when there was only a few hours of hard riding between themselves and freedom?' The sheriff scrunched up the paper in his right fist and leaned on the bars of Colt's cell nonchalantly. Colt hesitated.

'What will you do when they arrive?' he asked.

The sheriff smiled. 'We'll take it from your neck. Have you met our hangman, boy?'

Colt's eyes flickered past the sheriff to Jonesy, who was now sitting on the edge of his bed, watching this exchange with a strange look of entertained glee on his face. Who did he think he was, watching him this way, as though he were a fish in a bowl? Colt rolled his shoulders back, then leaned down to pick up the cup that still lay on the floor. He handed it out to the sheriff, who ogled him incredulously.

'A top-up would be great.'

The sheriff smiled and then turned away from Colt, facing Jonesy. He strode across the short distance and plucked the cup of coffee from the floor, passing it through the bars.

Jonesy took it, sipping it instantly, a nod of courtesy taking the place of a silent thank you.

'Jonesy,' the sheriff began, 'have you ever met our hangman?'

'Turner? I have. He's been doing the job since I was a boy.'

'That's right. He's a practised hand,' the sheriff said. 'How would you describe him for your fellow inmate here?'

'He's...' Jonesy faltered. 'Listen, I don't wanna say anything that's out of line. He's a good man, and it is not an easy job. He's the only one that I know of who'd be willing to do it – yourself excluded, Sheriff.'

The sheriff grinned, a genuine smile, and nodded. 'That's right. He is a good sort of man, but it takes its toll on you, don't it? How could it not? Turner and I, we think differently about some things. We've both killed men, but it's the manner of his killings that has stuck with him. He's haunted.' He glanced from Jonesy to Colt, stepping back across the divide, his boots clicking with every movement. 'It's the begging of the sinner on the walk to the gallows. It's the intimacy of placing the rope around his neck, against his skin, the whimpering, the smell of another man's piss that close to you. That's what it is. It's the drop. The wait. It's seeing the look in the audience's eyes, the faces of the mother, daughter, wife.' The sheriff was now up against the bars, the movement of a man completely certain that he won't be grabbed from the other side. 'Haunted. Do you believe in ghosts, boy?'

Colt shook his head. 'I do not.'

'Well then. You'll know soon enough.' The mood suddenly switched from tense to jovial as the sheriff clapped his hands. 'I'll go and see Turner, organise his coming by to measure you.'

A strange shiver ran through Colt's body, and he breathed slowly, determined not to let his worry show. It doesn't matter, he thought. When she arrives, I'll kill her.

Ida had ridden through the night, watching the empty horizon expand before her. Beneath her, Bullet had begun the journey as she had, rested after a night indoors, raring to go. He had sensed her nervous energy, and each time she checked behind her, heart pounding at the noises of unknown terrain, he appeared to move faster still, keen to get away.

The landscape had changed subtly on their way, and now, as the sun rose, Ida glanced around at the barren land. Single rocks and dead trees punctuated the earth, and she pulled the bearskin coat close around her, noticing that she was starting to see her breath before her, something that she had never before witnessed. Her eyes were heavy after the night of riding, and she still longed for the bed that was unslept in, way back in that strange arrogant town. She pulled Bullet to a halt and dismounted, her legs sore from the ride. He breathed out cold air, and she lay a hand on his neck, soft and warm beneath her skin.

There was a larger rock close by, big enough to lean against, and so Ida led Bullet toward it and then removed the saddle and saddlebags, indicating to him that this was a time for rest. He understood immediately, dropping a back hoof and closing his eyes. Ida smiled and began to pull together some small rocks and sticks. She knelt on the ground and carefully built a fire, the way her father had taught her to do in the hearth. It seemed to take a little longer than usual with the cold, damp air, but once it had gotten going, she rolled out her bedroll and lay down in relative warmth. The sky above glistened in the strange half-light between night and day. In many ways, she was freer than she had ever been at her father's house. Her father's house. When had it become that, instead of her homestead? Despite the sun's appearance, the moon was still lingering, and she smiled at this, the strangeness of the two seeing each other, saying hello.

'Mother,' she said, whispering it, her hot breath forming in the air as though the word had substance. 'I am glad that you are with me.'

She didn't look around her for traces of the woman, just stared at the sky instead, listening to the soft crackle of the fire and the heavy breathing of a sleeping Bullet. The earth was hard beneath her back, regardless of the bedroll. Her ears were cold and no longer kept warm by her long hair. Despite the tiredness she had felt when riding, the lack of sleep, she felt more awake now than she had in hours. She thought of them, that short man, trying to find her, a useless picture of the old Ida Vale. And yet, they had her name. She had given Colt a fake name on purpose. But of course, he cannot have been stupid, despite appearances.

Bullet gave a snort, almost a snore, and Ida smiled. Five hundred dollars. That was a lot of money. In fact, Ida thought, that was more than any bounty she had seen the Sheriff of Steepmount put on a head. When he did deign to help someone who wasn't a local, and that was rare, he certainly didn't usually give this much of a damn. Maybe Colt had gotten to him, gotten inside his head, offered him something. But what? The man seemed so meek when she had met him, barely able to look a woman in the eye. Could he have changed all that much? The moon was dipping lower now, the fire beside her no longer roaring.

'I shall close my eyes for an hour or so, and then we shall ride on,' she said as if to her mother, picturing her nodding. Ida closed her eyes and dreamed of a soft bed beneath her, a full meal in her stomach, and a cup of coffee and bourbon.

Chapter 13

In Incan's Brook saloon, the gunkeeper was trying desperately not to let himself slip into a comfortable sleep. Billy had given him explicit instruction not to let anyone come out of the establishment until he himself had searched each and every room. That had been hours and hours ago now, and yet he had heard no more words about it. He was starting to think that Billy and his men were just enjoying a night at the saloon, and the fact that the sun was coming up made him think that his instincts were right. He should have locked the door as he had wanted and gone to bed, only Billy would not account for it, telling him that a locked door didn't let anybody in, and what if the woman in question tried to enter? There was a mess of words anyway, them having lost the chap that had stolen Miss Daisy's precious heirloom necklace, and maybe lost Ida Vale as well. The gunkeeper's head dipped forward, waking him up. He opened his eyes, having not even realised they were closed, and saw that he was staring into the face of the bounty hunter.

'Billy,' he said sleepily, pushing himself up on the desk before him. 'Any luck?'

'No,' was the response.

'Ah, well. She must have left before you got here.'

'Do you think? Or do you suspect that she might have slipped out while you were sleeping on the job?' Billy raised his eyebrows. 'Give me my guns, now.'

'What was your number?' the gunkeeper asked, rubbing his eyes.

'Are you kidding me? Do you have any idea how much time you have wasted for me tonight? First with your nonsense about being armed and then by sleeping when you should be working. You oughta be embarrassed. Guns, now.'

The gunkeeper sighed and turned, staring into the cubbies. In truth, he did know which belonged to Billy; pretty much everyone in Incan's Brook did. He just didn't want to give the man the satisfaction of this. The guns were what you saw first when he entered the room. They were gold-plated, for a start, which seemed like a ridiculous waste of money. The gunkeeper reached for them and flinched at the bark of 'Careful!' from behind him. He turned and placed them down, watching as Billy reholstered with impressive speed.

'Now listen. If I don't find that woman, I'm coming back to see you, specifically. Do you understand, Mr Grebus?'

The gunkeeper nodded solemnly. He did understand quite well. Billy glared at him as though he were staring at a wayward child, not someone who was significantly older than him. He turned and stepped out of the saloon, where his two men were waiting for him, leaning lazily against the hitching post, hats pulled down over their eyes.

'Get the horses. I think she's left town, and it can't have been long ago,' he said, staring up at the early morning sun. One of the men lifted his hat and nodded, striding away with purpose. The other man yawned.

'We got time for a coffee, boss?' he asked, his hat still low, his body slumped in rest like a bag of sand.

'Coffee? No. No time for coffee. We ain't got time for anything but catching this woman and taking her up to Steepmount.' He pulled the bounty poster from his pocket and looked at it again.

'Let me see that,' his man said, lifting his hat from his eyes and taking the paper. 'Doesn't look the type.'

'Greyson, you don't think that any woman looks the type. Ever. And we've caught all sorts of miscreants.' Billy sighed, scratching his cheek and glancing off in the direction of his other flunky.

'Thieving. Isn't ladylike,' Greyson said, handing back the poster. He hocked up a phlegm ball in the back of his throat, causing Billy to wince, and spat it into the dirt.

'I gotta tell you, that really turns my stomach. And ladylike? I don't know anyone who is ladylike around these parts.'

'My pa always used to say a man has a right to spit.'

Billy rolled his eyes. 'You also got the right to shit in the street, but I don't see you doing that because it is impolite.'

'I got a right to shit in the street? Anyway, this woman, supposing she is armed?'

The other man came round the corner, three horses in tow. Billy nodded, leaving his colleague's questions hanging in the air, and went to grab his horse. All the while, he mused on female criminals and the likelihood of them being a better shot than he. Improbable, he thought, but not impossible.

Ida awoke to the sound of trundling wheels moving over the tiniest rocks, breaking them into even smaller ones. She sat up, staring about her for the culprit. There, in the near distance, was a stagecoach being pulled by two horses. Its driver was sitting up high, wrapped warmly, a scarf covering most of their face. Ida ducked down, trying to hide behind a rock. Her hands began to sweat, going clammy over the thought of Colt jumping from within the carriage. Bullet woke up at the noise and began to nudge the ground, searching for any signs of grass, of life. The coach sounded like it was coming closer, the noise becoming louder and louder. It stopped after a moment, and Ida heard a door open and close, footsteps walking nearby.

'It's just a horse. Wearing a head collar there. Draw your gun, Danny. The owner will be around here somewhere,' a woman's voice said. She spoke in an accent that Ida had never heard, clipped and sharp as flint, the words like a staccato song.

Ida took one last sharp breath and stood, drawing her pistols. Her eyes fell upon a middle-aged woman in an oversized blue satin day dress, who looked entirely unsurprised to see her. She didn't even move, her grey curls remaining piled on her head as though made from clay.

'Well, well,' she said softly, amused at the sight of Ida. 'You can lower your weapons, dear; I was simply intrigued by the sight of a lone horse standing in the morning sunshine.'

Ida kept one pistol pointed at the woman and wiped her nose with the sleeve of her bearskin coat, the cold air causing snot to run onto her top lip. The action, coupled with the woman's gaze, made her feel like a little girl, and she rounded her shoulders and lifted her chin, determined not to give herself away. 'I'm not looking for company.'

The woman laughed, a tinkling sort of noise, the air before her fogging. 'I'm not offering you company, dear. Though I must say, you look half-starved. Where are you heading?'

This had happened to her before, Ida thought. It was as though she were looking into her past, meeting Mrs Smithe for the first time. She clenched her jaw.

'I am not telling you, a stranger,' she said, throwing her voice deeper than Colton's usual, doing her best to appear threatening.

The woman pursed her lips and shrugged. 'I am going to The City of Glass. It's a cold journey, you should know. It's not a journey for the faint-hearted. Once you reach the Alask Wilds, you'll need more than that coat.'

Ida said nothing. The woman rolled her eyes dramatically as though she was being quite clear and direct, and Ida purposefully misunderstood her.

'Should you wish to take a ride in the coach with me, I would not find it disagreeable. I am known as a helpful and philanthropic woman in these parts. We'll get there in twice the time with my two steeds, and you can rest your eyes and enjoy the provisions that I have brought for the journey.' She spread her hands before her as though she were laying out the ideas for Ida to see. 'Some cheeses from the northland, spicy and fresh in flavour,' she added as an afterthought.

Up above, a large bird began to circle. It caught Ida's eye, and she glanced up, staring at the large wings spread above them, talons poised. The woman followed her gaze.

'The Whitchit bird. They've been known to attack lone travellers, steal children, that sort of thing. A dangerous bird.'

Ida pulled back the hammer on her left pistol. 'Gone are the days when I might trust a stranger such as yourself. Keep moving, old woman. I want nothing to do with you.'

The woman smiled a strange, iced grin that led Ida to trust her gut even more. She nodded, and picked up her skirts, turning back to the coach. As she turned, she laughed breezily. 'You will die out here.'

Ida watched her climb into the coach and close the door with a flourish. The driver tipped their hat to Ida and flicked the reins twice, causing the coach to spring forward into an instant trot. It weaved away. The air tingled around Ida's face, and she uncocked her pistol and reholstered, wiping her nose again. Bullet stepped forward and pushed his large velvet snout into her cold hand, warming it. She stroked his forehead and patted his neck, staring upwards for a sight of the bird. It was no longer there.

'Come on, boy, let's get going. We've got to make the most of the daylight,' she said softly, feeling the horse's heat beneath her hand, her stomach tight with the hangover of confrontation.

Turner was exactly as haunted as the sheriff had implied, if not worse. He was a surprisingly short man, although why this surprised Colt, he was not sure, only he had assumed that a man with such a responsibility would be much larger, in case there were any threats of escape from criminals. He stood before him with a measuring tape, and Colt assessed him readily. His ruddy pink skin implied that he either had a drinking problem or a standing outside in the sun problem and indeed, he was not wearing a hat, which was unusual. Apart from that small element, he appeared to have made some small effort in the rest of his clothing. He was dressed in a smart black suit with a bolo tie done up to the neck, the decorative metal piece being a golden hangman's noose. Colt frowned. This seemed to be in relatively poor taste, he thought. His head was hairless, as was his face, and his eyes peered out from behind little circular glasses with a yellowing tint.

'It would be best if you could lay down on the bed, young sir,' Turner said, his voice so soft and gentle that Colt had to strain to hear him. Colt scratched his head.

'Why's that?' he asked.

'Stops me straining my back.'

'Oh,' Colt said, nodding. He sat down on the bed and then lay down, catching eyes with Jonesy, who was watching the entire scene with the glazed look of a child in math class. Once he had lain down, Turner began to measure him. Colt thought that he would primarily measure his length, but this did not seem to be the way the man did it. He took each limb in turn, saying quiet numbers under his breath, moving slowly and precisely. Colt allowed him to do his work without a word, keeping a watchful eye on his ever-moving hands.

Eventually, he stood back and allowed Colt to sit up. For the first time, Turner made eye contact with him. There was something in his stare that gave Colt a proper understanding of the word haunted. His eyes were a cold blue, penetrating and bare. It wasn't the bags beneath them that belied a lack of sleep, rather the desperation that enclosed them. It was as though he was looking at a man who had not just slept poorly the night before but rather had never known the meaning of sleep. Colt shivered in the hot cell, unable to look away.

'Nervous?' Turner asked.

Colt nodded haphazardly.

'Don't be. I'll come get you when it's time,' Turner said.

Colt felt as though he suddenly came back to life and managed to break the stare between them. 'Oh, of the hanging? No, that's not going to happen.'

Turner gave him a grim smile, or rather, it was more of an impression of a smile, without it actually reaching his lips.

'Many have said it before you, but rarely am I called for the measurement before judgment has fallen.' He glanced around him then, eyes drawn and focusing on different sections of air as though assessing a full room before a speech. Colt observed him and winced as the short death bringer stuck out his right hand to offer a handshake. Colt laughed uncomfortably.

'Oh no, I don't.'

'Handy Rose?' Turner asked, his eyes momentarily dancing. Colt nodded, and Turner mirrored the movement, a real smile creeping onto his lips for the first time.

'I wouldn't worry about that. She was my first hanging.'

Chapter 14

The sun was now climbing in the sky at a steady progress, and yet as Ida moved forward, Bullet springing beneath her, she noticed that the air itself continued to grow colder. Bullet's coat was dry and warm, and she placed a hand on his shoulder every now and then to check his temperature. She would care for her horse with close attention in the cold months at the homestead, though it never got this cold, not even on the hardest of weeks. Her father would always cluck at her, telling her that horses were made to withstand such a change in the temperature, but then her horse had been her only friend, and she treated him as such.

Bullet was carrying enough weight to keep warm: herself, her roll mat, and the miscellaneous bag that she had taken from the trading post strapped to the saddle. She had barely given it a thought since and ignored it still. Now Bullet seemed to be fine beneath her, even quickening his step before she requested it, his movements agile and light.

As they moved forward at a fair lope, the scenery remained the same, except for one key element. The horizon was changing before them, at first just the tip of a white mountain and then the rest, like an iceberg rising from the ground. Ida had never seen snow before and had never even thought of its existence in her own reality. In one of her mother's books, there was a short story that she had read as a child. She thought of this as they rode closer for the first time in many years.

In the story, a man had lost everything, his family and his home, and had chosen to live in a cabin at the top of a snow-covered hill. The snow compounded his loneliness, and each day, he saw himself reflected in it – cold, solitary, uninhabitable. On the sixth day, he went to the river to catch himself some fish and, upon stamping on the ice to make a hole for his rod, fell through to his death. There seemed to be no moral to the tale, or if there was, Ida could not work out what it was that she should have taken from it. When she had asked her father, he had slapped her hand and told her that only those who had finished their working day were permitted to waste time on stories that went nowhere.

Ida smiled as they rode forward, pulling Bullet to a walk. The mountains seemed almost close enough to touch, and yet the distance between her and them was insurmountable. She glanced around her and noticed, with surprise, that the shape of her mother was walking beside her, a strange walk that seemed to lack any need for speed and yet kept up with their own four-legged wanderings.

'I was thinking of you just now,' Ida said softly. Her mother nodded and said nothing.

'I remembered one of your books about a man who lived in a cabin in the snow. Do you remember it?' she asked. Her mother nodded once.

'What was the moral of that sad tale?' Ida pulled Bullet to a halt, waiting for her mother's answer in the cold air. Her mother also stopped and turned to face her. It was hard to see her in the strange whiteness of the atmosphere.

'Good ideas and their execution are different things,' she said, and Ida strained to hear the words. She smiled.

'Of course.'

Her mother turned to face the mountains on the horizon, which were bearing down on them with their silent gaze. Ida had never seen anything like them and was both drawn to them and afraid. Her stomach growled in irritation. It had been almost twelve hours since she had last eaten anything substantial. The crackers in her saddlebag were less than effective at staving off real hunger. She swallowed and placed a hand on her right pistol. They were going to have to find some food.

The City of Glass was unlike any other city or town in The Nameless Stretch. It had the largest population, for a start, and the highest buildings. Some even stretched to four stories, made not just of wood, like the other buildings in the land, but also of bone, stone, and leather. The months of the year were filled with iced chills, and within each home and place of business, a fire crackled.

Maids and poverty-stricken children were hired under the title of Windbreakers to keep the fires burning throughout the night. From every place in the city, one could see the mountains of the Alask Wilds, though they were days away at least. The youngsters crowded around their parents to hear stories of those who had lost their lives there, of small children who wandered away from their parents at the market, who left home in the night searching for adventure, and many other tales of death and cold within the mountains. On occasion, there were the brave ones, usually the young adults, who spent months prepping for adventure and returned silent and strange, if they returned at all. The daytimes were darker than anywhere else in The Nameless Stretch, the sun doing a poor job of lighting the city, and struggling to reach over some of the tall buildings and stretch above the shapes of the Alask Wilds. Because of this, the people were used to the icy ground and cold walls, some unaware that on the other side of the land, there was a place where each day was filled with unbearable brightness, where water was revered and drunk in massive amounts, however cold.

Rumours abounded that the land beyond the Alask Wilds was worse than any icy dream the dwellers of The City of Glass could imagine. This was for a good reason; rarely did those who leave choose to return, especially once they hit upon the heat of Bleakhollow and got used to enjoying the long days and rare chill. Those who did return did so for family and rarely told the tales of beyond in a positive light. The general consensus among the returners was that if they told their fellow occupants of life beyond, the city would empty, and their inherited houses would crumble. Every few years or so, there was one who tried to tell the public of the Stretch, the feel of a cool bourbon on a hot day, the sensation of dust in the air. Every few years or so, that person is also hanged in the town square, their face unwrapped, icicles forming instantly on their extended tongue. Not every traveller from the other direction made it past the Alask Wilds to find The City of Glass. When they did find it, most travellers wondered why they made the journey.

The city inhabitants did leave, on occasion, for one main reason only: to bury their dead. Beyond the city's gates, around a day away by a single horse, lay the graveyard of the entire city. What began as a sensible practice – it was the first place the original undertakers reached where they found they could

127

genuinely break the cold ground with their shovels – turned into a superstition over the years. Burying the dead far away kept the city free of ghosts. Of course, some intuitive people knew that this did not hold the spirits from the door, but little could be done about that.

Tracking wanted criminals was easy, and Billy knew that as well as any bounty hunter. All he had to do was get inside their head, think about what scared them, what delighted them, where he might be likely to find them. The first place Billy found himself and his two men? Banging on the tailor's door before he opened up shop. Billy guessed the woman had probably left the area by now – but didn't Larry say something about the tailor? The man could be of great help. He banged on the door again and growled through the wooden front.

'Open this bloody door before I shoot it open!'

As if by magic, the door swung open to reveal the harassed-looking tailor. He nodded without a smile. 'You want a suit?' This question caused Greyson to burst into laughter inexplicably, and Billy turned to survey him with a glare that held the threat of a punch in the jaw.

'We want this woman,' Billy said, holding up the bounty poster. The tailor's eyes glanced to it and back again, and he gave a single nod.

'I don't believe I've had the pleasure. This is the poster that Larry showed me earlier – now he could have sworn that she was in this store, but if it was her, then she was not like that picture.'

'How do you figure?' Greyson asked, stepping forward.

The tailor glanced at the picture again. 'Well, they were much thinner. Strong jaw. Bought a gentleman's outfit. Shaved head.'

Billy raised his eyebrows. 'That's the thing about fugitives, though, isn't it? They don't want to be caught, and they'll do what it takes not to be. Did this person say where they were headed?'

The tailor shook his head. 'No. You know I would help you if I could, but I do not have much information.' His eyes were wide and bloodshot, as though he hadn't slept a wink. Billy squinted and stepped forward, inspecting him for clues.

'You do not look like a well man.'

'I have not slept,' the tailor responded.

'And why is that?' Billy asked, clenching his jaw. 'A guilty conscience? The pressure of keeping a secret?'

The tailor wiped his brow and squinted in the early morning sun. He hesitated. 'If you find her, and it is the person who was in my shop, please,' his voice was suddenly desperate, and he lurched forward, grasping Billy's lapels. 'Please bring her back here. I'm being haunted.'

Billy grimaced and stepped backwards in repulsion, letting the tailor fall to his knees. 'Have some goddamn self-respect, man,' he said. 'If we find her, we'll be taking her in for the bounty.'

'Yeah,' said Greyson, spitting on the ground beside the tailor, who flinched as though it had touched him. 'Have some self-respect. If we find her, we are not going to bring her back here to do some voodoo nonsense with you.'

'He's got nothing,' Billy said. 'I reckon she'll have left town.'

'Yeah...' said Greyson, scratching his head. 'But where to?'

'Where do you think? No sane person would head toward the place they committed the crime in. She'll be going south.'

The third man, who was in general quieter by nature, shook his head. 'I won't be coming with you. I'll stay here, make sure she isn't lurking in Incan's Brook.'

Billy nodded. 'Yup, good plan.'

'Oh,' said Greyson. 'Can I do that one instead? I wasn't really planning on heading south...'

Billy glared at him, a silent answer in his eyes. Greyson nodded. He was headed south.

Chapter 15

The sheriff sat on the porch of the jailhouse, leaning back in his old rocking chair, a pipe slotted between his teeth. It was a strange sort of morning, the type that suggested a hot day, and yet the breeze belied a certain chill, cold for these long, cloudless months. The chair creaked with each movement, and he sucked on his pipe, letting a cloud form before him every now and then.

What was Colt's plan? He had been far braver in the face of the executioner than the sheriff had intended. He was a strange man, unusually confident for one so weaselly looking. It was a wonder that he had ever been robbed by Ida at all, for she was barely a confident woman. Some of the witnesses to their illicit union that night, the barman, the other girls, had said that it was the first time Ida had truly made an effort with a man. They were impressed, all of them, as though she had been taking notes for months and finally understood how to put them into action. Rosetta, Mrs Smithe's bestseller, was even planning on buying her a drink the next day. A sort of 'well done' cheers. And Colt...they all said the same about him. He was barely more than a worm. That was the exact word the barman had used: *worm*. He expected him to have a shy night with Ida and to vanish the next day as though he had never arrived. Nice horse, though, he had mentioned, as a side note.

The sheriff snorted a stifled laugh. He could hear Jonesy singing in the jail cell behind him, something about women and fields and basking in the sunshine – the words only came through now and then. Jonesy was a good sort. It would be a shame to let him out eventually, the sheriff thought. He'd almost been reluctant to do so; he was turning into quite the friend. And yet, Jonesy couldn't work out what Colt's plan was either. They had spoken about it through hushed whispers the day before when the sheriff had taken him out of the cell for his monthly bath.

'He ain't said a word to me, Sheriff. I reckon he's hoping to see her hanged, that's all.'

But then what? He'd still be in jail. Of course, the sheriff now had a reason to hang the man. Fraud. Fraud was as good a reason as any – and there were a great many reasons to hang a man. In fact, he could probably find a reason for every single person in this town if he had to, he mused. Including himself. Oh, definitely. At that, Mrs Smithe walked past, a basket in hand. She nodded at him and paused, her cherry blossom perfume hitting him in the face like a punch. She must have bathed in the stuff, a hideous excuse for washing.

'Sheriff. I hear that my little runaway is being brought back to us within the next few days?' she said, her voice light and airy, as though it were a superficial matter of a shipment of tinned beans. The sheriff took another puff of his pipe, trying to fill his nostrils once more with the scent of the smoke.

'It may be, Mrs Smithe, but I would not set your watch to it.'

'Oh? And why's that?'

'You know how these things go. They ain't always as simple as you'd expect,' the sheriff said plainly, keeping his metaphorical cards close to his chest. 'Mrs Smithe...' he said, pausing. She looked at him with eager expectancy. 'How much was Ida in debt to you?'

'Oh, now, I'd have to look at the books.'

'Hmmm.'

'Why? Do you think you might be able to reclaim some of that money for me?'

'Oh no, quite the opposite. I wondered if she had balanced her books, as it were. In a little while, there will be some bounty hunters here asking for five hundred dollars. That is an amount that the jailhouse does not have, and it is one that the idiot who advertised it does not have.'

Mrs Smithe tutted and put one hand on her hip, grasping her woven basket with a neatly gloved hand. 'I think you are well aware that not many of my girls have balanced their books, Sheriff. It is an expensive position, mine.'

The sheriff raised one eyebrow and nodded. 'Perhaps, if they come, you can offer them something to stop them from burning this place to the ground.'

'If I catch your meaning, Sheriff, you are requesting that I offer some items on the house. This is not my usual practice, and at the risk of telling you how to do your job...if they cause trouble, just shoot them.' With a firm smile, the portly woman turned away and swished in the other direction.

The sheriff watched her go with a smirk, her many layers bouncing with each step she took. Just shoot them? That would set a dangerous precedent. Shooting a bounty hunter was asking for more than trouble; it was asking to be shot yourself. The sheriff sniffed and took another puff of his pipe. It was far safer to shoot a sheriff, he thought, than a bounty hunter. What a strange turn of events that was. Shoot a sheriff, and you gain yourself a promotion, and all the other lawmakers across the land blow out a long and slow whistle of gratitude, thankful that it wasn't them. Shoot a bounty hunter, and you receive the weight of the law. Thank goodness he had someone to blame this all on.

The air somehow grew stiller and quieter the further Ida rode. It was a strange sensation; the closer the mountains became, the more confident Ida was that they were being watched. Her mother's image flickered beside her, sometimes weak and then strong, a memory and a photograph all mixed up into one. The rune still lay against her skin, and she noticed that as the air around her grew colder, it began to heat up. Perhaps, she thought, it was merely reacting to the heat of her skin. The mountains were closing in around the horizon, forming a half-circle. There was something different there, too, Ida noticed after a moment. She squinted. The white backdrop made it hard to see exactly what she was looking at, and she nudged Bullet forward. It was...a sign, hammered into the earth just as the edge of the mountains began to climb from the stony and bare terrain. They pushed on, a continuous lope, edging nearer and nearer. Eventually, as the ground started to change beneath Bullet's hooves from dust to icing sugar, the words on the sign became visible. Ida pulled Bullet to a halt before it and felt him skid beneath her, the white stuff building in little piles before each hoof.

The sign was written in white paint, haphazard letters scrawled upon a piece of driftwood. The wood seemed aged and old, but the colour was fresher. Ida dismounted and stepped toward it, reaching a hand out to the letters before she had even read them. They were bumpy and ridged, belying a sign painted many times over. Ida stepped back again and read the words before her.

Take care. There is now but one road to The City of Glass.

Beneath the words, a wobbly arrow was painted. Ida followed it with her eyes. The path appeared to go to the left, across some flat land and disappeared into the mountains. She walked toward it and inspected the markings in the snow. There were carriage marks, hooves and wheels on the ground. That woman must have passed through this way, she thought, curiously bending down. She touched the print of a wheel and felt the cold dampness on her fingers. Intriguing. Ida stood back up and turned toward the sign. There, she noticed, was something smaller – something written beneath the arrow. She stepped back to it again and leaned in. It was faint, as though it had only been written once and long ago.

I didn't do it.

A cold breeze ran across Ida's face, and she shivered, though whether it was for the draft or the words and their meaning, she was not sure. What was the implication, anyway? Didn't do what? Ida turned to face Bullet, who stood with his head low, his nostrils snorting and wide.

'Are you cold, boy?' she asked, the type of rhetorical question one asks an animal. He glanced at her, and she nodded, taking it as an answer. 'Then we must take this path to the left, I suppose. I doubt that we will reach The City of Glass before nightfall.' Beneath her, her stomach rumbled. She had been ready to hunt, hoping to see an animal that might do for dinner, a rabbit, or even a bird.

Ida moved toward her horse, noting that the image of her mother still stood beside her, eyes locked on the mountains that reached above. She seemed distracted, staring at them in a strange way, preoccupied with the air around her. Ida mounted and took a breath. The path in the other direction, to the right, also had hoof marks, though not as many. It appeared to stretch into the mountains, though clearly without a known end. Ida pushed Bullet on and went to turn left when something caught her eye. She paused, glancing over her shoulder. It was a rabbit! No, wait, it was three rabbits. Three rabbits jumped across the path on the right, disappearing beyond a bend. Ida caught her breath. She could always turn back, she thought. She could always grab one and return to the sign and then onwards to The City of Glass. She pulled on Bullet's reins and squeezed her legs against his ribcage so that he reversed. Then, she turned him swiftly, pointing him to the path on the right. He seemed reluctant, but she placed a hand on his neck.

'We need food first. Then we shall travel to the city, where you will be stabled with a barrel of oats.'

Bullet snorted, unconvinced. Ida squeezed him forward, and he burst into a jog, moving doggedly along the iced snow. The path turned a corner quickly, the slope rising with reluctant steepness but flanked by ever-growing mountains. The air whipped about their faces as though in a frenzy; the mere act of turning a corner seemed to have plunged them into a greater winter still.

Ida pulled a pistol and slowed Bullet down to a walk, his restless energy pulsating beneath her. A rabbit darted before her, and Ida aimed her gun, but it had gone by the time she went to pull the trigger. Then, another burst forward. Ida pulled the trigger this time with impetus, and the bullet glided past the rabbit into the snow. Bullet's ears lay flat against his head at the noise, and he tossed his mane, his movement turning from a walk to a dance. There, up ahead, Ida saw something else on the track. It appeared to be an animal gazing at the distance. Was that right? Was it some sort of horse? The white of the snow around them clung to each rock and mountain face, making it hard to differentiate between animal and other. What other could it be, though? Ida thought grimly. Colt, perhaps.

The figure became a little clearer. It appeared to be a deer, a male, its horns reaching into the sky. Ida wasted no time; she aimed and fired without mercy. The first shot hit the animal's back leg, and she saw its head twist in her direction, and then it leapt, scattering away up the path. Ida leaned forward and pushed Bullet on despite his protests, which were becoming greater by the second. He fell into a gallop but tossed his head and whinnied in anger, cross with the cold, the sharp and sudden sounds that kept surprising him, and the long day that had led to this moment.

Ida kept the beast in her sight and noticed, as somewhat of an afterthought, that the animal's blood in the snow was easy to see. She aimed again and fired once more. The bullet hit the same leg again, though it was not necessarily planned, and the animal fell to the ground with a sound that burned through Ida. It was a strange and strangled moan, almost human in its delivery.

She reached the deer quickly, and Bullet twisted his body across the path, coming to a sudden halt and almost throwing Ida off. The deer looked at them both, and Ida climbed down, her feet hitting the cold white cushion and sinking further than she expected. She stared back at the creature, at its back leg mangled and bloody, showing some muscle beneath the wound. Ida blinked at it, noticing a shard of bone sticking through the fur. Though she had seen her father kill game, it was never like this. It was never at her hand, and it was never done so poorly. It was usually one shot, and then wash up for dinner.

'I am sorry,' she breathed, 'I am not a hunter.' With one last look at his desperate eyes, Ida turned and pulled a knife from the saddlebag. She had paid little attention to it before but now saw that the handle was engraved with one word. Colt. She swallowed and knelt, dragging the knife across the deer's throat with an easy movement, trying desperately not to look at its face. Blood spilt from the new cut and sank into the snow, melting it at speed in a circle before the deer. Ida gazed sadly at the mark. How was it that she could more easily imagine killing a man? How was it that she wouldn't hesitate to pull the trigger on a stranger on the path? She glanced up and saw the image of her mother on the other side of the beast, staring at it, her pale eyes sad and weary.

'I must eat,' Ida said softly, trying to justify the killing. Her mother nodded once, her eyes not moving. Ida shook herself, a sign that the mourning period was over. It had to be; there was too much to do. She grabbed Bullet's reins, steadied him beside her, and then reached down to the deer, bending her knees. She slid her hands beneath its warm body and attempted to stand. She staggered forward, barely able to lift the beast. It was far heavier than she imagined.

'Okay,' she said, breathing into her hands, trying to push some strength and warmth into them. She thought back to her father, who would occasionally bring back an animal of some kind from the nearby Gorman Forest. He never taught her to harvest the edible parts of the animals, only to cook them. He always told her that her husband would do the hunting, the killing, and that it would be her role to make the meat delicious. But what did he bring her on that old blood-stained piece of wood? She pinched her nose and thought back; it had been so long since she had prepared any type of food. In Steepmount, she had eaten with the other girls, stew from the kitchen, potatoes leftover from clients' plates. He would bring her the innards, she thought. He would get the liver, the kidney and would keep the entire heart for himself. She stared at the deer, dead on the snow before her, and picked up the knife once more, grateful now for its existence.

Ida sliced the torso, revealing more than she had ever seen of any being. Her stomach was rumbling so hard that she could only think of hunger as she pushed her right hand in, searching for the organs that she knew. She pulled and cut them out one by one, placing them on the cold snow beside her. The tangy smell of game filled her nostrils, earthy and musky together. Once she was confident that she had taken all she recognised, she pulled the saddlebag down from Bullet's rump and emptied one side into the other. With two stained bloody hands, she grabbed fistfuls of snow, packing the bag and placing the organs within. Though it may have seemed to an onlooker that she was doing this to preserve them, she was, in fact, trying to protect the leather of the bag. The less stained with blood, she thought, the more welcome she would be when she eventually came to find The City of Glass.

Once full, Ida placed the saddlebags back on Bullet and secured them. He was now standing with his eyes closed, taking a moment to rest as she worked. She turned back to the deer and surveyed the mess that she had created. It was a hideous sight to behold. Anyone who came along this path would be shocked. For the last time, she glanced at his head. The antlers, she thought. Her father would always come home with the antlers. Why was that? She couldn't think, but it was something. They must have had some use. She stepped over to the deer and, with a firm swallow, placed one boot on the base of the antler, near its eye. She leaned down and grasped the other end with both hands and then pulled hard. It gave up surprisingly easily, cracking and causing shards of bone to fall. The weight was light and touch smooth. In a moment, she took the other one, too, leaving the deer without either. They were large and unwieldy, and she felt unsure of how to hold them and secure them to Bullet without hurting him. He snoozed still in the cold, unaware of her predicament. The roll mat would do, she thought, if only for an hour until they were able to stop and build a fire off the path. She unfastened it and carefully rolled the antlers into it, covering their spikes and sharp prongs. With some rope, she secured it to the back of the saddle and climbed on gingerly. Bullet awoke when she mounted and blew hot air out of his nostrils, which filtered into space before them. It was getting dark, Ida thought. Her mother watched, ignored by Ida. Beneath Ida's clothing, the rune burned.

Chapter 16

The sheriff knew they had arrived before the door swung on its hinges. First, he heard the shouting outside, the beat of hooves on the dusted ground. It was a noise that would usually send him out with his gun drawn, ready to protect Steepmount in all its understated glory. Today, he simply stood and picked his hat up from his desk and placed it on his head with a smile. He turned to Colt and nodded once.

'Well, they've arrived, boy. Let's see just how reasonable they are, shall we?'

Colt stood and stepped toward the bars of his cell, staring at the closed door and holding his breath. This was it, he thought. He was about to see that woman again. He didn't care, not one bit, how angry the bounty hunters would be once they found out the five hundred dollars was not forthcoming. He couldn't care less, he realised with mild surprise, he just wanted to see that thief hang. The noise got louder, and it appeared that these were not your subtle bounty hunters. There was the sound of a gunshot, whooping and laughing. The sheriff shook his head.

'Sounds to me like they're celebrating already.'

Colt nodded. They listened to the footsteps and chatter in silence, now sounding as though it was directly outside the jailhouse. The sheriff stood back as though he knew what was coming and placed one hand on his gun, leaving it in the holster. Suddenly, the door flew open, smashing against the wall behind. The kerosene-lit lamps wavered in the breeze of the movement. Two men stood in the doorway, the one in front grinning widely, two gold teeth shining from his mouth. He tipped his hat and stepped in and then aside, making way for the other man, who was taller, wider, and holding the body of a woman over his shoulder.

'Sheriff, I have for you, Ida Vale,' the first man said, indicating the body.

The sheriff nodded and stepped forward, frowning. 'Is she alive?'

'Yes, I'm alive!' the body said, causing the sheriff to start.

'She's got a mouth on her,' said the first man, tutting. 'But it's her.'

'I am not Ida Vale!' the body said, the voice slightly muffled against the jacket of the man carrying her.

'My brother doesn't speak,' the first man said, 'but he can attest to the fact that this is Ida Vale. We asked all around Blackreach, and this is the woman.'

The sheriff nodded. 'Put her down. I know Ida.'

The large, quiet man looked at his brother, who nodded once. He placed her down firmly, keeping a hand on her shoulder. Her arms were tied behind her back with rope, her hair was swept into a strange mess of blonde and grey plaits, and her dress was filthy. The sheriff regarded the woman and frowned.

'What is your name?' he asked.

'Ida Vale,' said the bounty hunter, his gold teeth flashing as he spoke.

'Sir,' the sheriff turned to him with a blank stare. 'I would appreciate it if you would let the lady speak.'

The woman glared at the man and turned back to the sheriff. 'I said – I am not Ida Vale. My name is Isabelle Norma Vale, the last name taken from my husband, who is dead. These idiots came to my house, read the sign on the postbox, and carted me off without question! If my son had been visiting me, they would be dead by now.'

The sheriff nodded and sighed. 'Yup. Boys, Ida Vale is a younger woman. She is in her late twenties. Now listen, this woman, and I don't mean no offence by this, Mrs Vale, because I cannot vouch for your age, but she is not in her twenties. How old is your son, Mrs Vale?'

'He's twenty-nine,' the woman said, shaking her hands behind her back in an effort to get the large brute off her.

'Well, there you have it. It sounds to me like this is a case of mistaken identity. I hesitate to ask him because the man is a certified moron, but he did have relations with Ida Vale, so I imagine that he would have a fair impression of her image. Colt,' the sheriff turned around and fixed him with a dissatisfied stare, 'is this the woman that you were hoping to see come through the door?'

Colt narrowed his eyes. She was older than he remembered, that was true, but wasn't there something familiar about her? 'Bring her forward,' he said darkly.

The sheriff tutted and rolled his eyes but stepped aside for the quiet man to bring her front and centre. The woman glared at Colt, a danger in her eyes. Colt glared back. She was shaking her head at him ever so softly, a movement barely recognisable. Colt felt a fire in his stomach burning, one of rage at her disrespect.

'I am old enough to be your mother,' the woman snapped at him, hair scattered about her face. Colt could smell her from where he stood: body odour, dirt, and the lingering scent of cheap oily perfume.

Colt's lip curled, and he raised his eyebrows nonchalantly. 'I cannot say either way. But, Sheriff,' he said, his eyes remaining on the woman, 'I would suggest that given the similarity in name, this woman is taken in for questioning.'

'Yep.' The man with gold teeth stepped forward and nodded at Colt, 'I'm in this guy's camp. We have brought forward a key witness in this crime, maybe even the woman herself. If you would kindly pay us, then we shall head over the road to your saloon and pay some of that money back into the Steepmount economy. You cannot say fairer than that, Sheriff.'

The sheriff rolled his eyes and tutted. 'Oh, for goodness sake, Colt. I know Ida Vale, and this is not her. And you two? Even if there were money to give, you wouldn't be getting any. This is not Ida Vale.'

'What do you mean even if there was money to give? It said five hundred dollars on the poster,' the bounty hunter said with a frown.

'Yeah, well, this idiot right here put that down without asking. So Colt, if you're the one who wants this woman to be taken in so that you can decide whether or not she is, in fact, the woman that robbed you, I suggest you pay these gentlemen.' The sheriff cocked his head to one side thoughtfully, pleased with this sudden turn of events.

'Sirs,' Colt said, 'as you can see, I am currently not in a position to pay any money due to my being in jail...'

Silence fell across the group. The bounty hunter frowned at his brother and then at Colt. 'I really thought that sentence was going somewhere. Is that it?'

Colt scratched his head and shrugged. 'Well, you can see my predicament. I cannot pay you what has been taken away from me.'

The sheriff scoffed and pulled his right pistol from his holster, feeling the weight of it in his hand. 'Boys,' he said, not aiming the gun, merely holding it. The quiet brother eyed it. 'Mrs Smithe is the woman who runs our establishment over the road. She told me that you can expect some good service there, in fact, if you let her know I okayed it, you may have some discount. Leave Mrs Vale with me and come back tomorrow, where you will see this man hanged for his inability to pay you what he owes you.'

The brothers stared at the sheriff for a moment and then glanced at each other. The one with gold teeth turned his lips down in thought and then shrugged. 'Well, what if you decide it is Ida Vale? Will we be getting our money?'

'I can put that to rest right now – this is not Ida Vale,' the sheriff said. 'I can see how the confusion has taken place, but there is no denying it. I know the woman, and this ain't her.'

'I told you,' the woman hissed, her frenetic energy all but crackling in the air. 'Taking me away from my house for nothing but nonsense. Sheriff, they oughta be strung up themselves. They barely gave me food to live on out there, made me sleep on the cold hard ground.'

The sheriff sighed and focused his attention on her. 'Ma'am, if I may, I believe that it would be best at this juncture if you were quiet.'

'I told you she has a mouth on her,' the gold-toothed brother said, grinning a lazy smile. 'All right, Sheriff, we'll be back tomorrow morning. We have some thinking to do – I ain't sure that this arrangement is completely to my liking.' He glared at Colt for a moment. 'But you're right; the man has promised me what he cannot pay, and for that, I would like to see judgment done. Brother.' He nodded at his sibling and tipped his hat to the sheriff before heading out of the door. The brother shrugged and followed, letting the door swing behind him for a moment. Outside, the wind began to pick up, howling and blowing dust against the building, making it sound like hail and rain were hammering over the tin roof. Mrs Vale raised her eyebrows at the sheriff.

'Are you going to untie me then?'

'Mrs Vale, I will, but I should like you to take a seat with me first.'

'I don't see why I should,' she responded flatly, her brow creasing.

'Well, you might see why if you take a seat. In fact, I can offer you a drink. How about that?' The sheriff reholstered his gun and pulled up a stool in front of his desk for the bedraggled woman. She glared at him and then sat down, hands still behind her back. The sheriff nodded with a smile once she had seated and pulled out two small glasses, which he then filled with a golden liquid.

'This is a bottle I keep just for myself. I rarely allow a tot to another.' He placed the glass in front of the woman. Her eyes flicked from the glass to the sheriff, who was taking a long sip. Mrs Vale sighed and leaned forward and, to the sheriff's surprise, put her entire mouth over the top of the glass in a perfect O shape. In a single movement, she flung her head back, the golden liquid disappearing down her throat. She leaned back toward the desk and dropped the glass back down, letting it fall from her lips, and then nodded, sitting with a smile.

'Well. That's a new one on me,' the sheriff said, uncorking the bottle again. He poured a little more into her glass and smiled cordially. 'You see, I'm quite a nice man, really. People in these parts don't always say I am because of how I got this job. But I am quite a nice man, really.'

Mrs Vale kept a straight face.

'Mrs Vale. I believe that you know of Ida Vale, don't you?'

'The woman I was mistaken for? All I know is that she is a criminal and that you are offering five hundred dollars for her capture,' she responded.

'That ain't strictly true. We aren't offering anything for her capture, but we are hanging that idiot for sending out posters across the land inviting bounty hunters into our quiet town. But all the same – I've a feeling that you know exactly who she is.'

'I've never met the woman.' Mrs Vale shrugged.

'No. Perhaps not. Who was your husband, Mrs Vale? Could he be the same man that Ida told us of when she arrived in town? The man who was shot by his wayward son, a practical stranger to him?'

Mrs Vale cleared her throat. 'Sir, I have spent two days on the back of a horse with a couple of idiot brothers masquerading as bounty hunters. Untie me and allow me to be on my way.'

The sheriff nodded. 'I'll speak plainly then, Mrs Vale, as you clearly would like to be on your way. Months ago now, when the sun was high in the sky, a disordered young woman came riding into town. We had never seen her before, and she was desperate. She told us that her father had been shot by a man claiming to be her brother. She said this man had taken over her homestead and that she had been forced to flee. It seems rather interesting to me that just a town over from us was your own home and that you share a name and have a son. We helped this young woman restart her life, and yet, as this fool will attest,' the sheriff indicated to Colt, who stood behind the cell bars, watching, 'too much damage had been done by this event. She was an unhappy woman. In fact, perhaps the mere act turned her into a criminal.'

Mrs Vale scoffed. 'It seems an odd tale. If this were true, why was the man not arrested for murder?'

'It's not my jurisdiction, ma'am. And even if it was, I'm not sure what could be done. A son taking what is rightfully his property after his father's death. It's a complex issue. But as I say, not my business.'

'Then let me go.'

'It seems unusual though, don't you think? How did your husband die, Mrs Vale?'

'My husband was a complicated man. He was not often home. I heard of his death via word of mouth, if you must know. Who knows how that man died? He was a philanderer.'

The sheriff grinned. 'Yep. I think you know exactly how he died. It's unfortunate that I find you here, isn't it? I always trust my gut instinct, Mrs Vale. It's gotten me far in life. I believe that when I feel something is right, then it is usually so.'

'Sheriff, you said you would speak plainly, but I find your sentences filled with nonsense. Allow me to leave, or you shall regret it.'

The sheriff leaned forward, plucked the untouched glass from in front of Mrs Vale, and downed the liquid. He placed it back down with a flourish and shrugged. 'I am going to keep you in a cell for the night, Mrs Vale. If not longer. I believe that there is more to this tale…perhaps it is nothing, but in any case, a night in a cell is cheaper than a night at the saloon, and a lady would not travel back in the darkness, would she?'

Mrs Vale licked her dry, chapped lips with her tongue and sighed. She glanced at the cells behind her, both with a man in. 'I'll not share with a man,' she said.

'Of course not. It wouldn't be proper.' The sheriff stared at the cells and sniffed. Jonesy was asleep in his, and Colt watched them from within, his eyes shallow and glaring. 'And yet, you see our predicament right here. It's a small jail for a small town. That's why our hangman is such a busy chap. Here's what we'll do. Just for you, Mrs Vale, I'll stay up and at my desk to make sure there's no funny business. I'm sure Colt will let you have his bed for the night, ain't that so?'

Colt frowned at the idea. 'What? And where will I sleep?'

'Where do you think, boy? On the floor. You've not long left in this world, and I shouldn't be worrying about that sort of thing. Any aching back will be cured by the short drop of justice.'

Colt said nothing but lifted his chin in defiance. It was a motion that nobody noticed. Mrs Vale rolled her pale eyes. 'Will you at least untie me?'

The sheriff stood and sauntered around the back of the bound woman, helping her to her feet. 'You get that in that cell, and I'll send off to the saloon kitchen for a meal and some water. How does that sound?'

She mumbled an agreement and watched Colt step to one side.

Greyson squinted in the darkness. The small kerosene-filled lamp hooked to Billy's saddle did nothing for what he could actually see ahead of him, and it only plunged them into further shadow. He wiped his brow, a bad habit from the hot air of his hometown, Incan's Brook, but a habit that was, nonetheless, not needed now. The air was growing colder by the second, the nighttime not helping. He glanced up at the sky above him, smiling at the stars. It was the only great thing about leaving town and being out in the middle of nowhere. The stars above were his reward.

'Billy,' he said. The word fell into the air without answer, fully formed and alone. His ears pricked slightly, waiting for a reply, but none came. The hooves of the two horses on the dry path continued, occasionally interrupted by the far-off howl of a wolf or chirp of a cricket. After another moment, Greyson cleared his throat and tried again. 'Billy.'

'What?' the low voice responded.

'How can you tell where we're headed in the dark? We lost the chance to see hoofprints hours ago.'

'So you want to stop? Is that what you're telling me?' Billy replied with an edge of irritation.

'Well, it's getting cold. We should have a fire and a hot drink, at least.'

Billy sighed. 'It's weak to stop tracking. I ain't a weak man.'

The silence sat between the men for a moment, and Greyson ran the back of his hand along his dripping nose. 'Neither am I, but tracking in the dark is a tough game,' he said, a hint of regret shining through the words. He watched the lamp as it slowed and stopped in front of him. It was picked up, and Billy dismounted, holding it to his face. A few moths hit against his cheek, and he gazed unflinchingly at Greyson.

'Fine. We'll stop until dawn.'

Greyson nodded and dismounted, the cold air wrapping itself around him. He accepted the lamp from his boss and set about finding twigs and small pieces of wood with which to start a fire. When he had found enough, he returned to the horses, who were standing close to each other as though for warmth. He built a fire swiftly, under the close stare of Billy, who sat eating crackers with a grim expression on his face, only occasionally visible in the light. Once the fire was lit, Greyson began to warm a pot of coffee over the top and busied himself, laying out both bedrolls for the men. He noticed that Billy did nothing to help, as he rarely did, and thought about mentioning the glorious warmth that one could attain when they put their all into moving around, but there was something in the crackle of atmosphere that stopped him from speaking. Eventually, he poured a cup of coffee, handed it to his boss, and took a seat beside him, the fire warming his skin deliciously. The horses whickered beside them, their eyes closing.

'You tired, boss?' Greyson asked, taking a deep sip of his coffee.

'I'm always tired,' Billy responded, 'tired of no one else taking this job seriously.'

Greyson glanced at him in the firelight and said nothing. He got like this sometimes, the boss. It was clear that his favourite moments involved the catching of bounty and any time they were searching, he was angry and quiet, as though he expected the criminal to be waiting for him, politely pausing their day until they got picked up and taken to a jail cell.

'I just needed a break, is all,' Greyson said to his drink, just loud enough for Billy to hear. There was no response. The flames licked the wood, darkness in the distance. How many creatures were watching them now? he wondered. How many eyes were settled on their illuminated faces? He glanced at Billy and saw that his eyes were closed. The man often slept sitting up, and even though he was holding a cup between two hands, it appeared that it might have happened again. He grinned. Billy needed a rest also, then. Greyson drained his cup and lay down on the mat, closing his eyes and edging closer to the warmth of the fire.

Chapter 17

To the right of the track, Ida sat with Bullet, her mother standing nearby. They had travelled only a short distance, far enough away from the trail that those on it would not be able to see them, close enough that they should hear anyone coming. Beside them, a large rock stood, blocking the wind from blowing out the fire. The fire had taken a while to catch, the sticks and wood being damp from the snow. Now it had finally caught, Ida leaned in and closed her eyes, warming blood-stained hands.

She was grateful that she had taken the antlers of the deer with her. She had used each prong to spear the meat and innards that she had collected from the beast and had rested them over the fire, sticks holding them in place. They were cooking gently, smoke rising into the air, and the smell was clawing at Ida's senses. She closed her eyes. She was hungrier than a bear, but it seemed a waste to tuck into her limited supply of crackers and jerky. Just wait, she whispered aloud, wait for it to be cooked. There was more there than she could handle alone, she thought, but that was fine. She would pack it away for the journey to The City of Glass, where she would rent a room, sleep the day away and warm up by a real fire.

The thought of it made her skin tingle with anticipation. The scents would be similar, she thought, meat cooking on an open fire in the kitchens, drifting up through the floorboards. Her dinner being prepared. She opened her eyes again and stared at her hands. The blood was drying, and she took a breath and pushed them into the snow before her, using it to wipe them down. It turned red in front of her eyes, and she hastily moved to the fire to warm herself again, noticing with interest that the snow she had touched had made her hands wetter than she expected. Her skin dripped in front of the fire, and she laughed, jumping up and turning to the saddle that sat on the floor beside the snoozing Bullet. His middle was now covered in the bear pelt; Ida was committed to keeping him warm while she had the fire to make herself comfortable. She dug into the saddlebag and pulled out a small pan, no larger than two cupped hands, that she had, as yet, no need for. It was dented and old, and she wondered briefly at its history, its life with Colt. Then, she dug it into the snow, filling it to the brim, and sat down again. Ida pushed the pan into the fire, watching the flames lick the sides. The snow turned to water, and Ida chuckled with joy. She plucked the pan from the flames by the hot handle and took a deep and long sip. It was lukewarm and refreshing. She filled it again quickly and then took it to Bullet, waking him with a stroke on his soft velvet muzzle. He drank fast, and Ida made the journey five times until he refused more. She leaned forward, placed her forehead against his own, and closed her eyes, feeling his warm heat.

'Tomorrow, we will find you some grass,' she said.

She laid another stick on the fire and then picked up her knife and poked the meat, feeling the flesh of a liver having toughened up beneath the point. After a moment, when she could wait no more, she bit into the flesh, pulling the meat from the antler as a bear would. The taste of earth and mineral filled her mouth, and she chewed, her stomach gurgling with anticipation of its settling. She ate ruthlessly, almost forgetting that there was a need to save some for later. Just as she reached for the other antler, still cooking in the fire, she caught herself. Instead of putting it to her lips, which were now stained with blood and charred from the ash and burned sections, she moved it away from the fire, allowing it to cool fully.

Finally, she was full. Ida stood and wiped her brow, feeling warmer than she had in hours despite the dying firelight. She removed her boots and climbed inside her bedroll for the first time in days, pulling the canvas up to her chin. With one tired eye on the brightness of the fire, the warmness of its presence, she began to drift into a heavy, full sleep. Her mother watched, as she always had. Around them, others watched, too, although Ida was not aware of it.

The sheriff was already asleep, his feet resting on a stool in front of him, his hat low over his face. Mrs Vale glared at him from inside the cell she was sharing with Colt. Colt wondered how she was feeling, sharing with a criminal. She glanced at him every now and then, a warning look, daring him to come near her as if she wanted to show him exactly what she was made of. She placed her empty plate on the ground beside her. Colt had watched her eat a meagre meal of unknown meat and potatoes, possibly scraps from someone else's plate. It could have been anything, though, and he guessed Mrs Vale would have eaten it. The sheriff had given her three drinks to consume: coffee, water, and another tot of his drink, which he gave her graciously, his expression that of a priest blessing a child at birth. She had downed it in much the same way as the first. She turned to Colt, who was sitting on the floor beneath her.

'You know I'm not the woman who robbed you, you stupid child,' she hissed at him. The sheriff didn't stir at the noise.

Colt glanced up at Jonesy, who still slept in his bed, unaware of the entire event. 'I don't know anything,' he said, his voice barely at a lower decibel than usual.

'You're to be hanged tomorrow,' Mrs Vale replied, a statement rather than a question. Colt shifted his legs, stretching them out in front of him, and sighed, saying nothing. Mrs Vale looked at him. 'You have a plan?'

'I did have a plan. But as time goes on, that plan sort of...' he stopped speaking, letting his voice drift off.

'You thought what, that you could see the woman who shares my name hanged? That you would escape somehow?'

'Yup.'

'How were you going to escape?'

Colt scratched his head and sighed again, peering at the sheriff to see if he was still asleep. The man's chest rose up and down in a steady and slow pattern, his nose whistling occasionally. He was sleeping as soundly as if he were in a bed.

'Bounty hunters would bring her in. I'd see her hang. Get my money back. Tell them they'd get extra if they got me out.' He shrugged. 'It didn't seem like such a long shot at first. And it might still work. She's out there somewhere – only I didn't count on you coming in.'

'I didn't count on me coming in either, boy. A long shot indeed. You can't rely on bounty hunters – didn't you know that?

You can't rely on anyone, not these days.' Mrs Vale cracked her knuckles and took a seat on the lumpy bed.

'Listen, I heard what the sheriff was asking you. Was he right? Are you her mother?' Colt asked, his eyes narrowing.

'The sheriff wasn't asking if I was her mother, boy. He was asking if I was married to her father. Which I was, I suppose. Except he had some witch over at another homestead that he got knocked up after he met me, worse luck. The woman died soon enough, that's true, but I wasn't able to claim what was rightfully mine yet.'

Colt grinned, stuck his little finger in his ear, and scratched about. The sheriff snored, and the two glanced back at him. 'So it was your son who…?'

Mrs Vale shrugged. 'My son has been wanting his own land for a while, and it's normal for a man to leave his mother. He stayed too long as it is. That's all I'll say on the matter, and I ain't seen him in months. And anyway,' she grinned at him, 'I only tell you because you're going to hang tomorrow.'

Colt inspected his little finger for wax before wiping it on his trousers. 'I don't know about that. You might be in for it yourself. You're behind these bars, too.'

Mrs Vale watched Colt for a moment, a slow smile forming on her lips. Her stare was unflinching and so focused that Colt began shifting a little further away from her. The air around them was growing colder. Suddenly, she stood and padded toward him, crouching down, her skirts around her in the dirt.

'I've an idea,' she whispered. 'Such an idea that would mean you would not die tomorrow, and we could both leave tonight. But you must come with me.'

Colt flinched at her strong scent despite the fact that he himself had not washed in a long time. The low bags beneath her eyes and her papery skin were unbearable to be so close to. She reached out a hand, the long fingernails feeling his shirt sleeve, and he shuddered at her touch. 'I don't think so, lady…I reckon I've more chance of them bounty hunters—'

'You're a fool, boy. You want revenge? You want to find her?' she hissed. Colt nodded, his eyes wide. She looked like a witch, but those didn't even exist…even so, he felt genuinely afraid of her. 'You want revenge. What do you think she wants?'

'I have no idea. To hide?' Colt suggested, stuttering over the idea as it formed in his mouth.

'No, you idiot. She wants revenge, too. At some point, she will ride back to that homestead, where my boy is lighting the fire and starting his own independent life, and she will try and kill him. Imagine if you were waiting for her. Imagine the sweetness, the surprise. You are far more likely to find her there.' Mrs Vale began nodding, her smile wider than before.

Colt swallowed, his nose still stinging at her earthy scent. 'How can you be sure?'

'Because she'll dream of it. She'll dream of the killing, of the robbery. She'll dream of it, and she'll come back to claim what she believes is hers.'

Colt nodded. There was something in the old woman's eyes that told him that she was exactly right. He wasn't sure what it was. It was more than self-confidence. It was as though she knew everything, as though it had already happened. 'All right,' he said.

'So, you need to follow my lead. When I say the word, you take this,' she pulled a stained, plaid handkerchief from up her sleeve and handed it to him, 'and you shove it as far into his mouth as you can. Don't let him shout. We'll try not to startle the man in there. I don't know his crime, but I ain't in the habit of saving people – only I can see that to get us both out is a two-person job.'

Colt took the cloth and pocketed it. Mrs Vale stood up and rotated her neck one way and then the other like a boxer limbering up for a fight. She clicked her fingers gently at Colt, indicating that he should stand up. He got to his feet doggedly, amazed at her energy. The woman had been on the back of a horse for days. Perhaps that drink had done more than he could imagine. He stood staring at her, waiting for whatever was about to happen, with a nervous feeling in his stomach. Suddenly, Mrs Vale grabbed the plate from the floor and stepped toward Colt, throwing it down with a smash.

'Get away from me!' she yelped. Colt flinched, wide-eyed.

'What's going on in there?' Jonesy yelled, sitting up in his bed and peering through the dim light to the cell ahead of him.

'The man tried to touch me!' said Mrs Vale, batting at Colt with one hand. Colt just stood, staring at her. Acting never was one of his strong points, he thought.

The sheriff was sitting up now, wiping his eyes with his sleeve. He adjusted his hat and stood up, making his way over to the cell. 'Don't you worry yourself, Jonesy, you just head on back to sleep.'

'I wish I could with all this racket,' came the response. Despite this, the man lay back down, obedient to the last.

Mrs Vale held her hand to her throat, flustered, the image of a harassed woman.

'Sheriff, this miscreant laid his hands on me. I will not spend another second in this cell with him!'

The sheriff sighed heavily. 'Oh, good lord, boy, what is wrong with you? This woman is old enough to be your mother. I am ashamed of you, boy. You know we are short of space.' He pulled the cell keys from his pocket and selected one before noticing the plate. 'You smashed a plate and all. Mrs Smithe ain't going to be happy about that. Oh, you are determined to send me to the debtors. Mrs Vale, you will have to spend the night in Jonesy's cell, and he is a trustworthy man.'

'Oh, I don't doubt it, Sheriff. I am just grateful to get away from this scoundrel,' Mrs Vale said, wiping her brow with her hand. She gave Colt a stern look, and he felt his heart begin to beat faster in his chest, hammering away at the weight of expectation he found upon him.

The sheriff put the key in the lock and stared at Colt before he turned it. 'You ain't even got an apology for the lady? I am ashamed.'

'I- I'm sorry, ma'am,' Colt murmured.

Mrs Vale nodded. 'Well, truthfully, Sheriff, I did not expect it,' she said, turning her full attention to the man with the keys. He shook his head in a sorrowful way, pulling the cell door open. Mrs Vale stepped out and to one side and then widened her eyes at Colt, who took the moment as he saw it, the seconds seeming to stretch out into an eternity of opportunity. He moved forward and threw his body against the cell door, causing the sheriff to fall back with a jolt. As he hit the floor, his hat flew off, and the old woman turned on him, a gentle, motherly hand placed on his chest. Mrs Vale then promptly pulled a knife from her boot, much to Colt's surprise, and held it against the sheriff's neck.

'Don't move, sweetheart. I would hate for this to end horribly,' she said softly. As the sheriff opened his mouth to speak, Colt pulled the handkerchief from his pocket and stuffed it over the sheriff's tongue. Then, he noticed that the man's hands were reaching for his pistols. Colt did the only thing that he could think of at that moment and punched the sheriff in his ballsack, causing him to double over, the point of the knife cutting his skin ever so slightly. He groaned and spluttered against the cold floor, and Mrs Vale stood, nodding at her protege. Colt moved fast, grabbed the guns, pocketed them, and then pulled the groaning sheriff by his ankles into the cell. In one second, the door was locked again, Colt and Mrs Vale now on the outside. Jonesy stood in his cell, open-mouthed, watching the turmoil before him. Colt nodded at him.

'You ain't gonna leave me in here, boy?' Jonesy said, blinking hastily.

'I thought you liked it here,' Colt replied, heading toward the sheriff's desk. He picked up a pack of cigarettes and pulled one out, lighting it with a candle. Taking a deep drag, he turned back to Jonesy and held the keys aloft. 'Here they are, *boy*. I'll leave them right on the desk for you. Look me up when you get out of here.'

Mrs Vale took Colt's arm. 'Show a lady to the stables, won't you? My son will be waiting for us, and I hate to make us late.'

Together, the two left the prison behind, walking out into the dark and dusty street. The saloon lights glowed as they headed to the stables, the rest of the town either sleeping, drinking, or locked up with a soiled handkerchief stuffed in their mouth.

There he was. It had been so long since Ida had seen him that she had almost forgotten what he looked like. She stared at him, hard. His head was already smoking, a bullet hole straight through the middle of his forehead. She could smell the smoke, and the scent was overpowering – gunpowder and flesh, stinging her nostrils. He grinned and dismounted, stepping over and onto her beautiful flowers, her planned garden. The only thing that she had complete control over. The weight of the Winchester was heavy in her hand. She raised it to her eye, staring down the barrel. He laughed, a halo of smoke still surrounding his head, like a deity of some kind. He said something. What was it? She cocked the hammer. He spoke again.

'The land is lousy with snakes.'

And there, in her hands, the Winchester went soft, flopping into her palms. She stared down at the smooth feel of the new item. In the place of the barrel was a writhing, moving snake, its skin strangely soft, not the sticky feeling she had always expected. She let her hands fall to her sides, the snake dropping to her feet, and stared at him, her brother. He walked still, the ground beneath his feet covered in reptiles. Behind him, Ida saw the shape of her father, bending down to the soil, toiling the earth.

'Father,' she said, the noise coming out as barely a whisper.

Her brother stopped, his smile still creeping about his lips, the bullet wound in his head dry and unbleeding. The scent of smoke lingered. 'He is no longer your father. You are all alone.'

'I know everything about this house,' she said, the words more audible now. The snakes began to hiss, the strange noise filling Ida's ears with vibrating beats.

'It does not matter,' her brother said. 'You will never see it again.'

Ida awoke in a moment, sitting up swiftly. The sun was rearing its head above the mountains, the moon more than visible in the sky, and yet bright enough above the snow to give the impression of light. Bullet was sleeping. Ida noticed without surprise that her mother was still standing, staring. It was almost as though she was not there at all anymore, just an image of a woman who once was a real person. Ida frowned. She wished that the woman would lie down and at least pretend to sleep.

The fire had died down low, and Ida stared at the tiny flickering embers before her, the warmth no longer surrounding her. She pulled the canvas roll mat around her shoulders and stared at the snow, the harsh mountains. Her brother. What did he do now that he was at the homestead alone? Had he buried her father or called for his own mother to move in? Perhaps he was starting a family of some sort, finding a bride from a nearby town to take the place of Ida, who would scrub the floors and find her mother's strange markings carved beneath the table. Perhaps.

Ida quivered in the cold. Her bearskin was still over Bullet, and yet he looked so content that she left him a moment. The land is lousy with snakes, she thought. Who had told her that, before her brother? Where had that snippet of information come from, anyway? She closed her eyes and wrapped her arms around her body, thinking. A face hovered in front of her. It was the man in the trading post. The postman. She opened her eyes suddenly and frowned. She had forgotten all about the letters that she had stolen. She had the money, of course, but the letters were still tied haphazardly to the saddle, a strange reward for her callous behaviour. Colton's callous behaviour.

She pulled the canvas down, allowing in more cold, and stood. Laying one hand on Bullet's warm neck, she swiftly removed the bearskin and wrapped it about her, grateful for the body heat of the horse, the thick fur of the long-dead bear. Bullet opened his eyes and snorted in the moonlight. Ida moved toward the saddle and its various bags and wrapped objects and untied the postbag before retaking her seat beside the dying fire. She emptied the bag before her, its mass surprising. What a waste of weight, she thought. What a waste of a good bag and space.

She grabbed one envelope and opened it with a dirty fingernail, slicing the top. Inside was a letter from a mother to a daughter. It was from Incan's Brook by the address at the top and heading to Blackreach. It was short, with barely any information within its scrawled writing and haphazard letters. Something about a stew and the best way to cook meat. Ida stared at the end of the letter, the sign-off. It was written more heavily than the rest of the letter, as though the author had leaned hard on the paper when writing this particular section. They had written, *Believe me, my love for you is ever pure—your mother.* Ida noted the loops of the Y's, low and elaborate. This was a letter that the daughter would never see, she realised. Instead, this was in her hands, and she was reading the words as though they were meant for her.

The rest of the letters sat before her in a pile, too many to read. Her heart ached. For what kind of woman was she to take these letters, read them, and never give them away? Something within her stirred, and she flicked her eyes up to the mountains. Her mother still stood, staring into the distance, a strange expression on her face.

Ida scratched her head, noticing that the hair was starting to grow back ever so slightly, feeling like a rough sort of velvet beneath her fingers. She was not just Ida anymore; that was the issue. Ida would have gone out of her way to find the people waiting for these letters. She would have ridden for miles to provide them with the post, doing another's job. And what would she get for that? A half-hearted thank you as a daughter learned about her mother's favourite stew. No, she thought, the letter itself is one of love. She pulled her hat down firmly onto her head. If it was a message of love, it was more than she had received herself from the residents of The Nameless Stretch. Each one of them was out for themselves, her father included. No, she would not act as Ida would have. She would not be the gentle, subservient woman that she had been brought up to be. She would act as Colton, the being who took the letters, the being who could kill a deer and remove its organs. But Ida, she thought, you knew what organs to take because you had learned so from your father. She shook her head, starting to get a headache. No matter. Take what you need from both. Be Ida and Colton, but the strongest of each.

She threw the letter onto the burning embers and watched it light up before her, the looped letters dying in the flames. She then sat and went through each envelope, checking for money, for notes, for bonds. Anything else she flung into the embers, barely noting the words within. Birthday money, rent money, sales – it mattered not. Colton took what was needed to survive, warmed by the words on paper that lit the air. The sun began to rise in the sky, the nighttime turning to day. The sky was heavy with white clouds, a threat of snow lingering above them.

He had barely slept. Greyson drank the last of the bitter coffee, slightly cool from the flames of the fire, and sighed. The night had been a cold one, the hard ground scarcely making up for the late evening. He thought then, as he often did when out on the trail, of his mother. It was a habit he'd developed in the last few years, dreaming of his childhood home, the scents of bread baking in the kitchen, drifting up to his soft bed. He sighed again, which caused Billy to turn to him with a grimace.

'What are you sighing for?' he asked, his brow furrowed and eyes hard. Greyson stared at him. He was always a nightmare on the trail; one of the reasons he wanted to stay at Incan's Brook was so that he wouldn't have to deal with him. Greyson had only been out with him twice before, but both times, his mood had soured, and he had a strange habit of sitting back and waiting for everything to be done for him. Billy expected others to do his bidding for the opportunities he provided them.

'I didn't sleep well,' Greyson said, making a mental note not to sigh for a while.

'You don't get much sleep when you're working on the hunt,' Billy said, draining his cup and refilling it with the last of the coffee. Both men watched the final dregs drip into the cup, and Greyson fought not to say something along the lines of, 'Oh, don't worry, I've had my fill.' He knew it wasn't worth mentioning.

The sun was drifting up in the sky. Kissing the moon goodnight, Greyson thought. His mother used to say that to him when he had to get up early to help his pa on the farm. He stood and started packing up, rolling up the beds and securing them to the horses' saddles, taking a moment to check their legs and hooves for stones and the like. Billy watched him, still seated with his coffee.

'We'll head toward The City of Glass, might be a few more days. It's going to get cold,' he said, nodding.

'Yup,' Greyson responded, feeling no need to add anything. What else was there to say?

'Once there, we'll split up, organise a meeting place outside. I heard tell of a graveyard a day's ride beyond the gates. Maybe we meet there once we've got her, then we can ride on up to Bleakhollow. That'll be a journey.'

'Here's hoping she's got a horse.'

Billy stood up and kicked dust over the fire, watching it go out. 'It don't matter what she's got – it just matters that we've got her. And we will.'

Greyson nodded, tightening the girth on his horse. 'Yup.'

'Know how I know?'

Greyson turned and shook his head, watching the short man curl his lip.

'Because I ain't losing that kind of money for anyone,' Billy said, his eyes hard. He pushed his coffee cup into his satchel and mounted his horse swiftly, urging it forward on a long rein before Greyson had got a chance to mount himself. Greyson sighed again, but only the horse heard him this time.

'Come on then,' he said to the beast, who whickered in response, a comforting sound if Greyson had ever heard one.

Mrs Vale and Colt were now in the saddle, both delighted at the turn of events. Of course, Mrs Vale had told Colt, she would be more pleased if the circumstances had never actually occurred. Still, the horse she had stolen was a satisfactory recompense for the situation. Colt had chosen a dark bay steed, almost black, with a soft leather saddle with fancy tooling that suggested a wealthy owner. He had no qualms at all about taking it; after all, the person who owned this miraculous beast and expensive saddle clearly had the money to spend on it. And, he reminded Mrs Vale, the people of that town were goodfornuthins – selfish and lazy to the last. Mrs Vale had agreed, and had picked a shorter appaloosa, its spotted skin making up for the very plain and fairly old saddle that she was left with. Together, they had ridden out of the town without a backwards glance, the sheriff's two pistols shared between them and nestling over chaps and skirts alike.

As they predicted, the journey was fairly long, but they had taken some care to ensure that canteens were filled from the horses' trough, and Mrs Vale had assured Colt that she had the skills to survive in the wild. Colt asked about her experiences as they travelled through the dirt, Steepmount now not even a speck on the horizon. The sun was rising, and the people of the town would be starting to rise with it. Who would be the first to find the sheriff? Colt wondered. He placed a hand on his new pistol with a flicker of pride. He was really a man of action now, if only his mother could see what he had become. He glanced sideways at Mrs Vale, who was bouncing in her saddle, as though she wasn't used to riding.

'It helps to lift your pelvis, if you don't mind my saying,' Colt said. Mrs Vale glanced at him and then shifted in her seat, her body now more stable. Colt nodded. 'If you need to stop at any time, you just tell me. We're far enough away from the town now that we've got a good head start.'

'Oh, don't you worry about me; I've spent a long time alone in these parts. When I was a young slip, I used to take my horse right up the edge of the sea, right by the Docks of Astray. I was sweet on a fella up there, you see, and it would take me a few days. I'm tougher than I look.'

Colt nodded at her, noticing with strange surprise that it was the first time he had felt no animosity toward another human being in a while. Every conversation he had been involved with recently felt as though it was backed by hatred and suspicion. He smiled, feeling sort of tender toward her all of a sudden.

'You're still a young slip, ain't you?' he asked, smiling. Mrs Vale frowned in slight confusion and glanced at him.

'Oh, hush, boy. I'm old enough to be your mother,' she said. That was true, Colt thought, but she wasn't his mother. His mother would have kept him in jail if she'd had the chance, locked him up inside the farmhouse and kept the key out of reach.

'Yeah, but you ain't my mother,' Colt said, his confidence rising. Mrs Vale rolled her eyes dramatically.

'We've got a lot of ground to cover,' she responded, urging her horse into a steady lope. Beneath him, Colt's horse did the same before he could request it, and he tutted and pulled him back into a jog before allowing him back to a lope. He wasn't about to let a horse tell him what to do, he thought.

He watched the back of Mrs Vale, her grey bun bouncing with the beat of the horse's gait, her skirts flying behind her. The air was getting warmer, and the breeze that the speed offered was welcoming and almost blissful after so long in the jailhouse. Colt closed his eyes, feeling the sun on his face and skin, tasting the dust kicked up by the horse's hooves. The saddle beneath him was far comfier than his own, he thought with pleasure.

Ida's journey, wherever she was, would not be so sweet. And when she arrived at the homestead, what a surprise she would get. Perhaps he'd keep her alive and sell her to bounty hunters for a fraction of the fake reward. Now that was a sweet idea, he thought, laughing. He opened his eyes to see that he was now ahead of Mrs Vale, the bare and stony brown scenery flicking past them at a pace. He turned in his saddle and tipped his hat to the woman, who nodded in response. He liked her, he thought, she was a good sort. Perhaps she was the first woman he had ever thought that about, save the fake Elizabeth whom Ida had claimed to be. But then, liquor had been in his system, and hers was a young and beautiful face, easy to take at its word. No, he thought, slowing his horse down so the old woman could catch up. There was something about Mrs Vale. Beneath her aged and wrinkled skin was a spark that was like his own. And no one was going to take it from them.

Chapter 18

Ida stared at the path ahead of her and then turned in the saddle to stare at the rocky snow behind her. Which way was it again? The body of the deer was now gone, which had surprised her. She had remembered its location well, careful not to stray too far so that she could get back on track. The only thing remaining of it now was a pile of bloody snow, a hideous sight that turned Ida's stomach, despite her being responsible for the entire thing. Where had the creature gone? She wondered, resting a hand on the pommel of Bullet's saddle. Who would have wanted for the carcass of the beast? A bear, perhaps. A wolf. She strained to listen, wondering if such a creature might be watching her now. There was no sound, not really. It was perhaps the quietest place she had ever been, just the wind drifting between the mountains. It unnerved her.

She stared at the patch of blood and sniffed. She needed to turn back, head back down the track, and rejoin the other path, the one that went to The City of Glass. Yes, that was correct. She turned Bullet away from the display of horror, and he moved as directed without fuss. The rune against her chest began to heat up slightly, and she noticed it with a frown. It kept doing that, she thought; it kept heating up and cooling down at random. Perhaps it was broken somehow, although she still wasn't entirely sure what the thing was for. She nudged Bullet into a careful walk, aware that he might stagger if he took the path too fast, a horse unused to the slippery white floor below. She loosened her reins, letting him stretch his neck and search for the balance he needed to deliver them to safety. Beside them, Ida's mother appeared to walk slowly.

'Mother, are you well?' Ida asked, aware that her voice and Bullet's hooves were among the only sounds she could hear. Her mother barely turned.

'Well, it is not a thing that I can experience any longer. It is thoughts and feelings, but not as though I were alive,' she responded, the image of her body more potent than ever.

Ida nodded. 'I can see you more clearly than ever before here. Perhaps my powers are growing.'

Her mother shook her head. 'I do not believe so. It's this place. You cannot see what is here, but I can.'

Ida frowned and glanced around them. The snow-covered mountains and paths were empty apart from themselves. 'I see,' she said softly. 'Well, we are not far from the correct path now. Once we turn that corner up there, we shall reach the sign. And then, we'll be going in the right direction. What do you see, Mother?'

'Stay on the path,' her mother said, as though Ida hadn't spoken. That was all. Her voice drifted up into the air, disappearing with the wind. Ida leaned her weight back in the saddle, giving Bullet a chance to distribute his weight evenly down the path. The corner was coming up fast, and she noticed that now, no rabbits were darting across the invisible road before them. Perhaps they had seen what had happened to the deer, Ida thought. Animals were intelligent; she knew it. The ground began to flatten out and then turned the corner at a faster pace. Ida took advantage of this and nudged Bullet into a jog, which he took lightly, his hooves shifting through the mini drifts of snow with ease, almost a glide. There, ahead, Ida saw the pinprick that hinted at the sign.

'There it is!' she said aloud, noticing her hot words forming ahead of her in a fog. She smiled at this; such a trick was delightful for someone who had always lived in the sunshine. The excitement drove Bullet forward into a lope, and he cantered across the floor, the sign turning from pinprick to dot and from dot to wood. They skidded to a halt in front of it, Ida rereading the words.

Take care. There is but one road to The City of Glass.

She squinted and leaned forward, reading the scrawl of *I didn't do it* once more. She noticed beside her that her mother withdrew at something in the distance.

'Mother?'

She turned and stared at her, shaking her head. Her expression was one of concern, and Ida noticed that the gentle stares she had given her before were now rare, the tenderness replaced by something else.

'You should hurry to the city, Ida. You are wasting time.'

Ida snorted, irritated at the suggestion that she was wasting anything. She was an adult, damn it. 'I do not believe that stopping for rest and food is a waste of time, Mother. And unless I ask you your opinion, you would do well to keep it to yourself. I have a had a lifetime of—'

'Move,' her mother said, interrupting her. Ida glared at her and felt the rune burn against her skin, hotter than before. She pushed Bullet into a canter again, up the correct path, following the arrow on the sign. It was much like the other one, almost indistinguishable, though lesser in slope and with a slightly more beaten path. They moved at a steady speed, as fast as was possible for such slippery terrain, and Ida held her bear pelt coat around her with one hand, the other holding the reins, confident in Bullet's movements. She breathed in the cold air and smiled. Those bounty hunters from Incan's Brook would be far behind them, surely. What horse could move as Bullet could? She had complete faith in his abilities, their bond growing by the day.

The path began to narrow, and up ahead, a sharp corner showed itself, almost too late for Bullet to slow. Ida pulled on the reins suddenly, seeing the potential for a skid, and Bullet slowed so quickly that she almost fell forward on his neck. She steadied herself with the pommel again and took a breath, her heart beating hard. The corner was upon them, two rock faces on either side of the path, bearing down on them as though they were trying to press them into the earth. At a walk, they turned it, hooves slipping and sliding. Ida gathered herself, sitting still in the saddle, strengthening her core, and pushing her leg into Bullet's side – a comfort to him. He righted himself and stood still. Ida stared at the path. She saw the great wheel before seeing the rest of the wreckage, wooden and buried in the snow, its spokes broken and ruined.

They had found the remnants of a fire beside a large rock. It was only some charred earth, burned sticks and cold black embers, but Billy treated it as the strongest clue they had yet. Greyson shrugged. Perhaps it was. He watched as his boss knelt in the dirt, touched the dead fire and smelled the ashes. He stifled a yawn and frowned. What could be gained from smelling ashes?

'What are you smelling for?' Greyson asked bluntly, perhaps a little blunter than he had initially intended.

Billy didn't look at him. 'I'm seeing how old the fire is. At least a day.'

Greyson did his best not to roll his eyes. There was tracking, and then there was making stuff up. Of course, he would never say that. He tipped his hat back and glanced at the sun. Despite it now being higher in the sky, the air was chilled around him. It was making his nose run.

'We should head off,' he said, wondering how it had now fallen to him to nudge the journey along.

'I don't think she'll be far. Once she reaches the Alask Wilds, she'll struggle with the snow – they all do,' Billy said, standing up. He dusted his hands off on his trousers and remounted swiftly, his horse countering the weight by staggering.

'The Alask Wilds?' Greyson said. 'There's a way through the land to The City of Glass without going near them.'

Billy shook his head but answered in the affirmative. 'Yeah, we know that. We know that you can choose snakes and potential death or snow and potential death. But she won't. The map shows one way, that's through the Alask Wilds.' He nudged his horse forward, and Greyson followed alongside.

'They say they're haunted,' he said.

'Who do?' Billy asked with a snap.

'That's the rumour of the Alask Wilds – you gotta have heard it.'

'So what? They say the other way is haunted, too. All those people in that plague town. You believe in ghost stories? You afraid of ghosts when there's snakes and men tryin' to kill you?'

Greyson scratched his head and sighed. Yes, he was, he thought. He was terrified of ghosts, as most people were. Rumours abounded about the Alask Wilds when he was a small boy, of the dangers that could be found there. The City of Glass was not the only place in Hangman's Rest that tried to keep their youngsters at bay with threats of the wider world. They moved on, the unanswered question hanging in the air.

'We should be there by nightfall, eh?' Greyson said instead, choosing to avoid the ghost discussion.

Billy nodded. 'I suppose so. As long as we keep up a good pace.' They moved smoothly into a gallop as though the horses understood the need for urgency. Greyson leaned forward in the saddle, the cold wind hurting his eyes. He pulled his hat down a little so that the brim sliced through the gusts. Five hundred dollars, he thought. That was worth it for this, wasn't it? Worth a bit of discomfort, the rough nights of sleep, the wind. Was it worth the potential of ghosts, though? Five hundred dollars. Of course, most of it would be going to Billy. That was obvious. So how much would he be getting? He glanced over at his boss, his eyes beginning to stream in the wind. How much would his share be?

Ida dismounted and stared at the wreckage before her. The opulent spokes of the wheels stuck out of the snow at all angles, plush purple and black curtains lay abandoned. There were no horses, as though they had been cut away or perhaps had escaped the confines of their harnesses. The luxurious and large stagecoach was just stuck there, jutting out of the land like a discarded pebble, there and of no consequence to anyone. Her skin tingled. Glancing to the side of her, she noticed her mother watching, a strange and sad expression on her face. Against her skin, the rune burned, almost a blistering heat.

Ida moved toward the destruction and climbed up onto one of the heavy wooden wheels, pulling herself until she was face height with the broken window. It was iced up, and Ida noticed that the top section was not, in fact, ice but smashed glass. She pushed against it gingerly with her arm, protected by the bear pelt, and felt it give way beneath her force. It yielded and smashed back into the shell of the carriage. Ida looked inside. The velvet seating area and wallpaper were almost untouched despite being on a slant. However, there was one difference to its usual splendour. It held a dead body. The breath caught in Ida's throat as she stared at the woman. Her blue day dress now had dried blood trickled down the front, and her grey set curls had fallen from their high perch.

The woman's eyes were staring, unblinking. Ida shuddered, more from the sight than the cold. It was the very same woman that had offered her a lift. She closed her eyes for a moment, thankful that she had not accepted and that she had chosen to ride alone. She opened them again and saw in a flash a face before her, grey and pallid but as lifelike as any real face she had ever seen. Ida let out a single scream, falling back into the snow heavily, her heart racing within the cage of her chest. She stared up at the white sky, the snow causing cold to creep up her neck and skin. Bullet whinnied a sound that caused her to sit up. He stared at her, confused. Ida reached into the breast of her shirt with her right hand and pulled out the burning rune. It was glowing with heat, and she dropped into the snow as soon as she grabbed it. The snow around the stone wasn't melting, she noticed, as though the heat was not really there. She got up carefully, leaving it where it lay. Ida climbed back to her vantage point with a deep breath and pulled herself back to the window. There was the woman, only one body, dead and staring as before. She nodded, as though affirming to herself that this was the right way of things, that the moment before was a dream only.

'Ida,' her mother's voice said, floating to her ears. She held onto the window frame and turned, seeing her mother fainter but still there, the outlines of her seeming to blow in the wind. She was pointing at the rune. 'You must have that for protection, for nothing else will protect you here.'

Ida shook her head. 'I don't know about that. It burns my skin, Mother. I saw a face, a ghost.'

'Come, child. The Alask Wilds is haunted. Did your father never tell you? There is little that helps a stranger in these parts, but the rune will protect you some.'

Ida stared back into the carriage for a moment, though she didn't know why. It was like she had never seen a dead body before, though she had. There was something so shocking about the scene that she could barely look away.

'Ida,' her mother's voice said again. She ripped her eyes from the horrific scene and stared at her mother again, who pointed at the rune with more force. Ida felt, once more, like a child being admonished. What was this? she thought. Her mother finally having the opportunity to do some mothering and taking full advantage of the strange situation?

'I am trying to help you,' her mother said as though she could read her mind. Ida jumped down from the stagecoach, landing in the snow, her clothes still dripping from the fall. She stepped through the drift toward her mother and then reached into the unmelted snow to grasp the rune. It was still hot, despite being chilled.

'I don't want to see any ghosts,' Ida said, feeling more like a small child than ever before. Perhaps even more than in her actual childhood, she mused.

Her mother shook her head. 'No one has control over such a thing. The Alask Wilds have been haunted for years.'

Ida slipped the rune back under the shirt against her skin, where it settled in, burning. 'Why is it haunted? Surely not all of these people have been murdered?'

Her mother's image was a little more clear now but still fainter against the backdrop of white. 'I don't know, Ida. They are here, and I can see them all. They are here. They were around us last night. For whatever reason, they seem to be condemned to this land.'

Ida looked around her. She could only see the stagecoach on its side, broken luxury descending into disrepair. She stared at the box for a second and then let out a breath, its fog forming in the air before her.

'The driver,' she said, stepping back toward the wreckage. She moved up to the box and checked the surrounding snow. There were blood marks and footprints around her. Ida stared at them, the cold air prickling her eyes. She leaned down and picked up a piece of leather still attached to the stagecoach. It had been cut, without a doubt. Hoofprints scattered away from the scene. The driver was alive and had fled on horseback. She did not blame them for wanting to get out of there, but what had caused such a catastrophe in the first place? Ida turned and looked at the bend behind her, the one that had made Bullet skid on his steady hooves, and frowned. The woman had spoken to her as though she had done this trip many times before. In fact, Ida had assumed that she was from The City of Glass. Surely they had known this route, this journey, before they headed out?

The sun was forcing itself through the white sky. There was nothing that Ida could do except carry on. Then, something occurred to her. There would be food and goods in the stagecoach unless the driver had taken them all. How much could a single person carry, she wondered, even with two horses as companions? Not as much as a coach. She turned and headed to the back of the vehicle, where the luggage box was usually kept, and frowned to find it already unlocked. She yanked it open and sighed at the inside. It was cleared out. Ida wiped her brow and tapped her fingers against the wood. The woman, she thought. She was clearly well to do, and perhaps she had something on her that might be of use? Ida licked her lips and turned to her mother, scratching her head a little, nervous.

'Now listen, there's not much in the way of food left in this coach, so I'm going to search inside.'

'Ida...' her mother said, the voice quiet in the wind.

'I have said my piece,' Ida responded, 'and it is not up for discussion.' She raised her eyebrows, giving her mother the stern look of Colton, and rolled her shoulders back. That's right, she thought, that is precisely what a man would do. That is exactly what Colton would do. He would search the scene for what was rightfully his by way of finding. It was what her father would have done, too, she thought, and what her brother had done. That was what men did. They took, and they took, and they gave nothing back.

A rage suddenly bubbled up inside her chest, and she spat onto the ground, furious. How the hell had she ended up here, in this iced hell hole, searching a dead rich woman for pennies and food? Why had she been driven out of her homestead by a stranger with a gun? She placed a hand on her pistol and growled beneath her breath.

'Mother, after The City of Glass has given us what we need to recoup, we'll be heading back to the homestead. I'm not leaving a bastard to take over our land. Her mother simply nodded. Ida ran her hand beneath her nose and turned, pulling herself back up to the door. She yanked it open, the remaining glass smashing into the snow behind. She climbed in, noticing with interest that the woman didn't smell. Ida could barely smell anything. She knew little of ice and snow and how it worked, though she understood that it had preserved the food that she had collected from the deer. She stared at the woman for a second, those staring dead eyes, almost just to make sure that she wasn't about to move, and took a breath.

'Courage,' she said quietly. Ida steadied her feet and reached out, touching the woman. She didn't flinch, much to Ida's relief. Ida stared at the blue dress and grimaced. First, she lifted the sleeves from her wrists to check for jewellery. There was none, she found.

'That bloody driver,' she whispered, certain that they were the culprit. She pulled the shawl from the woman's neck and checked her decolletage. It was quite low, and Ida could see no necklace. There was one other place she could check, she thought, carefully dropping down lower. Her boots. Ida knelt and began to unlace the icy threads, trying to throw off the desire to leave immediately. There was something so carnal about this act, the searching of a body. It made her feel slightly sick, even as she pretended to be Colton. Her rage was now subsiding, and she was faltering in her actions. She pulled both boots off with a little struggle and tipped them upside down. From within, a few notes fell out, but that was all. Ida collected them up and pocketed them. They weren't as useful as food might have been, but it was something to add to her pile. One could never have enough money, she thought. Ida stood up and stared at the woman, who now looked somewhat in a state of undress, her shawl and shoes abandoned.

'Oh…' Ida whispered, the sight stinging her heart. She leaned forward and pulled the shawl back around the corpse, trying to give her some decency in death. As she did so, a cushion was knocked from beside her onto the floor. Ida saw what hid behind it and laughed, a singular bark of pleasure. It was an almost full bottle of bourbon. She grinned. It was worth it all for this moment, this one juncture. As she reached for the bottle in the strange cold light, the rune pulsed suddenly as though breathing out heat. Ida paused. That feeling again, the one that told her she was being watched. She stared upwards at her entryway, the door that she had yanked open. There, staring down at her, was a ghostly face, the one that she had seen before. She glared at it and grabbed the bottle of bourbon, holding it close.

'What do you want?' she growled, her voice more Colton than anything else. The face said nothing but stared at her with a strange smile. It was a woman, she thought, with her hair scraped back. A large nose jutted out in front of her. Her eyes were cruel and small, made smaller still by the nose. Ida hissed at her as if she were a cat, trying to get her to scatter in the same way. The woman just continued staring.

'I will shoot you. Get out of my way,' she tried, pulling her pistol and aiming it at the woman's head. The face just stared intently, blinking now and then. Ida cocked the hammer, aimed the gun and fired. The shot rang clean through the air, whistling past the door. She heard Bullet whinny in surprise somewhere outside the stagecoach. The face remained. The rune, Ida thought. Could that help her? She reached inside her shirt and pulled it out, the stone hot in her hand. She showed it to the woman, who gave her a strange, melancholic smile and disappeared. Ida steadied herself and then uncorked the bourbon, taking a deep sip. She glanced at the dead woman beside her and tipped her hat.

'Ma'am, I appreciate your generosity.'

The woman said nothing and stared into the distance for eternity.

Chapter 19

The unlikely pair eventually settled for the evening. It was a little earlier than Colt would have liked, but he was aware that the woman he travelled with was older than himself and was surviving on less sleep. There were moments when she reminded him of his mother in a strange, bossy way, and at those times, he found that he could be pretty sharp with her. At other times, she was expressive and nothing short of charming. He built a fire, occasionally stealing glances at her as she busied herself searching through the saddlebag they had stolen with one of the horses. She was not the woman he had envisaged himself with…but that didn't mean she couldn't be. After all, she owned land. She pulled out a packet of crackers and tutted, throwing it beside the small knife, piece of rag, and apple that she had already claimed.

'There's just trash in here,' she said crossly. 'Crackers and an apple. That won't last us until the next town.'

'Maybe we oughta go fishing,' said Colt, tapping his pockets. 'You got a light?'

'Fishing? Where do you see a fishing rod? Where do you see a lake? We ain't near the sea or anything,' Mrs Vale reprimanded him, giving him a look that showed her displeasure, her eyes small and cross, her brow furrowed deeply. She pulled a packet of matches from inside the breast of her dress and threw them underarm at Colt, who tried to grab them but missed. Mrs Vale rolled her eyes in disapproval. 'Well, I guess I'll take the crackers, and you take the apple,' she said, taking a sip from the canteen.

Colt nodded and lit a match, holding it up to the straw beneath the wood before him. His hands shook a little. He had a feeling that if he used more than one match, there would be a serious discussion to be had. There was a strangeness about Mrs Vale, an attitude that inspired within him a reaction he had not felt since his father had been alive. It was a desperation to impress, a longing to be approved of. The feeling created a strange potion of longing and irritation that Colt recognised as that of a lost son, forever attempting to establish love and respect, but falling short. As the fire caught, he sat back and removed his hat, nodding at the early evening sun as though it had said a word to him. It was still hot in the day, and Colt closed his eyes for a moment, enjoying the sensation of stillness about him. He breathed in the warm, humid air and smiled. Life seemed so much more joyous now he was no longer in the stale and stilted air of the jailhouse.

'Ha! Got the bastard,' he heard suddenly, and he opened his eyes to find Mrs Vale holding the small knife in one hand, up above her head. The sharp end was stuck clean through the head of a snake, its body dangling to the ground, blood dripping. The woman's eyes shone as she stared at the reptile. Colt felt his heart thump a little quicker in his ribcage as he stared at her, so capable was she.

'Lawsy! I didn't hear it coming,' Colt said.

Mrs Vale nodded, 'Yup, it would have bitten you had I not been here to help. And he's a nice bit of protein for our supper.' She flattened the snake out before her with surprising efficiency and then used the knife to slit its body from bottom to top. She removed its skin proficiently and chucked it at Colt, nodding. 'My boy would take that skin and turn it into something beautiful. A belt. Something like that. You got that skill, son?'

Colt stared, the bloody skin touching his boot and turning his stomach. Mrs Vale tipped a little water from the canteen into her hand before running it over the snake. Then, in a moment that seemed to truly lack planning, she threw its body onto the fire. It sizzled immediately, the flames lapping the greyish rope. Colt wrinkled his nose.

'You eat a lot of snake?' he asked hesitantly.

'You are not a man of the outdoors, are you, boy? You have to be prepared to look after yourself out here, nobody will do it for you. Now tell me, what is it that you plan to do once Ida has visited my son's home?'

Colt shrugged, watching the snake's underbelly (if that's what it was) change colour in the flames. 'I want my money back. My horse.'

Mrs Vale nodded. 'Hmm. Well, we might have to come up with a better plan for that, boy, because she's not coming back to give you the money and horse, is she? She's coming back to claim what is not lawfully hers. She wants that house, that land, and my boy's life – not to mention that the property should legally be his, as the male heir.' She picked up a stick from the front of the fire and poked at the snake half-heartedly, turning it. The scent of cooked potatoes filled the air.

'Well, I'll kill her if she tries anything,' Colt said firmly, pulling an expression that he thought represented his sincerity.

Mrs Vale smiled a little. 'That's more of a plan, sure. But don't you wanna have something foolproof? Don't you wanna make sure you have that sweet moment of justice?'

Colt stared at her, unsure of what to say. Her skin, wrinkled and age-spotted, was like dapples of sunlight before him. He shrugged. 'I don't know what to say. I'll shoot her when she comes in.'

'Dear boy,' Mrs Vale said, causing Colt to flush a little, 'we can do better. How about this, just off the top of my head. I wait outside, and I'll be doing my knitting, waiting. She'll ride up, full of fury, and then see me there and hesitate. 'Well, who is this old woman?' she will think. I am here to kill the man I saw last at this property. I will loudly explain that the man has moved on, that I bought it from him for a fair price, that I am sorry, but it is nothing to do with me. She will have had a long ride, and so I will invite her in for a drink, perhaps a bite to eat. Of course, she will comply, for women do not fear women. I will encourage her to leave her guns at the door, so they can cause no harm to a human inside. Once she is in, I will lock that door behind me. You will be sitting at the table, waiting for her. And that will be the shocking moment – that will be all yours. You will take the money, my boy will be outside securing the horse, and you shall deal with her.'

Colt listened and nodded, scratching his neck occasionally, flying insects chewing on his skin. 'It certainly sounds like a plan,' he said. 'When you say deal with her, what is it that you mean?'

'You shall kill her, boy. She has taken what is rightfully yours. This is the law of the land.'

Colt nodded. That was indeed the law of the land. And wasn't that what Ida was thinking, too, coming back to claim what she thought was hers? 'Well, Mrs Vale, I am thankful to be a man.'

Mrs Vale's right eye twitched, and she gave him a strange smile. 'What an odd thing to say. Why would you be thankful for such a thing?'

'The law is on my side, as it is on your son's side. We shall have justice.'

The old woman nodded and turned the snake over completely with the stick, a movement she had clearly done before. 'Justice,' she said. 'It's a strange thing in these parts. Different for each and every person who says the word. This snake would've bitten you, wouldn't it? Is it justice that we eat him now before he has had the opportunity?'

Colt stared at it and then at Mrs Vale, whose skin was glowing in the soft light of the fire. 'I suppose that is justice, yes.' He smiled. 'I must say, ma'am. You have a way with words that is most becoming.'

She snickered softly and blinked her watery eyes. 'It is a fact that I am destined to live with,' she said, fishing the snake out of the fire and onto the ground. Its skin was now charred and brown, and the woman grasped the knife. With one cut, she removed the head and, with another, sliced the body in two. She peeled the snake, then threw one half to Colt, who caught it and bit into the flesh. It was tough, dry. He chewed and swallowed, grateful not for the snake but for Mrs Vale's company.

Chapter 20

Greyson snuck a cracker from his pocket and chewed it as the horses loped forward. His back was aching. His neck was hurting. Heck, his whole body had just had enough of this journey. The stones beneath his horse's feet occasionally tripped it up, causing a rush of adrenaline to flush through Greyson's body. He stared at the grey sky above, the sun struggling to make its way through, and trembled in the cold air. He had something he wanted to ask the boss, but he was afraid to, already knowing what the answer would be. Money was always a sore point, he thought. The conversation about money was always a bad one. Up above, a large bird appeared to be circling. Billy glanced up and nodded at it.

'That's the Whitchit bird,' he said with a grin. 'Known to attack the weak. Actually…it may be that the woman has already fallen foul of it…if you pardon the pun.'

Greyson laughed, out of politeness only, as he couldn't see any pun in the words. 'Want me to shoot it?' he asked, reaching for his pistol half-heartedly.

'Nope. Just wait. Ain't no point in drawing attention to ourselves.'

Greyson let his reaching hand fall back onto his canvased thigh. He stared at the barren land before them. Attention from whom? The snow-covered mountains were starting to rise out of the horizon. Greyson grimaced, already cold from the ride. He just wanted to turn back, to go home.

'So, when we get to The City of Glass, we'll have time to stop off at a saloon right, time to refresh ourselves?' he asked Billy, bringing his horse up beside him.

Billy shrugged. 'I Dunno. It depends where she is.'

'Hmm. I look forward to a square meal and a nice bourbon.'

'The quicker you stop thinking of your stomach, the better. Think of the money. That's the only thing that should be driving you forward.'

Greyson nodded, thinking of his mother again. It was similar to something she used to say to him. Think of the pleasure of a shining floor, Greyson. That's the reason you should be helping your mother out, for the joy of that shining floor, not for the hope of your pocket money.

'So the money is five hundred dollars…'

'Right.' Billy gave him a glare that almost stopped him from speaking, but Greyson pushed forward, breathing in sharply through his nose.

'And…with that in mind, what's my cut?'

The words hung in the air for a moment. Neither of the men spoke. Above them, the Whitchit bird circled, its wings large and noiseless. Billy smiled, a strange turn up of his lips that didn't convey any pleasure.

'How much would you want, Greyson? How much do you think is fair?' he asked eventually. Greyson thought on this. It could, of course, be some strange sort of trap. It could be something like him saying a figure, and the figure that lingered in Billy's head was more, so he'd be doing himself an injustice. Greyson rested a hand on his horse's neck, the warmth and movement of the muscles a comfort.

'There's a bit of space I've had my eye on back near Incan's Brook. It's a little out of the way, but it's got a fair building attached, a bit of farming land. I got a feeling that it would be pretty sweet to plant some of my own vegetables, live off the land. Maybe own some livestock.'

Billy frowned at him. 'I don't see how that is relevant.'

'My point is, boss, that I got dreams that require money. I got hopes that require capital.'

The mountains glared at them from ahead, watching them ride ever closer, slight tracks along its cold flesh now becoming visible.

'And I've got a business to run. Bounty that needs collecting. I've got situations that require men with guns. Are you telling me that this is your last trip, that you're about to become a farmer?' Billy shook his head in a tiny display of irritation and disbelief, as though he could not find his way to understanding what the man beside him was saying.

'Not saying that for certain – I just mean—'

'Are you talking about the old farm up from Juniper Hill?' Billy interrupted. 'Well, it's cheap because of those murders, ain't it? What you want to buy a house like that for?'

Greyson sniffed and stared up at the bird again. 'The murders don't bother me, and I can always knock it down and rebuild. It's good land.'

'It ain't great land though, is it? That old farmer went mad because nothing would grow, I heard,' Billy said, pushing a cigarette into his mouth. He looped his reins around the pommel of his saddle and pulled a match out of his pocket, swiping it across the leather. A small flame appeared, and he protected it from the breeze of motion, lighting the tobacco. Greyson observed him. He hadn't heard the same. Sure, he'd heard that an accident had happened there, but accidents happened everywhere. You'd be lucky to find a house in The Nameless Stretch that hadn't housed a dead body at some time or another.

'Anyhow. I think that I deserve a fair cut. That's my point. If I could get a fair cut of this job, pay off my debts, buy this land. I'd be set up. And I think that given that it's just you and me out here, all on our own…the money should be split.' Greyson swallowed hard, aware that the last sentence was not what Billy wanted to hear. Despite being outside, tension crackled between the two men. Greyson winced a little at the stilted silence and tried to breathe through it. Leave it for him to break, he thought. Leave it to him. After a moment, the Whitchit bird cawed. In one swift movement, Billy pulled his pistol and shot into the air, looking as though he almost hadn't even aimed. The bird fell from the sky like a rock shattering a frozen lake, and smashed into the ground somewhere behind them. Greyson looked at the man beside him.

'I thought you didn't want to draw attention?' he hesitantly asked.

'At some point, the bird would draw attention, and we cannot have that. Anyhow – the money. If I split that amount with you, then it wouldn't make me the boss, would it? You see, Greyson, you think that what we're out here doing is sharing the workload. Now, I see it differently. You don't have the problems of expectation and decision making and plain responsibility laying heavy on your head. You don't have that problem at all. You get to ride and see the country, you get to sleep and build a fire, and the only thing you get to be concerned about truly is what time you get to lay your head down. My head is filled with much more important concerns.' He took a long drag from his cigarette and blew the smoke out into the air. It disappeared almost instantly, whipped away by the wind. 'To say that we were equal in this endeavour when it is I who found the bounty, who decided the route, who learned the skills to get us to the feet of this woman, would be wrong. Plain wrong. It is almost so wrong as to be found offensive by myself, but I give you the benefit of the doubt because I know you are not a cruel man by nature.'

Greyson nodded. He was not a cruel man by nature, he agreed silently. And yes, Billy was quite right. He could see that now. It was an error to think that the men were equals in this job.

'Billy, I agree. My apologies. I forgot myself thinking of the farm for a moment. If I could take one and fifty, I would be quite content with my lot.'

Billy glanced at him and took another suck on his cigarette before flicking it into the air. Greyson watched it fall to the floor in a sea of sparks and vanish behind them.

'You forget your expenses, Greyson. You forget my wife. Here's what we'll do. We find this woman, get that whore to the Sheriff of Steepmount and collect our five hundred dollars. Then, I'll make sure you get that farm. At whatever cost that is. Now, I don't want to lose a good man, so if the farm costs more than you earn on this trip, well, it ain't a problem. You just pay it off with another bounty, and we'll call it quits. Think of me as a bank extending my loan to you.'

The mountain was becoming ever steeper, the snow a little deeper, as they moved on. There were footprints in it, hoofprints, occasionally wheel prints, as though it were a busy thoroughfare in a town filled with people. Ida stared at the blanket of white before her, eyes dulled to the spectacular sight.

It was the same every moment, never changing, only growing a little more arduous, slowing Bullet down.

She swigged on the bottle again, now a quarter empty, enjoying the feeling of being warmed from within. It soothed her. She closed her eyes, feeling Bullet move beneath her as though he knew the way. It was, she supposed, either one way or the other. That he continued to agree it was uphill was a blessing in itself. She was entirely at his impulse. At this thought, Ida opened her eyes again and looked around her. The mountains were still stretching high into the sky, as though climbing further up them was doing nothing to actually move them along. She felt that they were so tiny in the world and the mountains so gigantic that it did not matter what they did to traverse them. They would still be a mere pinprick in the snow.

Her mother, the strange hovering shape beside her, was still staring ahead. The rune was now at a constant burn, as though working hard to protect them. Ida took another swig of the bourbon and hiccupped. It made her feel almost wondrously careless, and she held the bottle in one hand and then raised it to her mother in a sort of cheering action. Her mother barely looked over.

'I am guessing that they are everywhere…the ghosts?' she asked her.

'They are here and there,' her mother responded, not looking. Ida nodded. She had an undeniable impulse to pull the rune from inside her clothing again and to view the world as it truly was. No tricks. How small she was, she thought again in her slightly drunken stupor, how unimportant. And yet, the pressure she had been under thus far in her life, only to come to this mountain range, and realise that there was nothing within her that would ever scale the import and sheer size of this world. Perhaps there would have been, once. If she had been able to take the farm, she could have made it her own. How did one become so important in the world? They put their name on an unmovable and everlasting place. She hiccupped, again tasting the bourbon. The world was starting to look a little hazy, she thought, and she was pleased about it. It was a welcome break, a generous gift from the dead. Colton raged inside her, a strange battle between Ida and himself, a merging of the two.

'Mother,' Ida said, thinking aloud. 'When I take back my land, our land, I shall have to do something with that brother of mine.'

Her mother's eyes flickered over.

'But if I kill him, then he shall follow me as you do for the rest of my life, I guess. And I am not in the market for another ghost, another tagger-on to watch me while I live out my days in the fields.' They carried on in silence, Bullet trudging through the snow like a cart horse, his ears flickering back and forth every now and then as he listened to the surroundings and the cool air. Ida watched them, curious about what he could see.

'Perhaps there's a way that I could set up an accident,' she said with the vague air of a barfly. 'Some type of…fire. And yet, there's a satisfaction to be had in showing up as he did. No warning.'

'You do not need revenge,' her mother said, so gently that the words barely lifted themselves through the wind, hardly whispered in Ida's ears. She heard them and rolled her eyes, the inner Colton dismissing her. Of course, revenge was needed. That was all that was needed. If she continued to let the people of The Nameless Stretch treat her in this way, they would never stop. When the laws weren't made to be fair among the sexes, you had to take pistols into your own hands.

'Revenge is the only way I will acquire what is rightfully mine by blood. He has a mother. I had a father. Let her provide for him, and I will take what has been provided to me.'

They seemed to be nearing the top of a slope now, a strange steep corner up ahead. Ida loosened the reins and allowed Bullet some slack so that he could stretch his neck forward and climb with ease. After a few minutes of climbing, his hooves lifting high over each small snowdrift that formed against them, they reached the corner. There, Ida saw that the mountain fell away, almost straight down, a wide path sculpted into the cliff face at an angle. To her right, the snow-covered path they had travelled on thus far carried on up the mountain, but the sight before her showed which road was the right one. Far beyond the drop, in the icy distance, was a city larger than any Ida had ever seen. Despite it being daylight still, the city seemed to glow in the brightness of the white surroundings. Ida stared, her mouth ajar. It was unlike anything she had imagined, so used to the hot wooden towns of the north was she. Soft pinpricks of light shone from buildings, large and small, and collected together in a mishmash of directions. There were moving carts, as small as ants, being pulled through winding streets. She smiled. There was something about the image that warmed her, made her desperate to join in, to find the warmth of the light. She tucked the bottle of stolen bourbon into her saddlebag and licked her lips.

'Okay. Bullet, take it steady,' she said, collecting her reins in both hands and digging her heels softly into his underbelly. He stared at the steep path beneath him for a moment, clearly considering this new terrain. Then, with the confidence of his journey down the path of the Demon's Canyon, he began to step forward. Ida leaned back, daring herself to look down at the drop, to be brave.

Colt watched Mrs Vale in the glimmering darkness, her features lit subtly by the dying firelight. Each groove of her skin, each ravine of flesh that made way for a well-worn track, told him something else about her life. He noticed that she had more frown lines than laugh lines. The ever-present furrows in the middle of her brow showed her displeasure, even when she was sleeping soundly. The bags beneath her eyes were significant, swollen, dark.

How strange, he thought, how unusual that he should be drawn to her so. It was as though she was a beacon of light and warmth, drawing him in after a long time outside in the snow. He scolded himself. Don't be naïve, one side of his brain murmured. You are only feeling this way because she has shown you a little interest. True, the loving part of him thought, she was maybe the third woman in his life to do so. The first being his mother, and the second that lying whore Ida Vale. And yet, her interest was not just self-serving, he told himself. She helped him escape. He stared at her flickering eyelids, the gentle snore emanating from her nose. She was not a classically beautiful woman, no, but then he was not what you might call a handsome man. In fact, no one had ever told him he was handsome, least of all his mother. She used to say to him it was a shame that he looked so much like his grandfather, who, for all his charms, had never been called good-looking. But then, no one in his family had a face you might call pleasing.

And what of children? He noticed the detail on her chin, the tiny, white, straight hairs that sprouted from the skin. They clearly couldn't have children. Did that matter? Did he care? She had land, and he had farming experience. He had horse training experience, too, and they could be happy enough. Once Ida was out of the picture, they could live a comfortable life, and he would have his money back, his horse back, and his manhood would be back intact. Yes, he thought. That was a good plan. Then, he would propose. Not on a whim, not so that she might think it was a proposal of convenience or anything weird like that. He would ask her to marry him for the love that he felt, and she would agree.

How different she looked now to the woman who had entered the jailhouse. How much her image had changed through his getting to know her. She no longer looked like a witch to him and no longer held that threat. Even if she was a witch, he thought, at least he had her on side. There could be worse things than a witch as a wife, like a liar. A thief. Ida. He smiled at her peaceful sleeping and turned onto his back, feeling the small pebbles beneath him.

The night sky stretched across his eyeline, the stars blinking and falling into each other. One bright spark shot through the atmosphere, the fresh, humid air of a night in Bleakhollow. This was precisely what was in his mind when he imagined leaving his parent's house to travel. Staring at the sky on a warm night, stomach full, goals set. This was the dream, the fantasy. He felt something crawl up his arm and flicked it deftly, aiming for the dying fire. Tomorrow, they would ride together to the homestead, and he would meet Mrs Vale's son. They would dine together and laugh together, a type of family. Yes, he thought, that's exactly it. A family that takes revenge together stays together. There ain't nothing so beautiful as that. At that realisation, he closed his eyes and drifted into sleep, imagining that it was the first of many nights with Mrs Vale.

Chapter 21

The mountains were upon them now, stretching into the bleak night sky. Ahead was a sign, Greyson thought, though they were not close enough yet to work out the words that were written upon it. He was, once again, building a fire for the evening after what had been a long and challenging conversation about stopping for food and rest. The boss was like a workhorse, wanting only to ride and find bounty. Greyson suspected that, actually, Billy was as hungry and tired as he was, but his pride was so great that there was nothing that would stop him from moving forward. They had agreed on one stop between here and The City of Glass. This was it. A couple of hours to sleep, drink coffee, eat and get themselves back on track. Greyson stared at the white mountains beyond and swallowed.

'You want one of us to keep watch while the other sleeps?' he asked.

Billy shrugged and shoved a cracker into his mouth, chewing as he spoke. 'Do what you like. I'm sleeping, and in a few hours, we're moving on, so if you think you can last without sleep, that's on you.' Sprays of crumbs flew into the air, and Greyson watched their silhouette with a grimace.

'Right. I'll be sleeping then.'

'Just make sure you wake us up in a couple of hours. She'll be stopping and resting and all that. The way we get her is by catching less rest and taking more action,' Billy said, pulling a blanket up to his chin and settling into his canvas bedroll. He lay down and closed his eyes, yawning. Greyson gave a quiet snort of derision. He knew the man must be tired. He just knew it. He took a deep breath of the cold air and lay down to sleep, trying to get his body as close to the fire as he possibly could. It crackled comfortably, and he closed his eyes, pretending that he was at home beside the fireplace, listening to his mother fixing a hot chocolate over the stove. The thought warmed him.

In the distance, he heard a wolf howl and another strange sound. It was as though the wind was speaking around them. He kept his eyes closed, trying to focus on the cracklings of the fire only. Billy was right, he thought after a moment. This was how you caught bounty, by taking the risks and the chances that they weren't prepared to. Pushing to the limits that they weren't experiencing. The only thing was that Greyson didn't feel as though he thrived on it in the same way as Billy and the others in the gang. He would have much rather been something else. Maybe a postal worker, or a saloon owner or...Greyson drifted into an uncomfortable sleep, all the while thinking of what he could have been that would have delivered a safe bed for the evening.

Reader, the plan would have been a good one had Ida decided to stop for the evening for sleep and food. As it was, the bourbon had blurred her thought process, and she was comfortably warm and happy to chew on what leftovers she had in her saddlebag as they progressed on their journey. The City of Glass was now more lit than before, and the further they got down the winding path, the more Ida thought that she could hear noise from the buildings, however far away. It sounded jovial to her, joyful. It sounded like exactly where she wanted to be. Bullet was treading carefully, his hooves surefooted and steady. They couldn't stop now, anyway, Ida mused. Where would they set up camp? It was just a path as wide as a carriage, too steep for rest and sleep. She thought of the stagecoach behind them, the wreckage with the dead woman waiting in the back. If they hadn't crashed at that corner, there would have been ample opportunity for them to fall to their deaths here, she thought. Her eyelids were starting to get heavy, and Ida yawned.

'Bullet, you're doing a grand job,' she said, watching his ears flicker back at the sound of her voice. It seemed to be getting darker, and the moon was covered by white snow-filled clouds. Ida leaned over, pulled her kerosene lamp from the hoop on her saddlebag, and lit a match, lighting the gas with care. The flame seemed to darken the area around them, but she hooked it onto the front of the saddle, all the same, to help light Bullet's way. Then, she looped the reins around the pommel loosely so that they no longer needed holding and placed a hand over it, steadying herself. Ida let her eyelids close, allowing herself to fall into sleep, rocking with the steady rhythm of Bullet's steps, trusting him to deliver them to the ground floor.

Colt opened his eyes to see Mrs Vale already astride her horse. The sun was in the sky, and he frowned, sitting up. The fire was still going, coffee had been made, and there was suddenly some sort of bread on the floor beside him.

'Where did you get that?' he asked, frowning.

'A passer-by was generous enough to provide me with some things, and you have been sleeping for far too long, boy. Time waits for no man.' Her eyes were fresh and awake, and she gathered her reins with the speed of an experienced cowboy. Colt grabbed the cup of cooling coffee and took large gulps, hurrying himself in irritation. He stared at her, the old anger flaring again as though he hadn't spent the evening before imagining how he would marry the woman. She watched him incredulously.

'We've about a day's riding ahead of us, and then we should be there.' Her horse threw his head a few times, impatient to get going, and pawed the ground, kicking up orange dust that settled on Colt's piece of bread. He grabbed it, took a bite, and then pushed it to the side of his mouth.

'You shoulda woken me up, woman. Told me what time we were leaving instead of having a leisurely breakfast without me and then hurrying me to eat and pack up.' He chewed a little more and swallowed. 'I do not like being hurried.'

The old woman smirked, the skin on her face making way for the strange and rare expression – a type of smile. 'I would have woken you up had you fallen asleep at the same time as me,' she said. Colt stared at her and shrugged, pretending to be unsure of what she meant. He took another large bite and mixed it with a swig of coffee, now unable to answer.

'As it is,' Mrs Vale continued, 'I think you were up a little later than myself. To let you sleep in was a gift. I was not being quiet. You did it to yourself, and I am not responsible for anybody, not my son, not my horse, and certainly not you. You take responsibility for yourself from now on, boy. I am not your mother.'

Colt wiped his mouth and stared at her. She was right, he thought. She was his wife.

There he was again, that son of a bitch. Her flowers beneath his boots. Her land beneath his weight. His face looked eerily like her own, like her father, like her mother. But that couldn't be, she thought, for he was nothing like them. He was not one of them, not really.

'Our blood is not the same,' she said down the barrel of her gun, pressed to her shoulder, ready to fire. 'Don't take another step forward.'

He stepped. She fired. Clean, through the head once more, barely a blood splatter to show for it. He didn't even flinch, just stepped forward again, that steady walk to her porch.

'Sister,' he said, as though they were old friends, as though they had spent years playing in the fields together. Smoke rose from the back of his head. 'If we lived here together, would that be such a bad thing?'

Ida snarled. Of course, it would. She raised her gun again, feeling the soreness of her skin from the previous fire's kickback. 'I will kill you where you stand,' she said.

'My wife already moved in, woman. You need to remove yourself from the property.'

Ida turned, the world blurring and shifting before her in a strange, slow motion. Beside her, on the porch, stood the rotund figure of Mrs Smithe. The woman smiled and lifted a Winchester, aiming it right at her. She fired. Ida stared at the madam, swaying slightly. When had she moved in? How had she not realised?

Ida jerked awake. She had dreamt that she was falling, she thought, the shared dream of every beast, but made all the more likely by the fact that she was, in fact, astride a horse who was carrying them down an incredibly steep cliff path. She opened her eyes and stared at the surroundings, rubbing her sore neck. Bullet had stopped. Perhaps the surprise at his lack of movement was what had woken her? He appeared to be snoozing beneath her, his head dropped low, his ears flickering occasionally. She smiled at him. The poor thing, she thought, he must be exhausted. She glanced around her, the light still glistening on the small kerosene lamp that still sat hooked onto the saddle, though the sun was just rising. She turned the dial down and watched the light flicker out.

They were almost at the bottom, still on a slant but much diminished from the top. Ida stared out at the city just beyond, its lights glimmering. She could hear the distant noise now, a low, deep roar of people waking up, heading to work, markets beginning…at least, that was how she hoped it would be. The reality, she told herself, might be quite different. She thought momentarily of Steepmount in the morning, the general hubbub of farmers and workers. The women who drank coffee together, as those who had their addictions leaned against the bar, preferring something more substantial for breakfast.

Ida noticed that there was a feeling missing, a lack of something. The burning on her chest was no longer there. She lifted one side of her shirt and placed her hand on the rune, checking for its existence. Then, she turned and stared at the air around her. For the first time in days, she could not see her mother. It was a strange loss, one that she registered with a type of sadness. Perhaps this was what it was like when all the people you knew died. You knew they were there on some plane but preferred the land of the living for yourself. Ida placed a kind hand on Bullet's neck, stroking his warm coat. The heat spiked her fingers and trickled through the skin on her hand, and she felt how cold they were, how chilled her face was. The bourbon and its heady comfort had completely worn off. Bullet's head rose, and Ida leaned forward into his mane, breathing in the scent of earth and salt, a smell that was starting to mean safety and home. She collected the reins in one hand and squeezed ever so gently.

'Bullet,' she said, his ears flickered back to hear her voice. 'We are so close to rest. Once we reach that city, you can have a good meal, a quiet rest in a stall, a nice groom. I promise you.' He whickered in response, and Ida smiled, pretending for a moment that he understood her words.

They carried on down the mountain steadily, the flat earth becoming closer all the time. Eventually, they reached it, and Bullet placed his four hooves squarely on the ground for the first time in hours. Ida rounded her shoulders and pulled the bear pelt around her, staring at the city. It felt so close. The air was definitely colder now, her breath sharp and visible before her. She aimed Bullet and leaned forward, pushing him into a flat-out gallop across the frozen rubble.

'On the road, the grass is sharp,
  The dirt is mean, and the horses smart,
  The land, while flat, will break your bones,
  And there's no friend who can hear your moans.
  On the road, the track is bare,
  The wolves will take what you will not share—'
'Greyson, will you shut up, man?' Billy glared at his companion, who stopped singing immediately. Greyson shrugged. It was a bleak scene, all right, the snowy mountains surrounding them. Greyson had barely slept at all, waiting for the light to come, for Billy to kick him awake. He was more fearful of oversleeping than anything else, afraid of being blamed for missing out on the five hundred dollars. That blasted amount kept driving them through the cold, through the pain.
    'Just thought a little sing-song might help, boss. Clear away the cobwebs.' He scratched the cold skin on his cheek and sighed. Couldn't rest, couldn't stop, couldn't sing.
    'Yeah, and what do you think the woman might do if she heard you singing your way along the path? She could be just around the corner for all we know,' Billy responded in a low hiss, his dark eyes reflecting the brightness of the snow. Greyson nodded, feeling like a schoolboy, scolded for his attentions. He glared. They were on the right path now, he thought. A while ago, they had passed a sign for the city that pointed one way only. He had wondered, though he couldn't say why exactly, whether the sign was a strange sort of trick, maybe by the ghosts that they said frequented the mountains. That was another reason for the singing, too; he wanted to drown out his thoughts.

'Did you see that bit on the sign, boss – at the bottom?' He leaned forward in his saddle, trying to get closer to the horse in front. His horse sped up its gait at the movement.

'Hmmm,' Billy responded, with a lack of commitment common to the powerful man who longs to know it all.

'It said, "I didn't do it",' Greyson said.

'Could mean anything.'

'Yeah,' Greyson said. Could mean anything, that was right. It sat heavy in Greyson's mind, though, weighed on his thoughts. Who didn't do what? They were on a steep incline now, and Greyson shifted his right hand forward, resting it on the horse's neck, giving it more rein for the climb. It wasn't easy carrying a grown man up a hill, he imagined, and less so in the snow. They were taking it at a steady walk. Greyson was secretly fearful of sliding and falling to the iced ground, and he suspected that Billy felt the same, given his sudden agreement to slowing. There, up ahead, was a very tight corner. Billy went round it first, and Greyson was just close enough behind him to hear the words before he saw the wreckage.

'Dang my melt,' Billy breathed. Greyson craned his neck to see what lay before them. A stagecoach tipped onto its side, the horses gone, a few fancy wheels thrown into the snow. Greyson pulled his horse up alongside Billy's, and the two men sat and stared at the scene. The carriage door was yanked open into the air, as though gravity wasn't an issue, the glass smashed out.

'Check for cash,' Billy said briefly, and Greyson nodded, dismounting smoothly. He swallowed, nervous. For a bounty hunter, he certainly hated seeing dead bodies, and this wreckage looked terrible enough to warrant some. He stepped to the back of the carriage and checked the safety box, unlocked and empty, its lid hanging open and bearing no contents but wood.

'Empty,' he said aloud, turning to face Billy. Billy was sitting, smoking a cigarette now, watching.

'Check inside the carriage,' he responded, the smoke coming out of his mouth alongside the words. Greyson nodded and turned, putting one foot onto the side of the carriage and hauling himself up. He held himself prostrate over the gap where the door would once have snuggly fit in and stared into the dim space.

'Gosh, all hemlock,' he said, pausing. He glanced backwards, still holding himself out of the carriage. 'There's a woman in here.'

'Dead?' Billy asked. Greyson tried not to roll his eyes.

'Yeah, dead.' Of course, dead, he thought grimly.

'You gon check her for cash?'

Greyson leaned in a little further and looked at the woman. Her eyes were staring into the middle distance, and she was sitting on the plush seats as though the only thing unusual was her horizontal state. He glanced at her clothing, luxurious and…unkempt. The woman's boot sat on what would have been the other door, her stockinged feet out in the air. Greyson frowned.

'I've got a feeling she's already been shaken down.'

'A lot of women keep money in a garter beneath their skirt,' Billy said plainly, his voice light, as though what he had said was perfectly normal. Greyson pushed himself up and jumped back onto the ground.

'That is just not something that I am willing to do.'

Billy took a drag of his cigarette and moved his horse forward slightly. 'Well, ain't that a shame. I tell you what, if you do, I'll let you keep the most of it. Say it's one hundred dollars; I'll let you keep seventy. How about that?'

Greyson stared at his boss and thought of the offer. What would his mother say to see him pulling up a lady's skirt for the hope of a dollar? It was a hideous idea. 'And if I don't?'

Billy grinned, leaning forward in his saddle jovially. 'Well, if you don't, then I'm gonna have to do it, aren't I? And if I find a hundred dollars, then I'm keeping a hundred dollars.' He grinned and bit his bottom lip. This was the cheeriest Greyson had seen him in days. He shook his head and walked back toward his horse.

'You do what you need to do. I will not behave in that manner toward a lady, be she dead or alive.'

'You're a proud fool, Greyson. Ain't nobody here to see what we do,' Billy responded, dismounting into the snow. He trudged through to the door, hauled himself up, and then looked in. 'She's dead all right. Ain't got no need for anything in this world where she's gone.'

Greyson watched him as he lowered himself into the stagecoach. That man, he thought, was not brought up right. Even if the woman had a thousand dollars strapped to her leg, it wouldn't be worth the hunt for it. Greyson shivered at the thought of touching the cold flesh of that staring old woman. 'Hideous,' he whispered. He watched the carriage. There was no movement for a while. What happened to the coach, he wondered? An inexperienced driver, perhaps, a sharp corner. It appeared that the horses were gone and the stagecoach driver with them. Probably over the edge, Greyson thought as he glanced up at the mountain range about him, imagining falling off the steep path.

'By Harry!'

The shout made Greyson flinch and focus back in on the carriage. He winced.

'You okay, Billy?' he called, nudging his horse forward slightly. The horse's ears went back suddenly, flat against its head, and it began to dance backwards beneath him. Billy's horse, who had been calmly snoozing in the snow, began to do the same, jumping sideways into the mounted pair with a whinny of fright.

'Whoa, boys,' Greyson murmured, leaning over and grabbing the other horse's reins while he could. Greyson tried to soothe them with his voice, holding his legs firm against his own horse, a signal of calm.

'Billy!' he called through the chaos. He stared at the carriage shell, no movement. 'Whoa, boys, calm,' he said softly. Suddenly, they both stopped, standing upright, their ears pointing forward, alert and ready. Greyson frowned. Billy's head appeared out of the carriage door space, and Greyson watched as he pulled himself up and out. He was pale and pallid, his eyes sunken. He dropped into the snow, fell to his knees, and then picked himself up, not bothering to dust the white stuff off his canvas trousers.

He made his way to Greyson and grabbed the reins from his hand, mounting shakily.

'What did you yell for? You spooked the horses.'

'It wasn't me that spooked those horses,' Billy responded, wiping a sweating brow despite the cold. 'I saw a...face. I saw someone. There was someone with me.'

'Yeah, the old woman,' Greyson tried.

'No. No, it wasn't. It was...it wasn't...' Billy stuttered. He pushed his hat hard onto his head and closed his eyes for a moment. 'We have to get out of here.' He dug his heels into his horse's side, and he sprang forward from a walk to a canter almost immediately. Greyson followed, allowing his horse the time to work through the gaits and catch up to the other two. Cantering in the snow was not an easy feat, especially for horses so used to the hot ground.

'Billy!' Greyson called as his horse slipped a little beneath him. 'Was there any money then?'

Billy said nothing to Greyson, leaning forward in his saddle and yelling, 'Work, you damn nag!' at his horse instead. The horse fell into a gallop, and Greyson pushed his horse to match the speed, leaving snow spray falling behind them like heavy clouds threatening rain. Finally, they were closing in on their prey.

Chapter 22

Colt and Mrs Vale arrived at the lake to the east of Blackreach by lunchtime. A rickety bridge crossed over the centre, a pointless sort of bridge that existed only for those willing to risk their dryness. A journey around the outside was just as simple and potentially even made for a shorter time period. Colt stretched his right leg back behind him and dismounted, picking up a stone from the floor and throwing it into the lake with a plop. The water was cloudy, dirty even, misted and dark. The sun shining on its ripples added nothing to its overall impression. He sighed and glanced back at his companion, Mrs Vale, who had ridden at speed the entire time and was silent still. What was up with her? he wondered. Why didn't she want to know as much about him as he wanted to know about her?

'Should I catch us a fish for lunch?' he asked, attempting a smile. Mrs Vale dismounted and began searching in one of her saddlebags.

'No. There's no fish in that lake; it's just a dumping ground for excrement,' she responded, pulling out the canteen and taking a sip.

'Oh,' Colt said, squinting at the dark water. Disgusting, he thought. 'Looks like there's a chap over there fishing, though.' He raised his hand to his hat and tipped it up a little, staring into the distance. There did indeed appear to be a man just on the lake's edge further up, rod in hand, bait in the water. Mrs Vale turned and glanced at him and then shrugged.

'So what? I've lived at the neighbouring Blackreach for all my adult years, and I'm telling you, boy, eating any fish from this lake would be like eating your neighbour's dinner for breakfast.'

Colt wrinkled his nose. She had quite a way with words, he thought, however grim. Mrs Vale pulled some jerky out of the bag and took a bite of one, holding another out to Colt. He took it gratefully and bit into the tough exterior, the salty goodness filling his mouth, causing his taste buds to pop and dance. Where was she getting all these snacks from? he wondered. He took another bite. Wherever it was, he was grateful.

'So, are we going to head to your house now before we go on to your son's?'

Mrs Vale wrinkled her nose. 'You don't need to be seeing my house, boy, it's a waste of time. Anyway, that's exactly where those no-good assholes who caught me will be expecting me to be, and if the Sheriff of Steepmount is looking for us somewhere, he'll start there.'

Strange, Colt thought. The Sheriff of Steepmount. He had almost forgotten about him, and Jonesy. It was as though his head was now just filled with Mrs Vale and whatever she might want, need, desire. He hoped it was him, although something at the top of his mind told him that it was, in fact, not.

'What?' Mrs Vale asked, glancing at him. Colt shook himself. He was staring again.

'Yes, the sheriff. I shouldn't think he'll be looking for me. He's got his hands full with those bounty hunters, no doubt.'

Mrs Vale shook her head. 'Do not be so sure. There is nothing like the vitriol a man feels when a woman has bested him.' She took another bite of her jerky with gusto and strong teeth. 'He might have let you go without any trouble, for a boy escaping from jail? Well, that's just expected. But for me? No. A woman doing the same will cause pain in his heart. They're obsessed with it.' She snorted with derision.

'I don't know...' Colt tried.

'You don't know, boy? How you feel about Ida Vale, would you feel the same about a man that had robbed you in the night?' Mrs Vale asked, her dark eyes knowing and inquisitive.

Colt stared at his jerky and shrugged. 'I believe I would. That horse took me years to train. Anyway, she tried to make me fall in love with her. The insolence! Using my heart against me.'

Mrs Vale smiled, a long wide smile that showed a little teeth, and said nothing.

'And how about you? You want to help me get revenge on a woman? If you're so concerned with the fairer sex, why are you helping me?' Colt continued. The smile remained on Mrs Vale's wrinkled lips.

'Well, boy, I am just telling you how it is, in case you hadn't noticed. Being wronged by a woman in this lifetime causes men to go out of their way to get revenge. I've seen it with my own eyes. I see it now before me. And concerned with the fairer sex I am, because I am she. But be under no illusion; my main concern is, and will always be, my family. If anyone touches a hair on my son's head, then I will know about it. I married his father to get him the rights to that land, and I will not be flung aside in widowhood while an illegitimate thief takes what is rightfully my boy's.' She took a bite and chewed with her mouth open, thoughtfully, as though considering her next words. 'People are complicated, Colt. Didn't you know? They can know and think things that are at odds with each other. They can believe in justice for a sex, and they can kill a woman for trying to take what is rightfully theirs. And that is the point.' She pointed the jerky at him, like an extension of her finger. 'You have to do what you have to do to keep the people you care about safe in this land because there ain't nobody who cares for you. Put yourself first. Recognise that everyone else will do the same.'

Colt felt the sun beat down on the back of his neck and pulled a dirty handkerchief from his pocket, wiping it across the skin. He stared at it when he brought it back around, filthy with dust and wet with his sweat.

'Well, if I got married, I would put that woman first. Yes, I would. My wife would come first in everything, and I should endeavour to get her land, even.' He nodded a firm forward nod and grinned. Mrs Vale tutted at him.

'I shouldn't care myself.' She pushed her left foot into her stirrup and bounced once, elegantly rising into the saddle. Colt watched, impressed by her agility.

'We have a bit more of a ride, but if we reach the place at sundown, I should be happy. A hot meal is what I need, a comfy bed,' she said. Colt just stood, staring at her, chewing on his salted snack with the expression of a five-year-old.

'Get on your blasted horse, boy. We ain't got all the time in the world,' she hissed at him. Colt snapped back to life, nodding. She certainly had some grit. He liked that in a woman – like his mother. No, he thought crossly. Like his wife, that's right. He did as he was told. Mrs Vale moved into a jog, her face turned from Colt. She smiled darkly; the boy was coming along just as she had planned.

The city glistened in the distance. It was cold, but there was something different about it now, further removed from the ice of the hills. Up there, it was almost as if smell did not exist, as though there was nothing but cold and ice, a scentless atmosphere. Now, as she moved closer to The City of Glass, Ida began to smell new aromas.

There was the scent of smoke, almost like cigars, clinging to the air. There were some lingering remnants of roasting fat, too, cloying in the back of her throat, making her stomach rumble. It was getting closer with every stretch of Bullet's legs, and Ida lifted herself in the saddle, forgetting for a moment about the bounty, about revenge, about her mother. She thought only of what she would do once she arrived. She would stable Bullet, buy him a coat to protect him from the weather and allow him to rest and refuel, ready for the journey ahead of them. She would find an inn or saloon with a deep, plush chair settled in front of a roaring fire. She would order meat, bread, whatever the cook could muster. She would get a bottle of straight rye and a glass and would sit alone, enjoying the warmth and steady intoxication, a full stomach, a hazy mind, the ideal combination. She wriggled her toes, imagining the warmth of the fireside, the heat reaching them. They were happily unfrozen, though they had grown cold and were largely untouched by the journey so far.

Ida glanced around for her mother, but she was not to be seen. Ida wore boots that had belonged to her originally. The greatest gift she had ever been given, she often said to her father when he was listening. In reality, they were a last-minute gift, a forgotten birthday one year, when her body was growing faster than either of them could believe. Ida had watched her limbs expand beyond the lines of her clothing, her cotton dresses stretching at seams and pulling at fabric. Next, she noticed her shoes begin to stretch and hurt, her toes aching beneath the leather. The rain rarely came in the north; it was a once-a-year occurrence that the people of Bleakhollow prepared for with excitement. They would ready their buckets, their large containers, their land. In the towns, the people celebrated the idea of one full day of heavy rain to fill their yearly quota. They would stand in the street with open mouths, pointed at the sky. And then some would die, swept away in a flurry of dampness, catching colds and influenzas. The rain was a glorious moment in the year, and its gift was both in the giving and taking away.

At the homestead, the rain meant one thing only. Both Ida and her father would turn over the land, preparing the soil to drink. They would pull the large sheets off their rain barrels, flushing out the old into troughs for the horses. Because of the overspill of water at this time, the mud would come thick and fast. Ida's old boots sank steadily, and it was when she pulled out her feet at the end of the day she noticed that her stockings were covered in mud also, and her toes red and sore, wrinkled at their creases where she had shoved them into ill-fitting shoes. She had forlornly shown them to her father, aware that the response was likely to be that he might pick some up when he was next in town. Ida knew that this was no treat. A pair of tough, probably too large, worn boots would be winging their way to her. Instead, he looked at the scene and murmured that boots were essential, especially at this time of year. He had then disappeared for a moment, reappearing with a brown paper bag. He handed it to Ida with little celebration and told her that it was her birthday present. Ida frowned; her birthday had been two weeks previous, and nothing had been mentioned about it. She sat down and carefully unwrapped the brown paper, and pulled out the gift.

They were incredible. Soft leather, calf-high, a heel for keeping the foot in the stirrup. She pulled them to her nose and closed her eyes, breathing in the scent of the cowhide. She turned them upside down, fingers pressing into the skin of the boot, and saw that they had never been worn. To get a new item of clothing was almost unheard of. Even her father didn't wear clothes that another hadn't once worn. Eventually, she pulled them onto her feet and admired them from above. They were a little big, she thought, but that was a good thing. It was space to grow.

'They're your mother's,' her father said in a soft voice. 'She never got a chance to use 'em. A wedding present from her father, your grandfather, before he passed.'

Ida nodded, silent in her gratitude. And what gratitude she felt each time she viewed them, every time her feet sunk into the mud, each time the sun blared down onto her skin, and she felt no heat beneath the leather. They were ideal. She wriggled her toes again, thankful once more for their hardiness despite their years of wearing.

The city was now upon them. She pulled Bullet into an easy jog and pulled her neck scarf up around her mouth, covering half of her face. She had wondered how easy it might be to enter the city, whether there would be a large gate and guards, some sort of iced fortress as its name suggested, but found that the houses and buildings just started suddenly and that before she knew it, she was on a path riding between little huts and cabins. She pulled Bullet to a walk and nodded at a few strangers who were shuffling down the street, their faces also covered and their bodies wrapped in fur, much like her own. One nodded back, and the other fixed her with a steady and hard stare. Ida kept going.

The scents were much the same as before, only more potent now, woodsmoke and meat lingering in the air and drawing her into the ever-narrowing streets. It was a strange layout, she noticed. It was almost as though the city was once one broad road, and it had then had more and more buildings shoved into it, without any desire to widen the width of the borders. Offshoots of streets would appear to start somewhat randomly, and alleyways would appear before you, just wide enough to fit a horse down.

Ida kept moving forward, on toward the noises of the city, which spread through the air like smoke, flitting and growing as they walked toward the middle. Ida began to notice the buildings go from houses to shops, wooden signs swinging outside on frozen ropes, with pictures instead of words. A needle, a vegetable, an overflowing cup. Here, among the tight-fitting shops, more people roamed. All were covered from head to toe, making it impossible to see their features. Ida paid attention to their clothing, fur, thick leather, and boots that reached up beyond their knees. Unusual, she thought, interesting. She noticed a person staring at her, standing outside a dark shop, its sign bearing the carved image of a bottle. Ida cocked her head to one side and pulled Bullet in, stopping before them.

'Good day,' she said sincerely, leaning forward onto one thigh, casual. The person grunted a response and touched the tip of their hat with black-gloved hands. 'Could you tell me of a stableyard where I might rest my horse?'

'Hmm,' the person said, nodding. 'Go h'up to the left. Straight on. Horseshoe sign.' Their voice was higher than Ida had expected, with a soft, lilting cadence. They appeared to be wearing thick canvas trousers, as Ida was, their high boots muddied. Ida touched her hat in response and moved forward again, taking the narrow street at a steady walk. Bullet was slowing in the cold, and she was starting to worry for his health. He was now far more than a mode of travel to her. He was a friend, a travelling companion, and she would have been stranded long ago without him. Ida knew her debt. There, on the corner, she saw the horseshoe tied upside down and rattling against the wall in a slow rhythm, the wind smashing it from side to side. Bullet lifted his head, sensing it was time to collect.

The wind was getting strong. The horses had dropped from a gallop to a lope now, the steepness of the snowy slope and the strength of the wind battling with their manes. Greyson had called out to Billy, telling him to slow down, to watch his horse's steps. The man was riding like he was possessed, charging his horse and yelling now and then, as though the land before them was flat and green and there were no obstacles in the way at all. To their right side, the mountain stretched up into the sky, its snow-covered peaks disappearing into the clouds and giving the impression that it may never stop. To their left, the mountain fell away into whiteness. Neither Greyson nor Billy had ventured close to that side. Greyson especially did not want to see what lay below, fearing a drop into nothing. There were many things that he could handle, but nothingness was not one of them. His horse tossed his head wildly, and Greyson laid a hand on his neck.

'Billy!' he yelled through the growing wind. 'We have to slow down. The path is getting steeper still.' Billy's gaze flew around, and he glared at his protégé, shaking his head.

'Five hundred dollars,' he yelled. Greyson sucked in the cold air and leaned forward on his horse, driving him to match Billy's speed. The path was just wide enough for two horses, and a carriage would have been fine had the driver been wary.

'Slow down – if we lose these horses, we lose the money,' he shouted. Billy's eyes flickered to his face, and he leaned back in his saddle for a moment, allowing his horse's speed to drop back a little. 'Billy, what did you see back there? You have been riding like—'

'What I saw is a waste of our time. I saw something that you do not wish to know about. We have to get that woman and get out of here – I don't even want to talk to you about it,' Billy hissed. The wind flew alongside them, making his last words inaudible. Greyson nodded, feeling the tension between them, gathering the meaning of the words from his expressions and body movements. The horses were now moving at a fast jog, both sweating beneath the men. Greyson laid a hand on his horse's wet coat.

'Listen,' he called, trying to be heard over the wind and sound of the hooves in the snow. 'They're sweating. It's so cold that I'm afraid they could get sick before we even get there. We need to slow down and recover before we push them aga—'

'You are not the boss of this outfit!' yelled Billy, rage glowering across his face. He reached into his pocket and pulled out the bounty poster, shoving it into Greyson's chest with an outstretched arm. 'That is the only thing you need to worry about – catching that woman. Anything else does not concern you. I will hear no more from you!' He leaned forward again and pushed his horse onward into a struggling gallop up the slope. Ahead, Greyson noticed that the clouds had cleared, and he could finally see beyond the mountains, beyond their height. Dead ahead, it looked as though a city awaited them, just a glowing light in the blanket of white. Greyson pointed, though Billy wasn't looking.

'Look! Dead ahead – it's the City of—' he called out. Billy turned in the saddle, his face full of rage and bile, his horse still forging ahead and being kicked at every opportunity.

'I told you to keep your mouth—' and then, the land flattened out. The horse saw what Greyson had noticed moments before, that before them was a drop into a steep winding path. He pushed his four hooves into the snow, straightening his legs, and skidded from full gallop into a desperate attempt at stopping. His body slipped to the side, and he fell onto the ground, hitting the snow at a strange angle, whinnying in shock. Greyson watched as Billy turned too late, lost his balance, and slipped with his horse. The horse came to a stop on the knife-edge, where Ida had stood previously. Greyson pulled his own ride to a halt and watched open-mouthed as Billy carried on moving, his body flung from the unsteady horse straight over the side of the cliff. The horse stood up immediately, turning and walking back to Greyson, its side covered in snow. Greyson held the bounty poster with a shaking hand and looked at the face of the woman, Ida Vale, staring back at him.

Chapter 23

Bullet was wrapped in the finest coat the stables had available. It was third hand, the stable boy said with a shrug, and Ida shrugged back, caring not for new things or fancy items, as long as it was warm. She fingered the material, thick and soft against Bullet's coat and smiled. He had his head already deep into a bucket of oats and flaxseeds, and Ida lay her cheek against his neck, silently thanking him for his hard work. The stable was chilly but not as cold as the nights he had just experienced. The rest would do him well.

'So you want the full package?' the boy asked, kicking a bit of mud to the side of the stall.

'Yes,' Ida said, pulling her face away from Bullet's warm skin. 'Whatever it is you do – he has a big journey coming up, and he needs to recover. Food, water, warmth. That's it.'

'It'll cost,' said the boy, his chin jutting out as though he expected a fight.

'Who said it wouldn't? My name is Colton. I'll be staying nearby. This,' she reached into her pocket and pulled out a hundred-dollar bill, watching the boy's eyes widen, 'is for my horse. I expect him to be taken care of as you would a child, do you hear me? I want that saddle to be shining by the time I come back, that bridle to be as clean as the day I bought it.'

The boy's dirty hand reached out, and he snatched the money from her, nodding with wide eyes. It was a strange thing to have money, she thought. Obviously, it wasn't truly her own, not really. That hundred-dollar bill could have been in one of the envelopes that she stole for all she knew. She wasn't even confident of how much she had now, only that every time she reached into her pocket, there was money waiting for her. She gave Bullet one final pat and walked toward the door of the stable, pulling it open on its squeaking hinges. At the last moment, she turned back to the boy, who was still staring at the money, dumbstruck.

'Where is there to stay near here?' she asked, realising that she hadn't seen many saloons as yet.

'We got a place up the way that takes all sorts,' he said, glancing up. Then, he looked at the money again. 'But if you're handing out this kind of cash for a horse, it ain't for you. There's The Palisade in the centre of town. They won't even let me in.'

Ida grinned. 'Sounds just right.' And it did. She realised that she didn't care how much money she had left; what did it matter? She was staying in this ice town for one night only, and then the road back would be as rough as it had been on the way. Both Bullet and herself deserved something special for once, and not at the whim of Mrs Smithe. And then, she would take back her homestead. Every night would be the same from then on out, as she pleased.

The Palisade was a sizeable palatial building, grey and oppressive. The outside of it was like nothing Ida had ever seen, its walls curved and strange, with faces stuck on at odd angles. It was terrifying in a peculiar way. She stared up at the large oak door. There were no signs at all, no way of knowing that this was what she was looking for, and if it weren't for a couple of people pointing at the building, she would never have guessed. She swallowed and lifted her fist, knocking on the door. There was a creak, and a small hatch opened right before her face.

'Yes?' a voice said. Ida tried to peer in but could see nothing but darkness.

'I'm looking for a room for the night,' she said. There was a small silence in response. 'Hello? A room for the night,' she tried again.

'Have you booked?' the voice said.

'I don't know how I would have booked,' Ida replied, 'but I can pay.'

There was another creak, and the small hatch disappeared into a door, which swung open. A hatch, within a door, within a door, Ida thought. Odd. She stared at a tall, skinny man dressed in a smart suit, his shoulders somewhat hunched over. He looked her up and down.

'You don't look like you can pay,' he said. Ida smiled tightly.

'You don't look strong enough to open that door, but you managed it. I can pay, sir, for a room for the night.'

'Hmm,' he said and stepped aside finally to let her in. The space was minimal and dark, and when the door was closed, there was a moment when Ida reached for her pistol, ready to fire into the darkness. Then, the man pulled aside a curtain and light filled her senses. She stepped forward. Ida had never seen such opulence. Even the saloon at Incan's Brook, which was, by all Nameless Stretch standards, incredibly fancy, was nothing compared to this. Above her was a large chandelier, glistening and glinting in the sky. And it did indeed look like the sky, for a mural covered the ceiling, giving the impression of space and freedom. Ida tried not to look impressed and turned back to the man beside her.

'You do food?' she asked curtly.

'Of course,' he said in a similar tone.

'Good. I shan't eat here, in this hall. Show me to my room and fetch me a bottle of your finest straight rye, a prime cut of meat, and all the trimmings. Run me a bath for afterwards.' She pulled another note from her pocket and pushed it into his hands. His reaction was not the same as the stable hand's had been. He simply pocketed it and nodded without a smile.

'Follow me to your room. Do you have a bag, or is it just...' He indicated the worn saddlebag thrown over Ida's shoulder.

'I have all I need,' she responded, tipping her hat. It was pleasing, she thought, to be Colton. To be out in the world alone and trusted to be her own protector. The man barely showed a glimmer of recognition that Ida had spoken and stepped ahead of her, leading her through the bare yet luxurious foyer to a large staircase. Ida followed willingly, intrigued by what she might find, hoping for a plush bedroom. At the top of the staircase, the man directed her to a door, and she opened it to find herself facing a long corridor.

'Yours will be the last on the left. We will bring up your food and drink presently. A fire should already be lit, but do let us know if there is anything we can do.' The man nodded, gave

Ida a look as though she had just bad-mouthed his mother, and stepped away back down the stairs. She walked down the hallway, noting the dark mahogany walls. Occasionally, there were nails in it, as though a picture had been put up and then taken down in haste. The grandeur of downstairs already seemed to be lacking upstairs. Eventually, Ida reached the last door on the left. It had a sign hammered onto the front at an angle. It read *The Suite*. She turned the old handle and pushed, using her shoulder as the wood stuck a little in its frame. The room behind it may have been luxurious once, a hundred years ago, but now it was anything but. Ida stepped in and dropped her saddlebag, pushing the door closed. There was indeed a fire burning in the fireplace, with an oversized wooden rocking chair placed before it. The bed was a single iron frame, the blankets pulled tight around the mattress, displaying a few holes, wear and tear. Ida frowned and touched the wallpaper, which appeared to be wooden but was, in fact, fake, a flaking painting of wood. She sighed. Well, it was a warm bed for the night, and the door had a lock. What more had she expected? She took a seat in the rocking chair and felt the warmth of the fire wash over her. Ida closed her eyes, waiting for her meal.

Greyson stared. What was he going to do? What, in the wisdom of The Nameless Stretch, was he supposed to do now? He dismounted, stepping toward Billy's horse with a calming voice. The horse seemed unaware of what had just happened and stood in the snow with his head down, his eyelids dropping. Greyson stepped to his side and laid a hand on his neck, causing the horse to whicker. His skin was sweating, a light sheen having developed on the surface. Greyson pulled the reins forward and placed them into the snow so that the horse would understand that he had been hitched. Then, with a stomach full of bile, he stepped toward the edge that Billy had disappeared over. He leaned over, his feet almost at the drop, hoping to see the man holding on below, desperately staring upwards at him with angry and humiliated eyes. It was not to be.

Below, there was nothing, not even a patch of darkness. Greyson stepped back, his heart thumping so loudly that he could barely focus. He staggered forward, causing Billy's horse to throw back his head, ears flattened against it, and eye him.

'No boy, shhh. I just – I need…a moment,' he said, falling to his knees in the cold snow. Greyson stared at the two horses, the backdrop of the snowy mountain they had just climbed before him. *Five hundred dollars.* The words came to him as though they had been whispered in his ear. Greyson flinched and looked around him, certain somebody had just spoken. *Five hundred dollars,* the voice said again. Five hundred. Greyson wiped his eyes, streaming from the cold, and frantically turned his head. The whisper came again as though the lips were right up against his ear.

'Get up, you stupid sonofabitch.'

It was Billy's voice, and there was absolutely no doubt about it. Greyson staggered to his feet. Was he going mad? Was he losing his mind? There was no one there; he was alone on the mountain. He flicked around once more to make sure, but there was nothing but space, the two beasts staring at him, awaiting his next move.

'Right,' he said. 'Okay.' He grabbed Billy's horse's reins and pulled them over to his own horse, then mounted doggedly, pulling his weary body up. Ahead of him, in the distance, lay The City of Glass. It was time to collect, and at least now he had a horse to put the woman on. They began their steady descent, the three of them, Greyson clinging to the saddle with one hand and both sets of reins with the other. His heart smashed inside his chest, and he tried to ignore the slope to the left of him, the inevitable death that lay beyond the horse's hoofbeats. He heard Billy no more.

They were close now, Mrs Vale had said with a flash of a smile. She had spent the last hour or so talking about her son and his childhood in some great detail. It was the most she had spoken since they had met. Colt listened with a distracted ear, paying little attention to her actual words. Instead, he rode alongside her at a fast walk, the horses' heads bobbing up and down together in a pleasing rhythm. Colt made a great display of pretending to listen to the woman, watching her body language, nodding, and smiling at the right moments. It appeared that he was doing a good job, as Mrs Vale seemed pleased to continue. In reality, though, he was inspecting the curve of her neck, the blushed hue of her cheek. The way her lips pursed when she spoke of some memory that she disapproved of. The hollow laugh that never seemed to reach her eyes and yet showed her teeth, as grey as an overcast day. Each of these things was more beautiful to Colt by the moment. Eventually, she stopped talking with such enthused fervour, and Colt noticed that a pinprick took up her attention on the horizon.

'We are here,' she said, more to herself than to Colt. In an instant, she flew, her horse speeding into a gallop. Colt barely touched his own, but it sprang forward beneath him without being asked, which irked him somewhat. It was bad manners, something that his own Trigger would never have done. In any case, he allowed him to follow, coughing at the dust that Mrs Vale's horse kicked up. The pinprick quickly turned into a spot, and then Colt began to see the farm come to life before him. Mrs Vale showed no signs of slowing her horse down as they approached, and even as Colt pulled on his reins to slow his beast, he watched her skid into a stop from a full gallop, a cloud of dust announcing her arrival.

'Boy!' she yelled, dismounting and patting down her skirts. Colt stared at the house, or rather, hut. It was quite sweet, he thought. It was small, aged, but well-built and clearly with care, the little porch highlighted by charming details such as flowers carved into the step. Colt dismounted and walked toward it, leaning in closer to get a good look at the carvings. The door slammed open suddenly, causing him to stand to attention, his eyes wide and blinking. The man before him seemed huge. His arms were flexed, and large hands poised beneath a Winchester rifle, and he was pointing it right at Colt's head. It was his eyes, Colt thought, that were more terrifying than the gun. He looked as though he would kill a man for the joy of it, like there were no qualms at all to be had with hurting a stranger. Colt sniffed and raised his hands over his head. He thought about going to his pistols, but one look at those eyes turned him cold and fearful.

'Who's this?' the man asked, his voice gruff and deep. Mrs Vale stepped up onto the porch and gave her son a light kiss on the cheek before turning her attention to Colt. Colt noticed that she didn't immediately ask him to lower his gun, which seemed like an oversight and a bit of an insult.

'He's after your beloved sister, my dear boy. He's after revenge.'

The man frowned. 'Why is he here then? She won't be heading back this way soon. I took care of that.'

'Did you, boy?' asked Mrs Vale. 'Lower the gun, will you, and I'll make us all a nice stew.' She placed a motherly hand on one of his arms and smiled at him, apparently undisturbed by the manic look in his cruel eyes. The man nodded and lowered the gun to his side, a tight smile appearing on his face.

'You know my sister?' he asked Colt, stepping forward. Colt lowered his hands and did his best to stand up straight, rounding his shoulders back like a much braver man.

'Sort of. She robbed me, and I've got a bounty on her head.'

The man laughed as though it was the best joke he had heard in months. 'I like that. She robbed you? She's barely the size of you, man. You hear that, Mama?'

'Oh, I know all about it, son. This is Colt. He is a farmer from somewhere down south. Colt, this is my dear son, of whom I have told you so much about. We call him Trick.' She nodded at both of them and then flapped her hands at them as though they were schoolboys. 'Now off you go, leave me to make this here meal and sort out the rooms. I know all about my son's style of keeping house, and it leaves much to be desired.' She disappeared inside the hut, and Trick snorted with derision before pulling up one of the wooden chairs on the porch and sitting down. He pulled a cigarette from his pocket and lit it without offering Colt one. Colt took the other chair, feeling nervous about being without Mrs Vale and her protection. This man seemed to be unhinged.

'So, you've been riding with my mother,' Trick said, staring off into the darkening distance at the retreating sun. It wasn't a question, more a statement of truth.

'I have,' Colt said, patting down his pockets absentmindedly. He didn't appear to have any tobacco on him, though it certainly would have helped his nerves. He stared at the smoke forming before the two men greedily but was too afraid to ask. 'But uh – that's all we did.'

'What?' Trick said, staring sideways at him. 'What does that mean?'

Colt swallowed. 'I don't know.'

'What else would you do with my mother?' Trick asked, his full attention on him now.

'I didn't mean anything, I just meant…I don't know.'

Trick took a long, angry drag of his cigarette and jutted his chin forward as though looking for a fight. 'You don't seem that smart to me. What makes you think you can take on my sister? She is tough. She robbed you, after all.'

Colt scratched his head and sighed. 'She ain't so tough. She seemed more…' He ran out of words and just sat, staring at the horses, still tacked up, dozing in the dirt beyond them.

'What happened to her anyway? How'd you two meet?'

'She was a whore out at Steepmount. Robbed me in my sleep. Took my horse and everything. My clothes.'

Trick grinned widely and nodded. 'Well, ain't that something. I only met her once, but I feel sort of proud of her. Dad would be pleased.'

'Didn't you…um…' Colt tried.

'Kill him? Yeah. He did the dirty on my mother and me. Left us for some young witch, moved out here, visited every now and then and just…stopped. Seemed I might never get my hands on the land after that. I couldn't see how we would ever see the man again. It ain't right to have two wives. A wife and a mistress, that is to be expected, but two wives is too much trouble. What about my land? What about my rights? No point in being the firstborn son if you got nothing to show for it; you may as well be a woman.' He took another deep drag and then flicked the stub out ahead of him, watching the sparks spring from it as it hit the ground. Colt nodded and thought of his own mother. She would never have allowed another wife to be a part of his father's life, not for any money. She would have cleared the idea of a mistress out of his head with a bullet, too.

'Well, your mother reckons she's coming back for revenge on you,' Colt said, giving him a single, firm nod of the head to show he meant business.

'Ah yeah, well. Maybe that's the case. I ain't welcoming you both for too long, though. I got me a wife coming at some point.'

'You have?'

'Yup. Oh, from somewhere near the Docks of Astray, it is some farm woman. She's a bit younger than myself, but that's all right. Her father came along and said he heard someone had taken over the farm and was looking for a wife. I said not without seeing her, no. I ain't signing up to take on more pigs than I can keep in the sty, I said. He'd already made the journey, oh it's about a day or so, so he told me all about her, showed me a photo. If she ain't a beauty, then I don't know who is. Trust me, boy, you have never seen a woman like her.' He grinned. 'Let alone touched one. I am looking forward to having her here. A woman's touch is what this place needs.'

Colt tried a smile. 'What's her name?'

Trick scoffed and shrugged. 'Dunno. I don't really see why it matters. He tells me, but...' The man paused to pick something out of his teeth and flicked the invisible nothing into the air. 'I don't remember.' He gave Colt a sideways look. 'You got a wife?'

Colt found himself glancing at the house, thinking of Mrs Vale, working her magic behind closed doors. He imagined her making the bed with a clean, sharp edge, the soft mattress...her sinking into it.

'Oi,' Trick said, pulling him out of his fantasy. 'What's the matter with you?'

'Oh, no. I don't have a wife,' he said dumbly.

'Yeah, you don't look like you do.'

Colt stared down at his clothes, trying to work out what exactly that meant. He frowned. This man was a bully, he thought. He was a bit of a brute.

'What does that mean?' he asked, feeling suddenly angry and brave. Trick grinned from ear to ear, the happiest that Colt had seen him since he arrived, at the display of annoyance.

'It don't mean nothing, boy, you just look like you could use a wash. There's a bucket outback. Help yourself.'

The two men started as they heard the door swing shut behind them, and Colt turned to see Mrs Vale lighting the kerosene lamp out front. She had a cigarette hanging out of the corner of her mouth and was now wearing an apron, her grey hair neatened and piled expertly on top of her head. She looked even more stunning than before, Colt noticed. A wave of lilac hit his nose as she moved.

'You found her things then, Mama,' Trick said.

'I sure did. Stew is on the table, so just you boys come in and take your fill.'

The two men stood and made their way inside the house. The kitchen was as Colt had expected it: nothing but handmade rugs and wooden walls, a bright fire and a long table. The scent was rich and wonderful; meat and gravy filled his nose. There was something beautiful about the scene, he felt, as though he were stepping into a little slice of home. The table was laid, with bowls of steaming stew set before them and a bottle of liquor laid out beside three glasses. Colt's stomach rumbled, and he sat down gratefully, grabbing his spoon and starting. Mrs Vale sat down and rolled her eyes at Trick, indicating Colt with her head.

'You'll have to excuse his manners; I put it down to hunger.' She reached for her spoon without looking and inadvertently knocked it on the floor, causing it to clatter.

'You getting old, Mama,' Trick laughed as she leaned down to collect it. Reader, you can guess what happened next. She grasped the spoon with her right hand and then glanced up as she did so, staring at the bottom of the table. Neither of the men saw it or even noticed her pause, both so concerned with their supper. Mrs Vale stared at the crude carvings before her.

'Well, well,' she whispered with a grin. As you guessed, she knew those symbols all too well.

Chapter 24

Greyson flicked his collar up and pulled it around his face. Despite the chilled air, his hands were clammy and damp, and he shivered. What he needed was rest, he thought. Rest, a meal, a little warmth. All this was far too much. How was he supposed to find this woman, take her for the bounty, travel back this way...it just seemed so impossible all alone. And yet. Five hundred dollars. The voice was no longer whispering in his ears, and for that, he was grateful. He turned in the saddle and stared back up the long path they had traversed. His faith in the horses was just right. He had trusted them, and they were delivering him to safety. At times, they had broken into a trot, which had filled him with dread, but he had squeezed his pelvis upwards, closed his eyes, and rested a hand on the mane of his horse, trusting his body.

Greyson stared out at the city ahead. It glowed in the darkness, just out of reach. He longed for it, desperate to be wrapped up in a bed. But she was there, he thought. She was there somewhere, doing something, waiting for him to arrive. The horse beneath him lurched forward, and Greyson caught his breath, grabbing onto a fistful of mane with the reins. They were so close now, so close to the bottom, to levelling out, to being able to race to the city. Greyson would find her, and he wouldn't do it Billy's way either. He'd do it with a little bit of class, a little decorum. He would be polite but firm.

'You better come with me, woman. I'm not gonna hurt you. I've got this horse you can ride, and I promise that I will protect you on the road,' he said aloud, practising his speech. He nodded. Yes, that was it. Firm but fair. He pushed his heels down, feeling brave and ready. This was it.

'Yah boys!' he yelled, and beneath him, his horse moved up a gait, completing their journey down the steep path without a second wasted. They scattered onto the level floor, and Greyson pushed them into a gallop. Up ahead, The City of Glass waited for his arrival.

Ida stared at the auburn liquid in her glass, glinting in the firelight, and grinned. Finally. Her stomach was full, the residual slicks of gravy spread around her mouth. She licked her lips and sighed contentedly, sparing a thought for Bullet in the hopes that he was doing the same. She took a large sip of the straight rye and let the peppery taste dance around her tongue. She held it in her mouth and savoured it. This was an expensive bottle, she thought. This was no cheap homemade bourbon.

The room might not have been as luxurious as she had hoped, but the meal and the bottle made up for it. With a swallow came the welcome fire. It lingered in her throat and poured into her chest, warming it. Ida took another sip almost immediately, wanting the experience again. The fire cracked before her. A knock came at the door, and she sighed, picking up her hat from the table beside her and placing it on her head. Her hair was no longer a totally shaved scalp. It was starting to grow back and was taking on a strange velvety texture.

'Enter,' she said gruffly, placing down her glass. A young woman came into the room, dressed in a low-cut bodice and full skirt. She did a strange curtesy, and Ida frowned.

'Good evening. Are you in the market for some company?' the girl said. Ida shook her head.

'Nope.'

'Oh. Well, they told me to draw a bath for you, and it's been done. It's available just down the hallway there.' The woman smiled, waiting.

'Okay. I'll head on down when I'm ready. Listen, can you rustle me up a spare razor?'

The woman shifted. 'A razor?' There was a strange tension in the air suddenly, and Ida frowned, leaned forward to grab her glass again.

'A razor. You heard of one? Something that I would use to shave with.'

'Well, yes. Of course. I just um...' the woman stared at Ida for a moment and then glanced around the room. She appeared to shrug, a movement that was barely visible to the eye. 'I can get you one if you like.'

Ida sat up straight, drained her glass and swallowed with one loud gulp. 'I don't know why on earth I would have asked if I didn't want one,' she said in a deep, irritated voice.

'No, of course. I'll um…put one next to the bath, shall I?'

'Of course.'

The woman nodded and then cocked her head to one side, pausing. 'I did not mean to upset you.'

Ida shifted, taken aback. It was rare for such a moment to happen in The Nameless Stretch, a genuine, concerned action.

'No- no…' Ida felt for the woman, for her role in life. She had been there not months before. 'Listen, you have a tough job. I know it. I'm not here to make it harder. It's been a long time since I slept, I guess – if I was snappy with you, well, I am sorry.'

'Oh,' the woman waved her hands in front of her, dismissing the sentiment. 'You would not believe some of the people I have to deal with. You are not the worst of them.'

'I know exactly who you have to deal with, trust me.'

The two stared at each other for a moment, and then the young woman clapped her hands together, breaking the spell between them. 'I shall fetch you that razor, and your bath water is hot. Feel free to head on down when you are ready.' She left the room with a smile. Ida watched the door close. That was a strange interaction, she thought. It was almost as though she knew who she was. Perhaps she recognised her from the bounty posters? No…that couldn't be it. Surely. Ida removed her hat and scratched the short hairs that were growing from her scalp.

Colt stared at the dried old hessian sack that had been thrown before the fire. It wasn't quite what he had hoped for in terms of a bed. Mrs Vale had shown him around after dinner with stilted enthusiasm. She was very clear on where he was allowed to go and where he should stay. There were only three rooms anyway, he thought, but when she showed him her bedroom, what was clearly previously the master suite (although that was a grandiose term for a room with a straw mattress and wonky wardrobe without doors), she had given his arm a sharp pinch.

Trick was staying in the other room, which held a single iron bed, far too small for his frame. Colt lay down and sighed. The fire was dying beside him, and he could hear the scratch of critters beneath the floorboards. Rats, he thought. Or mice. Whatever it was, he didn't want anything to do with it. He pulled his gun from his holster, lay it across his chest, held onto it with one hand, and then pulled his jacket around him like a blanket. The floor was hard and unforgiving, but warm enough in the heat of Bleakhollow. Colt stared at the ceiling. His bones ached. Was this the adventure that he had hoped for when lying in bed at home, stifled by the family unit? It wasn't what he had envisaged, but still…it was undoubtedly adventure.

All he had dreamed of was the opportunity to fall in love. Love a woman, find a wife, ride his horse. All that stuff about the jailhouse, being robbed, that would be a fine story for another time. He was almost grateful for it now, becoming fond of the very uncomfortable moment he was currently in, in hindsight. Which was odd, he thought, given that the moment was still upon him. And hadn't he fallen in love? Absolutely. There she was, just next door, lying in bed and sleeping like an angel. Well, maybe not like an angel, but certainly like a wife. She was already trained in the ways of the household, a fine rider, brave and determined. What more could you ask for? Children didn't really appeal anyway, why would they? They were a woman's business, not a man's. They'd have more money for food, and that was the most important thing.

Yes. He closed his eyes. He could see them here once that whore had been dealt with. They would swiftly move the son out, send him packing, and claim the land. Or perhaps they would visit her own house, and he would become a city man, beloved by all who knew him. Yessiree, there were some opportunities to be had from becoming that woman's husband, and in the morning, he would ask for her hand in marriage. He opened his eyes and felt the weight of his gun in his hand. Maybe he could ask now. He strained his ears and listened. There was certainly some noise drifting in from next door, wasn't there? It was subtle and quiet, but all the same, it was something. She definitely wanted him to visit; that's why she had shown him where the room was, surely? Colt nodded to himself. Yup, quite right.

He stood up, holstered his gun and stepped lightly over the floorboards to the bedroom. Beneath the wooden frame, he saw the soft glow of light. He gave a light tap on the wood and turned the handle, pushing open the door gently. There sat the fully clothed and still awake Mrs Vale. She wasn't paying attention to the door, her eyes focused on a candle before her, hands hovering above it. It was as though she was in a trance. There appeared to be stones before her, Colt noticed, with interest. He stepped forward and hesitated. The air around her seemed to be growing misty, and a sort of fog appeared.

'Mrs...Mrs Vale?' Colt tried shyly, the words coming out as a whisper.

Suddenly, the fog disappeared, and her eyes flicked upwards and made contact with his. Her stare sliced through him, and he backed away, skin tingling. The door clicked behind him, and he turned, seeing that there was no one there. It was closed. He turned back to Mrs Vale and smiled apologetically.

'I uh...I didn't mean to interrupt your...um,' he stammered.

'I'm making sure that woman comes to find us,' she responded, still staring at him. Her eyes were larger than usual, the pupils dilated and steady. The candles flickered before her.

'How are you...how?' Colt asked, feeling cold despite the humidity.

'I have my ways.' She gave him a tight smile. 'What do you want, boy, why did you come in here?'

'I...' Colt swallowed and took a deep breath, straightening up his posture. 'Now, I know that you might not be expecting this, but I have to tell you that over the last few days, I have fallen in love with you. I have never felt anything like it, Mrs Vale. And I know...' He took a breath, feeling the rambling begin, 'I know that you are not the same age as me, and that I might not be a worthy prospect for a woman of such experience and…power. But I know I can make you happy, and I believe that you can make me happy. I don't have a ri—'

Mrs Vale raised her right hand, commanding silence. Colt obeyed with an uncomfortable nod of the head. She licked her dry lips thoughtfully, considering the words that were about to spring from them.

'Do not go on, boy. It is the middle of the night, and any such engagement could be a flight of fancy. An error. A haze of tiredness. You—'

'It is not so; I have been feeling this way—' Colt interrupted. Mrs Vale raised her hand again, silencing him.

'I am not finished. I know the way you feel. Stay until this woman is dealt with, and should you still feel the same, we shall discuss it then.' Mrs Vale nodded, stern and severe, not a glimmer of pleasure on her face from the compliment he had paid her. Colt stared in disbelief.

'I had hoped that—'

'Do not make me repeat myself, boy. Go, back to bed with you. Or you shall be sleeping in the stables.'

Colt's shoulders dropped, his confidence gone. He nodded and turned on his heel, exiting the room with little noise.

Mrs Vale stared at the closed door and curled her top lip, irritated. The spell had worked too well, if anything. In fact, it had never worked so well. The boy was just supposed to want to stay near her until she could break it, ensure they had someone else for Ida to haunt. He was not meant to come creeping into her bedroom in the night asking for her hand in marriage. She shuddered. He must have had nothing in his head but fluff, far easier to lead astray than anyone she had ever met. Marriage? Indeed! Even Mr Vale had taken more convincing. What an idiot boy.

She stared at the candles before her. Right, where was she? Ah yes. Ida. She stared at the runes before her and focused, calling on the winds. *Bring her back here. Make her dream of the revenge she seeks. Bring her back and bring her quickly, for we are sharpening our knives.* The runes glowed with heat, and the candles flickered, smoke rising from their flames. The Nameless Stretch listened.

Ida's eyes snapped open. She sat up in the cooling bath water. All that straight rye, she thought, raising her hand to her aching head. And that dream again. The same one as ever, her brother, riding through her flowers. The gunshot that never happened. The cold stare of his eyes as he stepped toward her. And that old woman, that was a new feature, reappearing with a gun on her porch. She had shot her, again. It had woken her up with a nasty shake.

Ida shivered and climbed out of the bathtub, reaching for a towel in the dying candlelight. As she dried her chilled and clammy skin, she thought of her homestead. Every dream made her more and more confident that she should be travelling back there to reclaim it. Every moment she didn't was starting to feel like another betrayal. She dressed quickly, re-binding her breasts, pulling on the now unclean canvas shirt. Ida ran a hand over her newly shaved head. It had been a small challenge for her, using a cut-throat razor for the first time. The back of her head was sore, and specks of blood were still forming over the fresh skin. Ida touched them and inspected her fingers. They would dry. For a first-time effort, it was fine. There were still places that she could feel were unshaven, but Ida cared not. Once she was back at her home and order had been restored, she could do what she wished with her hair.

She stared at the rune on the table beside the bath and picked it up, placing it back against her skin, beneath the binding. She could have sworn that her flesh was starting to look flatter when it was bound. The rune was cold, and Ida thought momentarily of her mother, somewhere in the room, ever watching. Since arriving in The City of Glass, she hadn't seen her at all. The straight rye probably wasn't helping in that area anyway, she thought. Ida pulled on the heavy door and headed back down the long corridor to her room. The fire had been stoked, another log placed on it, and the room crackled with a cosiness that Ida had not felt in such a long time. She sat down on the bed and lay back, watching the flames dance among the embers, licking the fresh wood like a grateful dog. She closed her eyes and fell into a heavy sleep almost immediately, her thoughts full of her homestead, the land, hers to reclaim.

Chapter 25

Greyson arrived at the city with little fanfare. It was unwelcomingly cold, the streets covered in slick ice and scattered grit, the day's footfall having made it more slippery. Occasionally, his horse would skid, and his heart would thud heavily in his chest, causing him to suck in the cold air, a sudden shock for his weary lungs. He pulled his jacket over the hand that held Billy's horse, making his way down the narrow alleyways. The shops and houses were lit up from within, causing the streets to be brighter still, aiding him in his journey. There were barely any people out, and Greyson struggled to see the signs in the light, searching for a stableyard of any kind. He rode on, squinting at the gently rocking wooden images.

'Lost something?' a voice said. Greyson paused, halting the horses and glanced around. There, in front of a darkened window, stood a figure shrouded in clothing. Their face was covered.

'Looking for a stable. You know where I can find one?' Greyson asked.

'Just down the way there. Not often we have so many strangers in the city,' the figure responded.

'You having a lot of strangers today?' Greyson leaned forward, smiling despite the pain of his cracking lips.

'Stables that way,' the figure said again, before turning and walking off in the opposite direction. Greyson watched for a moment, nodding. Now, that was good news. He nudged the horses forward. They slipped a little on the ice but held up well enough. It was time to collect his prey. Greyson was feeling braver now and lifted his chin against the elements, his dry tongue running over his lips. There it was, right ahead, the swinging image of a horseshoe.

Ida sat up suddenly, awake. What was this? She usually slept well, without all these bloody interruptions. She stared at the small window in her room. It was still dark, and the fire beside her still burned bright, the room warm and soft. But her stomach was uneasy, queasy even, beneath her. And then, the gentle pulse of the rune began. Against her skin, it started to heat. Ida swung her legs out of bed and put her hand to her head, scanning the room.

'Mother?' she whispered desperately, forcing herself to focus hard on the area. A very gentle outline began to sketch out beside her, just before the fire. Her mother's image was dim, but there. 'I don't feel so good,' Ida said. Her mother nodded, her expression still. 'The rune is beginning to heat up again.'

'Then danger is present, Ida. You must heed the warning.'

Ida nodded. Heed the warning. Where was the danger, though? She stood up and walked toward the door, checking that the sliding lock was still in place. It was. Ida span around. Perhaps it was time to leave.

'Oh sure, we can stable them all right. They're beauts.' The boy raised a hand and stroked the muzzle of Billy's horse.

'I'm surprised to see you're still open – grateful and all, but surprised,' he said, glancing around at the lamp-lit space. A few horses whickered in the lamplight, snoozing beneath their coats.

'We ain't usually up this late, it's true. Someone wanted their horse cared for overnight, so, you know. They got the money; we do the job.'

Greyson handed both reins to the boy and nodded, glancing around. 'That right. New horse to the area, was it?' The boy led both horses to a shared stable, and Greyson followed closely behind.

'Oh sure, he's a beauty. That one, right there.' The boy nodded in the direction of a bay Delath Walker, wearing a plush coat. Greyson stared at it for a moment.

'That's a beautiful horse.'

'Ain't it. The owner certainly cared that it had the best care, anyway.'

Greyson nodded, lifting his hat slightly off his head to reveal his hairline, a subtle indication of trust and nonchalance.

'You in the market for any horses at all? I got this spare one, as you see.'

The boy began to untack Billy's horse and shrugged. 'I can get my boss to come look at it tomorrow if you got the time.'

'Hmmm.' Greyson nodded, glancing at the Delath Walker again. 'Truthfully, I'd be interested in buying that horse. Don't suppose you could tell me about the owner so I can see if I could cut a deal with them?'

The stable boy shrugged and patted down Greyson's horses with a kind touch.

'Well, we ain't supposed to share that sort of information, really. But listen, he's only stayin' here one night. The owner said they had a big journey. Horse's name is Bullet. You never know, maybe you two could do some kind of a swap — wouldn't be the first to need a packhorse, and you got yourself a couple of sturdy rides right here.' He pulled a treat out of his pocket and held it beneath one of Greyson's horse's nose, smiling warmly.

'I would hate to miss them. Don't suppose you would mind if I just take a lay down in one of your spare stables for the rest of the night?' Greyson tried to smile with the same warmth and enthusiasm as the boy, nodding, trying to get him to copy his body language.

'I don't uh...we don't usually allow owners to sleep over. We ain't really kitted out for it. As I said to the owner of that one there, there's a few places to stay around here. You got a place up the way that'd take you at this time. The Palisades is a bit fancier, but I doubt they'd let you in at this hour.' The two stared at each other for a moment, and Greyson nodded to his supplies that had been removed from his horse.

'That is a bedroll, and it's a fine one. I slept all over this land in that thing. All I need is four walls in this cold, and I'll be right, especially with the horses to keep me company. In fact, boy, you could even head off to get some rest yourself — as you see,' Greyson indicated his pistols, 'I'm well primed to take care of any horse thieves in the area. You would be doing me a favour, and I would pay you for it. Shame to give money to them with a mattress up the way when you have fresher straw right here, right?'

The boy paused and scratched his head and then visibly relented. 'Well, I won't leave you here alone; the boss wouldn't let me hear the end of it. But there's an empty stall over there if you want it, and I don't suppose I'd charge much more than the cost of a horse for it. All right? But you gotta promise me you'll not tell no one, and it's only because it's already late. If the boss comes in, you act as though you ain't sleeping here. If I lose this job, then you got another mouth to feed, you understand?' The boy raised his eyebrows at this last statement as if daring Greyson to argue. Greyson grinned, feeling the middle of his bottom lip crack in the centre, pulling open a wound to the cold. He tipped his hat in agreement, leaned down to grab his bedroll and saddlebags, and then made his way to the empty stable right beside Bullet's. He paused as he passed him, watching the snoozing horse.

'You're a beaut,' he murmured. Bullet's ears flicked forward at the sound. 'And I cannot wait to meet your owner.'

Ida shoved the bottle of straight rye into her saddlebag and grabbed a piece of cold potato from the dinner plate she had almost cleared hours before. The image of her mother flickered in the light.

'You know what the danger is?' Ida asked wearily. Her mother shook her head.

'I can only see you and what is about you. I see no other beings here.'

'Fine,' Ida said, pushing the last of the potato into her mouth and chewing quickly. She wanted coffee. She wanted more rest. The rune pushed into her skin, the steady heat beginning to hurt. It was definitely a warning. Ida scanned the room, making sure that everything had been collected. The moon was getting lower in the sky outside, threatening the sunshine's arrival. She nodded at her strange image of her mother, who stared as usual, and moved toward the door, pulling it open. Ida caught her breath. Right outside stood the young woman who had visited her earlier. Ida watched her for a beat and then stepped out, pretending that she wasn't there at all. She began to walk down the corridor, only to hear the light step of the woman behind her. After a few footsteps, Ida turned.

'What do you want?' she said, raising her chin, her eyes emblazoned as Colton's own. The young woman stared back, her head cocked to one side.

'Are you leaving already?' she asked softly. Ida flinched, irritated.

'Answering questions with questions? Okay. You always lurk outside rooms?'

'I don't. I thought you were interesting, though.' The woman narrowed her eyes, and Ida frowned. What did that mean?

'I don't have time for this,' Ida responded in a deep, gruff voice. The rune was throbbing, and she shifted, readjusting the saddlebag that lay heavy on her shoulder. She raised her eyebrows at the woman and turned, continuing down the corridor.

'Take me with you,' the voice said, suddenly. Ida turned and shook her head.

'What?'

'I don't want to be here. Take me with you.' The woman moved toward her quickly, and Ida backed up along the corridor, glancing over her shoulder at the exit to the staircase.

'Listen,' Ida said, running a hand across her damp forehead. 'I can't do that. You wanna leave? Here's what you do. You take what you can get, you head out in the darkness, and you don't wait for permission. You don't need me to help you.'

'I've just never seen a woman as tough as you,' the young woman said, her eyes glinting with tears. Ida frowned and removed her hat, running a hand along her freshly shaved skin.

'I can't…' she said roughly before replacing the hat with a long sigh. 'I'll see you.'

She turned, stalking along the floorboards to the exit door. Behind, the stairs awaited in dim light, the area empty. Ida stepped down them lightly on her tiptoes until she reached the heavy curtain that hid the front door. The man who had welcomed her, in his strange, rude way, still sat behind the curtain and was snoring in a chair beside a small kerosene lamp.

Ida ignored him and pushed past, opening the door and stepping into the cold air. It hit her like a punch, making her eyes water and her skin tingle. She pulled her scarf up around her face and slipped through the dark streets, the floor now an ice rink, the grit of the day before barely in existence. As she walked toward the stable, Ida shook her head. That woman had known her secret. She had known that she wasn't Colton. Well, she thought, she was the first to know, wasn't she? Maybe she had seen her in the bath… perhaps she had – she remembered her reaction to the request of the razor. Ida rubbed her hands together, pulling as much material as she could over the cold skin. She was pretending to be Colton now, she told herself. She was an image of her father. She was still Ida; deep down inside, she knew this, still had those Ida feelings, and still wanted to be Ida. But Colton would survive in the world beyond.

Colt woke up to the sound of Mrs Vale moving a large kettle onto the stove and busily shifting items around in the kitchen. He sat up and stared at her, his back sore from sleeping on the uneven wooden floor. She didn't seem to notice him at all. He swallowed. What was it that he was feeling awkward about, sick over? Oh, right. It came flooding back as he stared at her busy shoulders. He had tried to propose, and she had shot him down, hadn't she? Colt snarled at her image and stood up, causing her to twist and face him.

'You making coffee, woman?' he said with a grimace, rolling the sleeves of his shirt up. He stepped over to the sink and nudged her to one side, pushing his hands into the bucket of water that awaited him. He cupped them together, creating a small bowl, and splashed his face. Mrs Vale watched him with an intrigued look. She had three cups out on the side.

'I am making coffee, yes,' she said brightly, ignoring his tone.

'Good,' he responded, his face dripping. He walked to the table and pulled out a chair, sitting with a thump. Colt watched and waited. Mrs Vale began the process, lighting the stove, readying the pot.

'While you're here, you can make yourself useful,' she said once it was heating steadily. Colt's stare in response was the polar opposite of the day before, he knew.

'I'll do what I please. What are you making me for breakfast?' he said, his lips pursed like a scolded child. Mrs Vale smiled and placed a hand on her hip.

'I've noticed something about you, boy. You have a problem, a real problem, with rejection from a woman. There ain't nothing to it, you know. It's just a part of life. I can only deduce that you have one complicated relationship with your mother – but let me be clear. If you think that I would ever marry a man who spoke to me in such a manner, then you have got another think coming. I did not refuse you last night, but I still may.' The coffee began to steam and bubble behind her, and she turned, taking it off the stove and pouring three cups with a slightly shaking hand.

As she poured, Colt watched her. She was quite right, he thought. Something inside him baulked at a woman who refused him or treated him as anything but the respectful man he was. He thought of Ida for a moment, her cloying hands, her lying words. Mrs Vale turned and placed a cup down in front of him, and he took it gratefully. So, he thought as she sat down beside him, blowing on her steaming liquid, there was still a chance. He sniffed, trying to allow himself to move past his intense anger. His humiliation subsided slightly, and he cleared his throat, raising the cup a little.

'I thank you for my coffee. I am never quite myself without it.'

Mrs Vale gave him a stern glance and nodded, raising her own cup in a sober cheer.

Chapter 26

Greyson lay on the floor, his eyes closed. He had his gun laid across his chest, and he was waiting patiently, listening to the soft sleeping snores of the horses and the stable boy going about his quiet work. When she came in, he thought, what would he do? He could jump out on her, aim the gun and wound her a little. That would stop her in her tracks. Or maybe he could make small talk, not tell her who he was. Or, he could just follow her, track her. His mind was starting to wander a little, he noticed. He mustn't let himself fall asleep, mustn't accidentally miss her, not now. *Five hundred dollars.* Billy's voice boomed the three words in his mind, and he nodded. *Five hundred dollars.* Suddenly, there was a click at the door. Greyson's eyes opened, and he stared at the shadows made on the wall opposite him. He stayed still, waiting to hear.

'Oh, hello. You're back sooner than I thought,' the stable boy said. Greyson grinned in the dim light.

'Yup. I have to make tracks. Saddle up my horse, will you boy, quick as you can,' the stranger's voice said. Greyson frowned. The voice was dull and deep, with a baritone hue. He sat up and shifted to the door of the stable in which he was hiding, peeking through a crack in the wood. He could only see a man's trousers and the stable boy's legs.

'There's a chap who mentioned he wants to buy your horse Bullet,' the stable boy said. Greyson winced. He would have to stand up any minute now. There was a pause in the conversation.

'What?' the voice said.

'A chap who wants to buy your horse Bullet—'

'What did you tell him?' the voice said.

'Well, he's right—'

Greyson took a breath and stood up, reholstering his gun. He had no idea what the next step was. It seemed like he had gotten the wrong person. In the dim kerosene lamplight, the stable boy and the stranger turned to look at him. Greyson pushed his hat on his head and nodded, stepping forward with a hand outstretched.

'Just sleepin' there. Nice to meet you. I'm Greyson. A fine horse you got,' he said. 'Bullet, is it?' The stranger stared at him, mouth twitching, and then glanced at the hand, making no move to shake it. 'Oh right, Handy Rose. My mother brought me up to shake a stranger's hand, so I apologise for the offence.'

'I don't shake hands. Not selling my horse,' the person said clearly, nodding at the stable boy to tack Bullet up. Greyson dropped his hand and shrugged.

'All right,' he said. 'What's your name?' He cocked his head to one side, staring hard. He had spent time memorising the woman's image in the picture. This person, though, he thought, was an interesting one. The eyes were harder than that of the woman he tracked, the face thinner. But there was something in the jawline, in the protected way that the stranger stood, that confused him.

'My name is Colton,' the stranger responded, eyes fierce. 'Roll up that horse blanket, boy, and fix it to the saddle.' They flicked their gaze to the stable boy and then back again, raising their chin. Greyson stared.

'You a bounty hunter, Colton?' he asked.

'What's it to you?' came the response.

'Well, I'll tell you.' He reached inside his coat pocket and pulled out the bounty poster of Ida, unfolding it carefully. He held it up and showed the image, settled above the words 'Five Hundred Dollar Reward.' Greyson watched the reaction. 'You hunting for this person?'

'Not a bounty hunter,' the stranger said, eyes glancing at the image. They scanned the name and then raised an eyebrow, hand resting on the handle of their pistol. 'What do you want?'

There was a silence in the stableyard suddenly, as though the question had lit the fuse of a piece of dynamite. The stable boy glanced over as he tightened Bullet's girth and frowned. The two men were just staring at each other in silence. Greyson licked his lips and turned the image around, holding it up beside the stranger's face. This is what Billy would tell him to do, he thought. This was precisely the type of thing you did as a bounty hunter: suspect everyone because disguise is easy. Swiftly, without warning, the stranger pulled a pistol and, grinning, aimed it at Greyson's head.

'You comparing me to that woman there, are you?' they said sharply, cocking the hammer. Greyson's eyes flicked to the image and then back again. There was definitely something there.

'Well, I would be remiss if I didn't check somebody for a disguise now. After all, I hear they don't get many strangers in this town, and I am certain that this person is here and that you are one of the few strangers who have ridden in the last couple of days. You understand, of course. Five hundred dollars,' he said with a shrug as though a pistol wasn't pointing at his head. The stable boy hastily did up the straps on Bullet's bridle, wanting the strangers to get out of his stableyard once and for all. Greyson smiled. 'You're either Ida Vale, or you are after Ida Vale.'

The stranger glared. 'Drop your guns on the floor, now. Drop your guns, or I'll shoot.'

'So you have got something to do with it. Always trust your gut, my mama said.' Greyson laughed, his hand hovering over the handle of his pistol. The stranger glanced down quickly and dropped their gun to the right, firing a single shot into his shoulder. It took a moment for the action to register, and Greyson stood staring at the weapon as though in disbelief.

'Did you just…?' he asked, and then he felt it. The pain. It seared through his left shoulder, and he winced, moving his hand up to protect it. Hastily, he pocketed the bounty poster.

'Drop your guns, or I will shoot you again.'

Greyson undid his holster and let the belt fall to the ground. The stranger stepped forward and kicked it away and then glanced at the stable boy.

'You, bring me some rope. You know how to hogtie?'

The stable boy nodded awkwardly and grabbed the nearest lunging rope, stepping up to the pair. Greyson stood clutching his arm, eyes burning.

'Make it easy on the boy; put your hands in front of you.' The stranger cocked the hammer again, and Greyson did as he was told. 'Tie him up.' The stable boy proceeded to tie Greyson's hands. 'Don't forget his feet.'

'Now listen here – I am a bounty hunter. That makes me a man of the law,' Greyson tried, watching this bear-clad stranger tighten their jaw with a grimace.

'You're no man of the law. Tie his feet, boy.' The stranger watched as the stable boy roped Greyson's ankles together and tied them securely. 'Did he come with a horse?'

The stable boy stood up. 'He came with two.' He pointed at them, waiting in the stable. The stranger followed the boy's gaze and nodded at the horse that just so happened to be Greyson's.

'Saddle up that one. The other you can keep for your trouble.' The stranger turned their attention back to Greyson, reholstering the gun now that he was tied, and leaned down to pick up Greyson's weapons. 'Not the best, but they'll do. All right,' they said, glancing around them. 'Ah, that'll work.' They leaned down and plucked an offcut of rope from the floor and then stepped up to Greyson.

'You—' Greyson began, but the stranger quickly drew a gun and smashed the frame of the pistol into his mouth. Greyson reeled backwards, silent and spitting blood. The stranger took that opportunity to tie the rope around his mouth, securing it at the back with a knot. Then, they removed the scarf from their neck and wrapped it around Greyson's face, so that he looked every inch the criminal, and there was no sight of the bloody bind that silenced him. The stable boy brought the horse over, and the stranger nodded at him in appreciation.

'Thank you. All right, Greyson. You can use that mounting block over there. We're going on a little journey.'

Greyson frowned and glanced at the block. What the hell was happening? He'd lost his control over the situation so quickly. His shoulder and mouth throbbed, and he coughed a little, feeling the blood seep into the rope between his teeth. Whomever this person was, he thought, they were not what he had been expecting. He needed Billy. What would Billy do? He would have shot them already, Greyson realised. He'd been too slow on the draw, too eager to work out if it was the right person. Still, they had something to do with Ida Vale, and that was a certainty. If he just stuck with them, he could try and regain some of that control.

'Get on the block, Greyson. I don't have all the time in the world,' the stranger said harshly. The stable boy brought the soft bay horse to the mountain block and held him, and Greyson did the only thing he could do. He hopped up onto the mounting block in an impressive feat of leg strength and then paused.

'Just lay across the saddle there. You'll be all right,' the stranger said as though to a friend. Greyson half jumped, half pushed himself across the saddle and groaned in pain.

'Straighten him up and secure him on there, boy; you gotta earn that horse if you want to keep him.' The stable boy had tied another lunge rope around Greyson, securing him to the horse's saddle. He lay on his stomach, his head hanging over the side.

Greyson felt the wounds burn and claw at his skin, his eyes stinging with tears. Did this person even feel an ounce of empathy? Perhaps when they were further out, they would let him sit normally, let him tend to his wounds. And yet...what would he have done?

'Pass me the reins, boy,' the stranger said to the stable boy, who handed them over wordlessly. 'Enjoy your new horse. You deserve it.'

Chapter 27

Colt found himself growing more comfortable throughout the morning. There was something in the way that Mrs Vale had responded earlier that comforted him. Perhaps they were bound to be a couple, he thought. Maybe she really was going to be his wife. He watched from the porch as she brushed the horses that they had stolen, talking at length to her son about whatever popped into her mind. Her speech with him was far more relaxed, Colt realised. She spoke as though there was no filter whatsoever, nothing between her thoughts and her mouth.

Colt leaned back in his chair, feeling the weight of the Winchester rifle over his knee. It was an old type, a little rust around the end. Trick said he had found it here when he'd arrived, dropped on the porch. Ida must have left it, they agreed. And now, Colt thought as he rested a hand on the grip of the gun, she would come to face the barrel of her own gun. He was excited by the thought of it. Real men take revenge, he thought, with a nod. Real men see what has been done to them, and they respond with fervour. He thought of Ida, standing at the bar in the Steepmount saloon, a memory that he revisited often. She had a strange beauty, he had thought at the time. It was a rugged appeal, a sort of strong and yet tender face. She had been wearing a lot of blush, that much he remembered.

Colt hocked up a phlegm ball and spat it onto the dirt, firing it out of his mouth like a bullet from a chamber. It was all he could do not to spit every time he thought of the woman, the thief. He glanced at Mrs Vale again, who was absentmindedly brushing the horse's tail with a wide-toothed comb while chatting about the possibilities of rain. Trick was leaning against the fence near her, murmuring in agreement now and then, his eyes fixed ahead on nothing in particular. It was quite a nice life, Colt thought, one that he could get used to.

The day was becoming brighter by the moment, and Ida gave a small smile to everyone who stopped and gawked at the pair leaving town. There was a surprising amount of people on the street, she realised, making their way to work, fetching coffee, and watching them with steady and fearful eyes. At one point, a young boy had gasped loudly, pulling his mother round to see them.

'Oh, he will have done something frightful. That must be a bounty,' the mother replied, ruffling the boy's hair. Ida had nodded, giving them a wink of agreement. That seemed to be the general consensus, and yet they still stared as though unsure of whether what they were seeing was legal and proper. When the well-walked paths became a little broader and less icy, she pushed Bullet into a jog, clicking her tongue for the horse she led behind. He followed obediently, unperturbed by the fact that his owner was lying across him in an unusual manner. By the time they reached the threshold of The City of Glass and stared out across the barren snowscape before them, the mountains in the distance, the sun was well and truly bright. The cold air wrapped about them, and Ida held her coat close and then paused, pulling Bullet to a halt.

'Whoa, boy,' she said to Greyson's horse. 'All right, Greyson. I see you there, and I know how cold it is. Would you appreciate a horse blanket over you, or are you determined to freeze?' She waited, hearing the murmur from his bloodied and covered lips. She smiled.

'Determined to freeze, is it?'

He moaned again in response, this time a little louder. Ida felt the burn of the rune against her skin throb hotter than ever before. She stared out at the white landscape and saw the image of her mother appear, who stood with a heavy gaze, staring at her hard. She shook her head. Ida sniffed, wiping her hand beneath her nose. She understood what her mother's glare was about, of course. But her mother wasn't considering how this would be the other way around. She would almost certainly be the one tied up. She would definitely be powerless in the situation. Ida rolled her eyes and dismounted, pulling the rolled-up horse coat from the back of Bullet's saddle. She moved to the other horse and glanced for a moment at the bright lights of The City of Glass, now alive behind them. There was a part of her that wanted to go back, to drink at a bar all day long, to sleep deeply with a boozy air. But no, Ida thought, remembering her dreams. Revenge must be sought first. It was in revenge that one had found satisfaction, not at the bottom of a bottle. She stared at the body of Greyson and pulled a knife from her holster, cutting the ropes at his feet. Then, she cut the ropes that secured him to the saddle, leaving his hands tied. She heard him murmur in surprise and stepped back.

'You can shift yourself about if you can and sit in the saddle properly. I'm going to keep your hands bound, and you should heed this warning – I am a better horse rider than you. My horse is faster. If you try anything, I will shoot both you and your horse. You won't have a moment to think about it.'

Greyson let his body fall back slightly and then pushed himself up on his elbows, manoeuvring around until he was sitting firmly in the saddle. He held his bound hands before him and glanced down at Ida. She nodded and stepped forward, tying the hands to the pommel. Then, she flicked out the horse blanket and wrapped it around Greyson, securing that to the front of the saddle, too. He stared at her with appreciative eyes, half of his face still covered by her scarf. His eyes told her that his shoulder was still throbbing with pain, the bullet lodged in there, but the blanket would already be warming his steadily freezing body. Ida cocked her head to one side and stared at him for a moment.

'I mean it, Greyson. I will kill you both. And if you nudge that horse on a little bit faster than my own, I will take that as a sign. I will shoot it in the legs, and I will leave you on that mountain to freeze.' Ida lay a hand on the warm, soft coat. 'And that mountain is haunted, did you know?'

Greyson nodded. Ida grinned. She turned to face her mother, to see if she was happier with this scenario than the other but found that she was no longer there, no longer watching. Ida turned back.

'All right. I have some business to take care of in Bleakhollow. It'll be a bit of a gunfight, and I'm reckoning that if you can keep yourself alive, it would be helpful to have another finger on the trigger beside me. If you listen to me, if you pay attention and adhere to what I am saying, I will tell you where Ida Vale is. I know her well. After that, you can claim your bounty.' Ida licked her lips and tipped her hat back slightly, staring at Greyson from beneath the brim. 'What do you say?'

'Hmmm,' Greyson said, a murmur of agreement. Ida clasped her hands together, satisfied. She turned back to Bullet, mounting smoothly, and picked up the reins of Greyson's horse, clicking her tongue. Bullet threw his head, the sight of the open white plains and the night of rest and food spurring him on. Ida leaned forward in her saddle and pushed him forward, feeling his steady gait move into a gallop beneath her. She turned to see if Greyson was still aboard his ride. He was clearly an experienced horseman, stable in the saddle despite the wounds and bound hands.

In Steepmount, the sheriff sat behind his desk, smoking his cigar and watching Jonesy go about his daily business of sitting, reading, and talking to himself. He stared at the empty cell and grimaced. It had not been a pretty evening, but time had passed, and he was starting to get over the outrage of it. An old woman and an idiot who had thrown himself in jail? It was ridiculous. He had wanted their heads for the first day and then had sent word out among the other towns in the Bleakhollow area. No one had seen them. Horses stolen from the stables, a sheriff bound and left for dead, and no one had seen them.

The sheriff sighed and took a drag of his cigar, watching the smoke rise around his face. The bounty hunters had come back the following day after the sheriff had been freed, and the sheriff had seen them off with rage inside him. It was their fault, he'd said, bringing that woman in here. He'd aimed a gun at their heads and told them to run, boys, or face the wrath of Steepmount. And run they had. The sheriff had even fired a shot into the dirt at the soles of their shoes. Jonesy had lamented that he had been left behind for a while.

'Ain't you gonna find them, Sheriff? Ain't you going to hang that man?' he'd asked, furious that he had been denied his freedom. The sheriff had sighed and scratched his head.

'There's something about that woman. She gives me the spooks. I'll think on it – the less I have to think of that idiot Colt, the better.'

And so, the sheriff had still done nothing. He was in two minds. In a way, he thought, he knew that they would be back at some point. Colt was not a smart man, and if he believed that Ida Vale was making her way to the town on the back of a bounty hunter's horse, there was no chance that he would miss that eventuality. If the man strolled back in, he'd shoot him, clean in the head. Maybe that's all there was to be decided.

Chapter 28

They arrived at the Alask Wilds by sundown, the occasional groan coming from behind. Ida stared up at the steep winding path and then paused. There was something in the wind, a noise that floated through the air to her ears, making her skin prickle and tingle uncomfortably. She glanced at Bullet's ears, which began to flicker before her. He threw his head up and whinnied.

'Steady boy. Steady,' she soothed, but it was too late. The sound came almost immediately and told her what the uneasy feeling was. Wolves. A single low howl began, followed closely by another. Ida glanced about her, and saw a few grey shapes to the right, crowding around something on the ground. She squinted her eyes—another howl. Bullet's ears flattened against his head, and he began to skitter beneath her. Ida grabbed a pistol from her holster and turned, staring at Greyson. His eyes were wild between his mask and hat, desperate and afraid.

'All right,' Ida said, 'hold on.' She dug her heels into Bullet's sides and pushed him onto the steep track ahead. He moved like his namesake straight into a gallop. Ida turned and saw in a flash that the wolves were indeed paying attention.

'Ya!' she shouted at Bullet, who stretched his neck and legs out further, pulling himself up with speed. Ida held the rope of the horse behind and turned to see it keeping pace. Greyson was not looking ahead but turning his head to watch the wolves that were now chasing them. They were making a good pace, too, their grey shapes focused and threatening, yellow eyes narrowing. Ida wrapped the rope of Greyson's horse around the pommel of her saddle and pulled it, drawing in her lower belly so her body remained stable on Bullet's back.

They were coming to a corner on the steepening hill, the snow getting thicker. She turned in the saddle and closed one eye, aiming behind her with the pistol. She shot, Greyson flinched. One of the wolves fell, blood-red in the white snow. Three more to go, she thought, as Bullet began to turn the corner. Ida leaned her body forward in the saddle and focused, taking a deep breath, the cold air stinging her lungs. Suddenly, she was around the bend, slightly higher than the others, and turned back on herself, climbing up ever faster. Bullet's ears were still slicked back onto his head. His gallop was one of fear, and both horses knew exactly what was chasing them. Ida aimed again and shot, this time missing. She heard Greyson try and shout. This would be so much easier if he were free, she thought. And yet, there was nothing that could be done now, and there was no time to free him.

Ida pulled one of Greyson's pistols out of the second holster that she had removed from him earlier and began to fire at the wolves, half aiming and half recklessly hoping to hit fur and flesh. One more down. She fired again. Another one was shot in the leg and began to whine, falling back behind the other. Greyson's horse began to whinny, throwing its head as it galloped behind. In one incredible swift movement, he bucked, kicking his legs out behind him. The wolf that Ida had failed to shoot was swept off the rocky white hillside and plunged into the snow below. Greyson groaned, still aboard his ride, his hands bound. Ida leaned back, feeling Bullet slow his gallop, and reholstered, picking up her reins in one hand. She turned to face Greyson.

'Once we're up there, I'll untie you,' she said clearly. He frowned in reply and nodded, as though not understanding but grateful for the offer. Ida loosened Bullet's reins and allowed him to find his own gait. He continued to gallop, his ears still flicking from front to back, his coat damp and sweating, body steaming in the cold air. She could feel his heart beating beneath her legs.

They reached the top in a daze. Both horses had slowed down, sweating from their steady charge up the steep slope, their hooves now less sure, slipping in the snow. Ida stared at the familiar sight, a faint path still left by hooves in the white, wet ground, the sudden and intimidating impression of being on top of a mountain, and yet surrounded by mountains. She filled her lungs with the cold air and pulled Bullet to a halt, feeling the horse behind do the same, the rope slack. He had learned quickly. Dismounting, Ida stepped toward her captive and pulled out a knife, noticing him recoil as she did so. She rolled her eyes at him and then sliced the rope that secured his hands to the saddle, ensuring that they were still bound. She removed the horse coat from him and placed it momentarily onto Bullet, his damp skin glistening.

'You can dismount,' she said, taking a step back. He shifted his bound wrists forward and leaned on his horse's neck, before shifting one leg over the saddle and landing on the ground. Ida stepped forward again and untied the back of the scarf. The rope that she had tied into his mouth was a little frayed, and it took a minute or so before it was removed. Ida threw the bloodied rope onto the floor and observed Greyson. He spat blood on the snow before him and then turned and brandished his wrists, holding them out.

'Will you untie me?' he asked, the skin around his lips worn and cut. Ida stared at the marks and winced. They looked sore and cracked in the cold air, as though he may never look the same again. She shook her head.

'I'm sorry, but no. I can't trust you. I've unbound most of you, and you can still use those hands to drink coffee. You'll be all right.'

Greyson spat onto the ground again and then used his tongue to inspect a wobbly front tooth.

'Fine,' he said, his eyes resting on the guns that he had lost, now wrapped around Ida's hips. Ida nodded and began to tramp down the snow beneath her feet. She observed Greyson after a moment.

'A hand?' She stamped her feet and nodded in appreciation as he did the same. Once it was flat beneath them, she stared around them. 'There should be some wood, stones, around here somewhere. There's a tree over there. Fetch what you can carry and bring it back for the fire.'

'I'm tied up,' Greyson responded, his eyes dim and tired. There was barely a flash left.

Ida reminded herself once more that she was Colton and that if it had been the other way around, the man would not be so meek. 'Yup. Better that you're there collecting sticks with your wrists bound than here stealing the horses. Go.' She watched him, his shoulders hunched over, defeated. He walked through the snow to a small tree and carefully began to collect what he could find, a few sticks by the burgeoning roots, which stretched and pinged out of the ground. Some stones that had fallen from rocks, their smaller siblings. It took no more than fifteen minutes for the entire process to be complete, before Ida was on her knees in the snow, focusing on building the stony base and building the small fire on top of it. Beside her, Greyson stood and watched in silence.

Once it was built, Ida stared up at him and tried a smile. He could have killed her by now, she thought, and he hadn't. He could have taken a rock and cracked it across her head as she worked on the fire, but he didn't. That said something for the man, whether he was broken from the bullet wound in his shoulder and the smashed teeth, or was more trustworthy than she initially suspected. He glanced at her and then looked back to the fire.

'Listen, I'm not all bad. And I need your help to take down the sonsofbitches that we're heading to visit. So sit down, get warm. I'll put a pot of coffee on. You got food in that saddlebag of yours?'

Greyson nodded. 'Some.'

'Well, all right. Sit down, Greyson, I mean it. Or I'll shoot you.' Ida laughed, still playing her role as Colton. Greyson didn't seem to find the comment funny and reached for his shoulder as though remembering the moment when she had, in fact, shot him. He sat down heavily by the fire and closed his eyes. Ida watched him.

'Greyson, how is your arm? Would you let me look at it, clean it?'

'It's a flesh wound,' he said, his eyes opening sharply.

'How do you know if I haven't inspected it?'

'Because I'm not dead. I haven't bled out.'

Ida stood, stepping over to Bullet. She pulled the bottle of straight rye from her saddlebag and turned back to Greyson. 'Here, take a swig of this for the pain. I'll use a little to clean the wound; it's sterile.' She pulled the cork out and handed the bottle to him, and he took it with his bound hands.

Greyson knocked back a few clean gulps and swallowed, satisfied.

'Whoever you are, at least you know about rest.' He jerked back as Ida knelt beside him and glared at her.

'Hold still then,' she said. Ida had only tended to this sort of wound once before, a flesh wound, her father's. He had stood on a spike, and it had gone right through his foot. At first, Ida had thought it was perfect, the ideal moment to take him into town, to see some of the world. But no, he refused. He took swigs of whisky and got her to clean the wound with the stuff, flinching and swearing the entire time. And he survived that. She stared at the blood-soaked shirt before her, ripped when the bullet had entered the skin. Carefully, she ripped it a little further, inspecting the area as best she could. There was an entry hole and an exit hole. Lucky chap, she thought. She grabbed the bottle from him and poured a little onto both sides of the wound. He flinched, of course, but said nothing, not even allowing a murmur of discomfort. Ida sat back, impressed.

'If you want, I could pack the snow around it, might numb it a little,' she said, shrugging. Greyson shook his head.

'I'm cold enough.'

Ida nodded and glanced around. The air was different up here; it was not just dryer and colder, but something else, too. Strange and a little unsettling. Ida noticed that the rune against her chest had cooled down from burning. It was no longer throbbing, but still warm. She looked for her mother and could not see her. Interesting, and unlike before, she thought. She must be near them now. Ida began to busy herself around the fire, making a pot of coffee with water from her canteen. She kept a close eye on Greyson and eventually handed him a cup of the black liquid in silence. No smile. She sat on the other side of the fire and watched as he blew on the steaming drink.

'Well...' Ida began, feeling a little unsure. Despite her dalliances with the various staff at saloons and more, she hadn't had a proper conversation in a while with anyone but her mother and Bullet, who rarely answered back. She felt unsure of what to say, but there was a tension between them that was thick. If she wanted him to shoot her brother and not her when he was finally handed a gun, she might need to create a friendship beyond the promise of delivering Ida Vale.

'You know it's haunted up here?' she said again.

Greyson took a sip of coffee and nodded. 'Yup.'

'Hmm. You must have been through here before. It's a tough road to travel alone...' Ida paused. She thought of the second horse at the stable, its saddle and saddlebags. Clearly, he did not travel alone.

'Yup.' Was the only response she got.

'Where did your partner go?' she asked, taking a nonchalant sip of her coffee. The wind picked up around them, whipping past her ears.

'Over that edge,' came the response, with a small nod behind them. Ida shifted and looked at the direction they had just come from. 'That'll be what the wolves were snacking on, I reckon. Billy,' Greyson said. For the first time in a while, he raised his sight to her and stared. Ida nodded and cleared her throat.

'Not a nice way to go. Your brother?'

'No. My boss. Once you show me Ida Vale, I'll be collecting the money for the rest of 'em back home.'

Ida drained her cup and swallowed, the now warm liquid only slightly improving her temperature. 'All right.'

'You do know where she is then?' Greyson asked, his attention still firmly on her. Ida nodded.

'Yeah, I know.'

'Oh, right. So what were you doing in The City of Glass then, if that isn't where Ida is?'

Ida smiled. 'That is my business alone.'

'It's my business too,' Greyson said.

'Not yet. I promised you Ida Vale. I will deliver. You can get your damned money and be off, once you've helped me.'

The fire crackled before them, and Ida stood up and went to the horses and began to remove their saddles for the night. The moon was bright in the clear sky, bouncing off the snow and creating a light reminiscent of early morning. As she worked, she paused for a moment, staring about her. For one second, she thought that she saw the image of her mother next to the fire. When she checked again, she was gone. Perhaps it was something to do with Greyson, Ida mused. Maybe her focus had been distracted too much.

The woman had begun locking her door. There was nothing mentioned about it, but Colt had noticed all the same. She was locking her door at night. He lay next to the dying fire and heard the slick movement of metal chink across the wooden frame. It irked him. Something about her was irrational, he thought. He ensured that he was the picture of delight, even helping to wash up in the evenings. He'd cut a carrot up, poured her cup of bourbon. Mrs Vale still treated him with a weary distance, being polite and occasionally hinting at their relationship being more than one of convenience and revenge and, at other times, hardly hearing the words that came out of his mouth.

Trick was just as bad. He would say things like, 'I can't wait to get this place back to myself,' and 'Once my wife comes, you two are out on your ears. If you think I can't shoot that thieving woman when she visits, you got another thing coming.'

At these times, Mrs Vale would cluck and smooth down the material on her son's shoulders, telling him not to be silly and that a mother's place was with her son where she could look after him. Besides, she wanted to meet this wife of his, and she was certain that Colt would be no issue at all. Time would move quickly, she said. Time would tell. Colt turned onto his side and listened. He could hear her murmuring through the wooden door, the crack beneath showing lamplight. Every night was the same. He would lay and listen to a strange, dull chanting, almost like she was singing a hymn of some kind. Then, silence. The light would go out. Next came the sound of the rats, their claws on the wooden floor beside him as they tried to discover what had been left over from dinner. He sighed. The sooner he could get into Mrs Vale's bed, the better. If only for the lack of sleep he got out here.

He lay a hand across his chest and thought of the wedding day. It would be simple, he thought. Perhaps he could get a person to come along and do it right here at this homestead. Trick could give her away. They could celebrate with some choice rye. Yup, that would be just fine. He smiled as he closed his eyes, the chanting still going on next door.

Chapter 29

The night was cold and blissfully short, and Ida slept in her roll bag fitfully, waking every now and then to check that Greyson was still there and that he hadn't stolen the horses. He appeared to be asleep each time she woke to see. By the time the morning came and Greyson woke, Ida had already made the coffee and handed him a cup. She was turning a wooden spit that she had created with some kind of small-skinned animal on it, and Greyson sat up, surprised to see the scene before him.

'Got myself a squirrel of some kind,' Ida said, watching the skin turn from blood red to brown. 'It'll do for breakfast. Then we'll head off, try and get out of here before the night comes again. Might not be possible – in fact, I doubt it. Horses being slower downhill.' The smell of the meat wafted beneath Greyson's nose, and he closed his eyes, clearly enjoying it. He took a sip of the coffee that had been placed before him.

'You put rye in the coffee?' he asked.

'Yup. For the pain in your shoulder, your mouth.' Ida didn't look at him while she spoke, just carried on turning the spit.

'Thank you,' Greyson said.

Ida turned and noticed his tongue at the front of his mouth, pushing on the teeth that still wobbled. She thought of suggesting that he try to pull them out himself but thought better of it. They glanced at each other, two strangers sitting beside a fire. It was weird, Ida thought, that this man was waiting for her with rye in his cup of warm coffee and breakfast on the way. As though they were old friends. She took another sip of her drink, feeling the warmth of the booze slip down her gullet nicely. The man was a prisoner of sorts, his hands still bound before him, and yet a prisoner with breakfast may just be preferable to a bounty hunter without.

'You sleep okay?' Ida asked, pulling the spit rod onto a plate and slicing the meat off in chunks. The steam rose into the cold air, making it appear even more appetising. Greyson nodded.

'I slept better than I thought I would, what with the shoulder, the hands.'

'Hmm.' Ida peered briefly up at the man in front of her, noticing the dried blood that still sat on his beard. She thought about her own face, about her disguise, and hesitated.

'Well, I got a lot done this morning before you woke up. Shaved, caught this critter.'

She moved over and placed a bowl before him, filled with chunks of meat, and sat back down, popping one into her mouth. The taste of the warm squirrel made her stomach tingle, and she was grateful for the feeling of slow fullness that came from chewing. They ate in silence, Greyson not mentioning the comment about shaving, which had stuck in Ida's throat like a lie waiting to be outed. Once finished, Ida stood and kicked out the fire, then began to ready the horses, who were grateful for a handful of oats and generous in their whickers. When they were ready, Ida held Greyson's horse steady while he mounted. He looked weary despite the night of sleep he claimed to have had. Ida felt the opposite, the rye and coffee having done their job. She felt as though she could gallop from here to Bleakhollow in a day, despite the reality of it. Greyson was finally mounted, and he nodded down at Ida.

'Pass me the reins. I'll be a better companion if I can ride by myself,' he said, his gaze warmer than yesterday. Ida shook her head and mounted Bullet in a single smooth motion, still holding onto Greyson's reins. She looped them around the pommel and collected her own.

'Sorry, but I don't know you yet. Best we stick together until I'm a little more comfortable with what you are bringing to the team here. Now listen, around one of these corners is a coach that has crashed. Take my word for it; I do not recommend that we stop, look in, or do anything of the type.' Ida raised her eyebrows in sincerity.

'I know it. My boss put his head in, came out all funny. Like he'd seen a ghost,' Greyson responded, lifting both of his bound hands to his chin to scratch.

'Yeah…' Ida looked around her, looking for her mother. She was nowhere to be seen. It was a little infuriating, in a way.

Had she lost her focus so fast? Wasn't she here before on the Alask Wilds without effort? Ida clicked her tongue and moved Bullet forward. They rode in silence, the riders trusting their horses' movements as they travelled, allowing them to decide on the path and their footfall.

The sun moved across at surprising speed. Ida glanced up occasionally, wishing its rays would warm her cold skin. And yet, she thought, she must be much warmer than her companion, who sat steadily enough and didn't complain, but had no bear pelt to cover him. Then, as the sun began to dip in the sky, Ida saw it on the horizon. The image of a black shape. It was the carriage coach, she thought, waiting for them, hidden in the snow. The body of that woman. The face. Ida reached up beneath her clothing and pressed the rune to her skin, checking for heat. It began to tingle ever so slightly, but whether that was from herself or anything else, Ida could not decide. Behind her, Greyson cleared his throat.

'My horse is beginning to dance a little, and I would appreciate the reins just for this section. He does not spook easily, but there is something around this area that he does not like.'

Bullet began to spook as well as they got closer, his ears springing back against his head, his nose lifting in the air. Ida scanned behind her.

'I've got him, don't worry.'

'I mean, we shouldn't linger, when I came through this way—'

'I've got him,' Ida interrupted, clicking her tongue at the horse behind as though that might make a difference to him. It didn't. Both horses still threw their heads and shifted beneath. They were coming closer to the carriage now, and Ida sat heavy in her saddle, using her weight to try and calm Bullet beneath her. As they neared the door, where she had previously climbed, she couldn't help but glance over at the door. It was flung open, the window still smashed on the ground, as she believed that she had left it. Ida twitched. What was that? A noise on the wind reached her ears, it almost transfixed her. She stared at the carriage door.

…Back again?

The words seemed to appear in her mind, and she shook her head, turning back to Greyson. His face was pale and dropped, his hands desperately holding onto the saddle.

'Did you hear that?' Ida asked.

He didn't answer, just squinted at the hole in the carriage as though he couldn't take his eyes off it. Ida swallowed and turned back, the rune pulsating with heat against her flesh. There, her mother now stood by a wheel cast adrift in the snow. Her faded image was one that Ida could just make out, and she stared with a grimace. Bullet threw his head and reared slightly, his front hooves hesitating on the icy ground.

'Run,' her mother said, the word as strange as the voice she had heard before.

Ida took one last glance at Greyson, whose eyes were wide with a peculiar horror, and dug her heels into Bullet's stomach. He reared again and pounced forward like an alley cat running from a bucket of water. The rope pulled taught from Ida's pommel to Greyson's horse, and both held on as the horses flew down the mountain path, hooves skidding on snow and flinging ice behind them as they galloped. Ida squinted and breathed in the air as it flew at her face, the cold land and iced backdrop of the mountains disappearing with every beat. The horses ran as though they were being chased.

Mrs Vale sat at the small table in her adopted bedroom and frowned. Before her, the tea leaves were muddying the dirty water, the candlelight not helping with its dull glow. Where was she? Where was the woman who was coming to exact unlawful revenge on her son? Although, she thought, as she absentmindedly danced her fingertips over the flame, she couldn't blame her. She would have done the same if she were in her situation, no doubt. And yet, she wasn't. So that was that. The woman had no claim to this land and no claim to her father, really…who could say who he had met first, her or his fake, second wife? She shrugged. She cared not. It did not matter. All men were weak enough when a new woman came along, regardless. Just look at Colt, the fool.

She picked up a little bag of herbs from the table before her and sprinkled them into the tea, whispering some words. Each day, when he woke up, he found himself more and more distracted by thoughts of their life together. She knew this because she was responsible for the dreams that he had, just as she was responsible for Ida's. So easy to infiltrate a mind when you had years of practice. She'd have done the same with those bloody bounty hunters if they hadn't bound her so tightly. Still, no matter now. The sheriff wouldn't come after her. She was sure of that. His dreams were filled with blasé thoughts; the big job of finding the runaways was determined to be barely worth the hassle.

Mrs Vale tensed, hearing the floorboards in the kitchen next door moving. Ah, she thought. His nightly check on her door. She knew it was up to her, that the only reason he hung about as he did was because of her actions, and yet…he was definitely the creepiest chap she had ever put a spell on. The way he watched her was unnerving. Yesterday he had even called Trick 'son', despite them being of a similar age. He'd almost got his head punched off for that until Mrs Vale had stepped in, laying a hand on both men's arms.

'No point in fighting, dear,' she had said to her boy, her look meaningful and transparent. Let him live until she comes, and then he can do our bidding for us. Of course, Trick didn't fully understand the plan, and Mrs Vale watched him with interest. She knew that his father was haunting him; there was no doubt. And yet, nothing had come of it. He had said no words to her about it. Perhaps his father's ghost was silent and weak, as in life. Maybe he lacked at the haunting game as well as the farming one. She let out a small laugh at the thought of this, a pleasure to think of him failing in death. But Ida was vengeful, her spirit strong. There was no way that she would be an easy haunt, and if Mrs Vale could save her son that, it would be worth it. The footsteps outside the door crept away again, and she heard Colt lie down before the fire. Strange boy. He'd be delivered to the sheriff soon enough for murder. No harm in that sweet drop of justice.

Chapter 30

The way down was quick. Despite the darkness and the strange noises that whipped past their ears – flesh-eating animals, the baying of wolves, the threat of the undead – Ida let Bullet carry her at his own speed, keeping the rope tied to the horse behind taut and strong. Now and then, she would turn to see if they were still okay and would glance at Greyson's grey palette, still wide-eyed and blinking in the brightness of the night. Eventually, they reached the sign that Ida had inspected before. One road, she thought, pulling on Bullet's reins and turning him in a tight circle, getting him to calm and slow down, shushing both horses. They stopped, both breathing hard after their desperate runs. Ida dismounted and pulled her canteen out, pouring some water into her hand and holding it beneath Bullet's mouth. He lapped it up.

'Here, dismount. Start collecting things for a fire. We can melt some of this white stuff, get the horses a long drink,' Ida said, nodding. Greyson sat still, his eyes still glazed in a type of fear. The rune against Ida's skin was no longer burning, and she took a sip of the canteen and stepped forward. 'Greyson?' she said. His eyes suddenly flicked to hers.

'Did you see it?' he asked, his face shaking, though whether it was from cold or fear, Ida could not tell.

'Tell me…'

'It was a face. It was the cruellest face I ever saw. And it said my name. It said my name. My full name.' Greyson pulled his bound hands up to his face, wiping away the run from beneath his nose. Ida stared at him and took a sharp breath in.

'All right.' She pulled the knife from her holster and reached up, slicing through the rope that bound his wrists. He watched her as she removed them. 'Now listen, I have your guns, and I can ride faster than you. If you try anything, anything at all, that'll be it. You've more of a chance of getting that five hundred dollars if you help me than if you go it alone anyway. If you go it alone, you'll find your face on a bounty poster soon enough.' She passed up the canteen and watched Greyson take a drink before he handed it back. He stared at her.

'Did you not hear what I said?' he asked. The wind began to whip around them again, and Ida pulled the bear pelt close.

'I heard all right. The Alask Wilds are haunted. You knew that.'

'Yeah...' He turned around and glanced at the snow-covered mountains that they had just left, towering above them. 'But...that's where Billy saw something last time. That's where he lost his mind, and he galloped up that hill...he pushed that horse and...' Greyson trailed off and licked his lips. Then, he seemed to remember that his wrists were now untied and began patting his pockets. He pulled out a cigarette, offered one to Ida, who refused, and lit it. With it hanging from his mouth, he dismounted, his heavy boots falling into the snow.

'How's your arm?' Ida asked.

'It's...a dull ache.' He drew on his cigarette, the effect the same as his breath was before, the cold air and smoke lingering.

'Listen, we need to get that fire lit, eat some, rest if we can. We shouldn't hang around here,' Ida prompted. Greyson didn't move and stared back at the hills.

'Greyson,' she said. 'You're all right. You're alive, but you won't be without a little warmth. I'll sort out the horses. You build a fire. If I have to ask you again, I'll shoot you in the other arm.' Ida grinned with mock cruelty and saw Greyson's face break for the first time since she met him. He gave a small scoff, a slight upturn in his lips. It made Ida give a genuine smile, perhaps the first in quite a while, too.

Once the fire was lit and the horses rugged, the two sat in the firelight, warming themselves. There was no fresh meat to be had today, but they snacked on the crackers and some salted meat that Greyson had found in his saddlebag, apparently forgotten about until now. They passed the straight rye between them soundlessly, the crackling of the fire the backdrop of the gentle glug of liquid against glass.

'You know what I don't know about you?' Greyson said. Ida glanced up and shrugged. 'I don't even know your last name.'

'John.'

'Sounds to me like your names are the wrong way round, don't you think? Colton John. Should be John Colton.'

Ida shrugged and stared into the fire.

'John Colton. Colton John,' Greyson said, playing with the words.

'Doesn't matter either way,' Ida said.

'I suppose not. And there's another thing, you know— your voice. Sometimes, you speak as though you just swallowed a lit match, and at other times, it's like…you forget…or something. It's lighter.'

Ida sighed and took a swig of rye, feeling the heat run down her throat and into her chest, and then passed the bottle over. 'Yeah, well. While we're making observations…you don't seem like much of a bounty hunter to me.' She gave Greyson a hard stare and a shrug, noticing that her voice had, in fact, slipped from Colton's into Ida's. It would be the rye, she thought. And her tiredness.

'Not having a go at you. I'm just curious about how you are,' Greyson said, offering a tight smile.

'Well, it's not for you to be curious about. Get some sleep. We got a long ride up to the top of The Nameless Stretch.' Ida stood up, picked up the top of her canvas roll mat, and climbed inside, pulling it up to her chin. She dropped to the floor and lay down, placed her hat over her face and closed her eyes, breathing in. How much did the man know? She wasn't sure.

When Ida woke up, she was surprised to see Greyson already awake and making coffee over the still-lit fire. That meant he had at least tended to it a little overnight. The first thing she did was check that she still had both holsters with their guns beneath her roll mat. She did. He hadn't robbed her then, perhaps he was better than that. He passed Ida a cup of coffee with a nod of the head, and she took it, trying to remember the last time someone had made her something without her asking. It had indeed been a while, that was for sure. Greyson nudged a piece of burning wood, watching it crackle.

'So I've been thinking,' he said.

'Hmmm.' Ida made a noise to show that she was at least listening.

'You haven't given me no proof that you know Ida Vale. I would like to see some.'

'You're not in a position to ask for proof. Anyway, what proof do you need? Prove to me that you're the son of your mother.'

'Well, I can't,' Greyson responded, shrugging.

'Exactly. No proof. You just have to wait.'

They sat in silence for a moment, and Greyson drained his cup. Then he reached into his pocket and pulled out the bounty poster, unfolding it and inspecting the picture. 'Five hundred dollars,' he said.

Ida took a fleeting look at him. 'She must've done something terrible to be worth such a high bounty,' she said.

Greyson held the picture in front of him, his eyes moving between Ida and the photograph. Then, he winced slightly and dropped the arm, reaching for the wound.

'What are you looking for?' Ida asked, fighting the urge to pull her pistol.

'I don't know. I got my suspicions.'

'Go on.'

'Well, Colton. My old boss told me to suspect everyone. You kind of have the same jaw as this woman here in the photograph. You know her by relation?' Greyson began to prod his loose tooth with his tongue again, a habit that was now becoming a staple.

'You think what, she's my sister?'

'Maybe so. Five hundred dollars is a lot of money. Maybe you're just trying to get rid of a bounty hunter so that you can hand her in yourself for the dough.'

'So what, she's my sister, or am I after her?' Ida laughed, finishing her drink and standing up.

'I don't know.'

'Exactly. You don't know. Saddle up your horse; we've got a journey.'

The horses were keen to warm themselves up; a slight nudge was all it took for them to break into a hard gallop across the flat and barren land of Hangman's Rest. Now that Greyson was no longer tethered to Ida and Bullet, he occasionally edged forward. Ida observed him, grateful that Bullet was a horse not to be usurped in leadership. In a way, it was like a race, though Ida couldn't imagine where Greyson was running to. Perhaps just away from her. Slowly, Ida saw that there was something on the horizon. The town of Incan's Brook began to show, and she pulled Bullet to a jog and then a walk, indicating that Greyson should do the same.

'We're going to turn right across Hangman's Rest. We should end up coming out at the end of the Derelict Woods, and if we travel between there and Demon's Canyon, we'll reach Bleakhollow eventually. Where we're visiting is at the north end.' She pulled the bottle of straight rye from her saddlebag for no reason at all and took a deep sip, replacing the cork without offering Greyson any.

'No, no, no,' he responded, 'Right there is Incan's Brook. I know people there, we can get a good meal, a firm bed. We'll be better off resting there for the night.' The air billowed around them, significantly warmer than it had been in the south. Ida lay a hand on Bullet's neck and felt the sweat beading beneath his coat.

'No,' she said. 'We are not heading somewhere where you have a gang waiting for you to return with Ida Vale. Absolutely not. Do you think I'm a fool?'

Greyson pulled his horse to a halt and glared. 'Colton, a warm bed. A meal. Are you honest—'

'I said no. My word is final. I don't much trust even being this close to a town filled with your friends.' As if to finalise the thought, Ida pulled Bullet swiftly to the right and cut in front of Greyson with a sharp smile. 'You go that way, and I'll shoot you with your own pistol,' she said, raising her eyebrows in defiance. Greyson's lip curled, and he allowed his horse to follow.

'Yes,' he said to her back.

'What?'

'I'm answering your question. Yes, I do think you're a fool.'

Ida said nothing and reached into her saddlebag once more, pulling out some salted meat from the night before and chewing on it casually. Once more, she didn't offer anything to Greyson. He pulled his horse up beside her and sighed.

'We should stop soon; the sun is low in the sky.'

'Oh, we're not stopping. We won't stop until we reach the border of Bleakhollow, at the very least,' Ida responded with a full mouth.

'That seems foolish.'

'And so it would make sense, wouldn't it? A foolish act from a fool.' Ida raised her eyebrows, daring him to argue, and felt Bullet move into a lope beneath her without the need to touch his sides. He was basking in the warmer weather already, keen to stretch his legs and run. Ida let him, the reins loose in her hand. She checked back on Greyson now and then, who rode after them with a scowl, into the darkness.

The footsteps on the flowers, treading them into the dirt. The gun, heavy in her hand. Ida stared down the barrel once more and got ready to fire. Wait, she thought, hold on. What if, this time, you didn't? This was a new thought. She lowered the gun and squinted at the figure, making his way through her flower patch, the one that she had so carefully curated all those years ago. Who was that? It wasn't the brother whose face was etched in her mind, despite the fact that she had only seen him once for real. It wasn't his strange face, almost like that of her father's, almost like her own, but nothing like her mother's. It was someone else entirely. It was that man from the saloon. Ida frowned, lifting her gun again. Colt, wasn't it? There he stood, his weaselly expression blinking back at her, his thin and sallow cheeks. She remembered it from their hideous dalliance.

'You stole from me.' The words drifted from his still mouth, and Ida blinked, shaking her head. The words came again. He was carrying his own gun, she noticed, and now aiming it at her. Ida stepped backwards and shot, hitting him in the shoulder. He shifted back to the left.

'You stole from me.' The words came again, sifting through her brain. There was a sense of somebody beside her, someone standing next to her. She turned and stared at the stranger, an old woman, standing with a placating smile. Wasn't this the one who had shot her previously? Who was this? She had an odd familiarity about her. The woman turned to Colt as though moving through water, her body gliding in slow motion.

'So shoot her,' she said, her lips parting to form a grimace, her hands flailing before her. Ida turned back to the man who stood in her garden and shouted.

'Oi!' Greyson said, prodding her in the arm. Ida flinched, opening her eyes. She was hunched over the saddle, the quarter-full bottle of straight rye in her left hand, the reins in her right.

'Eh?' she said quietly, staring at Greyson's dimly lit face in the kerosene lamplight.

'You were asleep, shouting. Dreaming, were you?'

Ida nodded and stared out at the darkness. She turned in the saddle and wiped her brow, sweating in the ever-growing temperature. Even at night, the land that lay in the centre of The Nameless Stretch was hotter than the daytime of The City of Glass. She shifted in her bearskin pelt and wrapped the reins around the pommel of her saddle, re-securing the bottle in the saddlebag.

'Yeah, I was dreaming. Dreaming about that place we are going to.' She looked at Greyson. 'I'll be grateful to have your help. I need another gun out there.' There was a strange feeling when you awoke next to a stranger, she thought. It was unusual. Even though you didn't know them, it was as though you had shared something different. Like your guard had been lowered without your knowledge, and now you awoke as a new person.

'Well, you deliver on your promise, and I'll be a spare gun. Is that where Ida is hiding out, where we're heading?' Greyson asked.

'Sure,' Ida responded. She turned in her saddle and stared back from the direction they had come from. There in the distance behind them was Incan's Brook, the town lit up in the nighttime. Ida couldn't help but think of the beds there, the saloon, the meals and the bourbon. But still, she thought, she had made the right call. It wasn't going to be a restful night's sleep if you woke up to a gang of bounty hunters comparing your face to a bounty on a poster, that was for sure. She turned back to Greyson.

'Maybe we should bed down for the rest of the night, get a little shut-eye before the sun comes up. The horses are labouring a bit anyway now,' he said.

Ida yawned. It was true; Bullet had undoubtedly slowed. And yet, she didn't trust Greyson yet. They were not so far away from Incan's Brook that he couldn't ride back while she slept. She shook her head. They wouldn't stop.

Chapter 31

Mrs Vale licked her lips and took a sip of the tea. There, she thought, that'll do the trick. The girl would be dreaming of killing Colt over her son already. The herbs were potent, collected in the woods to the west of the homestead, doubtless where the girl had spent time when she was growing up. That might even make them stronger, Mrs Vale speculated. She heard the footsteps next door again and rolled her eyes, blowing out the candle before her.

She made her way to the bed and climbed beneath the heavy woollen covers, closing her eyes. The mattress was cold against the skin on her legs, and she pulled the covers tighter, smelling that strange scent that the previous occupant had left behind. Dust, tobacco smoke. Her husband. She thought of him in this bed. How strange to think of him now, as she slept, after so many years of sleeping beside him. Of course, those times were few and far between, what with his second wife over here.

It was a scent that took her back, far back, to when Trick was born, and the man who was responsible for getting her pregnant slept heavily beside her. A lazy man, an unhelpful man, but a man all the same. And then, he was gone. His visits were limited after that, a flash in the night, a week here and there, mostly after the death of his new wife. She would watch him when he slept during those times and wonder about the daughter. The new family member he had brought into his life. How selfish. How cruel. The second wife was barely a mother before she succumbed to her injuries, and even that didn't bring him back into her bed. Mrs Vale breathed in the scent of the pillow and sighed. Things could have been so different if only he'd listened. If only he had paid attention and chosen the right family, the rightful heir, his own son, then they would all be happy together. How foolish men are. How readily they follow youth.

The ride through the night was tough on all of them. Whether it was the sounds or the exhaustion, Ida did not know, but the horses were flighty, their ears laying against their heads often, their movements light and powerful. At times, Ida felt as though she had no control at all, as though Bullet was deciding on their speed and direction alone, and she was merely there for the ride. Occasionally, she would slip into a strange type of sleep, and her body could not keep her awake for anything.

They crept across the land, in fits and bursts and jogs and lopes, until they finally reached the border of Bleakhollow. By then, the sun was once more in the sky, having crept up without being noticed by either traveller. Ida looked at the barren desert, feeling the heat hit her skin. She pulled on Bullet's reins and dismounted clumsily, half falling to her feet. She pulled the bear pelt off her skin, rolling it and fixing it to the back of her saddle. Greyson watched her, circling his horse.

'It's hot,' he said, as though the words needed to be said, as though the phrase would make anything easier. Ida stared at him over Bullet's sweating back and sighed, removing her canteen and taking a drink.

'Yeah. We're at the border now. There's a cave over that way,' she gestured toward Demon's Canyon, and Greyson turned in his saddle to stare at the grey rocks in the distance. 'It's got water. I don't know. It's quite cool. Maybe we should head there for a rest.'

'Who's this?' Greyson said suddenly, his eyes narrowing. Ida flinched and stared in the direction that he was looking in. It was a couple of horses with people astride in the distance on the Bleakhollow side. They appeared to have seen them and were making some kind of gesture toward them. Ida quickly mounted.

'Listen—' She swallowed, thinking of the posters that had made their way across the map, bearing her face. 'I'm not sure how this is going to go down—'

'Hand me my guns,' Greyson interrupted. Ida hesitated and glanced at the approaching strangers, who were now galloping toward them, dust billowing behind.

'I don't know.'

'You have my word. You're gonna need backup if this goes south, and it appears to me that you're a little concerned. I don't know what trouble you got yourself into, Colton, but I know a few reasons someone might be scared of a couple of strangers and rather hang out in a cave for rest than a bed in a saloon.'

Ida swallowed and began to undo Greyson's holster, which still sat around her hips. She nudged Bullet toward him and handed it over with a stern stare. 'I'm quick on the draw, have my back and do not cross me. You will have your reward.'

'As I said, you have my word.'

The strangers were upon them. Ida pulled her hat down and hunched in her saddle, hunching her shoulders. They were men, it appeared, which did not surprise her. They rounded on them, one white horse, one palomino. Both men were stout and chunky, scraggly hair sprouting from beneath their hats.

'Where you come from?' the one on the white horse said.

'Who's asking?' responded Greyson, still doing up the buckle on his holster.

'We're looking for someone, that's all. You seen any strangers on your travels?'

'Only the ones in front of us now,' Ida said deeply, doing her best to embody Colton entirely.

The man on the palomino horse grinned a toothless smile and laughed, moving closer to Ida.

'We are looking for this person – you seen her?' The first man held up the poster that Ida knew all too well, the one bearing her face with the five hundred dollar reward. She shook her head. Greyson pulled the same poster from his pocket.

'Boys, you're not the only ones,' he said. Both men flicked their attention to him and frowned.

'You bounty hunters? That's our bounty. We thought we had her at one point. Lost the trail,' said the man on the white horse.

'Well, if you've not got her, then she's not your bounty, is she?' Ida responded.

The man hocked up some phlegm from the back of his throat and spat it on the ground. 'Where you been looking? We could share information. We already searched Steepmount, Blackreach, ain't made it as far as the Docks.'

Greyson scratched his head and shrugged. 'She's in The City of Glass. Mark my word.'

The man on the palomino horse frowned and shook his head, looking to his colleague, who rolled his eyes. 'You liar,' he said plainly. 'What you doing here if that's where you think she is?'

'She's holed up on the other side of the mountain. She's got a gang. She's no normal whore, they got supplies, guns, and it's gonna take more than just us two to clear her out and bring her back for that money. We're just on our way to Steepmount – that's where the sheriff who's paying is – see if we can't get us a gang to travel back up that way.'

Ida looked at Greyson; it was some excellent lying and quickly done. She shrugged and made a murmuring sound of agreement.

'You two couldn't take her, that's what you're saying?' the man on the white horse said.

'She scared us off a little, and we wanted back up,' Ida said.

'Oh...so you didn't try. You just got scared.' The two men laughed, the one on the white horse smacking his leg and hooting. Ida stared at the strangers and nodded.

'Listen, this whole land is lousy with people looking for Ida Vale. You feeling brave? You head there yourself and claim her. We all got our ways.'

The men looked at each other, both still grinning. 'Well, you two,' the man on the white horse said, 'are idiots.' Then, in a flash, they disappeared beyond, their horses' hooves hammering across the dusty ground.

Ida and Greyson watched them go in silence, and then Greyson turned back to her.

'Shame. Seemed like nice men.' They began to laugh, the lack of sleep and heat making them both feel a little hysterical. Through her laughing tears, Ida noticed that the figure of her mother was standing before her again. She smiled, genuinely pleased to see her. Whatever focus she had lost was suddenly back. Her mother gave her a gentle nod in response.

'If we can ride up the left side of Bleakhollow, we should make it past the towns to the edge of Gorman Forest. That's just a little way from where we're headed.'

Greyson nodded. 'How do you know?'

'My father had a map of Bleakhollow. I used to spend time memorising it, but you know, since travelling through Hangman's Rest, I seem to have been able to add to it a little. It's like my mind has filled in the gaps.'

'All right. We're avoiding towns then…'

Ida nodded in response and clicked her tongue, feeling Bullet move beneath her. 'Avoiding towns. We'll travel by day. Rest a little. Come up upon the homestead at night.'

'We robbin' a homestead? That don't seem like a lawful thing to do.'

'Lawful? It's my land, stolen from me. The least they could do is give it back.'

Greyson said nothing and moved along beside her. They crossed the border into Bleakhollow, and began to head to the left, a diagonal line meant to avoid all towns. The ground here was well worn, hoofprints littering the dirt land. Ida thought of the money inside her bag for a moment, remembering all that she had taken from Colt, from the trading post. It might even make up five hundred, she thought, enough to pay Greyson off. She glanced over at him, his tired eyes fixed on the road ahead. How greedy was the man, though? Would he be paid off and then demand the extra five hundred from the sheriff for the location of Ida? Her eyes travelled down to his gun, now resting on his hip. Perhaps it had been a foolish thing to do, to hand them back. But still, surely he had no idea who she really was.

When the evening came again, Colt fixed himself coffee for the first time since his arrival. Mrs Vale watched him curiously as she came out of her adopted bedroom, removing her apron. It was a glimmer of responsibility, perhaps the first since helping himself to whisky and cigarettes.

'So,' Colt said as he saw her settle at the table. 'When do you reckon she'll arrive? It's been a fair bit of time, ain't it?' He put a cup down in front of her, a thump of porcelain on wood. 'I'm thinkin' maybe you were wrong about it.'

'She's coming all right. Trust me in that. I am rarely wrong, boy.' She took a sip of the too-hot liquid and sighed.

'That floor is getting mighty uncomfortable,' Colt said, his stare lingering. Mrs Vale gave him a tight smile.

'It won't be for much longer. Best to have someone front and centre in case she arrives in the night.'

'Hmm. I suppose so.'

They sat in silence, Mrs Vale staring at the door, waiting for it to burst open. She focused on the handle, imagining it turning, the woman on the other side. Colt watched her as if he were studying the lines on her face. Then, as though her mind had brought the image to life, the door handle turned. Mrs Vale jumped to her feet. It swung open to reveal her son. Trick stood on the other side of the threshold, scratching his head.

'All right?' he asked tetchily.

'Yes, son. Yes. I thought you might have been…thirsty. Here, have some coffee.' Mrs Vale pushed her cup toward the other side of the table with a weary look. Trick looked at it and scoffed.

'It's whisky hour,' he responded with a curled lip, pulling a half-empty bottle from the cupboard beneath the sink and pouring himself a healthy shot. He sat down, downing the molten fire. 'My wife is arriving within the week. I have been so informed. I want you out of here by this time next week, no arguing.' He slammed the glass on the table and stood up, the chair screeching along the wooden floor. 'And that means especially you,' he said to Colt, jabbing a finger into his arm. Colt recoiled.

'It's enough time, son. She'll be here,' Mrs Vale said, an appeasing smile resting on her lips.

Chapter 32

Avoiding the bright lights of the towns was easy enough. They advertised themselves with a song as well as brightness, and as Ida passed by, she thought of all of those years spent locked in the homestead, imagining the map of Bleakhollow come to life before her. Back then, the towns were twinkling stars in the distance, masses of far-off danger. Her father would warn her so often of what lay beyond the gates that she would look at the images as otherworldly. As long as she stayed at home, she knew she was safe. Now, as she rode to the edge of Gorman Forest, Ida noticed that she no longer flinched at the noise of far-off gunfire and yelling. Now, it was what she had come to expect, the same as any town in The Nameless Stretch. She watched the night sky, the moon rising above them, the bright lights pinpricked through the clouds.

'We should rest here for an hour or so, regain our strength,' she said. Bullet's ears flicked backwards. They rode in the darkness, no kerosene lamp lit at all, for fear of being spotted on the horizon. There was no response. Ida turned in her saddle to stare back at Greyson, who appeared to be sleeping, holding onto the pommel of his saddle and snoring quietly with every movement. She nodded; he was in agreement then.

The trees ahead offered a strange mix of darkness and comfort. Ida longed for a bit of cover, somewhere to hide for a while. She nudged Bullet forward a little before pulling up in a small clearing. As yet, she could not see the homestead, and estimated that it was an hour's ride away.

There had been times when she had come to this forest with her father by her side, to pick herbs for the kitchen. It was odd to think of those moments now, so close to her home, and know that it was no longer her own. She dismounted and rolled her shoulders back, hitching Bullet to a tree. Then, she turned and hitched Greyson's horse too, careful not to disturb him. She was ready. Ready to reclaim what belonged to her. She pulled her bedroll from the back of the saddle and laid it on the ground, climbing in and leaving Greyson to sleep. As she was about to close her eyes, she started. There was her mother again, standing before her. She had a strange expression on her face, one of concern, and yet there was something in her eyes that Ida had never seen before. She sat up and stared at the strange figure in the moonlight. Her mother nodded at her and smiled. Ida's breath caught in her throat. It was a look she had never seen but somehow understood within her bones. It was pride. She nodded back at her and lay down, allowing the heat of the Bleakhollow night to warm her skin as it had done when she was a child. She slept immediately.

As wholly as sleep had enveloped her, it released her a couple of hours later. Ida awoke to see Greyson leaning against his horse, eyes closed, hat pulled forward. She sat up and began to pack up the bedroll, feeling as refreshed as though she had slept all night long. Greyson heard the slight noise and opened his eyes, blinking in the moonlight.

'You shoulda woken me up,' he said, removing his hat and replacing it squarely.

'Didn't seem much point in waking you to sleep,' Ida responded, fixing the bedroll to the back of the saddle.

'Hmm. So what's the plan then, Colton John?' Greyson asked. There was something in the way he said it that made her look up and stare at him. There was something beneath his tone, a suggestion of mocking that Ida didn't care for. She glared at him for a beat.

'The man that took my home and killed my father is in the house. I'm going to head in through the front door, and you go in the back.' She paused. 'Listen, you want to make an extra hundred?'

Greyson looked up at the mention of this and frowned. 'You got an extra hundred to give? Where you got that kind of money from?' His eyes flickered to the saddlebag, and Ida mounted, turning Bullet to face him.

'I can get you the extra if you kill the man.'

There was silence between them. Ida swallowed, thinking of what she was really offering. She knew two things: her brother would need to be killed to give up the homestead and that she did not want to be haunted by that man. Greyson scratched his head.

'Aren't you a bounty hunter, Greyson? You never killed a man before?' Ida asked. Greyson sighed.

'Yeah, I killed a man. I didn't enjoy it.'

'Well, you don't seem marked by the consequences,' Ida responded, turning in her saddle as if to look for ghosts. If the man was not aware he was being haunted, what were the chances he would notice one more? Still, she thought, her brother would doubtless be a malevolent man in the afterlife.

'The man in that house is my brother, and I do not want to be responsible for his death. Do you understand me?' The lies were dripping from her tongue with such ease that Ida could barely notice them. She thought of her mother's look of pride and glanced around. She wasn't there now, but she was watching. Greyson scratched his beard and shrugged.

'I'll do what I can,' he said finally, mounting his horse.

Together, they moved through the trees, heading north. Ida played the version of events that she expected to happen on repeat. She would knock on the door, and her brother would answer it. Greyson would sneak in the back way. Ida would hold up her gun and reveal herself. Greyson would shoot. She thought about the aftermath. Maybe it would be best to get Greyson to shoot in the yard, less mess. Then, Ida would live in the house, only the ghost of her mother for company. She frowned at this last part. It didn't sound like the ideal version of her life.

There was sound at the homestead as Trick slept, as loudly as ever. His snores punctuated what little silence there was. The rats helped with the nighttime noise, trying as they did to find the food in the kitchen that wasn't all cleared away at supper time.

Colt lay in front of the dying fire, as usual, sleeping in fits and starts, unsure as to when sleep would take him with its whole self. Usually, it was at around three in the morning. Currently, it was only around two. Mrs Vale slept quietly enough, the occasional murmur at a strange dream, some that she would remember, and some that she would not. As Ida and Greyson arrived at the gate, the house appeared to be all in silence.

The gate was open already, hoofprints scattering the dirt, the sides that used to be filled with bright and beautiful flowers now empty of anything but soil. Ida held her hand up to Greyson and dismounted, hitching Bullet to the gate. Greyson did the same. They walked down the path and stood in silence, watching the house. No movement at all.

How strange it was to see the old place, definitely looking worse than when Ida had left it. The paint on the front was peeling off the old wood, and she frowned upon seeing it. It was something that she and her father did every year: paint the house. The more you look after a place, her father would say, the more it looks after you. Ida had taken that to heart, understanding that this would be her heritage. This home. As she looked at it now, a stranger to its wooden charms, it seemed so different. This was her heritage? This stack of wood in the middle of nowhere? She turned and observed the view that she was so used to and frowned. She thought of the strange charms of The City of Glass, the way that the icicles hung from the buildings. She remembered the scent of fish from the market in Incan's Brook, the pride of the people as they marched through. She considered the strange trees in the forests, the jagged, dangerous edges of Demon's Canyon. Ida thought of the map and all that she had seen and had yet to see. And yet…what was rightfully hers was her own indeed. She drew her pistols and turned to Greyson.

'You head round the back. There's a door to the scullery, leads to the kitchen. I'll head in the front. Wait when you get there. You'll know when to enter,' she said.

Greyson tipped his hat and drew his guns, too, leaving her alone to walk to the other side of the house. Ida swallowed. So this was it. Her father's old chair was sitting on the porch, the divot in which it rocked still visible. Beside it was a small stool. Ida glanced at it. Then, she stepped onto the porch and reached for the door. She grasped hold of the cold handle, turning it. It was, of course, unlocked. In a homestead, so far from anywhere, in a land where guns rested on thighs, locks were just an inconvenience for those who needed the toilet in the nighttime.

Ida pushed the door ajar, the moonlight bathing the front room in cold light. The scent was different from when she was there herself, and yet she breathed in lavender, honey, and sweat. She took it all in: the table, where it was before, the sink, the fire…still lit – the man, lying before it, staring at her. Ida focused. The face of the man was familiar, but why? It wasn't the brother that she had been expecting to see. And then, it clicked. An image of this weasel-faced brute above her, sweating over her body. As this realisation hit her, the man sat up and parted his lips.

'SHE'S ARRIVED!' he yelled, an almighty sound dropping through the air and causing Ida to shudder back to reality. She raised her gun and aimed it, and he scrambled to his feet. The bedroom door smashed open, a different man tumbling out. Now, this one was her brother, Ida saw. This was the man she had expected to see. He glared at her and then shook his head.

'You what? This ain't her.'

The other bedroom door swung open to reveal an old woman, smiling from ear to ear. She paused when she looked at Ida and then laughed.

'Oh, it is. But a beautiful disguise, no doubt. You look like your father. In fact,' the woman glanced between Trick and Ida, 'the resemblance is uncanny.'

Ida glared at the three before her and lifted her chin. 'This house is mine.'

'You stole my horse and my money, you b—' Colt began, and Ida cut him off with a single bullet fired into his shin. He screamed and fell to the floor, clutching his bloody leg.

'Wasn't it a fair deal? What did you take from me, exactly?' she responded before aiming the gun at her brother. His lip curled, and he reached beneath his shirt, pulling his own small pistol.

'Now, now,' the old woman said, raising her hands. 'Can't we settle this like civilised people? Ida Vale, isn't it?'

Ida glanced at the woman and said nothing. Trick sat down at the kitchen table like he was waiting for coffee, his gun still aimed. Beside them all, Colt groaned, clutching his leg.

'Oh shut up, boy,' the old woman barked. 'You got a gun, haven't you?'

Colt shook his head, beads of sweat forming on his forehead. 'I left it in the latrine earlier.' The old woman sucked in her cheeks and then sighed, muttering about a waste of time.

'Ida Vale, sit down,' she said. 'My name is Mrs Vale. I was married to your father.'

Ida baulked at the suggestion and remained standing. She shook her head.

'You sit down. This is not your home. My father and mother own this home, and it is rightfully mine. You may leave now or face the consequences.' She raised her eyebrows at Colt. 'And I don't even know why you are here.'

'He's here to kill you,' Mrs Vale said with a kind smile. It was strange to see such words come from her mouth. 'And yet, you know that legally, this home goes to the firstborn male. That would be my son. In fact, you are trespassing.'

'The law is certainly kinder to men,' Ida responded.

'Oh, and don't I know it, and yet, what are we to do?' Mrs Vale grinned.

At that, the back door flew open, and Greyson stepped in, holding his guns aloft. With one clean shot, and without any warning, he fired a bullet directly through the back of Trick's head. Blood splattered across the wooden table where Ida had eaten her first meal, and Trick fell forward, his body slumping over. The spectators paused at the sight, including Ida, staring at the scene with disbelief. She had almost forgotten that Greyson was there at all, waiting out back. Mrs Vale beheld her son, lying dead on the table, before turning her full attention back to Ida.

'You want this old house so much that you killed my son?' she asked, her strange mirth-like glow now dissipated and replaced with a rage. 'You want this heap of junk that much?! We were supposed to get rid of you so I could go to the grave, knowing you would never return.'

'He killed my father.'

'And I'll kill your father's daughter,' she hissed.

Ida breathed out sharply, a strange realisation that the rune that still lay against her skin had started burning once more. It was as though she just plunged her hand into a fire, so sudden and sharp was the pain. She sucked the dank air into her mouth and aimed her pistol at the old woman with one hand, using the other to grasp the smooth shape that blistered her skin. As she grabbed it, the woman sneered.

'Just like you killed your own mother.' The words were so simple, so short, and yet they pierced a part of Ida as she looked at the woman. She pulled the rune out and grasped it in her hand, feeling it tear at her skin. She focused on the woman before her.

'Greyson, s-s-shoot her,' Ida said, faltering over the word in pain. The burning was pulling away all of her attention, and she shivered against the sensation.

'I'm not killin' an old woman, Colton,' Greyson responded.

'Colton?' Mrs Vale said with an amused grimace. 'So what, you think you can dress up and rename yourself, come back here and kill my son? Claim what is not yours? You haven't even begun to understand what revenge is. And yet...when you killed your mother, it was a work of art. The young thing didn't even know what she was dealing with.'

Ida stared at the words coming from the wrinkled mouth, the heat of the rune rising still. And yet, she held onto it.

The old woman shook her head in disbelief and growled, pulling her hand from her pocket. She opened her palm. Ida glanced down at it and saw that she, too, was carrying a rune with a strange emblem emblazoned on it that Ida did not recognise. It glowed in the dim light.

'You should be dead, girl. What witchcraft are you using?' she said furiously.

Ida looked up at the woman's contorted face and saw beads of sweat forming on her brow.

'You're a witch,' she said, feeling the power of her rune pulsate and shiver down her arm.

'As was your mother,' Mrs Vale responded before muttering something beneath her breath.

Behind her, something began to appear in the air, and Ida saw with great pleasure that it was the shape of her mother. Her mother's eyes were bright and still, no longer staring into nothing as they had for so long. With a single step forward, she reached out with her strange shadowed hands and pushed the rune from the old woman's claw, causing it to fall to the floor.

Mrs Vale's lips parted in disbelief, and as she began to speak in protest, she fell to the floor, still. The rune in Ida's hand stopped burning almost instantly, and she opened her fingers, staring at it. It has just become an old stone in her palm, as though the power within it were spent.

'Thank you, Mother,' she said, nodding at the image. Her mother's kind eyes stared back.

'You killed her,' Colt said, turning Ida's attention back to the man she had almost forgotten was there. 'We were gonna marry. We were gonna get married,' he gabbled.

Greyson stepped toward, surveying the scene. The old woman was now crumpled on the floor, her eyes plain and staring. 'You were gonna marry this old woman?' he asked, scratching his beard.

Colt scowled at him and then clutched his leg once more. 'I loved her – I reckon.'

'Well, that's…that's up to you. Um, Colton, what do you want I should do with this man?'

Ida glanced up at Greyson and shook her head. 'Ida,' she said plainly. Greyson gave her a small smile, unsurprised by the grand reveal.

'Well, I know that. I've known that since…oh, must be up in the mountains. Nothing to do with me what you call yourself. You want me to kill this chap, or should we just put him on a horse and send him on his way?'

Ida smiled, grateful for his assistance. Without him, she already knew that she would most likely be dead. Three against two, one of whom is a ghost.

'My horse!' Colt shouted, 'My Trigger! You got him?'

Ida nodded. 'Yeah, Bullet, I renamed him. He's a good horse, and I came to care for him greatly.'

'I don't care,' Colt responded, rocking back and forth on the floor. 'You stole my everything. You stole my adventure. My money. My horse. Why did you do that to me?'

Ida pulled out a chair and sat down at the table, removing her hat and placing it on the wood, trying to avoid the streaks of blood.

'I'll tell you. It was because everything was taken from me. It was the only way out, as far as I could see it. But that doesn't make it right. I know that. Listen, I've got enough to give you what I stole from you, and I can see to it that you got a horse for your travels, though if you left me with Bullet, I would be grateful. If forgiveness is what I deserve, then I request that you provide it to me and put yourself in my position, just for a moment.'

Colt shook his head and wiped his nose, saying nothing. Greyson stepped forward and reholstered his gun smoothly.

'From what I hear, you just said, boy, that you wanted an adventure. Let me tell you, travelling through The Nameless Stretch isn't an adventure unless something happens to you. You don't wanna go from town to town trying different cuts of meat and meeting a bunch of old folks. You want something that keeps you on your toes, something that makes you grateful for that quiet life. I don't know how you came to end up here, but having everything you own stolen from you, managing to make your way across the map, falling in love with… an ancient, well…she was a witch, eh? That sounds like an adventure to me.'

Colt regarded the body before him and shrugged, a slight nod forming. 'I want my horse,' he said sullenly.

'Yeah,' said Ida. 'I think it's fair. But you must promise me one thing, Colt. I know that there are bounty hunters out there looking for Ida Vale because of you. If you tell one person who I am, where I live, or mention my name again, I will find you. Do we have a deal?'

Colt nodded, a heavy head swinging. He tried to stand up and failed.

'Right,' said Greyson, 'I'm gonna get him to a doctor. You want I should um…' he glanced around the kitchen at the bodies, 'clean up before I leave?'

Ida nodded, 'Yeah, I would appreciate it.'

Chapter 33

The sun was rising by the time the three stepped out onto the porch. Greyson had carefully laid the bodies of Trick and Mrs Vale out in a shallow ditch somewhere, unbeknownst to Ida, who said she couldn't think of wanting to know. He had helped Colt into the saddle of Bullet, who now fell forward and whispered into the horse's mane, the only audible words being 'Trigger' now and again. Ida stepped forward and raised a hand to Bullet's muzzle, touching the soft velvet for the last time. She leaned her head against his coat and breathed in that scent she had become so accustomed to. Hay, sweat, home.

'So, best of luck,' Greyson said, touching his hat. Ida nodded, handing over the saddlebag that she had carried around with her all this time. Greyson peered into it, seeing the piles of notes climbing over each other, and nodded. 'I appreciate this. I'll see that he gets his.'

'I know that you will, Greyson.'

'Colton John, it has been a pleasure riding with you. You ever find yourself up at Incan's Brook again, I hope you won't be a stranger.'

Ida nodded and watched Greyson mount. He grabbed the reins of Bullet and pulled him along, Colt grumbling all the while, his leg causing him pain.

Ida stood for hours in that one spot, just watching the figures of the pair get smaller and smaller on the horizon. How strange it felt to be the one left behind, as though she were watching her father ride away for another week in a town she wasn't allowed to visit. She couldn't help but wish it was her there too, riding off for another adventure.

Eventually, Ida turned and stepped back into the homestead. She fixed herself a coffee and some stew out of the vegetables she found in a cupboard and then scrubbed the kitchen table of the blood that had stained it. It barely came up, despite her scrubbing for hours. A tablecloth, she thought, that would have to do. She stepped into her room and pulled open the cabinet where they had always been kept, displaying her old dresses and hand-downs from her mother. She lay a hand on one and felt a strange sickness hit her stomach. It wasn't right. None of it felt right. The dresses, hanging in the closet, waiting to be worn by a quiet, lonely woman. The tablecloths waiting to cover up an act of revenge. There was just nothingness, an empty future.

Ida stepped back, leaving the closet open, and reached inside her shirt again and pulled out the rune, staring at it. She looked up to see her mother standing there, before the dresses, a strange, sad expression on her face. Ida smiled at her.

"No Mrs Vale haunting me then, Mother?"

Her mother shook her head. "You didn't kill her, I did."

'And I appreciate it. But I'm not the same anymore,' Ida said. There was a small mirror nailed to the wall beside the closet, and she stepped up, staring into it. Her face was different from what she remembered, the dirt-smudged onto her skin the least of it. Her shaved hair was starting to grow back.

'I'm not for this life.'

She turned, grabbing her hat from the side. Ida grasped the half-empty bottle of bourbon that sat on the draining board on her way out and stepped out of the front door.

It was about a half-day ride to the nearest stableyard and who knows how long a walk. Maybe she'd be able to catch a lift, Ida thought. She raised her chin and adjusted the holster that lay heavy on her hips. One foot in front of another, she began to walk.

The End

Dedications

Books are created by villages of people, all of whom help the writer in many ways. My village is ever supportive, and I am so grateful.

To Daniel, my best friend and husband, who talks to me about plots and characters and asks difficult questions about my story ideas, all of which make me a better writer. Thank you for supporting me endlessly.

To my mother, Hilary, of course. Thank you for always supporting me and reading all of my words, whether or not they are in a genre and style you enjoy. Thank you for pointing out things that aren't working and for making me a better writer.

To my sister, Marilyn. Thank you for helping me understand what one might enjoy about the smell of meat and for discussing ideas with me with such enthusiasm.

Thank you to The Sunset Cartographer for the beautiful map of The Nameless Stretch.

To Sadie, Arthur, and John, who don't exist in this world, but who have been the greatest comforts during hard times.

Biography

Rachel Grosvenor is a writer from Birmingham, UK, with a PhD, MA, and BA in Creative Writing. Passionate about fantastical tales, Rachel favours writing stories about strong women, and her work can be found in good bookshops and anthologies worldwide. Her 'wry wit and vicious imagination' has been praised, and when she's not writing, she edits, coaches, and wonders what's for elevenses.

Printed in Great Britain
by Amazon

44754450R00159